THE BLACK SHEEP
and the
ENGLISH ROSE

THE BLACK SHEEP
and the
ENGLISH ROSE

DONNA KAUFFMAN

KENSINGTON PUBLISHING CORP.
http://www.kensingtonbooks.com

BRAVA BOOKS are published by

Kensington Publishing Corp.
850 Third Avenue
New York, NY 10022

All Kensington titles, imprints and distributed lines are available at special quantity discounts for bulk purchases for sales promotion, premiums, fund-raising, educational or institutional use.

Special book excerpts or customized printings can also be created to fit specific needs. For details, write or phone the office of the Kensington Special Sales Manager: Kensington Publishing Corp., 850 Third Avenue, New York, NY 10022. Attn. Special Sales Department. Phone: 1-800-221-2647.

Brava and the B logo Reg. U.S. Pat. & TM Off.

ISBN-13: 978-0-7582-1729-5
ISBN-10: 0-7582-1729-3

First Kensington Trade Paperback Printing: August 2008
10 9 8 7 6 5 4 3 2 1

Printed in the United States of America

THE BLACK SHEEP
and the
ENGLISH ROSE

Chapter 1

Someone else had gotten to her first.

It. Someone else had gotten to *it* first. She had nothing to do with it. Or shouldn't have. But then, he could be forgiven for being slightly distracted. He'd just broken into one of New York City's finer five star hotel suites expecting to be dazzled by a sapphire sparkler . . . only he'd thought the gorgeous gem would come in the form of a priceless Byzantine necklace. Not a stunning redhead tied to a bed in little more than midnight blue satin and lace.

If she was surprised to see him, her scowl didn't let on.

The last time Finn Dalton had laid eyes on Felicity Jane Trent, she'd been dripping in diamonds. Someone else's diamonds. Two years had passed since that stormy winter night in Prague. Her penchant for hot gemstones, however, apparently had not.

The only difference was that this time, someone else had gotten to her first. So, rather than rescuing a priceless antiquity, Finn was left with the option of rescuing Felicity Jane.

He leaned against the doorway of the elegantly appointed bedroom and folded his arms. "Hello, Jane." He smiled when she bristled. He was certain she felt that was far too common a name for a woman like her, which was mostly why he'd used it. Jane was a strong, no-nonsense moniker, much like its owner. Felicity, on the other hand, was a name that conjured up images of a beautiful, innocent sprite whose most pressing problem was attempting to find the heels she'd kicked off the night before.

The only resemblance Felicity Jane bore to a beautiful, innocent sprite was the beautiful part.

"I didn't steal it," she informed him, her crisp English accent reflecting both her Oxford education and a pedigree that would make even the royals gush in approval. Not that they would approve of her if they knew. Knew what only Finn knew.

"Well, not to state the obvious," he said, "but whatever it was you didn't steal is clearly no longer in your possession, so it's rather a moot point now, isn't it?"

"Whatever it was?" She all but spat his words back at him.

But then, he already knew from personal experience how much she hated to lose.

"You're honestly going to stand there and pretend that we aren't here for the same purpose?" She laughed then, but there was little humor in it.

"Actually, I'm standing here wondering why he didn't gag you. And why you aren't screaming bloody murder. Given that, you know, you weren't here to steal anything."

"Rather a sexist observation, don't you think?"

"What, that I assumed you were outsmarted by a man?" He smiled. "Again?"

"Not outsmarted. Everything was perfectly planned. I merely turned my attention away for a single moment and—" She'd instantly leapt to defend herself, then, realizing the trap, wisely clammed up.

"Not sexist," he went on, nodding at her clothing. Or lack thereof. And enjoying the moment far more than he knew was wise. "I simply deduced that it wasn't likely you'd been entertaining someone of the same sex." He cocked his head. "But I've been wrong before."

She sniffed. "Pig."

"Just a man. I hope you don't mind if I take a brief moment

to imagine . . ." He closed his eyes and let his smile slowly spread to a grin.

"A pig and a scoundrel, but then I learned as much in Prague."

He opened his eyes, his smile not wavering so much as a tic. He wondered if she'd noted his heightened awareness, though. She didn't miss much. "Funny, I don't recall you using either of those terms to describe me that night. In fact, as I remember it, the terms you used were more along the lines of life-altering and—"

"Nothing more than an ego stroke, I assure you. Men like to hear what they want to hear, after all." Her tone had become quite clipped, but her skin tone had warmed. And she couldn't seem to keep her gaze from dipping below his chin. Possibly recalling, as was he, that last night they'd been together. It had been rather . . . memorable. And for far more reasons than the manner in which it had unfortunately ended.

"Had it only been my ego you were stroking at the time, perhaps I'd agree, but that kind of sincerity—and, well, the word 'awe' comes to mind—really can't be faked."

Her gaze jerked to his. This time she looked him up and down quite insolently. "You'd be amazed by what can be faked."

He gave her the same once-over. "Perhaps." He smiled. "I don't believe I've ever had the opportunity to learn much about that, however."

"So certain of your prowess, are you? Or is it simply a lack of experience?"

He pushed away from the door frame. "Why don't I let you be the judge of that."

She didn't so much as squirm when he walked into the room, despite being at a very distinct disadvantage. In fact, she easily held his gaze as he approached, her own demeanor far more that of someone conducting a boardroom coup than a woman presently shackled to a bed with little more than an ounce of silk keeping her dignity intact. Hell, Felicity Jane could have been completely naked, and somehow she'd still manage to appear as unruffled and in control as if she were the one doing the interrogating.

He should know.

It was one of the many complexities about her that he used as his excuse for acting so completely out of character whenever he got within five feet of her. He paused at the foot of the bed.

"I would be happy to recite the terms of endearment I used after we parted," she informed him. "Nothing you haven't heard before, I'm certain."

He sighed then. "At least I had the foresight to gag you. Although your uses for that bow tie from my tux were certainly more creative, I must say. Still, I'd thought myself so original, leaving you as I did." He let his gaze slide slowly down her body, then just as slowly back up again. He was rewarded with a gleam in her green eyes that was only partially homicidal. "I do believe I left you with a little less modesty, though. Of course, given, well . . . everything, I suppose I didn't think you'd mind."

"Oh, it was quite amusing, indeed. The poor bellman almost had heart failure when he came to collect my luggage. Gallant of you to send him, by the way." The corners of her mouth twitched, and a real smile threatened.

And that was it. Right there. The reason Finn got himself into trouble whenever Felicity Jane was involved. She was the only woman he'd ever met who viewed the world with the same sort of detached amusement he did. The only difference—and it was a hefty one—was that his detachment came in handy in his line of work. Well, he supposed hers did, too. It was just, in his line of work, he had a vested interest in making sure the good guys won. As far as he could tell, in Felicity Jane's world, it was only important that Felicity Jane won.

"Yes, well, I had thought, perhaps, you could use a hand."

"I'd forgotten what a charming bastard you could be." She did smile now, and the warmth of it reached her eyes. But he was smart enough to know that all was not forgiven. Nor would it ever be. That was the other thing he liked about prowling around Felicity Jane. She kept him on his toes. Even when she was keeping him on his back. Maybe especially then.

"I'm wounded," he said. "I'd hoped you hadn't forgotten a single thing about me." He sat on the corner of the bed, by her feet. Her ankles had been bound with what looked like a man's silk tie. He fingered the edge of the silk without touching her skin. She didn't flinch or shift away from his touch. Not that she could have escaped him completely, but she could have made her feelings on the matter clear if she'd wanted to. He kept his gaze casually fixed on her ankles, though there was nothing remotely casual about the way his body was responding to her barely clad proximity.

Seeing her bound, even if it was with a monogrammed, designer silk tie, wasn't helping matters much, either. He wasn't normally into such things, but then, where the two of them were concerned, normal didn't often come into play. If ever. Play, however . . . that was something they knew more than a little about. And playing with Felicity Jane was as intoxicating as it was dangerous.

He flipped the end of the tie over her toes. "I see you still have a penchant for men's neckwear." There was a slight roughness to his tone, one he knew damn well she would pick up on. Just as he knew she'd use every advantage she had with him. And she had more than a few.

He wished like hell that knowledge perturbed him a bit more than it did. Because, right at that very moment, he should have been interrogating her in order to figure out how best to continue tracking down the Byzantine piece.

Not entangling himself once again in Felicity Jane's very enticing web.

As if reading his mind—and he wasn't too certain she couldn't; it would go a long way toward explaining her uncanny ability to keep herself one step ahead of him—she lifted her foot and lightly stroked her perfectly painted toes along the inside of his wrist.

She waited until he looked at her, then smiled and said, "I wasn't nearly as creative with his tie as I was with yours."

Finn's body sprang to full attention, just as she'd wanted it to. He forced himself to hold her gaze and tried to ignore the obvious bulge in his pants, knowing she wouldn't.

Two could play, however, and he knew right then he was definitely going to be one of them. He stroked a finger along the arch of her foot, well aware he was walking too fine a line to likely come out unscathed. And not particularly caring. It had been too long for him. Too long without putting his wants first, even for a night. And, if he was being completely honest, too long without someone like Felicity Jane.

And, as two long years of ultimately unfulfilling liaisons would attest, he'd learned that there was no one like Felicity Jane.

He trailed his fingers over the fine bones of her ankle, somewhat surprised his fingers weren't trembling a little. After all, he'd imagined this moment more times than he cared to admit, all the while never letting himself believe it would actually come to pass. They'd tangled only twice before, both of them during a time in his life he thought of now as purgatory, his life suspended between the one he'd always thought he'd be leading and the one he was leading now. It had been a time of dealing with his past, with his family, and discovering what he truly believed in. He had always known what he didn't want, which was a life like his father had led. One driven by greed and a hunger for more power. It had taken his father's death to teach him what he truly did want in life.

Now he had people counting on him, people who meant the world to him. He had a business to run, and work that was more important to him than anything he'd done before. Running Trinity, Inc., with his two closest friends, using his father's amassed wealth to help those who couldn't otherwise win against a system that was good, but not foolproof—the very same types his father had exploited whenever possible—

was easily the most personal thing he'd ever done. And the most rewarding.

He lifted his gaze to hers, wondering just what he was putting at risk here. There was the inescapable sense that now that he had everything else in order, he'd simply been waiting for her, for this moment, all along. Which, considering how their past liaisons had ended, should have sent him bolting from the room, yet kept him riveted to the bed as if he were the one shackled to it, not her.

Her eyes flashed like bright sparkling gems themselves as he continued his slow exploration. Using only his fingertips, he drew them slowly up the back of her calf, watching as her pale skin glowed a soft pink across the bridge of her nose, before tinting her cheeks. An oh-so-innocent reaction, when he knew oh-so differently. In some ways, they were too much alike. Innocent didn't describe either of them. They'd done too much, seen too much. Just as she had to know he was already diamond hard and ready to pick up right where they left off in Prague, he knew that if he drew his fingertips along the creamy, endless length of her legs, he'd likely encounter a soaking wet strip of expensive silk stretched between them.

"A shame we can't see our way toward working together," she said, her voice having also taken on a rather husky edge.

"A tempting offer," he replied, surprised she'd made it. He'd made that offer before, but she was stubbornly independent. Never willing to so much as discuss the offer, much less take him into her confidence. He wondered if the offer now was an indication of how desperate she was. And if that was why she was tolerating his touch right now. Not because she'd been wanting this moment to happen as ridiculously much as he had.

"Temptation is something we both know more than a little about," she said in a voice filled with all the carnal knowledge she had of him, making him twitch hard inside his now snug trousers.

He had to work to keep from adjusting his position. "True," he managed. "However, my client wouldn't be too thrilled if I came home empty-handed. And your client—" He paused and stilled his fingers, too, then cocked his head. "Oh, that's right. You don't have a client."

She held his gaze easily, her smile growing. "At least you credit me with the ability to come out the victor this go-around."

It wasn't lost on him that she hadn't refuted his assessment that her motives for being involved in this little caper were purely selfish. "I credit you with thinking you can, and that makes you just as dangerous. And I still haven't forgotten Bogota, what was it, almost three years ago now?"

"About that. And I hadn't thought you would." She pushed her bound feet downward, so she could dig her toes into the hard muscle of his thigh. She might as well have been pushing them between his legs for the reaction he had.

No, he hadn't forgotten Bogota. Not one sultry second of it.

"I simply thought you'd credit your uncustomary loss that morning to bad luck. Or bad, what was it, clams, I believe?"

There were, however, parts of that ill-fated assignment he'd rather never recall. "A pretty heartless solution considering that if we hadn't called for room service, in another hour or so you'd have likely had me so depleted I wouldn't have cared what you took."

"Darling," she purred, running her toes down along his thigh, then dragging them back up again. "Nothing about you is ever depleted. I should know. At least I left you clothed."

"I seem to recall wishing you'd left me dead. At least for the following eighteen or so hours."

She pursed her perfectly sculpted lips into a pout, which was so out of character for her, it actually made him smile. "I'd apologize, but that would be insincere of me."

He resisted—barely—the urge to yank her underneath him, shred the flimsy scraps of silk covering her, and bury himself so deeply inside her they'd both forget, at least for the moment, why they were really there. He had carnal knowledge, too. And he knew she'd be wet enough, tight enough, everything enough to fit him perfectly. "And I'd certainly never want anything less than complete honesty from you."

Something flashed across her eyes then, so swiftly he'd have missed it if he hadn't been paying close attention. And, where Felicity was involved, he always paid close attention.

"So noted," was all she said. But she shifted her feet away from his touch then. "In the name of honesty, then, I'll admit I'm surprised to see you here."

"Here in the city, or here in your bedroom?"

Her lips curved slightly at that. "Both, actually, but I meant the city. Or, perhaps I should say I was surprised to discover we're after the same quarry."

"And why is that? I know our paths haven't crossed of late—"

"I thought I'd read somewhere that you'd abandoned your vaunted post in the city as well as your . . . other travails, to start something, shall we say, a bit more legitimate. Haven't you started some sort of charitable foundation with the inheritance from your father?"

Now it was his turn to bristle, though he tried like hell to keep from responding to her obvious tactics. "I've never been anything less than legitimate, as you call it. I was an assistant district attorney when we first met."

Her eyebrows lifted. "In Bogota? Rather far afield for a city worker, isn't it?"

"Not in Bogota. We first met here. At a charity gala event, thrown by the mayor." He smiled, surprised. "You don't remember that, do you?"

"When, exactly?" She immediately shook her head, and he couldn't help but notice the way it made all those auburn curls of hers tumble about her pale, delicately defined shoulders. "Impossible. I would have remembered."

"It was quite crowded, and our introduction was made in a rather large group. The mayor can be somewhat pompous, and he was rather enjoying showing off, if I recall, to the lovely Brit."

"Namely because the 'lovely Brit' had a rather large checkbook attached to a very generous foundation that he was hoping I'd dip into for him. And I still can't believe our paths crossed before Bogota. I'd have remembered you."

"I can't see why."

She lowered her gaze, then lifted it once again, her eyes much darker now as her pupils expanded. "Let's just say there are occasions when I want to dip into things on a more personal level. I'd have remembered you."

He hadn't thought he could be any harder. Where she was involved, there apparently were no limits. That shouldn't have surprised him. After all, she lived her life the same way. "As I recall, you were otherwise engaged at the time. Unless, that is, you like to double dip."

It was her turn to bristle. "Think what you will, but no, that isn't something I'd ever entertain." She looked around the room, presumably seeing the scatter of her clothing on the floor, then looked back at him. "If you're concerned that could be the case here, let me assure you, it's not. Appearances can be, and often are, deceiving."

"Because you have no interest in . . . dipping?"

She drew her toes along his thigh again. "Because I haven't dipped in some time. And, where you are concerned, it seems I always have an interest." She drew her legs up before he could lay his hands on her again.

It was taking great willpower to sit and chat, as if the explosive chemistry between them wasn't electrifying every atom and air particle in the room. "Interesting," he said, "considering the state in which I've discovered you."

"If you're intimating that I used my wiles to that great a length as a means to get what I'm after, then I'm afraid you don't know me at all."

"So Bogota, Prague . . ."

"I'd have succeeded or failed in either case based on my

own skills, thank you. I don't use sex as a ploy. But then, I don't have to."

"So your involvement with me was incidental? Now I'm the one who finds that hard to believe."

"I didn't say that. You were critical to my success in Bogota, and an unfortunately ill-timed distraction in Prague. But sex was never part of the plan."

"So you'd have succeeded in Bogota with or without . . . dipping?"

"Most assuredly." She smiled. "One can have bad clams without great sex."

He shuddered slightly, but nodded. "True. And Prague?"

"Most assuredly not in Prague. Had I stuck to my usual plan, I'd have walked away the victor there. It's only because I let myself get distracted by you that I failed."

Finn wasn't so certain of that, but he let the comment pass. "And here? You mentioned earlier you allowed yourself to get distracted . . . Seems you might have a little problem with that, then."

Now she cocked her head. "Do you know who it is you're tracking?"

"I thought I did." No way was he giving her a name.

"Then you know how high the stakes are. And that the playing field is a rather . . . challenging one."

"If you say so." Finn had never gone up against this particular adversary, but after even the least bit of research, he'd realized that for once, he might be getting in over his head. A little. But he'd taken the case anyway. At the time, he'd have said that he'd signed on because he was certain that he was as capable as anyone to retrieve the priceless gemstone, regardless of who else was after it. He certainly had the best platform to work from, in both financing and talent. And, frankly, if he didn't get it back for his client, no one would. No one else had the interests of a bastard child at heart. The rest of the players were motivated only by greed. Not by doing what was right.

But now that he was here, it was impossible to deny that the entire time he'd been compiling the information he used to make such decisions, he'd wondered, given the players he'd discovered could potentially be in play on this, if Felicity would be in the game as well.

In the end, it had been an opportunity he couldn't pass up. His partners had no idea how big a risk he was taking. For the first time, he'd been less than completely open with them regarding the details, assuring them he was on top of things as they both had their hands full with other matters. He only hoped they, not to mention his client, wouldn't be the ones ultimately paying the price. Whatever the case, it was too late now. He was committed. And he was here. He'd have to find some way to deal with Felicity Jane, along with whoever else popped up, and see that the job got done, with him walking away the victor.

"So," she went on, drawing lazy patterns on his thigh with her toes. "If you know who you're up against, why aren't you off continuing the chase rather than sitting here, chatting with me? I've got nothing left to offer you, I'm afraid."

Finn abruptly clamped down on her ankles, trapping her there, keeping her toes pressed hard against his thigh. Their gazes locked, and he was gratified to see the knowledge dawn in her eyes that perhaps she was playing with fire here. The problem was she didn't appear any more put off by the idea than he was.

He slowly drew her down the bed, until her arms were stretched over her head. The shackles locking her wrists to the wrought-iron headboard kept her in place as he smoothly rolled to straddle her thighs, releasing her legs only when the weight of his body replaced his hands in pinning her down.

She didn't fight him, or look remotely alarmed. If anything, she looked . . . excited.

He levered his body over hers, tracing his hands up along her arms, over the wrist shackles, until he could weave his fingers through hers. She arched up into him, causing him to swallow a groan of satisfaction as the rigid length of him came into contact with the softest part of her. He managed to find the strength to resist the urge—like a primal directive—to drill his hips into hers.

Instead, he brought his mouth within a whisper of her lips. "I would never say you have nothing to offer."

Her lips parted, and she moved sinuously beneath him, torturing them both. "Who said I was offering anything? You have me at quite the disadvantage."

He released one of her hands and slid his hand to his belt. Two quick flicks of a lethal-looking little penknife later, she was free. He tossed his knife on the nightstand and immediately trapped her hands to the bed, once again weaving his fingers through hers. She didn't take the forced intimacy passively, but curled her fingers to hold his hands just as tightly. Their gazes were once again locked. Fused, almost, it seemed. He wouldn't have been remotely surprised to see steam fill the room, just from the look they were sharing.

"And now?" he asked.

She used the sides of his shoes to loosen the tie binding her ankles, then slipped her feet from the silk noose. An instant later, she was digging her toes into the backs of his calves as she wound her legs around his, tightening the pressure of his hips against hers.

She moved beneath him, and, this time, he was helpless not to move in response. Less than forty-eight hours on the job and he was jeopardizing everything. She was right. He had no business here, certainly none with her. And he didn't give a flat damn. He'd waited two years for this. For her. Or maybe he'd waited his entire life.

"Now," she said, gasping herself as he pushed against her, "now I want to know what you have to offer me."

Chapter 2

She'd lost her mind. It was the only explanation.

Two years had passed. Two years. Yet, nothing had changed. One grin—one flash of those white teeth—and the calculating professional who always put mission first, self second, vanished. And some inner sex kitten she didn't even know took over. What in the hell did she think she was doing?

She could lie to herself and say she was just doing what she had to in order to extricate herself from a less than promising situation.

And a lie it would be.

Two years. She'd almost managed to get the charming bastard out of her thoughts. She'd never get him out of her dreams. That, she could live with. She'd reconciled herself to that much. But now here he was, still larger than life, still cocky as hell, and pulling her right back into that same sexual fog she'd barely escaped from last time. If you could call being left naked and shackled an escape. Lord only knew where she'd have ended up if he hadn't chosen to leave her when he did. She couldn't even be all that angry at the manner in which he'd left her. She'd certainly deserved worse, considering the clams. Besides, he'd done her a favor. Another few hours spent wrapped around him and who knew what secrets she might have been tempted to spill? He already knew far too much about her, and she was still clueless as to why he'd let her get away with it. Twice.

She'd teased him about his business integrity, but she'd always known Finn Dalton was one of the good guys. Which, considering that he was also the epitome of a bad boy, was quite an intoxicating mix. And doubly dangerous. To her, and to her mission. That night in Prague, she'd been oh-so tempted to do what she'd never done before: confide in someone, bring him in on her secret.

Thank God he'd left her when he had. Naked or not.

That had been her mantra every day since. For a time, she'd thought she actually believed it.

She moved her hips beneath his, fighting the internal battle of want over need, losing it handily, and not particularly caring. He made it easy to play the siren. One look from him and she felt like some primal creature whose only directive was to melt him down to his most basic essence. It was a wonder they both hadn't gone up in flames the last time they'd tangled. Twice now they'd danced on the edge, twice now she'd been lucky to get out unscathed. The first time had been pure luck. But that last time . . . He could have ruined her, personally and professionally, had he chosen to. She had no idea why he hadn't. Which made what she was doing right now the epitome of foolishness.

If she entertained the thought, even for a second, that she could control him through sex, then she deserved whatever she got.

"Actually," he said, teasing the corner of her mouth with a brush of his lips, "I want to take you up on your proposition."

Her entire body shuddered at the mere thought that he wanted more of her. Her head knew it was business. But tell that to the rest of her. She was in dire need of an edge. More of an edge than the knowledge his raging erection gave her. She hooked her foot around his ankle and rolled him to his back.

Only his extreme agility kept them both from dropping off

the edge of the bed. Not exactly the edge she'd had in mind. She tried to straddle him, but he wrapped his legs around her and kept her fully pinned to him, his fingers still entwined with hers. So much for controlling things.

"I seem to remember you have a penchant for being on top," he said, his grin resurfacing.

Her pulse doubled. She was in so much trouble. She could extract the rarest of artifacts from the trickiest of locations leaving nary a trace. She couldn't be around Finn Dalton for more than five seconds without losing every ounce of intellect she possessed. "I don't seem to recall you minding all that much."

He laughed. "No. No, I didn't." He slid his arms up over his head, drawing their joined hands higher, pulling her face closer to his. "So, about this partnership you proposed. I was thinking we should . . . hammer out some of the details."

"I'm pretty sure I know what you want from this . . . partnership."

"Now, now. Like you, I don't conduct business in bed. That's strictly personal time." He abruptly rolled, and she found herself flat on her back again, pinned down by his weight, now fully on top of her.

She wished it didn't feel so damn good.

"However," he went on, "all work and no play can make for a very dull boy."

"Dull. Hmm." She pushed her hips up, making them both groan a little. "Apparently you've been taking a lot of time for play, then."

"Unfortunately, no." His grin was as unabashed as ever. "Though it's a problem I'd be more than happy for you to assist me with."

"How could a girl resist such an offer?"

He moved a little, until they were both breathing a bit more heavily. "I'm sure we'll spend some time figuring out the answer to that." He shifted his weight off of her slightly. "But for now, talk to me about this stone we're both after."

Her eyes widened in surprise as some of the fog blessedly lifted. She hadn't thought he'd be so open about it. For all they'd both known, during each of their encounters, exactly why their paths had crossed they hadn't exactly talked about. Much less shared any intel on it. "First off," she said, "what happened to the no-business-in-bed rule? And secondly, we haven't yet discussed what would be in this partnership for me."

Now he moved his hips and gave her his most hopeful, innocent smile, which didn't come close to reaching his eyes. She couldn't help it, she laughed. "You're incredibly incorrigible. A trait I admire, by the way. But, quite obviously I could get that from you without the promise of business."

He sighed, but his eyes still twinkled. She'd forgotten how incessantly blue they were. It was like staring into an endless sea, sparkling with sunlight.

"True," he said. "But think of how much more fun it would be to work and play together."

She disengaged her hands from his and tried to wriggle out from underneath him. She hadn't expected to feel such a strong tug. A tug that wasn't entirely physical. It was bad enough that he could make her body tremble in need with nothing more than a glance and a smile. Her heart absolutely could not—would not—come into play. And yet she was looking at him and feeling something that was undeniably affectionate.

Foolhardy, indeed.

She needed to get some distance from him, and quickly, if she was going to think even remotely clearly on the matter. For whatever reason, and she was certain he had them, he let her go and rolled to his back as she quickly slid off the bed and moved several feet away.

She'd thought she'd been having a bad day when she'd so badly bungled her one prime opportunity in this case earlier this evening. Now she was standing in her own room, wearing nothing more than a few flimsy pieces of lingerie, her body riled up in ways it hadn't been for two long years, her heart in a surprising little tangle of its own, and, furthermore, contemplating joining forces with the one man who'd proven himself to be her most formidable adversary. She hadn't known the meaning of bad day.

"Allow me to dress, then we'll talk."

"Don't feel you have to on my account." He propped his hands behind his head and crossed his ankles. "You know, I rather like you in blue." He said it casually, matter-of-factly. "Something about the contrast with that pale skin and all that amazing hair."

She shouldn't blush. Lord knew the things they'd already done together made blushing a bit after the fact. But for all that their main connection thus far had been purely animal in nature, he'd still occasionally say something so sincere, and so . . . uncalculated, she'd find herself reacting in ways that were dangerous, to say the least. Like wondering what it would be like to be with Finn in regular, day-to-day circumstances. Where every word, every move, didn't have to be examined and analyzed for potential danger to the mission at hand. It was a dangerous notion, indeed. Of course, even in her real life she lived nothing remotely close to what people would consider a normal routine, so it was all moot anyway. Still . . .

She turned her back to him and walked to her closet. "I appreciate the sentiment," she informed him, still struggling to reclaim that distance even now that his hands weren't on her. "However, though you have good reason to assume otherwise, if it's business we're to discuss, then I'd prefer to be dressed for such."

He shrugged. "Fine by me. All the better to imagine you like this underneath whatever tailored little suit you decide to put on. In some cases, more can still be less."

She rolled her eyes. Truly incorrigible. But his smile was one of pure fun and mischief, and she wished like hell it didn't make her want to be just as mischievous in return. Like surprise him by running back and leaping on top of him, and simply having her way with him for the next few hours. The images that immediately played through her now feverish mind made her leap for her walk-in closet instead. She did manage to pull herself together enough to pause before stepping inside. The only chance she had here was to keep him believing she thought she had the upper hand at all times.

She looked back at him. "Perhaps I should shackle you to the bed, to ensure you'll still be here when I return. At the very least, to make certain neither of us gets a head start."

"Oh, I'm not going anywhere."

She stepped in the closet and closed the door behind her. "Yeah," she whispered shakily. "That's what I'm most afraid of."

She skimmed over the array of clothing hanging in front of her, which was about as complete a wardrobe as anyone could hope to have at home, much less while traveling. She was an heiress and, as such, was expected to travel in a certain fashion. Had it been up to her, she'd have been thrilled with throwing a comfortable pair of trousers and a few shirts in a satchel and taking off. But that wasn't how things worked. "And I'm so heartily sick of how things have to work."

"Do you always mutter while you dress?"

She jumped. His voice was close. Just-on-the-other-side-of-the-door close. "I realize that my past manner of conduct around you might give a differing point of view, but, at the moment, I'd appreciate a bit of privacy, if you don't mind."

"Not in the least. That's why I left the door closed."

"Big of you."

"You have no idea."

She didn't know whether to laugh or rap her forehead repeatedly against the closet wall. If she thought it would instill the least bit of sense, she'd have been happy to do the latter, but, as usual, it was the former that he provoked. "Actually," she retorted, knowing better even as she spoke, "I believe I have a better idea than most. Well, assuming you don't spend all of your time as you do when you're with me."

"I should be so fortunate."

"I believe I'll take that as a compliment."

"It was intended as one. Are you decent yet?"

She laughed again. "You have no idea."

His laugh was rich, and deep, and so incredibly sexy that she grabbed for the closest hanger to keep from yanking the door open and dragging him into the closet with her. She quickly pulled on a crisply tailored, button-front, sleeveless white sundress, the full skirt decorated with a lush green and rust floral pattern, knowing something stiffer and more formal would have probably been a far smarter choice, but he had this way of looking at her that made her feel naked anyway, so what did it matter? At least this way she'd be comfortable.

She slipped her feet into matching green, low-heeled sandals, then made an attempt at fixing her hair, but with the mirror on the outside of the door, it was a blind attempt at best. Finally she faced the door, but paused before going out. She took a moment to remind herself why she'd come all the way to New York. She had a dual role here, her first time risking trying to pull off her public job and her private one at the same time. It was vitally important she complete both tasks successfully, and she'd already made a massive error in judgment on one part. Two, actually, if she counted severely underestimating her other opponent, earlier today.

She opened the door, expecting him to be looming on the other side. Instead, she was surprised to find him on the opposite side of the room, looking out at the expansive view of Central Park provided by her penthouse lodging. Of course, it was his very unpredictability that drew her in. Most men of her acquaintance were fairly basic, their motives and intent easily analyzed and determined. Not Finn.

"Nice view," he said as she walked up behind him.

She'd considered staying on the opposite side of the room, but for her own personal test, and to indicate to him that she wasn't the least bit affected by him now that she'd been released from her unsavory situation, she'd closed the distance between them.

"I thought it was rather lovely, yes," she said, then immediately cursed her flawed strategy when he glanced over his shoulder and did a quick head-to-toe rundown that left her feeling slightly flushed and fully stripped.

"Ditto," he said, leaving her to wonder whether he was referring to the view below or the one standing in front of him. She chose the former, but the continual involuntary flickering of the muscles between her thighs said she hoped otherwise.

"So, about the details of this proposed collaboration," she began. "Let's elaborate." From now on, business would rule the day.

She'd deal with the night when the time came.

He turned to face her. "We're both here for the same reason."

She wondered if he knew just how complex her reasons really were. "Continue."

"You were right earlier. Our adversary—assuming that is who left you in such a . . . bind, earlier, and is who I think it is—is a challenging one."

Her lips curved in a wry smile. "To say the least."

"So, it follows, that if we combine our skill sets and collective knowledge, we might prove a more formidable opponent than we would individually."

"Exactly my thinking on the matter. However, in keeping with your request for honesty, given how my last encounter turned out, are you certain you want me as a partner?"

His blue eyes twinkled. "Let's just say you do more for blue silk than I do."

Now her eyes widened. "So, you think I'm going to barter myself for—"

His gaze darkened. "No, that's not what I meant. I simply meant you're far more attractive bait in this particular scenario. Once our fish is hooked, we can proceed in any manner of directions, none of which will require you to—"

"Dip?"

"Right. In fact, I'd have a little problem if you felt otherwise."

"Then we're square on that. But it should also be stated that my appearance obviously didn't get me very far last time. Not that I'd banked on it."

Finn grinned. "Then the man must have other proclivities. Or he's dead from the waist down."

She did smile a bit at that. "Perhaps he simply has more discipline and an ability to stay focused on the prize."

Finn's gaze narrowed down so tightly on hers she thought she could feel him touching her. Everywhere.

"I suppose it would depend on your definition of 'prize.'"

She could have sworn her heart rate tripled. "You of all people should know I'm no prize."

He gave a little involuntary shudder, and she knew he was remembering the clams. She did feel badly about that, but she'd more than apologized back in Prague. And, had she to do it over again, though she'd try to be less punitive, if push came to shove, the job always came first and she'd do whatever she had to do. Bad clams included.

"Regardless of past exit strategies, I think we might complement one another in this particular endeavor." He gave her another once-over. "Great dress, by the way. Makes your eyes this amazing shade of green."

There it was again. That offhand sincerity that did odd things to her equilibrium. She was used to meaningless flattery, delivered by men hoping for benevolence from her foundation, or from her directly, of a more personal nature. Either way, it was always a calculated maneuver. It never seemed as such with Finn. When, of all people, it most certainly should.

"Thank you," she said, finding she meant it. Despite the mischievous and playful side of him that was always near the surface, she knew him to be an honorable man with a highly regarded level of personal integrity. She doubted he'd sink to useless and hollow flattery as a means to get what he wanted.

Certainly not from her, at any rate. "But continuing here, given our past, don't you think there might be a wee problem with trust?"

"We were opponents then."

"To a degree, we still are. We each want the stone, and there is only one to be had."

"I only ask for one thing."

She arched a brow and decided to give him the benefit of the doubt. "Which is?"

"Until the sapphire is in our hands, we operate as a team. No secret maneuvers, no hidden agendas."

Her whole life was a hidden agenda. Well, half of it anyway. "And when we have the necklace? Then what?"

"See? I like how you think. When, not if."

"Which doesn't answer my question."

"I don't have an answer for that. Yet."

She laughed. "Oh, great. I'm supposed to sign on to help you recover a priceless artifact, in the hopes that when we retrieve it, you'll just let me have it out of the kindness of your heart? Why would I sign on for that deal?"

He turned more fully and stepped into her personal space. She should have backed up. She should have made it clear he wouldn't be taking any liberties with her, regardless of Prague. Or Bogota. Or what they'd just done on her bed. Hell, she should have never involved herself with him in the first place. But it was far too late for that regret now.

"Because I found you tied to your own hotel room bed and I let you go. Because you need me." He toyed with the end of a tendril of her hair. "Just as much, I'm afraid, as I need you."

"What are you afraid of?" she asked, hating the breathy catch in her voice, but incapable of stifling it.

"Oh, any number of things. More bad clams, for one."

"Touché," she said, refusing to apologize again. "So why are you willing to risk that? Or any number of other exit strategies I might come up with this time around? You're quite good at your job, however you choose to label it these days.

Why is it you really want my help? And don't tell me it's because you need me to get close to our quarry. You could just as easily pay someone to do that. Someone who he isn't already on the alert about and whose charms he's not immune to."

"Maybe I want to keep my enemies close. At least those that I can."

"Ah. Now we're getting somewhere. You think that by working together, you can reduce the chance that I'll come out with the win this time. I can't believe you just handed that over to me and still expect me to agree to this arrangement."

"I said maybe. I also said there were myriad reasons why I think this is the best plan of action. For both of us. I never said it was great, or foolproof. Just the best option we happen to have at this time."

"Why should I trust you? Why should I trust that you'll keep to this no-secret-maneuvers, no-hidden-agenda deal? More to the point, why would you think I would? No matter what I stand here and promise you?"

"Have you ever lied to me?"

She started to laugh, incredulous, given their history, then stopped, paused, and thought about the question. She looked at him, almost as surprised by the actual answer as she'd been by the question itself. "No. No, I don't suppose, when it comes down to it, that I have." Not outright, anyway. But then, they'd been careful not to pose too many questions of each other, either.

"Exactly."

"But—"

"Yes, I know we've played to win, and we've done whatever was necessary to come out on top. No pun intended," he added, the flash of humor crinkling the corners of his eyes despite the dead seriousness of his tone. "But we've never pretended otherwise. And we've never pretended to be anything other than what we are."

"Honor among thieves, you mean."

"In a manner of speaking, yes."

"I still don't think this is wise. Our agendas—and we have

them, no matter that you'd like to spin that differently—are at cross purposes."

"We'll sort out who gets what after we succeed in—"

"Who gets what?" she broke in. "There is only one thing we both want."

"That's where you're wrong."

She opened her mouth, then closed it again. "Wrong, how? Are you saying there are two priceless artifacts in the offing here? Or that you can somehow divide the one without destroying its value?"

He moved closer still, and her breath caught in her throat. He traced his fingertips down the side of her cheek, then cupped her face with both hands, tilting her head back as he kept his gaze directly on hers. "I'm saying there are other things I want. Things that have nothing to do with gemstones, rare or otherwise."

She couldn't breathe, couldn't so much as swallow. She definitely couldn't look away. He was mesmerizing at all times, but none more so than right that very second. She wanted to ask him what he meant, and blamed her sudden lack of oxygen for her inability to do so. When, in fact, it was absolute cowardice that prevented her from speaking. She didn't want him to put into words what he desired.

Because then she might be forced to reconcile herself to the fact that she could want other things, too.

"Do we have a deal?" he asked, his gaze dropping briefly to her mouth as he tipped her face closer to his.

Every shred of common sense, every flicker of rational thought she possessed screamed at her to turn him down flat. To walk away, run if necessary, and never look back. But she did neither of those things and was already damning herself even as she nodded. Barely more than a dip of her chin. But that was all it took. Her deal with the devil had been made.

"Good. Then let's seal it, shall we?"

She didn't have to respond this time. His mouth was already on hers.

Chapter 3

So much for playing it safe.

She tasted better than he'd remembered. And he'd remembered her tasting pretty damn sweet. "You know," he said, moving his lips to the corner of her mouth, "for someone with a tart tongue—"

The rest of his sentiment was lost as she turned ever-so-slightly and slid that tart tongue of hers along his own, making him groan as he accepted her deep into his mouth. God, what in the hell had he gotten himself into here?

She lifted her head first. "Deal sealed, I'd say."

His response was more along the lines of a hoarse grunt, which was all he could manage. That made her smile.

Serious trouble, that's what.

"So," he began, paused to clear his throat, then said, "let's order up an early dinner and discuss our strategy."

She walked across the room, paused in front of the mirror to apply fresh lipstick, then continued to the door leading to the penthouse suite's private elevator. "Why don't we go to Antoine's, have his chef prepare us something perfect, perhaps add a bottle from his wine cellar as an accompaniment, and let the rest take care of itself?"

She didn't wait for his response. She merely pressed the button to summon the elevator.

Finn didn't bother with a debate on the pros and cons of

their being seen together in a high profile spot like Antoine's, which was the latest on the list of Manhattan's hot spots. Instead, he crossed the room, paused in front of the same mirror, decided there was no hope for his now crumpled linen shirt and somewhat wrinkled trousers, raked his fingers through his thick blond mess instead, then gave up altogether and followed her into the elevator. "Why Antoine's?" He knew she hadn't just picked that one at random.

"If we want to snag the attention of one Mr. John Reese, then having dinner at his favorite spot could be the perfect place to start."

Already two steps past him in planning. Hell, she'd probably had this all figured out while still shackled to the bed, with him on top of her. It shouldn't have surprised him. From what he knew of Felicity Jane, which, admittedly, wasn't nearly as much as he wanted to, she rarely did anything that wasn't directly related to benefiting her bottom line. Dinner at a five star restaurant was nice, but she could do that any night of the week. Beating an international artifact dealer—reputed to work deals on both sides of the law—at his own game while enjoying mouth-watering chicken marsala and a wonderful sauvignon? Far more satisfying.

He should be picking her brain on what else she knew about Reese besides his dining habits. He'd researched all the possible players in this game, Reese being the prime one, but hadn't stumbled across that little fact. Which was, arguably, why he wanted to team up with Felicity in the first place. But didn't explain why just the thought of how she'd conducted her personal research made him want to put a fist through a wall. Or square into John Reese's smug, smiling bastard of a face.

Quite the revelation for a man who prided himself on relying on quick thinking and fast reflexes rather than the use of brutality when it came to problem solving in tricky situations.

And he'd been back in her presence for an hour.

Once inside the elevator, he stabbed the button for the private parking lot level, then folded his arms. He didn't dare so much as look at her, much less touch her. He wasn't sure he could be responsible for his actions if she were to look at him with even a hint of that self-satisfied smile of hers. They'd be back behind locked doors and on the bed, the floor, or up against the nearest wall before either one of them could blink. By the time they came up for air, that satisfied smile would be there for an entirely different reason.

And Mr. John Reese could go fuck himself.

The doors slid open, and she stepped past him without pause, walking into the parking garage as if she owned the place. Which, for all he knew, she did. As could he, frankly, had he wanted to. But acquiring things for the sheer sake of ownership had been more his father's style.

"Let me call for a car," he told her. "I have a service we use when we're in the city that's quite—"

He stopped when a long, sleek black limo purred up to the elevator landing. She glanced over her shoulder. "I brought my own."

"Of course you did," he murmured, waving the driver back into the car and opening her door himself. "Convenient," he said.

"I always thought so. The Foundation prefers that I use private transportation when conducting business, so we've set up our own drivers in the cities we frequent most often."

He wanted to ask her if stealing priceless gemstones could be considered Foundation business, but managed to refrain.

The Foundation was the Trent Foundation, started by a duke-of-something ancestor of hers over a century before. Finn had done a little digging after their initial introduction and had learned that it mostly funded charitable trusts and various other philanthropic endeavors around the globe, but also maintained the Trent family holdings, of which there were many. He'd had some experience with managing a global-scale family inheritance and didn't envy her position as the sole remaining Trent descendant. He knew what an immense responsibility that was.

It had taken him several years of intense, and often elaborate, planning to dismantle and disseminate what his father had spent half a lifetime building. Of course, had he built it honestly and with some benefit to someone other than himself, Finn might have seen fit to find some way to keep the empire intact, even if run by someone other than himself.

Felicity had opted to run hers. To be fair, there had been far more public attention paid to the choices she'd made upon inheriting, as the British loved nothing more than lavishing media attention on their more highly pedigreed subjects. At least Finn had stirred things up only in the business world with his decision to break apart the billion-dollar industries his father had assembled.

What he didn't understand was, given her rather high-scale global profile, how it was no one had ever discovered what he'd discovered within the first twenty-fours he'd spent with her. Which was that Felicity Jane Trent, media princess, heiress to billions, benefactor to thousands, was also a very talented, very dedicated, and very successful jewel thief.

He had no idea what she did with her loot, or how long she'd been in that particular line of work. He was fairly certain it was the thrill of the hunt, not the prize itself, that was the lure. It had to be. More wealth she didn't need. He'd looked into that after Bogota, wondering if perhaps her inheritance was more burden than actual asset. But her wealth rivaled, if not outdid, that of the queen, so she wasn't in it for the money.

He didn't need more wealth either, but then he wasn't acting in his own best interests. He was in it for the benefit of others. His own benevolent foundation of sorts, he supposed. He didn't charge his clients for the services provided to them by either himself or his two partners, as their goals were tied to righting wrongs for those who couldn't do it themselves, not increasing his bottom line. He'd retained enough wealth that his company supported itself in the form of a vast array of investments.

He had no idea what Felicity Jane's goals were, other than to find something exciting to do in her spare time. Except he couldn't seem to make that image line up exactly right either.

She reached out her hand to him. "Joining me? Or are you just going to stand there and scowl because my car is bigger than yours?"

He slid in, careful to seat himself at a diagonal, on the far side of the roomy, beautifully appointed interior. If he had any hope of regaining control, he had to get his shit together and get it there fast.

She crossed her legs. He looked out the window. It didn't help much. He could still see them reflected in the glass. Maybe he should just crawl across the damn seat, drag her underneath him and get it out of his system. Problem was, last time he'd tried that they'd still been going at each other two days later.

Right now there was an ancient artifact floating around the city, with a very limited window of opportunity for retrieval before it likely took off overseas in the pocket of a private collector's agent. Finn's client, who happened to be the rightful owner of the stone, if not the necklace itself, regardless of what various legal entities had declared, wouldn't be too happy if he lost what might likely be his only chance at regaining possession of a precious family heirloom because Finn had been too busy fucking his brains out.

"Perhaps later," Felicity said, drawing his attention back to her. "After dessert. Or for dessert."

"Perhaps later, what?"

She glanced down, below his belt, then back at him, with a private smile curving her lips.

He shifted slightly, but there was no hiding what was obvious to them both. "About this dinner," he said, determined to get them both talking business at the same time. Even if it killed him. Which, given the relentless state of his aching hard-on, it just might. "Do you know who he might be dining with?"

"You mean, who is he going to sell the stone to? I don't

know what courier he'll be using, but I have a fair idea of who the actual buyer is, yes."

She'd said stone, not necklace, making him wonder if she knew about the contested nature of this specific artifact. And what impact that might have had on her decision to go after it.

She cocked her head slightly when he didn't respond right away. "I rather thought you'd be on the same page. After all, you were just behind John when you tracked him to me."

And Finn should have kept on tracking him, leaving Felicity to deal with her unfortunate incarceration. Now all he could think about was damned dessert. "I have my own ideas on who the other players are, but I wanted your input. You seem to have a direct connection to Reese. If we both know what we're dealing with, all the better in terms of being successful in getting the piece back."

She lifted one slender shoulder and picked at the folds of her dress. "As you said, there are several key players, but I'm fairly certain he's going with the Russian."

Finn said nothing. She could be telling him the truth, or she could be purposely steering him off the right path. It was true, she'd never directly lied to him in the past, but, despite the adversarial nature of their relationship, she hadn't had reason to. In both cases during their previous meetings, they'd already known the whereabouts of the quarry in question and hadn't needed the information or discussed the topic with the other. Had she bested Reese earlier today, she'd have likely beaten him to the prize this time. Only she hadn't. Which meant it was a race now, to see who got to it first. And he wasn't entirely sure what she was capable of doing in her quest to win.

What the hell had he been thinking, partnering with her? His cock twitched when she recrossed her legs, reminding him exactly what he'd been thinking with.

"You're certain he has it?"

She nodded. "I was close, but I'd hoped to get a key piece of information from him and beat him at his own game."

"He wasn't aware you were . . . in the market for the same piece?"

"I let him think I had heard about it and was interested in buying it."

"And he'd give you just enough information on who he was getting it from?"

"Something like that."

Finn thought on that for a moment. "Have you used his . . . services before?"

She smiled then. "You're adorable when you're jealous. I assure you, however, there is nothing to be jealous of. Yes, I have worked with him in the past, Foundation business mostly."

"Mostly."

"Yes," she reiterated, "mostly. Some family business as well. Nothing of a personal nature."

He wondered how foolish he was to believe her. But, holding her direct gaze as he was, he did. "Of course you're aware of his reputation for playing a bit outside the lines, when it comes to direct line of ownership with some of his more . . . unique artifacts. Not that this would be a problem for you personally, but how does the Foundation feel about working with someone whose character has been described as less than sterling?"

She laughed. "You'd have to understand British peerage and the Trents' very rich personal history to know that someone like John Reese causes barely a blip on the discomfort scale. The fact that he's a very powerful man building quite the trade empire is of more interest than whatever means he might have used to secure some of it. Of course, everyone maintains quite the upper crust appearance on the surface, but that doesn't mean they don't wallow in all the gossip once the evening's event is over. Everyone loves a good story, and John Reese comes packaged with quite a rich one."

"He'd have gotten along well with my father," Finn muttered. "Perhaps your family would have as well."

"Perhaps," she said, not taking the least offense. "Of course,

I'm the last in the line," she added, her own smile mischievous, "so I more or less dictate what the Foundation will deal with."

Finn smiled at that. "So, you think the trade itself will take place at Antoine's?" he said, keeping his gaze anywhere but on her damn legs. "Rather high profile."

"Which is what he's counting on, to be certain. Only someone with an . . . ego the size of John's would dream of pulling that off."

Finn scowled, not wanting to think about Felicity having direct knowledge of the size of any part of John Reese. "Won't seeing you there thwart that particular plan?"

Her smile spread. "I most certainly hope so."

Finn propped his ankle on the opposite knee and willed his hard-on to subside. Jesus, it was as if he'd never had sex before.

"Not only do I hope to unsettle Mr. Reese, I hope that by seeing that I have not only rebounded from the unfortunate circumstances he left me in this afternoon, but having come back stronger and more determined than ever, he will realize that there is no place that he, or that lovely piece of sapphire, can hide."

Finn noted that she'd made it sound as if this were still all her game, with him playing the role of nothing more than a convenient escort. He didn't bother to correct that assumption, thinking perhaps that would be to his advantage later. And God knew he needed one right about now.

"Seeing you pop up might make him that much more eager to dump the stone," Finn warned. "Once he makes his deal, he's out of it, and the chase moves on to the buyer and the courier. Which gets tricky with Russian import/export laws being what they are."

"I don't think Chesnokov will be as eager to take possession of an artifact with a less-than-pristine provenance if there is suddenly some less-than-discreet public attention being paid to it."

"Less-than-discreet public attention?" Finn leaned forward. "What scheme are you cooking up now?"

"Why look, darling. We've arrived." Felicity turned her attention to the side window, beyond which was the slowly rolling scene of the nightly line that formed outside Antoine's.

The car rolled to a stop at the entrance. Finn waited for the chauffeur to come around this time, using the extra few minutes to prepare himself for the gauntlet that lay ahead. He was used to operating behind the scenes, preferring to handle his affairs—both business and personal—in a one-on-one setting, without the attendant glare of public attention or speculation. He'd had enough of that during his days as an assistant district attorney in this very city, and even more so during the long months following his father's death.

He was several years into the private sector now, and his father had been gone long enough, his empire long since dismantled, that Finn rarely drew any attention beyond the local variety back home in Virginia. And even then, he kept a low profile. His neighbors in the privileged Middleburg horse community had never accepted his return upon his father's death, mostly because they considered what he'd done with his inheritance to be a sacrilege to success. The fact that he was using the remaining Dalton wealth to help people less fortunate than themselves didn't seem to up his social ante in the least. Which could have something to do with the fact that he didn't give flat damn what any of them thought.

The driver helped Felicity out of the car, eliciting a wave of murmurs from the crowd as they craned their necks to see who was emerging from the sleek, black town car. Finn followed, and immediately placed a hand on the small of her back, using his body as a shield between her and the crowd, who were now flashing cameras and cell phones, snapping pictures and calling out for her to stop and pose in case she was someone famous. There was a scattering of paparazzi as well, but not likely being aware of her stature in Britain, they were only minimally interested, which was perfectly fine with Finn.

Of course, Felicity didn't allow him to shepherd her into the restaurant with the minimum of fuss. She slipped from his protective stance and smiled and waved at the people in line, none of whom seemed to be the least bit offended that she was getting preferential treatment, as the mountain of a man governing the line slipped the rope free and motioned them both to go directly inside.

Finn leaned down and whispered in her ear, "I thought the sideshow began inside, for the benefit of Reese."

"The show begins now, darling." Keeping her smile intact, she added, "Do your best to keep up."

It should have pissed him off, her insouciance and dangerously placed bravado. Instead it made him laugh. Because he had little doubt she could pull off whatever scheme she had planned. His reaction set off a whole new wave of pictures, but when she would have paused again, he shuffled her ahead of him, corralling her through the front door, effectively using his broad shoulders to block out the barrage of flashes. He bent his head closer to her ear. "Keeping it up has never exactly been an issue for us."

She slowed just enough so that his hips bumped into the curve of her backside. She exerted the slightest bit of pressure, which had the immediate result of making him hard all over again. She glanced up at him. "Why, it appears you have a point. A hearty one, at that. We should discuss it in greater . . . depth, after dinner."

He really had to remember who he was playing with.

Finn shifted to her side, using the fullness of her skirt as camouflage, thanking God he was wearing loosely pleated trousers. He turned to the maitre d'. "We'd like a table in the main room, preferably on the far side of—"

"Bon soir, Jacques," Felicity said, leaning past Finn and placing her perfectly manicured fingers on the maitre d's forearm. "Could you please seat us at Mr. Reese's table."

Finn glanced down at her. "That's rather . . . direct."

"Darling, the man left me in a bit of a bind at the end of our previous engagement. I do believe he owes me a glass of champagne, at the very least."

Less than discreet, indeed. Finn smiled at Jacques. "As the lady insists."

Jacques frowned ever-so-slightly, clearly uncomfortable with the news he had to deliver. He cleared his throat and looked quite contrite as he said, "I'm sorry, Miss Trent. I believe Mr. Reese is already entertaining a dinner guest. They are on their second course. Perhaps you confused your meeting time?"

Felicity smiled, all charm and British polish. "I assure you, he'll be delighted to have us join him. Is Jason working this evening?" She glanced at Finn. "Antoine's has the most wonderful sommelier." She looked back to the maitre d'. "Please have him bring us your best Chantal Neuf."

"I'm not familiar with that one," Finn said.

"It's relatively rare." She smiled up at him. "And quite expensive." She peered around Jacques's shoulder, and they both spied Reese at the same time, seated prominently, dead center in the main room.

Perfect, just perfect.

A brief wave from her elicited a nod from the rather serious-looking, dark-haired man, which apparently was enough to appease the maitre d', who proceeded to lead them directly to his table.

Finn had seen several photos of John Reese in his preparation for the case, but in those he had been smiling. Definitely a different vibe at the table this evening. Finn had no idea what her plan of attack would be, but had every expectation that it would be an interesting one. He decided the best plan, at least initially, was to sit back and watch her work, take mental notes, then decide how best to proceed.

This partnership wasn't exactly panning out as he'd hoped, but why he'd ever thought she'd defer to his judgment or even attempt to work as an actual team, he had no idea. At least they were in it together, where he could keep close tabs on her.

"John, how lovely to see you again."

Reese stood and extended a well-manicured hand. He was tall, tan, and wearing a very expensively tailored suit. "An unexpected pleasure, to be certain." His accent was much the same as Felicity's; polished and well-educated. He had still yet to smile.

She stepped back so that Finn could move in next to her. "Allow me to introduce a friend of mine, Finn Dalton."

Finn accepted Reese's offer of a handshake. They were close to the same age, matched in height and build, except Reese had dark hair and gray eyes, whereas Finn was blond and blue. They were a contrast as well in their approach to business. Finn knew Reese's reputation to be all work and no play. Finn, on the other hand, thought that when work was done right, there was no better playground in the world.

Reese shook his hand firmly, without any overt power play. Finn hadn't expected anything so blatant anyway. Reese nodded to his dining companion across the table, who had also stood as Felicity approached. "Allow me to introduce Yvgeny Andreev." He didn't add anything else, but Finn didn't require further information, and was betting Felicity had done her homework as well. At least Reese hadn't insulted them by pretending Chesnokov's agent was someone else. Or maybe he simply thought they wouldn't recognize the name.

Finn had. Andreev was a well-known mule used by several European buyers. He was reputed to be excellent at his job; quiet, efficient, and, when required, very good at remaining undetected by those who might otherwise have a quibble with his possession of certain cargo.

Finn extended his hand to the slight man and received a tepid, at best, handshake in return. Andreev had thin, sandy brown hair and skin that was almost too smooth, without a hint of beard. His eyes were such a pale blue they appeared almost translucent, framed with lashes so blond as to be invisible. Finn had stood in courtrooms and boardrooms filled with all manner of human beings, ranging from the stone cold and psychotic to the wounded and broken. He'd observed enough in his life to know that this man with the dead eyes was essentially soulless.

Suddenly John Reese wasn't the biggest threat in the room.

Finn pulled out Felicity's chair, seating her on one side, between Reese and the Russian, then taking the only other available seat, which was opposite hers. His wait-and-see strategy was no longer an option. He trusted Felicity to hold her own, but in this case, he was taking no chances. He took the heavy linen dinner napkin from Felicity's plate and handed it to her before picking up his own. "So, Reese, I understand you have an interest in international trade."

If the Brit was surprised by Finn's direct offensive, his smooth expression didn't give it away. Felicity, on the other hand, paused ever-so-slightly spreading her napkin in her lap, but did nothing more than shoot him a quick, expressionless glance, before continuing to settle herself in. Good to know she was willing to follow his lead on occasion.

Finn turned his attention exclusively to Reese then, though he kept Andreev in his peripheral vision. He was frankly more interested in what the Russian was thinking at the moment than what was going through Reese's mind. Reese would likely react to this disruption somewhat predictably. He'd want to mitigate the fallout of Felicity's unplanned intrusion so as not to lose the sale. Not that he couldn't get another buyer for such a precious piece. But setting up another transfer would take time. And that was the one thing Reese couldn't afford now that he had possession of the artifact. Especially not with Felicity Jane smiling at him so guilelessly.

"Yes, I do," Reese said, casually shifting his gaze from the gentle swell of Felicity's creamy breasts, to Finn's face. He hadn't bothered to hide his prurient interest in her, but there was no gleam of challenge in his clear gray eyes, either.

Finn struggled a little with the fact that though Felicity claimed Reese had shown no sexual interest in her, there was both the manner in which he'd left her, and that blatant stare just now, that said perhaps it was otherwise. And yet, Finn still believed that Felicity had been telling the truth. Perhaps Reese just wanted to stir the pot. Finn supposed time would tell who the fool was. Time was becoming quite the precious commodity all the way around, it seemed.

"Do you have a specific area of interest?" Finn asked, not expecting a straight answer, but wanting Reese to know he wasn't simply Felicity's man candy for the evening.

Reese easily held Finn's gaze, not the least bit intimidated. "Oh, I dabble in quite a few areas."

Finn merely smiled. Perhaps it was better if Reese underestimated him. "A man of many talents, then."

Reese shot Felicity a brief, but surprisingly personal smile, then turned back to Finn. "So it's been said."

Finn dug his fingers into the napkin he'd been spreading on his lap, but otherwise did nothing to give away the surprisingly strong impulse he had to suddenly rearrange Reese's aristocratic nose. "Anything specific capturing your interest of late?" He kept his tone harmless. His gaze, if Reese was even a remotely good judge of character, was anything but. "I understand you are tapped in quite well to the international grapevine. Any good tips on currently available . . . commodities?"

From the corner of his eye, Finn noted the Russian's jaw visibly tighten. He didn't make eye contact, but Finn had little doubt when Andreev speared a stalk of asparagus on his plate, he was imagining cleanly skewering something else entirely. Good. Finn wanted him pissed off, wondering if Reese was playing him, worrying that this deal might slip right out from under him. Because even a soulless man like Andreev had to be a little unnerved at the prospect of returning to Chesnokov with his pockets empty. That was bad for business.

"There are always items of interest available," Reese said smoothly, as if oblivious to the tension circling the intimate setting. "The global market moves swiftly. You really need to stay on top of things if you want to succeed." He glanced at Felicity again as he said that last part.

Finn knew he was being baited. What he hadn't expected was how hard it was not to let it get to him.

"Oh, John, don't sound so pompous," Felicity teased, interjecting herself into the conversation with casual ease. She spoke to Reese quite comfortably, like old friends. Or lovers.

Finn hated the doubt that began to creep in.

She rested a hand briefly on Reese's forearm. "Tell us what exciting deal you're cooking up with Yvgeny, here." She gifted the Russian with a fast, charming smile. "We're being quite rude, intruding on your business dinner, but it's so rare John and I get the chance to catch up, what with him always in a rush, and me being so tied up all the time."

Her smile spread, and Finn felt her toe nuzzle his ankle as she continued talking. Flirting was more like it, not that the Russian was buying anything she had to sell. Yet. Finn would have enjoyed sitting back and watching her work the table if he hadn't had to stay so alert to every nuance of even the slightest reaction in either man.

"Come now," she continued, "the least we can do is allow you a moment to gloat over whatever wonderful item it is that John has craftily secured for you. I'm certain I'll be jealous and wish it were mine."

It amazed Finn how innocent and sincerely enthusiastic she came off. Not that either Reese or Andreev were falling for it, but it was good to know just how broad her range of acting skills was. They both might need them before the evening was over.

"I promise to pout only for the briefest of moments when I hear what fabulous find I've missed out on." She looked at Yvgeny. "I'm afraid I'm quite the spoiled child my father—bless his departed soul—always accused me of being when it comes to acquiring new baubles. I can be ever so determined, to the point of petulance, when I don't get my way. But never let it be said that on the rare occasion I don't emerge the victor, that I don't extend the lucky winner my heartiest congratulations for a battle fiercely won." Her smile spread. "Though, I'll admit that I do keep track of those lost opportunities. You never know when they might surface again." She glanced at Reese. "And I so hate to lose anything twice."

Andreev gave up eating all together, his dead stare presently pinning Reese squarely to his seat.

To his credit, Reese didn't exhibit the slightest shred of panic, despite the fact that it was clear the Russian was visibly quite unhappy now. "My darling Felicity Jane, I'm well aware of your rather obsessive proclivities, but, as even you must know, you can't have all the toys." He turned his most charming smile on the three of them, white teeth flashing now. It was a striking difference from the man they'd first walked in on, and very effective. "Whatever would the rest of us do for fun?"

Felicity rewarded his blatant attempt to lighten the suddenly tense mood with a delighted laugh and swat at his arm. They were saved from further conversation when the sommelier arrived with Felicity's requested bottle of champagne. She turned a charming, confident smile on all three men, as if commanding the attention of a room full of admirers was quite the normal evening activity for her. For all Finn knew, it probably was.

"I thought it only fair that I come bearing gifts. I hope you'll see fit to forgive me, Yvgeny," she went on, favoring the Russian with the full force of her charm. "Please, enjoy a glass of some wonderful champagne, won't you?"

Andreev stared at her for a second that stretched quite uncomfortably. Finn was a heartbeat away from coming out of his chair, as every protective instinct he owned flared to life. But Andreev abruptly stood instead and turned his attention to Reese. He spoke in rapid Russian, then ended in English with, "I'm afraid I shall no longer be requiring your services. I'm certain you will be hearing from my employer." He shoved his chair back roughly enough to draw attention from several nearby diners, but exited the dining room swiftly and quietly, with no further dramatics.

The noise in the room quickly resumed normal levels. Except at their table, where the tension remained high, as did the resulting echoing silence.

Reese very calmly folded his napkin and laid it across his plate, his dinner half eaten. "I'm afraid I've also lost my appetite."

Felicity's lips formed a distressed little moue, but the light in her eyes gave away her true feelings. "I'm so sorry if our intrusion had anything to do with that."

Reese signaled the waiter, then stood as the young man crossed the room. "Enjoy yourselves," he said to them, then looked to the waiter. "Please include their dinner and anything else they desire on my bill, Edgar." He pushed in his chair, then lifted a satchel Finn hadn't noticed he'd tucked under the table. "I trust you'll also enjoy the remainder of your stay in New York. You'll have to forgive me if I say I hope our paths don't cross again." He looked to Finn. "Pleasure meeting you, Dalton." He glanced at Felicity, held her gaze for a moment longer than necessary, then favored her with a brief smile before turning and exiting the dining room as well.

Felicity picked up a menu left behind by the waiter and flipped it open. Not so much as glancing in the direction of the departing Reese. "Well," she said, sounding quite satisfied, "that went rather splendidly."

Finn didn't know whether to throttle her, go after Reese, or order dinner. Chasing Reese right now would be pointless, as the man almost certainly had a town car waiting at the curb and would be long gone before Finn could exit the room. Felicity Jane could be supremely frustrating, but she was far from stupid, so he trusted she already had a few ideas about where Reese was likely to go next. Which left dinner.

He opened his menu and skimmed over the list of entrees.

A moment later he felt Felicity's toes stroking the inside of his ankle. He didn't look up.

She merely laughed and stroked his leg a bit higher. His body—traitor that it was—leapt to life.

"Don't be put out with me," she said, amusement still clear in her voice.

He continued to look over the menu.

She sighed, and stopped toying with his pant leg. A moment later she folded her menu, took a sip of champagne, then quite casually said, "Order quickly, darling. We have a hotel room to break into."

Chapter 4

"He won't come back here." Finn crouched in front of the hotel door and slipped the demagnetizer through the key card slot. "We're breaking and entering for no reason."

Felicity angled her body so anyone exiting the elevator wouldn't immediately see what Finn was doing. Or trying to do. "I could have gotten the key card from the bellman; then we wouldn't be breaking into anything. Technically."

Finn stood and opened the hotel door, motioning her inside first. "After you."

"Always a gentleman." She moved past him with a swish of her skirt. "And I agree with you. It's doubtful he'd come back here after our little dinner party earlier. I'm sure he's changed hotels by now."

"If not cities," Finn groused, following her inside. "So, pray tell, what are we doing here?"

"Looking for clues before the cleaning service gets to work."

Finn glanced around, taking in the perfectly pristine dresser top and nightstand. "Because someone like John Reese would write fully detailed directions on hotel stationery and leave it carelessly by the bedside telephone?"

Felicity wandered slowly around the room, eyeing every detail, from the clean surfaces to the way the blinds were set.

Then she turned and walked over to the ice bucket and lifted the lid. "Ah."

Finn was in the process of opening every drawer in the place, but paused to look at her. "Ah, what?"

"Ice bucket with melted ice." She turned once again in a slow rotation. "Gauging from the water left and the state of the ice cubes, I'd say he did come back here after dinner. Surprising."

"To pack and check out, most likely, so he could get the hell out of the city."

"If so, why get ice?"

Finn folded his arms. "Maybe he needed a drink to calm himself down after his lovely dinner plans went to hell."

"Possibly. Except . . . I'm thinking he didn't just come back here to pack." She wandered into the master bathroom. "Bingo."

Finn came to the door and leaned against the frame. "Because?"

Felicity turned, holding a long-stemmed crystal glass that still had a sip or two left in it. She swirled it, then sniffed. "Champagne. And quite a good vintage."

"You can tell that from a sniff?"

She smiled. "I'm sure some dedicated enthusiasts probably could. Not me." She stepped around the partitioned shower and picked up the black and gold bottle. "Chantal Neuf. Distinctive packaging. I guess he must have liked the one sip he had at dinner. Or, knowing John, he's had it before. I'm surprised the hotel would have it in their cellar, though."

It was on the tip of his tongue to ask her just how well she really knew John Reese, but instead, Finn walked over and picked up the second glass, careful to use a napkin so as not to smudge prints. "Nice shade of red lipstick."

Felicity glanced over her shoulder. "A bit tarty if you ask me."

Finn grinned. "What, Reese didn't treat you to expensive champagne?"

She set the bottle down and opened the shower door. "The only thing I want from John Reese is that lovely little bauble he's squiring about town." She leaned back to look at him around the frosted glass door. "And I'm not talking about the two-legged, tarty one."

Finn laughed. "Any ideas who the woman is?"

"I was rather hoping that was something you'd uncovered in your background search. I wasn't able to learn anything about his personal life, other than he didn't seem to have much of one. Apparently he takes being discreet quite seriously. Bully for him, but not so lovely for us."

At least that smudge of lipstick somewhat explained his complete disinterest in her earlier this afternoon. She'd oh-so-cleverly had him meet her for tea in her penthouse suite, ostensibly to discuss Foundation business, then make small talk about why he was in town, wheedle a little information. She'd met him at the door with her hair in a towel, covered head-to-toe in a hotel bathrobe, claiming she'd lost track of time after her massage and would he be a dear and pour tea while she dressed?

She wasn't one to use sex as a ploy, in either of her avocations, but then, she hadn't actually planned to have sex with the man. Though, if she were a different sort of woman, it admittedly wouldn't have been much of a sacrifice. He did have a way about him. A far too clever way, as it turned out.

She'd left the door to her bedroom carefully ajar, enough to allow him a glimpse of her in her lingerie as she moved from bathroom to closet to dress. She'd called out for him to take off his jacket and make himself at home, hoping her casual slip-into-something-comfortable demeanor would encourage him to let his guard down, perhaps turn his attention more to her personal needs than her business ones.

Her backup plan if he hadn't been feeling chatty was to ply him with as much tea as she could muster while drawing him out on the subject of Foundation business, and, if she was lucky, slip a hand into his jacket pockets later while he was making use of the bathroom facilities.

And her backup plan had worked beautifully, too, netting her a small card case that had included, among other things, a card from Antoine's and, beneath the cards, a small silver key. She recognized it as a train station locker key, probably belonging to the locker where her lovely sapphire was currently residing. She'd been overjoyed with her finds and quite happy with herself. Right up until the moment she'd heard the private penthouse lift kick into gear, signaling the return of their waiter. And, unfortunately, causing her to completely miss the sound of the toilet flushing. She'd been caught red-handed, as it were. A rare slip for her, but a very costly one.

She'd tried to talk her way out of it, but Reese was no fool. He'd put two and two together and come to the conclusion that Foundation business wasn't really why she'd been maintaining contact with him for the past several years.

To his credit, Reese had been quite the gentleman while divesting her of her dress and hosiery. He'd already retrieved the card case, with key, from her possession, but had ignored her offer to let bygones be bygones. Five minutes later she'd been bound quite efficiently to the bed with her own stockings and his tie.

Less than ten minutes later, Finn had found her.

"I do know he doesn't work with a partner," Finn said, drawing her attention back to the matter at hand. He was turning the glass so he could look at it under the bright bathroom lighting. "Which makes this either a business meeting to set up another buy"—he carefully set down the glass on the counter, then leaned down to scoop up two damp bath towels from the hamper—"or something more personal."

"With the Russian connection dissolving at dinner, I seriously doubt he came back here to dally around with someone just for the fun of it," she said. "It had to be business of some sort."

"Of course," Finn added, smiling, "you don't work with a partner, either. Until now. Desperate times, and all that."

She arched a brow. "Meaning you think he was backed into a corner? Calling in a few favors?"

"Or performing them." Finn shrugged, and grinned in the face of her glare. "Whatever works."

"Honestly, Finn."

"Here," he said, clearly enjoying her huff far too much, but then he was handing her the glass with the lipstick, a napkin wrapped carefully around the stem and saying, "Let's get back to my place and see what we can find out about our tarty mystery guest."

"Where are you staying?"

"I keep a place in town."

Her surprise must have shown, because he lifted a broad shoulder and said, "You keep a car; I keep a brownstone. We need what we need."

"Are you in town all that often?" A tingle of heightened awareness shivered over her as she wondered how many times their paths might have crossed in the past two years, given how often she'd done Foundation business in Manhattan. She'd thought him buried in the rural pastures of the Virginia countryside, running his little charitable organization or some such. In fact, she'd prided herself on not doing more than a cursory check or two on him after he'd left her in Prague. But the truth was, even though she'd thought that not giving him more of her actual time and effort would help to diminish the continued impact he had on her thoughts and quiet moments, it hadn't helped one bit.

She thought about him every time she accepted a new assignment, wondering if this was going to be the time he'd pop up again. And there were other times, usually when she woke up too early, restless and pent up, feeling needy and more alone than a woman of her means had any right to complain about. It was during those times she'd close her eyes and remember what it had been like, what it had felt like, to be with him. She was a confident woman, who handled her affairs, both private and public, with relative ease. But only with Finn had she been such a complete and total wanton. No one had tapped in to her inner core as he had done, and he'd done so almost effortlessly.

"Shall we?"

She snapped out of her reverie, realizing she'd been staring at the champagne glass in her hand. Finn likely thought she was brooding over not getting the attentions of John Reese. *Fine*, she thought, *let him think that*. More the better for her if Finn never knew the level of fascination she'd had for him. Still had, apparently. Dammit.

She tried her best to appear unaffected and coolly in control as she sailed out of the hotel room in front of him, the carefully wrapped glass tucked into the Hermes tote she kept stashed in the town car in case of spontaneous shopping trips. But Finn's long-legged stride kept him right at her back. And she could feel him there, just behind her, in a rather primal way that had no bearing whatsoever on what was actually taking place. She blamed it on the damp towels and lipstick-smeared champagne glass. All too suggestive for her suddenly overheated imagination.

Finn reached past her and pressed the elevator button. When he stepped in after her, she felt a bit claustrophobic, as if he was suddenly taking up way too much space, using up way too much of her precious air. And yet, he was standing a respectable distance from her, not so much as looking at her. Which did nothing to stop the little mini fantasy from playing out in her mind. She couldn't seem to keep herself from imagining what would happen if she suddenly jammed the emergency button, stopping the lift between floors, then catching his reflected gaze in the mirrored walls.

Mirrored walls that would show them from every angle as he saw the need in her eyes, pushed her up against the silvery tiles, and pulled her legs up around his hips. He'd shove her skirt up her thighs as she wove her fingers into his hair and took the weight of his mouth on hers. Their tongues would be dueling, mirrors steaming, her panties—snapped from her hips—in a crumple on the tiled lift floor.

She knew exactly, remembered perfectly, the depth and breadth of him, the way he filled her so fully, so completely. She would arch into him, taking him as he drove her back up the wall, spine arched, chin tilted, exposing her neck to his greedy mouth, gasping as he shoved her higher so he could nip and tear at the tiny row of buttons keeping her dress closed, her nipples aching to the point of pain from wanting his warm breath, his damp tongue, caressing them, sucking them. She'd moan, and thrust her hips, and—

"Have a problem with tight spaces?"

She blinked her eyes open at the sound of his voice, then flushed furiously as she realized that last little moan hadn't taken place in the fevered depths of her highly realized fantasy. "Not usually," she managed, wishing her own tight spaces would stop reminding her of the problem she was currently experiencing. Namely wanting the man next to her to invade them. Often, and with great fortitude.

Finn let her lead from the elevator, though the cooler, damp air of the underground parking garage did little to calm her steamed thoughts. Or body. He held the door to her town car open as he had before, only this time she wasn't nearly as composed. It was lack of food, she was certain, causing her to experience such dodgy behavior. They'd ended up skipping John's offer at Antoine's, leaving the tea and biscuits she'd shared with him earlier as her only source of energy for the day.

"I don't suppose you have a chef on duty at your place?" she inquired, wanting like mad to find her way back to solid ground.

"Hungry?"

Ravenous, she thought, only she wasn't picturing food as she had the thought. She glanced out the window and summoned up her most regal intonation. "I could do with a light meal, a sandwich or salad perhaps. I'm afraid all I've had today is tea and champagne, and a few biscuits."

"And here I was hoping you were thinking about dessert."

She wouldn't look at him. Couldn't. The last thing she needed right now was him baiting her in any way that was remotely sexual. She was baiting herself quite well, all on her own. "First things first," she somehow managed, knowing full well she'd likely need a whole lot more than a full meal to give her the strength she apparently needed to deal with him on a continued one-on-one basis. Especially seeing as she was going to be behind closed doors, in private with him, at least for the next several hours. With a bed handily nearby. She sighed a little, not caring at this point what he thought.

"I'll see what I can scrounge up," he said, a hint of concern in his voice. "We shouldn't dally too long, though. Reese has to be making plans to set up a buy as we speak. We need to get a handle on his partner and/or buyer, then move on it as fast as we can."

She trembled with a bit of relief. No dallying. She was perfectly fine with no dallying. She didn't even feel bad for making him worry just a little about her. The fact that he did made it just as hard on her anyway. "You have equipment to do a fingerprint trace from the glass?"

"I have access there to a lot of things."

She let that bit of news sink in, wondering now if his reasons for keeping a place in town were more business oriented than sentimental or personal. A convenient way to keep the various tools and technology one needed in a profession such as his handy and available. If her every move wasn't so keenly followed by either her Foundation board or the folks who employed her for her other services, she'd consider making a similar investment herself.

The more she thought about it, the more the idea of having her own private little oasis appealed to her. Imagine a place where no one could track her every moment, her every scheduled breath. Not an impersonal hotel room, or one of her family's ancestral holdings, complete with gossipy staff, but her very own, very private, very personal little place.

She allowed herself a few indulgent moments to imagine such a thing, telling herself that from a practical standpoint, it would make great sense to have such a base of operations to work from. Of course, there was no way she could hide herself away in London, as she was far too high profile there. The press would ferret out her hidey-hole in minutes. And though she spent considerable time in New York, D.C. and L.A. when she was in the States, if it was Foundation business, she was usually so heavily scheduled, with her time stretched over more than one city, that she'd have little enough time in any one place for a permanent residence to do her much good. The same could be said for Milan, Paris, and Rome.

And when she visited a city on her other business, she rarely stayed in the same spot for more than a night or two before moving on, and never in the same place twice on consecutive visits. Friends and Foundation members assumed she was on one of her many shopping sprees. And, in a fashion, she was, in fact, usually hunting for a new bauble.

The town car rolled to a stop in front of a tidily maintained but otherwise nondescript row house. "Yours?" she asked, somewhat surprised. She hadn't known what to expect, but perhaps something a bit more elegant, something in the more fashionable Greenwich or SoHo neighborhoods.

Finn nodded. "Home away from home."

"What made you choose this area?" They were in Chelsea, if she had her bearings right.

"Interesting neighborhood. I had some friends who lived here when I worked for the city, and I always enjoyed the energy here."

The area was definitely a mixed bag between high brow and low brow, which, when she thought about Finn's more rumpled elegance, perhaps made more sense than she'd originally thought.

He slid out and held the door for her. She stared up at the

building in front of her, and he stepped in behind her, his hand on the small of her back, making it almost impossible to keep track of what he was saying. Something about the place being one of the few restored nineteenth-century brownstones still privately owned. All she could think about was how warm and large his palm felt against the curve of her spine.

She might have taken the steps a bit more quickly than recommended for someone with heels on, but the sooner they got into his place and did what had to be done, the sooner they'd be back in the car, back on the hunt for Reese and that Byzantine sapphire. If it wasn't already too late.

Thoughts of the phone call she'd be forced to make to London later, explaining the details of her first failed mission, helped keep her head in the game . . . and out of Finn's bed.

Finn stepped in front of her and typed a quick series into the keypad by the front door handle. She didn't miss the fact that he'd shielded her from seeing exactly what he'd keyed in. So much for trust among thieves. Of course, if she was being honest, it had already crossed her mind that she might not need her own city oasis if she could simply find a way to access the one Finn already, so helpfully, had. Three layers of entry security later, she decided that wasn't going to be such an easy task.

But then, she did so love a challenge.

"My, my," she said, when they finally entered his inner sanctum. "How . . . bohemian of you."

Finn laughed, not remotely put off by her less than enthusiastic reaction to his personal space. "I spent enough time in stuffy law libraries and leather-bound offices. I don't like feeling constricted."

She wandered into the expansive foyer and looked up. Where there would have traditionally been a crystal chandelier hanging from the second-story, open ceiling, instead there hung a huge, brightly patterned parachute, somehow lit from behind, so the colors of the billowing silk played along the foyer walls, and those of the broad staircase leading to the second and third floors. She turned back to him. "You have the whole building, then?"

He nodded. "We all make use of it from time to time, when needed, but it's mine, yes."

"Who is 'we'?" She wandered into the front parlor off the foyer, half expecting to see hammocks slung rather than the more traditional settee and high-backed chairs, and so was only partially surprised to see a series of low-slung suede chairs and ottomans scattered about, with a huge brass platter balanced on a gnarl of mahogany root as a coffee table of sorts, and a pile of various types of rugs scattered about in front of the fireplace mantel. "Well, I see you're all prepared for your next orgy."

"I like comfortable things," was all he said, still sounding vastly amused by her reaction. "And the 'we' in question are my two partners, Rafe and Mac. We sort of grew up together."

"And your business in Virginia brings you here?"

"What do you think this is?"

She lifted a shoulder. "A personal jaunt, perhaps? After all, I'm not aware of too many charities that encourage breaking and entering, fingerprinting and stalking, as appropriate methods of philanthropy."

"I never said I ran a charity. You did."

That gave her pause. She might not have obsessively followed his every move, much as she'd have liked to, but she felt pretty sure of the little research she had done. "What, then, is Trinity, Inc., if not a charitable foundation?"

"We help people, just not in the traditional sense."

She felt him enter the room behind her, but kept her focus on the series of fascinating framed photographs lining the walls.

He stopped just behind her, so close she could feel his breath stir the ends of her curls. "And what do you know of Trinity? Checking up on me, are you?"

"I've found it's never a bad thing to know at least a little about my adversaries."

He leaned a bit closer, and she stared that much harder at a matted shot of Finn in mid leap out of an airplane. "Is that what I am to you, Felicity Jane? An adversary?"

She tried not to visibly shudder in pleasure at the feel of his breath on her neck, his body heat warming her even from the slight distance there still was between them. "We certainly have been in the past."

He moved an infinitesimal bit closer. "And now?"

She paused, long enough to draw on whatever reserves she had left, knowing she had to answer him with cool detachment if she didn't want to end up flat on her back in his bed. Or draped across one of those sumptuous-looking ottomans. "And now we have to figure out who John is working with before our little blue quarry leaves the country for points unknown and likely far more difficult to extract it from. I'd much rather wrap this up on American soil, if you don't mind."

He reached past her and tapped the photograph she'd been staring at. "My first jump. It was about four years ago, right after my father died. Amazing how clearly you can see things from ten thousand feet in the air."

"I—I can only imagine," she managed, wondering how to shift away from him without touching him.

"And I'm sure you have a rather well developed one." He ran his finger along the lines of the parachute in the picture, and it was as if he were touching her instead. "Have you ever?" he asked.

"Ever . . . what?" Could he read her mind? Did he know how hard her nipples were at this moment? How damp her panties?

"Jumped."

"From—an airplane? A perfectly functional one? No. I rather like to stay in touch with my own sanity, thank you." Like she would right now, she thought, wishing she felt more tightly tethered to reality than she happened to at that moment.

"Given your predilection for adrenaline-based activities, I'd think you'd find it incredibly satisfying."

"You think I'm an adrenaline junkie?"

"I think you have to have a certain appreciation for the rush to do what you do."

"Running the Trent Foundation is quite rewarding, but I wouldn't exactly say it gets the adrenaline pumping."

"I'm not talking about your charitable works."

Which, of course, she knew. So, he was calling her out, was he? Pushing her to put her cards on the table, as it were. She turned now, perhaps very unwisely, but she wanted to hear, directly from his lips, while looking into his eyes, just what it was he thought of her alternate occupation. "And what is it, exactly, that you think I do?"

She was neatly tucked between the wall of photos behind her and the wall of broad chest in front of her. His hand was still touching the picture beside her head, but he moved it now, fingering the ends of her curls instead, in a way that sent a tingling sensation along every nerve ending she possessed. It was a delicious feeling, and one she'd have loved to indulge in further, encouraged even, if the stakes weren't so high.

"I don't exactly know," he said. He twined more of her hair around his finger and leaned in a bit closer, his crystal blue eyes gazing intently into her own. "Why don't you help me understand why a woman of your means feels the need to steal those priceless little baubles, as you call them? My guess is it has to be the rush, the danger. Am I wrong?"

It shouldn't have offended her in the least, the conclusion he'd drawn. In reverse circumstances, she'd have drawn the exact same one herself. She wanted to confide in him, which would serve the dual purpose of finally having someone to discuss this secret life with, as well as give her the supreme pleasure of tossing his presumptions back into his beautiful face. That was dangerous enough, but even more, she perversely wished she didn't have to explain herself at all. She wanted him to think better of her than that, when, of course, she'd given him absolutely no reason to.

"One might wonder the same of you," she said. "We've

crossed paths several times now, in quest of, shall we say, off market property, using less than orthodox methods for retrieval. If the organization you formed with your childhood acquaintances isn't a charity or a trust, then what, exactly, is it? You've been in business with them for two years, but it's been longer than that since our paths first crossed in Bogota. Do you have other business interests of a more solo nature? And if you are here in the city on business, as you claim, then why would said business include mirroring the very same activities as me, pursuing the very same bauble, in fact, if not for the same reason? Client or no client. After all, you're an admitted adrenaline junkie, as the many photos on these walls would attest."

"Perhaps it takes one to know one," he said, his gaze not wavering in the least, despite the casual tone.

So, he was going to let her think him some sort of common thief. Well, perhaps common wasn't fair, as their quarry required a far higher skill set than that of the average jewel thief. "Perhaps, but from what I know of you, adrenaline junkie or no, international jewel thief doesn't seem to fit your otherwise helper-of-the-people profile."

"The same could be said of you."

She smiled now, a slow curve of the lips. "I know." She used the momentary confusion in his eyes as her opportunity to finally slip free of his immediate proximity. "So, time being a precious commodity, shouldn't we get on with doing whatever testing can be done to this fine piece of stemware?" She retrieved the wineglass from her tote and held it out to him.

He crossed the room and reached out for the glass, but she pulled it back, her smile growing wider with his frown. "You are going to let me assist, right?"

She could see from the look on his face that that hadn't exactly been his plan.

"If you're worried about giving up all the secrets to your little bat cave here, have no fear. I have my own set of resources. I can assure you I won't be requiring yours."

He held her gaze for a long moment.

"If we're to be partners, the trust has to start somewhere," she said.

"Partners," he repeated. His gaze dropped to her lips, long enough to make her squirm a little. Then he abruptly turned around and walked out of the room. "Follow me," was all he said.

Chapter 5

Finn didn't know what to do with her, but he damn well knew what he wanted to do. He didn't bother to look up the staircase, knowing full well there was quite the decadent lair waiting for them both upstairs. Knowing equally well just how good a use the two of them could make of such lodgings. If he chose to nudge her in that direction, which he wouldn't. Not if he had any sense in his head.

It was risky enough, bringing someone like her here, to his inner sanctum. It wasn't smart, giving someone with her proclivities even the most limited invitation to what was available within these old, renovated walls. It was true that both Rafe and Mac had availed themselves of the technology housed here, but, unlike the vast compound at Dalton Downs, this wasn't Trinity property. This place was his, had been long before his father had passed. The one thing he still had left from his former life, the one thing that had never been anyone else's. And he was already regretting bringing her here. Even in such a short time, he knew she'd find a way to imprint herself on his space, making her even more unforgettable, in the last place he needed her to be.

He stepped into the foyer and turned toward the hallway leading under the stairs to the rear of the house. Only he paused beneath the staircase itself and pushed on a panel hidden there. There was a soft click; then the entire wall panel swung inward. A cool rush of air from the lower realms of the below stairs brushed his skin as he crouched to step inside, then down the first several of the iron spiral steps leading downward. "Mind your head," was all he said to her, not even turning to see if she followed. Certain she would. "Use the handrail. Those shoes you're wearing aren't the most functional things for an operation like this."

"We all have our tools of the trade," she said. "You'd be surprised what a nicely tailored pair of Italian leather pumps can do for a mission."

Picturing those long legs of hers in Italian heels and nothing more than the lingerie he'd discovered her in earlier—was it only today?—he was inclined to agree with her assessment. He kept that bit of information to himself, however, and continued his descent.

"Watch the last step," he warned as he reached the bottom. "It's a bit steeper than the others." He would have turned and offered her a hand, had he been willing to risk even that much contact. He wasn't. Not at the moment anyway. He was sporting quite the raging hard-on. Again. And was growing concerned that the condition was going to be permanent as long as she was around. The solution, of course, was to end their less-than-strictly-business working relationship as soon as possible. Which was his goal, of course.

His thoughts strayed again to the third floor. To the huge, king-size bed he'd had specially made. It was built into a frame set directly on the floor and was covered in blankets and linens of various weaves and textures. There were pillows of all sizes, scattered everywhere. Panels of sheer curtains and netting hung from the ceiling, shrouding the bed in a filmy mist of ivory and pale blue. He rarely slept there, but when he did, he enjoyed the reminders of some of the places he'd been. Nepal, Peru, Indonesia.

Now he was picturing her there, beautifully splayed amongst the plush pillows and Egyptian cotton. The use he could make of some of those cushions, arching her body just so, getting caught up in the way her skin would look, so creamy and smooth against the bold jewel tones and exotic weaves.

"So," she said, a bit of wonder in her tone as she lightly hopped off the last step. "You really do have a Bat Cave right here in Gotham City."

He kept his back to her and his twitching erection from view. He walked over to a computer monitor, pressed a button so a keypad eased out of the console beneath, and typed in a series of pass codes. Lights came on in the cabinets surrounding the lab part of the room, and the countertop glowed a cerulean blue. A large screen was revealed over the desk and shelving units when wall panels slid apart. Incongruously, there was a pinball machine at one end of the panel of high technology, and Pac Man at the other. Smiling as he watched her take it all in, he pulled a small kit from one of the cabinets and flipped it open. "Why, yes, Girl Wonder," he said, "yes, I do."

He held out his hand. "Know anything about fingerprint-ing?"

She absently dragged her gaze back to his as she handed him the stemware. "Mostly about how not to leave any behind."

He shouldn't grin at that, but he did.

She didn't peer over his shoulder when he turned and placed the glass on the countertop. Instead, she came to stand directly beside him. "I pick things up pretty quickly, however."

"That much, I knew."

Now it was her turn to smile. "So," she said, "where did a former assistant district attorney/current adrenaline junkie part-time jewel thief learn how to process fingerprints? I won't ask where you got all the expensive toys."

"My partner, Mac, used to be a detective with the NYPD. As for the electronic gadgets, that's also Mac's specialty." He brushed lightly over one set of prints, then carefully placed a piece of specially treated, clear tape over the powder. "The computer system is Rafe. If you want to know anything about anything, or anyone, he's the guy. Given enough time, he can uncover anything. If he can't find it, it's not out there to be found."

She leaned over to examine his actions more closely, and a waft of spicy lavender scent tickled his nose, among other things. "Which makes you the bankroll guy, I'm guessing," she said.

He wasn't insulted by the remark. Mostly because it was true. "Initially, yes. The company funds itself now."

"Big buck clients?"

"Smart investments. We don't charge for our services."

That gave her pause. Good. He discovered he liked shaking her up, being unpredictable. Lord knew she was often that for him.

"Interesting way to run a company that's not a charitable foundation."

"Yes, I thought so myself." Smiling, he went back to work. He motioned her to follow him over to another small table, where he peeled off the fingerprint tape and processed it.

"You have access, I assume, to some kind of fingerprint database."

"We do."

"So, if John's shower and champagne companion is in that database, that means she's not likely to be your run-of-the mill Susie Secretary."

"Or Dora Desk Clerk," he teased, making her roll her lovely green eyes. "Highly doubtful that's the case anyway. I don't think Reese would stop in the midst of a full-scale deal melt-down to have a little fling with the hotel receptionist. Whoever was in that shower with him is, at the very least, involved in some aspect of his world. Whether it's the part that's a little shaky on legalities, I don't know. But the timing of this meeting certainly suggests it is."

He scanned the image into the computer, then sat back and keyed in the information to start the system searching. Once it was running, he swung around in his chair to look at her. Not surprisingly, she was presently looking over the various tools and equipment lining tables, walls, and a large lab center. Knowing Felicity, she either had a photographic memory, or some kind of recording chip buried in her earring. He certainly wouldn't put it past her, anyway. In fact, it wouldn't be a bad idea to revamp the entire setup down here after this was over. He'd have Mac rewire the entire security system. Mac had been bugging him to update to a newer technology anyway.

He glanced at the computer screen, then turned his attention fully back to her, and contemplated the fact that he was already planning a complete security overhaul designed specifically to keep out the very woman he'd invited in. He could say it was all about keeping his enemies closer, but that was a lie he wouldn't even pretend to tell himself.

"So, if we find this woman, then what?" she asked, still wandering around. She wasn't poking into anything, or even touching anything, but he doubted she was missing much anyway.

"We dig up as much information on her as possible. Then we find her."

Felicity looked over at him. "Find her. In a city of millions."

"You track things a lot smaller than people."

"But there aren't generally a million or so of them running around. And we have to do this before the piece leaves the country. Either you have access to a lot more data than even I could imagine, or you know more than you're letting on."

"I'm pretty well connected."

She held his gaze for a moment longer, looking as if she wanted to say something, then went back to wandering around his office and lab space. "You say you don't use this place often? A lot of gear here for the occasional user. Nice toys, too," she added, with a quizzical glance in his direction, as she walked past the pinball machine.

"Helps me think. It's a left brain-right brain thing."

"Not a stunted childhood thing?" she asked, smiling this time.

He smiled back. "Oh, no, that, too. Definitely didn't get enough toys growing up. But then, who does?" He gestured to the rest. "As to that stuff, well, we have the means to own some pretty nice gear. So, it's not a bad thing to have it when you need it."

She glanced over at him, a smile playing around her mouth. "There's a sentiment I can agree with."

His body stirred.

She nodded toward the computer. "I think we have something."

Surprised, he turned to look at the monitor and discovered she was right. "Usually takes longer." A lot longer. He chalked it up to luck and rolled his chair back over to the screen and began to scroll through the information. Felicity came to stand behind him and read over his shoulder.

"Julia Forsythe," Finn said, reading out loud.

"American," she said as he continued to scroll. "Interesting."

He glanced over his shoulder. "Why do you say it like that?"

"Nothing specific, just that I haven't discovered too many of you Yanks in this line of work, that's all. At least at such an advanced level." She smiled at him. "You being the exception, of course."

He didn't bother to correct her assumption, thinking she was baiting him for precisely that purpose. "My experience is that it doesn't seem to hold to gender or race." Now he smiled. "A thief is a thief."

She didn't respond to his baiting either. And he found himself regretting they would never fully be able to just be themselves with each other. Too much was at stake, for people who mattered. Well, in his case anyway.

He turned away to another computer and began typing in the pertinent information. She was still standing at the other monitor, scanning through what little info there was on the hit.

"One prior arrest. Grand theft. A felony," she said, making a humming noise, but no other comment. "Charges were dropped."

"The arrest was enough to get her prints in the system. That's all we needed."

"You're not going to find much then, are you?"

"I'm not researching her criminal history."

Felicity looked up at that. "Oh?"

"As you said, not much there to look into, and what is there isn't exactly a surprise, on the surface anyway."

"Says here, last known address is San Francisco."

"Still is," he said.

She walked over to stand behind him. "My, my. You are rather connected, aren't you?" She leaned down to peer more closely over his shoulder as additional information about one Julia Dawn Forsythe, age thirty-three, single, scrolled onto the screen in front of him now. "Impressive."

It was that, he thought. Knowing what their setup was capable of didn't mean he still didn't enjoy watching it in action every now and again. He'd sent the information back to their home system, with an alert to Mac, who'd set up a direct link into Rafe's database, which extended well into realms it probably shouldn't. Finn didn't ask questions. He just enjoyed the results.

"She's an art dealer," Felicity said. "How convenient."

"With a rather impressive private studio," Finn followed.

"I'm surprised her arrest wasn't more of a put off to her clientele."

"She was arrested four years ago. She opened this studio just under two years ago."

"And already such a success. Interesting."

He shifted to look at her, but she kept her attention on the monitor. "I launched Trinity around the same time."

"But you said you're not-for-profit. Your funding comes from investments made from your inheritance."

"True, but—"

"It says here her taxes last year showed her to be in the red by almost a million dollars."

"Maybe she had private funding as well."

Felicity looked dubious. "And shall we make a bet on the likely method used to secure this private funding?"

"She could just be a dealer who uses Reese to obtain objets d' art for certain clients who wish to remain anonymous."

"For a hefty finder's fee. And dealers willing to take risks can make an even better turnaround for their investment."

"You sound as if you know something about this." He looked at Felicity, who'd straightened and taken a step back.

"Hardly, darling." Rather than take offense, though, she laughed quite naturally. "Why ever would I want to part with something I worked so hard to obtain?"

It was a classic Felicity Jane response; confident and self-effacing, all at once. And yet, he wasn't buying it this time. "Money?" he said.

"I have more than I could spend in several lifetimes, so that would hardly provide motivation."

"Maybe not for you, maybe for the Foundation. It can't be easy maintaining your ancestral holdings."

She tilted her head. "Someone's been doing a bit of digging, too, I see. But to answer your query, no. The Foundation and my ancestral holdings, as you so quaintly call them, are maintaining themselves as well as can be expected, without my turning to a life of crime to help uphold them."

So then why have you? he wanted to shout. He'd already asked her once, outright, but she'd danced around the answer by turning it back on him. Perhaps if he hit close enough, he'd see the truth of it in her eyes. "Maybe it's the thrill of obtaining the piece, and, once secured, it no longer holds any fascination. So it would only make sense, then, to get rid of it. Enter John Reese."

"I told you, we've worked together on Foundation business. And his work with, and for, them would pass the closest scrutiny." She didn't respond to the rest, other than to say, "I thought we were in a race to track down the whereabouts of one Julia Forsythe? Surely your prurient interest in the motivation behind my recreational pursuits can wait until we've located our quarry."

Recreational pursuits. "I am tracking. If you worked with John in the past as a client, rather than as a peer hunting the same piece, then it holds that you might know something of Miss Forsythe."

She sighed. "I knew of John and his reputation—both good and bad—prior to this little adventure, yes, but, and I say this for the last time, I've never purchased anything from him personally, regardless of provenance. I've never dealt with Miss Forsythe in any manner. Anything else?"

She held his gaze with ease, her tone flat, indicating her displeasure with the direction of his questioning, but nothing more. Or less.

"But you know of her?"

She shook her head. "I know of her kind. There are a lot of less-than-scrupulous art dealers in the world. In this city alone, in fact. It doesn't say more or less for her that I've not heard of her. She could be quite the big thing in the States, for all I know."

Every question he asked seemed to net him no information, other than to add more questions to his list. It was frustrating on several levels, mainly the one that needed to be successful in solving this case in order to do the right thing by his client . . . and the other part of him that wanted to understand her better. Instead, he was more confused than ever. Instinct told him there was a lot more at play here than she was letting on. But that could be wishful thinking, based on the near constant hard-on he'd been sporting since seeing her again.

"So, what's next, Mr. Holmes?"

Finn turned his attention back to the report. With a little more time, he could get quite an extensive dossier on Miss Forsythe, but time was a commodity he didn't have. He was also itching to do a more thorough search on his current partner-in-not-quite-crime. Though not so much for the purposes of the case at hand. If he'd been smart, he'd have dug more deeply a long time ago. And he'd been tempted many times over the intervening years to do just that. Mostly it had been fear of what he'd discover, and what it might lead him to do about it, that caused him to opt to leave himself in the dark. What he didn't know couldn't hurt either one of them.

But now that he'd made a more direct connection, one he couldn't ignore, it was well past the time for burying his head in the sand. Or anywhere else. It was time for answers. One way or the other, he'd get them. Just as soon as he found Julia Forsythe.

"What's the next step?" she asked.

He started tapping at the keyboard again. "Next, we search for any information pertaining to previous visits she's made to the city."

"And you're going to get this—wow." She leaned over again as information began scrolling onto the screen. "How in the name of heaven can you access flight information like that? Particularly after 9/11?"

He leaned forward to get a closer look. "She's a regular visitor, it seems. Comes to the East Coast, New York City in particular, half a dozen times a year or more. All in the past two years since going into the art business." He scrolled down. "Bingo. I love the Internet and travel package deals."

"Meaning?"

"Meaning I don't have to dance around Homeland Security and flight databases. Avalon Travel's Web site is much less secure."

"Avalon Travel?"

"Small San Francisco agency, it appears. They book her flights and hotel."

"Hotel?" Felicity repeated.

He felt the sudden spike in tension and smiled. "And car rental." He tapped a few more keys, then abruptly pushed his chair back. "Come on."

"You don't think she'd still be there, do you?"

"Nope, she checked out earlier today."

"But—wait up a second, will you?" She kicked off her heels and grabbed them before hurrying up the steps behind him. "Where are we going?"

"Airport."

"She has a flight leaving tonight? Which one?"

"Yep."

"But airport security, you can't get out to her gate—"

"It's a private airfield, but we're not going there. At least not yet." He held the front door for her, never more thankful for Felicity's limo sitting curbside, awaiting its mistress's next whim. "She has to return her car first."

Felicity paused. "Who rents a car in the city?"

He gave her a sardonic smile as they climbed in and closed the door. "I don't know. Someone who wants to avoid using public forms of transportation for whatever reason?" He stretched out his legs. "You tell me."

"It's true, I use my own town car, but it's not quite the same as driving yourself about in this horrible traffic. Given the alternate forms of transportation, I'm simply surprised Miss Forsythe would choose to squire herself about."

He shrugged. "Maybe she likes to be in control of things."

"Perhaps. With all your whiz-bang technology, can you find out how many miles she put on her little rental?"

Finn sat up a bit straighter. "Why?"

"If the mileage seems exceptionally high for around-the-town driving, it could be worth noting."

"Meaning you think she rented a car to do out-of-town business, while in town?"

Now it was Felicity's turn to shrug.

Finn pulled out his iPhone and tapped at the screen. "Hopefully those are questions we'll be able to ask her ourselves."

"How close are we cutting it?"

"Too close for comfort, but unless she drives like she's in an Indy race, we should cross paths."

Felicity settled into her seat and crossed her legs. Finn kept his attention focused on the small, illuminated screen.

"Do you think it's coincidental that she happened to be in town at the same time as our Mr. Reese?"

"I'm not a big fan of coincidence."

There was a pause, and he looked up to find her smiling. "And yet, here we are."

"Hardly the same thing."

She lifted a shoulder. "Perhaps."

"Meaning what?"

"I've been in New York many times in the past two years. And yet, our paths haven't crossed until now. Are you saying you showed up in New York, in my hotel room, by plan?"

"No, I was tracking Reese—"

"Did you know I was in the hunt this time?"

"I—" He faltered. He hadn't known. Not for sure. But he'd hoped. There had been only a few times that his cases had involved something she might have also had an interest in. Each time, he'd certainly wondered if she'd pop up, had even anticipated the moment.

"So . . . a coincidence, then," she said.

"Only in that I wasn't intending to cross your path, but it's not all that surprising that I did. Given what we found in Reese's hotel room, I highly doubt it was just coincidence that he and Julia Forsythe ended up in the city at the same time."

"I don't know about that."

"Reese was trying to secure a big exchange at Antoine's, which fell through. I seriously doubt he just bumped into Julia in the hotel bar on the way back and figured, what the heck, might as well have a little fun."

"I simply meant that you bumped into me, and with a little less restraint, we might have left similar evidence behind. Perhaps more."

Finn couldn't exactly refute that statement. "You think they've worked together before, or knew of each other, hap-

THE BLACK SHEEP AND THE ENGLISH ROSE　71

pened to bump into each other at a time when he had no time to spare, and couldn't resist temptation?"

Felicity's smile was both knowing and challenging. "You tell me."

"What I think, is that maybe they were working together all along, and what we saw in the hotel room were the remnants of a celebration of a major deal being made."

"Which fell through."

"We don't know if they had that celebration before or after his dinner at Antoine's."

"Except for the ice. And the still damp towels."

"Not entirely conclusive."

"True, I suppose. But not likely."

"Did you have any information on Reese flying out tonight?" Finn asked.

"No proof, but I hardly think he'd stay in town. He's based in London, so it's the perfect time to get a flight over."

"I haven't been able to track anything down." He went back to tapping on his screen. "He's a lot more circumspect in how he makes his travel arrangements than Miss Forsythe."

"Wouldn't you think, if she was a high stakes roller, or in any way associated with one, she'd be more circumspect herself?"

"Not if her traveling to New York was already a well-established routine, which it was. Deviating from that suddenly would have looked more suspicious."

"If she flies privately, that takes a pretty good travel expense account. She's done well for herself, but that's pretty steep. Reese, on the other hand . . ."

Finn looked sharply at her, then clicked back to the reports he'd downloaded onto his iPhone. "She didn't always. Fly privately, I mean. That was noted on the last two trips, and this one. No other details about the flights, just a note from the agent that private arrangements were made. By noting the time of the car rental return, you could guess the flight times. The drop-off location is a private field just outside the city."

"So, maybe we'll get two for the price of one," Felicity said. "The big question is, do they still have the stone?"

The driver pulled in past a small discreet sign announcing the private field. They passed a small restaurant and gift shop, then a gas station. A few minutes later, they were pulling up at a small building with a car rental sign on the front. Just beyond, he could see the shadows of the larger plane hangars. The tarmac was just to their left, and the runways just beyond that.

When the town car came to a stop, Felicity didn't wait for someone to come open her door. Finn barely caught up to her at the rental agency door. There was a woman in a red blazer behind the counter inside. "I'd prefer it if you let me handle this one."

Felicity smiled sweetly at him. "You think I can only make things happen when there are men involved?"

He pushed open the agency door for her. "No. I just think I can make things happen better when women are involved."

She opened her mouth, then closed it again.

"What? No smart retort?"

She brushed by him, leaving a brief whiff of lavender in her wake. "No."

When had she put that on, anyway? It was incredibly . . . lingering. Not to mention arousing. "Because?"

She glanced over her shoulder. "Because you might be right. This time."

He laughed, and they shared a smile that was both knowing and intimate and made him desperately wish they were anywhere but where they were. They approached the desk together. "Excuse me," Finn began, before Felicity could start in. "We'd like to rent a white Lexus. Two door, if you have it. Would you happen to have one available?"

The young woman smiled rather mildly at Finn. "I'd have to look, sir."

"Thank you, Andrea," he said, catching the tag on her blazer pocket. "Much appreciated."

Clearly not impressed with his attention to detail, much less charmed by it, she gave a rather short glance Felicity's way, then began tapping on the monitor screen in front of her.

Another clerk stepped out of an office door behind the counter. His name tag read BRIAN, and he was younger than Finn's new friend, Andrea, enough that he didn't appear to be shaving yet. But not so young that he didn't get hung up, at least briefly, when he caught a glimpse of Felicity Jane. Maybe they should take turns, he thought, depending on gender.

"Whatcha need?" he asked, all willing to provide the cheerful customer service Andrea was not.

"I have it," she said, at the same time Felicity smiled at Brian and said, "Lexus, white, two-door?"

"I—I do have one," Brian said, all but beaming with pride. He stepped over to another terminal and began tapping on a keyboard.

Felicity followed him, after casting a brief, smug smile Finn's way.

He was pretty sure his responding smirk rivaled Andrea's. Or was a close second.

"It was just turned in, but it's not done being cleaned," Brian continued, looking a bit more tentative now.

"Dammit," Felicity murmured, but not so low that it didn't carry to the young rental agent.

"I'm really sorry, ma'am," the agent rushed to add. "But regulations state that we have to go through a check list of items before we can release it for rental again."

She looked up at Finn, all plaintive and uncertain. Damn, she really was good. "What do we do now?" she asked, as if their only other choice might be life-threatening. Given the barely suppressed level of hostility Andrea was aiming at Felicity Jane, that might not be an exaggeration.

"It won't take that long, ma'am," Brian hurried to assure

her. "I can get them to put a rush on it; it's just we had to go retrieve it from one of the hangars—" He broke off when both Finn and Felicity turned to look at him. "What? What did I say?"

"It was left at a hangar?"

"Yeah, some hot shot called and informed us we'd have to go pick up the car ourselves, like we have that kind of crew available. Some people just aren't considerate, but I'm sure we can accommodate you. How about I offer you an upgrade, free of charge? I have a nice—"

"That's quite kind of you," Felicity responded, this time with a smile only Finn knew was forced. "We need to go discuss this; then we'll get back to you."

"Sure, no problem. Let me know if there's anything else I can do. I'll put a rush on the Caddy for you, just in case. It's a convertible!"

"Much appreciated," Finn said, then steered Felicity back outside, leaning down to speak quietly in her ear. "I saw a sign pointing to the main flight office. It's over there, about halfway down the line of private hangars. We'll head there and see what we can find out."

"If she's on Reese's plane, they could be heading anywhere. He doesn't fly in anything small."

"I'll bet," Finn muttered.

Felicity let that pass. "We'd be lucky to find anyone in the office who'd talk to us."

Finn smiled as they both ducked into the waiting town car. "You underestimate yourself. You had the car rental kid ready to offer marriage if it would keep you in his proximity a minute longer."

She did smile at that, despite the concern still clear in her eyes. "It's the accent. You Yanks just don't know what to do with it."

"It does hold a certain charm." He sat back and pulled his iPhone out once more, his smile fading as he went back to work. "You know, I'm going to have to rethink the whole leased limo thing. This is coming in pretty handy."

"It does that," she responded, still sitting on the edge of the seat, looking out the window as the driver maneuvered along the narrow road leading toward the hangars and other outbuildings.

Finn noticed the pensive look on her face. "We'll track them down."

"I wish I had your confidence. I'm concerned that we're heading off in the wrong direction. If it turns out Julia isn't involved, or doesn't know who John sold it to, then we've wasted valuable time, and the stone will have left the country."

"I'm betting the private plane belongs to Reese. We find the plane, we'll find Reese and, hopefully, the stone. My gut says Julia helped him broker a deal with one of her clients back home and they're headed to California."

"And if you're wrong?"

He waited for her to glance his way, then grinned and said, "Well . . . we could always discuss dessert."

Chapter 6

The town car swung around toward the final hangar, mercifully preventing her from responding. Dessert. Like they weren't in the midst of racing about, trying to track down a priceless gem before it disappeared again. Like they had time for some frivolous liaison.

She kept her gaze focused out the side window . . . and away from the temptation seated across from her.

They pulled up in front of the small office, which was wedged between the much bigger metal structures that were the hangars. Most were relatively small, the ones they could see anyway, but there were a few in the distance that were rather large. Large enough to house a decent size jet.

Once again, Felicity exited the car before either the driver or Finn could assist. This time, she was going to do all the talking. And, again, Finn caught up to her just before she pushed open the glass door. The room on the other side was decorated with a few fake palms, a row of airport chairs, and a table with several magazines scattered on it. Behind the counter stood yet another pair of people wearing blazers. This time in navy blue. No one else was in the small waiting room area. Felicity tried not to feel disappointed, but it sure would have made things so much easier if Julia or Reese happened to still be making flight arrangements. No such luck.

Finn placed his hand over hers on the door, keeping her

from pulling it open. "I'd go for finding out what plane Julia is booked on, as we know she's brought her car back, so she's here somewhere, or was. Leave Reese out of it, for now. I'm sure you'll come up with some plausible story."

"And you'll be where?"

"I'm going to jog over to the big hangars and nose about."

Momentarily surprised at his decision to leave her to handle any part of this alone, it took her a second to regroup. She looked over her shoulder at him, catching his gaze long enough to gauge if this was some kind of test, or if he was trying to pull a fast one of some sort. Maybe he'd recognized something with one of the jets as they'd driven in . . . She was tempted to keep him with her; then they could head out together to check on the hangars and planes, but with time ticking down, dividing and conquering was the best plan. She just hoped it was a plan she could trust. "Okay," she said, knowing she sounded less than confident, despite its being her desire to divide and conquer in the first place. It was easier to trust when it was her idea. "I'll meet you outside when I'm done."

He smiled a little, as if amused by her wariness. "Good."

He stepped back and let her open the door. She waited for him to head off toward the private hangars, then signaled to her driver to wait specifically for her. If Finn had to count on her for transportation, that gave her at least a bit of an edge. She approached the counter with her most engaging smile and a slightly flustered demeanor. "Cheers, I'm hoping you can help me. It seems a friend of mine has changed her plans at the last moment, and only a part of her cell message came through." She put on her most crisply accented tone and proceeded with her tall tale. "We were supposed to dine in town tonight, then fly out to Paris tomorrow. We purposely decided to rent private so we could fly on our own schedule." She laughed gaily. "But, of course, it's just like Julia to get a wild hair and want to fly out tonight, instead." She leaned forward. "Or a wild man. I wouldn't be the least bit surprised if she's flying out on Sir John's plane." She leaned farther over the counter, all best pals and seemingly unaware of the boundaries she was crossing. "Could you be ever-so-kind and help me track her down before she flies out? Reese is his last name. John Reese. And Miss Julia Forsythe. I really need to get a better cell service when I'm in the States."

She scanned the papers on the desk as quickly as she could, before they could cover them up, but there was too much there, too much scrawled rather than typed, for her to absorb much of it before one of the agents deftly scooped the paperwork into his hands. "I'm sorry, ma'am—"

"Oh, my, I must look more dreadful than I thought," she said, patting at her hair. "Ma'am, is it now?" She laughed as self-consciously as she could.

The young man blushed and stammered. "No, ma'am. I mean, miss. I mean—I was just being polite, it wasn't—"

The other agent, unfortunately female and, while pleasant looking enough, not quite as entranced by Felicity's Britishness—at least once she saw her coworker tripping over his tongue, anyway—stepped forward and butted into the conversation. "We can't give out any manifest information, I'm sorry. It's very strictly regulated."

The crestfallen look Felicity gave them both wasn't hard to pull off. "Oh, dear. I certainly understand, but however am I to find her, then? I'll be stranded here and, well—" She looked back toward the door, to the tarmac beyond, then back to the agents. "Is this the only area serving private jets? Can you tell me if there are any planning to leave shortly, or that have just left? You list arrival and departure information for commercial flights; surely it's not against any regulation to give me that much."

"It is when it's a privately owned plane," the woman agent informed her. "I'm sorry," she added, and seemed to mean it. Mostly. Andrea could take lessons. For a brief moment she wondered if Finn could have swayed her, then snapped out of that. It would be unwise to get used to having him around. In any capacity. Surely she could handle this much on her own. She'd tackled far more challenging obstacles and won. Most of the time.

Felicity's shoulders slumped, but not overly dramatically, as she placed her bag on the counter. "Whatever am I to do?" She pulled out her cell phone and pretended to look at the screen. "No signal at all now. Oh, dear. Oh dear, oh dear, oh dear." She once again scanned a longing look outside, then back to the agents. "Would it be possible for me to book a private flight from here? Is there a service I can contact or another office?" She sighed. "Although, what if I book to Paris and Julia's gotten it in her head to fly back to San Francisco instead?"

From the corner of her eye, she watched both agents and noted the way the male agent's eyes darted to the papers in his hand when she said, "San Francisco." Bingo. She tucked her cell phone back into her purse and pulled out a slender wallet. "If I could just reach her to find out what the rest of her message said. She's going to feel awful for stranding me here." She kept the male agent in her sights as she let go with another aggrieved sigh. "Of course, if Sir John is with her, she's likely distracted and—"

"Is he truly a knight?" the young man blurted, eyes almost glowing with interest. He took the sharp elbow of his coworker with a little wince, but didn't take his eyes off Felicity. "I'm sorry, it's just you called him sir and I wondered, and—"

"The Queen herself thinks so," Felicity said, which, for all she knew, was true, as John was known to be quite the charmer when he wanted to be and, despite his less-than-lily-white reputation, had been known to grace more than one royal function. The fact that he hadn't exactly been knighted in the traditional sense and likely never would be wasn't really important. He was quite young for that honor anyway. Something the even younger agent here obviously wasn't aware of, and about which she had little regret in harmlessly exploiting if it got her the information she needed. No harm was being done, after all.

"Have you met her? The Queen, I mean?" he asked, eyebrows climbing halfway up his forehead.

Felicity ignored the aggrieved glances of his coworker, who was clearly embarrassed by his outburst, but fortunately was forced to duck away to answer a ringing phone. Felicity knew that this was her only chance, so she turned all of her attention on the young man in front of her, who had no name plate on. More was the pity. "We've met on several occasions," Felicity said, this time quite truthfully. She had graced a number of royal function guest lists, as well, but her attendance with the Queen had been limited to long receiving lines and very brief curtsies. "She's quite awe-inspiring."

"I bet," he gushed. "Do you know any other knights?"

"I've met my fair share, yes. Mostly I just need to reconnect with this particular one." She leaned farther forward and braced her arms on the counter, pushing her advantage as she lowered her voice conspiratorially. "To be perfectly honest, Sir John can be quite the scoundrel, and I'm very much afraid my friend Julia will fall prey to his rather finely honed charms. She's not quite . . . worldly enough, if you take my meaning."

"I thought she seemed pretty sharp," the agent said, so entranced by Felicity's let's-gossip chumminess that he seemed to forget what he was letting on. "I overheard them discussing something when they walked in, and she wasn't letting him walk over her, that's for certain. Although she did let him do the talking when it came to setting up their flight."

"See?" She threw up her hands in mock disgust. "Here we were supposed to fly out together, a girlfriends-only European weekend in the offing, and he's already got her head all turned around. I'm just afraid what else he might get turned around once he gets her twenty thousand feet up."

"She didn't seem to be that big a pushover to me," the agent told her, trying to reassure her.

Felicity wrung her hands. "When it comes to business, she's a shark, but as her best friend, I know her history with men, and trust me, she loses all common sense. Sir John is way out of her league, and I'll simply never forgive myself if I don't at least warn her as to what she's getting herself into."

The young man looked over his shoulder, to where his co-worker had disappeared into an adjoining office, then back to Felicity, clearly torn. "I wish I could help you, but even if I told you what hangar they were using, you'd never get there in time."

"If she leaves the States with him—"

The agent darted another quick look over his shoulder, then quickly shook his head at Felicity, his expression quite earnest, as if trying to signal her in some way.

"They're not leaving the States?"

He smiled, looking relieved that she'd picked up on his oh-so-clever signal.

She laid her hand on his arm. "Thank you for doing what you could. I appreciate it."

"I—I'm sorry I couldn't do more," he stammered, obviously a little overcome by her touching him.

"It's more than I had. Cheers." Felicity squeezed his arm, then quickly turned and headed toward the door.

"Cheers!" the agent called out behind her.

She didn't have to look far for Finn. He was presently running toward her in a long, loping stride. He had the natural kind of athleticism a person could only be born with. Any other time, she'd have taken pleasure in watching him move. She hurried toward him.

"I tracked down two flights, both leaving in the next forty-five minutes. Then nothing till morning. Nothing international tonight."

"They're not flying out of the country. I got that much. Was one of them to San Francisco?"

He shook his head. "Detroit, and Dallas."

"Maybe they're making a stopover for gas midway. Did you get a peek at the passengers for either flight?"

"I don't think either of those flights are theirs. I think they've already taken off. There were three flights out in the past hour."

Felicity swore under her breath, then noticed Finn was grinning. "What could possibly be amusing?"

"One of those flights was to San Francisco. It left about ten minutes before we got here."

Her eyes widened. "Then what are we standing here for? We should go back into the office and arrange something with whoever can get us up in the air first. I've managed to build some rapport with the agent in there. I'm sure for the right price, we can find someone to fly us out of here tonight." She turned around to head back to the office. "If nothing else is available, we can go commercial and take a red-eye shuttle out."

"Already done," he told her, snagging her elbow, and neatly turned her back around. "We leave in forty-five minutes."

She gave him a surprised look. "Quite certain of yourself. What if I'd come out and said it was Paris?"

"Flight plans can be cancelled." He grinned. "Your faith in me is touching. You could give a guy a complex, you know."

She couldn't help it; she glanced down, then quickly back up. "I hardly think that will ever be a concern of yours."

His grin only broadened, and made her quickly shift the subject back on topic. "Besides, you'd have to care what people think to develop a complex. And if you were so damn clever out here being one of the boys with your fellow adrenaline jockeys, then why did you leave me in there, making googly eyes at that poor young man, when you knew all along—"

"I was coming to your rescue when you hustled out the door. And never underestimate the potential future help of the freshly googly eyed. I'm sure, along with Brian, he'll be your devoted fan for life. You never know when you might need a car or another last minute flight. They could come in handy at some point."

She rolled her eyes, but she was thinking that she wished

Finn was as easily "googled" as the young agent had been. She wasn't used to dealing with someone as sharp as he was. Hell, she wasn't used to dealing with a partner at all. "Which one is our hangar?"

"About fifty yards, that way," he said, nodding. "We'll be about an hour or so behind them, depending on the weather between here and the West Coast."

"And when we land? Private flight, small airfield means they'll easily be out of the airport by the time we land."

He pulled her closer, until she was almost flush up against him. She shouldn't allow him the familiarity, but he was already talking before she could convince the rest of her body that she didn't want to be so deeply into his personal space. Mostly because it was a lie. And she was a terrible liar.

"We can plot and strategize once we're in the air. Right now, I'm more interested in finding something to eat before we take off."

"I couldn't possibly," she said, pressing her hand to her stomach.

"You have a fear of flying?"

She gave him an admonishing look. "Why do you say it like that? Like you couldn't believe me capable of such a weakness."

"It wasn't that. It's just that you do an inordinate amount of flying, so it would seem to be something you'd have adapted to by now."

"I don't fear flying. I enjoy it, actually."

"So . . ." Then he smiled as understanding dawned. "You're nervous." He said it with something akin to marvel in his tone. As if it were even more improbable than her having a relatively normal issue such as fear of flying.

She tried to take it as a compliment, that he saw her as that indomitable. She would never tell him the truth, which was that despite the nerves of steel sometimes required by someone in her moonlighting profession, she was just like anyone else.

Susceptible to doubt and insecurity, still vulnerable as the next person. "Are you so certain of success in this that you can honestly say you're not nervous?"

"I'm . . . concerned. And I certainly am geared to do whatever it takes to make sure we succeed. But my stomach isn't in knots over our eventual success, no."

Must be nice, she thought, but didn't give him the satisfaction of saying it out loud. She'd been working privately for MI-8 for three years past now, and had handled a number of cases for them quite successfully, but she still got butterflies when things got intense. Having Finn stare at her like the famished man he was, with her in the role of juicy drumstick, wasn't helping matters any. "If you'll point me to the plane, I'll go settle in before takeoff. Will they have tea or water?"

"No in-flight service on last minute charters." He drew her a bit closer. "Unless I can talk you into considering dessert."

"We haven't even had a proper dinner," she said. She smacked at his hand when he slid one past the small of her back. "And your fixation with dessert is becoming wearisome."

He laughed. She really was a terrible liar.

"I believe you were the one to first mention it."

"Well, I was preparing for battle then and feeling my oats a bit."

"And now? We have a transcontinental flight ahead of us." He wiggled his eyebrows. "Much plotting and strategizing to be done."

"Hardly the same thing," she replied coolly, though her body temperature was anything but. She was envisioning all sorts of things that could happen over a long, late night flight across the country. None of them designed to cool her off.

"The hangar is just that way," he said. "Number nineteen. I'll be back before we take off."

Given the nature of their banter, the state of his pants for the better part of the past few hours, and his tenacity, she was wary of his seemingly easy acquiescence. "See that you are."

He raised his brows, but his grin didn't abate a whit. "Why, yes, Your Royal Highness."

"I'm just saying that there is a lot at stake here, and I won't have the pilot waiting around while you find yourself a burger and chips."

"The pilot will wait for me."

She merely gave him a challenging look.

"Stacy has worked with Trinity before. She likes us."

Felicity scowled. "Only you."

Finn merely nodded. "I do have that kind of luck."

She went to slip her arm free of his grasp, very determined to walk away with her chin up and integrity intact. What did she care who he flirted with and what he did when she wasn't looking?

He neatly turned her right back around and flush up against him. "Would it take that adorable pout off your face if I told you Stacy was fifty-two and a grandmother of three?"

"I'm sure I have no idea what you're talking about."

He slid his arm along her back and snuggled her between his legs. "Have I ever mentioned that your queen-of-the-realm tone really turns me on?"

"I'm fairly certain a stiff breeze could do the same," she said, but the way her body immediately responded to the hard length of him made her retort less than stinging.

He leaned down and kissed the tip of her nose, which shouldn't have charmed her nearly as much as it did. "Save me a window seat." Then he was gone, climbing into the limo. She opened her mouth to warn him that she'd given her driver instructions to wait for her, but saved her breath. She spat out only a few very inelegant swear words when her car—with her driver—smoothly pulled away from the curb moments later. "Why?" she muttered. "Why did I think this was a good idea?"

She headed off to find Hangar 19, determined not to think about Finn, his luck, or what kind of dessert he might dream up, thirty thousand feet in the air.

Chapter 7

Finn hopped the stairs into the plane two at a time, then ducked inside, nodding to the pilot as he did. "Hey, Steve. Thanks for waiting."

The older man just smiled and tipped his fingers to his forehead. "Ready when you are."

Finn grinned. "I'm always ready."

Steve just chuckled, shook his head, then closed the door to the cockpit. Finn shuffled the bags in his hands, then made his way into the main section of the small private jet.

Felicity was seated in the central area, where there was a large round table surrounded by four cushy leather chairs. There were also seats along either side of the plane, situated next to the windows. He happened to know that in the back, there was a small private meeting area, a fairly nicely appointed bathroom, and a bedroom, which was pretty much all bed.

He smiled at Felicity, who had both her arms and legs crossed, and didn't look particularly happy with him. She glared at the closed cockpit door, then back at Finn. "A grandmother, huh?"

"I didn't say it was Stacy, just that it could have been. As it happens, Steve doesn't play for your team either."

She tried to maintain her frosty expression, but he saw her fight the smile. "No wonder I couldn't get him to move the plane one hangar over."

Finn shoved the bags into a bin under the table and extended his hand to her. "We need to buckle in for takeoff; then we can get cozy."

"Cozy?"

"Here," he said, motioning to the table. "No reason to stay shackled into those little seats when we can fly in comfort."

"Yes, further shackling I could do without."

Finn barked a laugh, and took her offered hand in his. She was such an interesting mix of blue blood and street smart, he never knew quite what to expect from her. He drew her up, but resisted the temptation to pull her directly into his arms. They had a five-hour flight ahead of them. Pacing was everything.

"Window or aisle?" he asked.

"Either is fine with me."

He led her to a window seat and waited until she got comfortable, but rather than taking the seat next to her, he sat next to the window on the opposite side of the plane. She looked surprised, and perhaps even a little disappointed. He smiled to himself and buckled up.

They were rolling toward the runway when she finally spoke. "So, I take it you know Steve? Lucky coincidence he was here."

"I fly in and out of here a lot, so I know several of the pilots."

"You always fly privately? Why not have your own plane?"

"I fly my own helicopter. We have several. In fact, one of them is parked on the roof of a certain hotel in town, as we speak."

"I suppose that shouldn't surprise me."

"Meaning?"

Her lips did curve slightly. "You do like your toys."

He tried very hard not to look at the bag stowed under the table. "Work hard, play harder. After all, what's the point of work if you never get to appreciate play?"

"Some would say their work is their play."

"Some would. Is that how you view your . . . occupation?"

She looked at him and parroted an earlier response, slightly modified. "My work for the Foundation is very involved and rewarding, but I don't consider it play."

"I wasn't referring to that occupation."

She looked back out the window as they taxied around to prepare for takeoff. She was smiling. "I know."

Finn was just about done with the enigmatic responses and Mona Lisa smiles. He just couldn't put the two sides of her together. She was understandably proud of one career . . . and so blatantly unrepentant about the other.

"Why didn't you invest in a private plane?" she asked.

"Too much to maintain. It's easier to just keep a few pilots on call and work things out when needed. I know it comes as a shock, but we still fly commercial a lot of the time."

"So do I."

He looked surprised; he couldn't help it. She laughed.

The pilot interrupted them with instructions for takeoff, and they fell silent as the plane accelerated, then lifted into the night sky. Finn loved this part, leaving the pull of the earth and gliding freely into the empty skies. He'd gotten a pilot's license when he was quite young, but it had been only a handful of years since he'd gotten his license for the helicopter. It was still a thrill, taking off in that thing, like he was flying himself, free of restrictions.

He glanced over at Felicity. Her hands were relaxed on the arm rests, and she was peering out of the window. No fear of flying. He wondered what she'd think of taking a ride in his new little black bird. He imagined it, taking off on a clear spring day, showing off a little, earning a few eye rolls from her, but also, hopefully a laugh or two, and an honest smile. He wondered what that would take.

Despite the intimacy they'd shared, he had no idea who she really was. Her background was so intensely privileged, far more so than his State-side version of the same. Her education was impeccable. She was sharp, smart, fearless. Which was both impressive and, he imagined, potentially quite intimidating when she wanted it to be. But that was the part of her he knew, the part the whole world knew, if they cared to. What he wanted to know—was suddenly dying to know—was who she was, and what she'd be like on a regular, everyday level. Then he laughed at himself. Felicity Jane Trent didn't have a regular, everyday level.

Still . . . he tried to picture her back at his home in Virginia. Dalton Downs had a lavish main house, stables, and enough acreage to satisfy an earl or two, and yet he really couldn't bring her into focus there. Partly because he'd worked very hard to remove the lord-of-the-manor vibe of the place after his father had died and left it to him. His partner, Mac, had moved his significant other, Kate, onto the property over a year ago, along with her school for seriously challenged young children. His other partner, Rafe, who typically involved himself with high-powered supermodel types, had apparently fallen for Kate's new head horse trainer. He couldn't wait to get back and witness that interesting union in action.

But he couldn't see Felicity Jane being in tow with him.

It shouldn't have dispirited him. After all, she'd always been more fantasy than reality. Larger than life. Certainly not part of anything having to do with his normal one. If you could call anything about his life normal, either.

"Quite the scowl you have over there. Something amiss?"

He glanced over at her, and found her staring at him in that intent, open way she sometimes did. He could imagine others found it a tad unnerving, that sort of overt directness. And that she'd intended it to be. For him it was more unsettling than unnerving. Despite the fact that they'd once again found themselves on a little adventure together, where, for a brief span of time, they'd be in each other's orbit, and more than likely each other's bed, only to drift apart once the adventure came to its natural conclusion . . . this time he wasn't so willing to leave it at that. The problem was, he had no earthly idea how he did want to leave it.

Or if he wanted to leave it at all.

The two intervening years since he'd seen her had vanished the moment he'd laid eyes on her again, and yet, he had no desire to repeat that cycle. Now that she was part of his world again, he found he wanted to keep her there indefinitely.

"No," he said. "Nothing's amiss." Frustrating, intriguing, and confusing as all hell . . . but not amiss.

He thought about the bag he'd stowed in the compartment under the table. He'd been quite happy with himself as he'd assembled his array of goodies, thinking about the various directions the following five hours could go, and how prepared he was going to be for any eventual outcome. Now his mood had shifted. Inexplicably so, really, as nothing had changed between them.

The captain's voice filtered into the cabin, announcing they had reached altitude and could move freely around the cabin.

She was still staring at him, clearly not appeased by his less than enthusiastically delivered response. But what was he going to say? He could hardly reveal his actual thoughts. Hell, he didn't even understand them himself.

"I know we have plenty of time to get down to business," she said, quite crisply, "but if it's all right with you, I'd like to go over possible scenarios on how we're going to proceed once we land, now, rather than later. I'm thinking it would be a good idea to get some rest before we push onward, and I know I'll rest better if there is a plan in place." When he didn't immediately respond, she smiled a little and added, "You do have a plan, I presume? Or are you going to depend on me to do everything in this partnership?"

She was teasing, but as he looked at her, all he could think about was the bed in the back, and how little rest he'd planned on either of them getting. And how much he'd counted on their partnership being quite equal. At least for the next five hours. Now . . . he had no idea what he wanted. "I don't know if you investigated when you boarded, but there is a small bedroom in the back, if you want some rest. I can bunk out here. The seats in the center recline."

She lifted her eyebrow at that, but didn't bait him any further. He knew he was confusing her. *Welcome to the club*, he wanted to say.

"I was going to link up and connect in with my partners back home," he said by way of explanation, though they both knew it was hardly that. "I want to see what they can dig up for me—us—while we're in the air. I can do some research on the unit I have with me, but they have access to far better equipment and can retrieve it far more swiftly."

Now it was her turn not to immediately respond. Instead, she looked merely bemused.

"What?" he finally asked, although he knew damn well what. Given their past history, by now, confined to close quarters with nothing else to do for some time, one or the other of them would have instigated something that required the removal of most of their clothes . . . and the other would have gone along quite willingly with the suggestion.

"While I would like to think that the gentleman in you listened to my repeated pleas to focus on the issue at hand, and steer our attention away from the rather explosive chemistry we share, our history precludes me from drawing that conclusion."

"You feel I'm not a gentleman?"

"You once left me chained, naked, to my bed—our bed, actually."

"I sent a bellman," he responded.

"My point is that you are a man who goes after what he wants. You can be both courtly and aggressive, depending on the situation, but—"

"You don't think I'd put your desires before my own? I'm wounded. I thought I was rather adept at meeting your . . . needs."

"I am merely saying—"

"That I'm a selfish bastard who can't keep his hands off of you, so if I am keeping them off now, something must be terribly wrong. You don't think, perhaps, that, like you, I'm wanting to focus on the case at hand?"

"There is a bed in the back of this plane. Can you look me straight in the eye and tell me you didn't think of, or at least imagine, in great detail most likely, spending a few minutes there during this flight? And not for the purposes of rest."

"Of course I thought about it."

"And that bag you brought aboard . . . ?"

"Again, my thoughts might have strayed beyond satisfying my immediate hunger. Would you like to see what I brought?"

"I'm certain you'll show me regardless."

"Your high regard of me is so challenging. How will I ever maintain such a vaunted image?"

"Everything I'm saying is true, is it not?"

He conceded her point with a nod. It shouldn't bother him, either. In fact, he had no idea why he wasn't pushing this repartee to its natural and all but foregone conclusion.

"But now . . . you're all business. And so I asked, and I shall ask again, why the sudden shift?"

He had no answer for that. Getting naked with Felicity Jane would be a great way to spend time, especially now as neither one of them had the stone nor could have it in the next half dozen hours, so neither was in danger of being poisoned or shackled, or God knew what else. It was as trustworthy a position as they were ever likely to be in. And yet, he found himself not overly interested in getting naked with her for the sake of getting naked. Oh, he wanted her. Kind of hard to deny that one, given the ongoing rock-hard state of his body. He just didn't want her casually. Which was ridiculous, considering there was no other basis for them to be together.

"You don't seem particularly dismayed, one way or the other," he said, going on the defensive rather than trying to come up with a suitable answer when he had none. "Perhaps my ego couldn't take the constant threat of rejection."

"Yes," she said drolly, "I can see where that's so often an issue with you."

"You have to admit, you have been rather fickle. Tormenting me one moment, pushing me away the next. If I didn't know better, I'd think you were a tease."

Her smile was slow, knowing, and did things to him that were impossible to ignore. Which she likely knew and was quite enjoying.

"You, of all men, should know the answer to that."

The hell with it, he wanted to say. *Just do it already*. The sexual tension between them was all but shrieking, as it always was. He'd be doing them both a favor by taking her to bed, where they could take the edge off for a prolonged and quite gratifying length of time, thereby enabling them to focus more clearly on the task at hand afterward.

And yet . . .

He held her gaze for a moment, then said, "If you had, say, an afternoon. No appointments, no grants to award, no gems to steal. Nothing on your agenda at all. You're alone, without anyone observing you, completely private. How would you spend the time? If you could be doing anything you wanted."

She tilted her head, as apparently surprised by his sudden question as he'd surprised himself by asking it. "Is this a trick question? Am I supposed to fawn, and bat my eyelashes, and say, 'Oh, my darling, of course I'd choose to be naked, in bed, with you'?"

"No, you're supposed to be absolutely honest. In fact, I'll alter the question to add, if you had to spend the afternoon alone, doing something just for you, by yourself, that you enjoy, what would it be?"

She frowned, then looked somewhat pensive. Gone was the teasing, knowing smile. It was the first time he'd ever seen her look uncertain. About anything. Finally, he thought, finally he was getting a glimpse of the real Felicity Jane. And he realized that that was exactly what he was after. That was what he wanted. To know her. In ways that had nothing to do with car-

nal knowledge and everything to do with becoming more intimate than they'd ever been before. It was a dangerous path to
pursue. Mostly because, rather than hope her answers diminished her appeal, thereby giving him the eventual easy exit
he'd like to think he wanted, he was hoping a better understanding of her would give him a clue as to what to do about
his already impossible attraction to her. Somehow he doubted
there was going to be anything easy about any of it.

But then, that was part of her charm.

He waited, as patient as he knew how to be, but just watching the play of emotions across her face, he was already more
interested in her than he'd ever been before. Which was saying
quite a lot.

"The truth?" she asked, looking at him, for once, like the
stranger he truly still was to her.

"Please."

"Gardening," she said without hesitation, then looked back
toward the window, as if she didn't want to face the ridicule
she was certain was about to follow. "Followed by a nice tea,
made and served by myself, out amongst my flowers. Then
reading. An entire afternoon of it. A grand adventure of the
mind, while never having to leave your own patio chaise."

Finn had no idea what he'd expected her to say. Shopping in
Milan with friends. Jetting off to the Amalfi coast. A visit with
the Queen. An afternoon safari in Africa, followed by pearl
diving in Madagascar. He thought she could have said pretty
much anything, and he would easily be able to imagine her
doing it. Nothing would be out of bounds for a woman who
had access to the world, and often took advantage of it.

He'd never expected it would be something so simple, so . . .
basic. Essential, even. He was having an even harder time envisioning it. She was a woman who had gardeners to tend her
flowers, and butlers to serve tea. And what could she possibly
read that would be more adventurous than the exploits she herself had experienced?

He continued to watch her, as intrigued by her obvious dis-comfort as he was charmed by her honesty. "Vegetables or flowers?"

She darted a look at him, and for the first time he saw past the perfectly arched brows and expertly applied makeup, to the core of the woman beneath. It was barely a glimpse, and only the beginning. But he couldn't have been more intrigued, wanting to uncover even more.

"What?" she queried, blinking at him.

"Your fantasy garden. Vegetables? Or flowers?"

"What makes you think it's a fantasy?" She didn't let him answer that. "Flowers. An abundance of them. Untamed, thriving naturally."

"No formal English garden?"

She shook her head, then asked, "Does that surprise you?"

"I don't know what surprises me about you. I don't really know you."

"Ah," she said, understanding dawning. "Is that what this is, then? Let's play twenty questions, get to know the real Fe-licity?"

"Would that be a bad thing?"

"Only if you're doing so hoping to find a chink in my com-petitive armor. I should know better than to lower any de-fenses around you."

She sat back in her seat, and he saw the moment she shifted gears, returning to the woman he did know. The knowing look was back, the confident attitude. She'd crossed her legs, and her arms. Her whole posture had shifted back into super-woman mode.

"Don't," he said, giving voice to the thought before he could think better of it.

"Don't what?"

"That." He gestured to how she was sitting. "It's almost like a persona you adopt."

"What in the world are you talking about?" She didn't uncross her legs, but she did uncross her arms, looking a little self-conscious, even as she blustered a little. "This is exactly who I am."

"When you're running empires or taking possession of priceless antiquities, maybe."

"And you think that is somehow not who I really am? I hate to break this to you, but that is very much a part of who I am."

"It's a large part of what you do. Not necessarily who you are."

The walls were up in full force now, and the predatory gleam completely filled her eyes. How was it he'd never noticed that? That she used the tension between them almost like a shield. Like it was a safe place of sorts, working that attraction, working him, so she didn't have to . . . What? Reveal herself? Be truly intimate? Intimate in a way that actually might mean something. Or compromise a part of her she couldn't risk compromising?

"When did you become such an expert?"

"I'm not," he said, but what he was thinking, what he was realizing, was that he was recognizing all this in her only because he was, and had been, doing the same thing with her. That had him sitting back in his seat, and he had to consciously not cross his arms, or put up his own shield. And he wasn't liking the feeling, the feeling of being exposed somehow, even though she had no idea what he was thinking or the realizations he was making. But it was enough to understand why she wasn't all that keen on pursuing the conversation. It was . . . threatening.

It would be so much easier to simply flirt back, play on the sexual attraction, seduce them both into bed. How interesting that that was turning out to be the safe place for them both. Naked and intimately entwined. Yet, not really vulnerable or intimate at all.

She held his gaze. "What brought all this on?"

He thought about deflecting the question, about making it

easier on them both and going the expected route, by saying something intentionally provocative and flirtatious. With what they were likely going to be up against in the next day or two, the reality of the parameters of their temporary partnership should be at the forefront of his thoughts. The probable outcome of the mission they were on, and the fact that only one of them was going to be getting what they wanted, wasn't exactly conducive to forming any kind of ongoing relationship. So deflect and seduce, enjoy what they could have, and be happy with that, would certainly be the wise course of action. It was certainly the course of action he'd have always expected himself to take in such a situation.

So, no one was more surprised than him, when, instead, he heard himself say, "What brought all this on is that I'm realizing that while I'd very much like to spend the next five hours naked and sweaty with you, and should be doing everything in my power to convince you of the same . . . I also know it's going to frustrate the hell out of me. And I'm not sure I ultimately want that."

"A man with a conscience?" she queried, trying to sound amused, but mostly looking a bit alarmed. "I don't believe it. The next thing you'll be saying is you want to—"

"I want to have you, don't mistake that." He unlatched and swiveled his seat so it angled directly toward her.

She stopped, then simply shut her mouth and stared at him.

"It's been two years, and yet one look at you, one whiff of your scent, and it might as well have been yesterday when I had you last. I'm so distracted by the constant raging hard-on I've had since laying eyes on you in that hotel room that I can hardly think straight. So, clearly, the best course of action here is to get you naked and bury myself as deeply inside of you as I can, for as long as I can, until I can get myself back under control. Then, and only then, might I have a prayer of thinking only about the job I'm on, and how I'm going to accomplish my goals. And not how badly I want to hear that little gasp you make in the back of your throat before you come."

Her lips parted slightly at that, and his body sprang even more fully and achingly to life. He wanted to taste those lips. Badly. He wanted to feel them on him. Every part of him. He wanted to watch, he wanted to participate. He wanted her. Fully, completely, and for as long as his body would hold up.

"So," she said, her voice not remotely steady now as she gave voice to the very thought he was having, "what's stopping you?"

"I don't know you. And what I do know shouldn't attract me as much as it does. I don't know how to square myself with that. Because you're right, I do have a conscience. One that shouldn't allow me to want all the things I want, with someone who chooses to do things that I don't believe in or support."

"Meaning my . . . penchant for certain antiquities."

He nodded. "But that doesn't seem to be stopping me. Which confuses me."

"So you thought that perhaps, if you asked a few questions, scratched beneath the surface, all would be revealed, and all would suddenly make sense."

"Something like that."

"So this is about assuaging your guilty conscience before you bed me, not about truly wanting to get to know me."

"I didn't say that. I do want to get to know you. I want to know everything about you. You fascinate me."

"I like to garden. You find that fascinating?"

"Far more than anything else I've learned about you so far."

She blinked at that, but he knew she heard the complete sincerity in his tone. "Don't you think that perhaps it's the mystery of who I am that makes me so fascinating to you? Perhaps if you knew me, and discovered that I'm not all that special or different, that, in fact, I'm rather mundane, it would dampen your . . . enthusiasm?" Her gaze drifted lower and settled on the now straining zipper of his trousers.

Her gaze alone made him twitch. It took enormous will not to shift in his seat. Not to touch himself, stroke his hand along that part of him she was looking at almost hungrily, just to see what she'd do.

"I'm not sure there is anything I could learn about you that would dampen . . . this." He laid his hand along the inside of his thigh, his fingertips close to brushing against his erection, but not quite.

He watched as she instinctively shifted her legs, pressing them closer together. Assuaging her own ache, perhaps. He waited, then, until she lifted her gaze to his, and said, "But I'm thinking I want to find out."

Chapter 8

Of all the things he could have said, he'd chosen the one most guaranteed to raise every defensive wall she owned. Partly as an instinctive security measure to protect her against the possibility that any element of her other life could or would be ferreted out. She could never allow herself to be exposed in such a way. Not if she wanted to continue with the work she was doing. And she did. Both for her own very selfish reasons and for the more noble goal of helping her country. She was somewhat ashamed to admit that it was the former that drove her far more than the latter, but then, she was already more than fulfilling her philanthropic duties to those less fortunate with her position as the head of the Trent Foundation. Surely she could be allowed a small measure of selfishness in her other vocation without its reflecting too poorly on her soul.

And here was poor Finn, whose soul was pure, as were his motivations in all avenues of his life, conflicted because he'd found himself attracted to a thief and had no way to square his moral self with that knowledge. It should amuse or gratify her in some way that despite his misgivings about her seemingly less than legal frolics, he wanted her anyway. Not only did he want her; he wanted all of her.

She did shift in her seat then, despite willing herself not to.

Because she was unable to find that place inside of her that would let her lie to herself, or at least come up with some small thing, anything really, that she could latch on to as a means of protecting herself. The truth of the matter—her instinctive and almost overwhelming immediate response to his baldly and intently stated desire—was that she wanted the very same thing.

It was shocking, really, and hard to even admit as much to herself. It shouldn't be. He'd never been far from her waking thoughts, despite the elapsed time since their last meeting, and with no promise of ever seeing each other again. And Lord knew he'd consumed her unconscious thoughts for far, far too many nights.

But still, she'd never allowed herself the fantasy of this. Of them seeing each other again and reaching out for more than each other's willing and quite ready body.

What he wanted was dangerous bordering on terrifying, and she discovered she was ill prepared to deal with any part of it. She had a job to do. An important one. People were counting on her to deliver, as she always did. This was no time for selfish pursuits, much less delusional ideas that there could ever be more here than a very intense, deeply passionate and fulfilling physical relationship. Hell, she didn't even think she could handle that and keep her head on straight, which was why she'd run so hot and cold with him already.

There was no way she could bring him in and tell him anything, no matter how badly she realized she wanted to. Not because she cared what he thought of her—though it mattered more than it should—but to ease his own conscience and allow him the peace of mind of knowing that his instincts were still on track, despite surface appearances.

Which left her sitting there, with no idea what to say. Or what to do. So, for the first time in her life, she took the coward's way out. It was the only course of action she could think of that wouldn't cause further risk of either of them being compromised.

She stood, and made far too great a deal out of smoothing

her skirt. "I think I'm going to take advantage of that room in the back. Alone." She forced herself to look at him. "I've heard all that you're saying, and I'm . . . I'm flattered."

"Flattered," he repeated, his voice toneless.

She shouldn't give him the slightest of edges. All of her training, and every bit of her hard-won experience, screamed at her to raise her guard and give him not so much as a toehold to latch on to. "If the circumstances were different . . ." She trailed off only for a second, then quickly went on, albeit far more shakily than she'd have liked. "But they aren't. And they won't ever be. So I don't see the point in pursuing anything beyond a strict working relationship. I do respect you, and because I respect you, and your directness and honesty, it's only fair to give you the same. Therefore, I'm telling you that I think it would be best if we made every effort to stay focused on the business we have between us. And nothing else."

She didn't realize she was trembling until she had to take a moment to get herself under control before risking taking so much as a step toward the back room in the heels she was wearing. That she might have been stalling to give him time to respond also crossed her mind . . . and the thought wasn't easily dismissed.

"Okay," he said at length.

She'd just steadied herself by placing her hand on the back of her seat, and was about to take a step, when he'd oh so calmly delivered his answer. So her consequent stumble would have been comical if not so mortifying, especially as it was accompanied, no doubt, by an obvious look of surprise on her face. It was just that given his temperament and drive, she supposed she'd expected at least a little battle.

She couldn't look at him, couldn't take the amused, perhaps even smug, expression she'd surely discover on his face. Well-deserved, but presently beyond her scope to endure.

But not looking up cost her even more, as she didn't see that he'd risen from his seat until he took her elbow in his hand and steadied her himself. She should have recoiled from his touch. After all, she'd just delivered her quite magnificent speech about how they were going to remain partners in business only. If he pressed his suit now, she wasn't entirely certain she wouldn't end up the biggest hypocrite ever.

"I understand," he said, his tone quiet, even sincere, if not particularly warm.

She did look at him then, wishing mightily that he'd take his hand off of her so she might have a shred of a chance at straightening out her thoughts and feelings. But he didn't. And she found she couldn't quite pull away. "Do you?" she heard herself ask.

He merely nodded. But when she thought he would drop his hand and step away, he instead said, "I just want to know one thing."

Danger, danger, her inner voice screamed, but it didn't stop her from responding. "Which is?"

"Have you ever wondered?"

"About?"

"Me. The rest of me. Or the possibility of us."

She should lie. It would end this. He wouldn't like it, but she knew a man with his code of honor would respect it. "There would be no point to it," she said instead.

Of course he saw through that. "A conclusion you could only draw if you had. Thought about it, that is."

"Avoiding the obvious doesn't require much thinking."

Rather than look hurt or dismayed, he smiled. It was slow to start, but grew steadily, reaching fully to his eyes, which twinkled quite charmingly. "If only we could. Avoid it, I mean."

" 'Business only' means just that. No sex, Finn," she warned, quite shakily as it happened. Damn it all.

"Mixing the two never seemed to bother you before."

"I didn't know you wanted more. I wouldn't—that changes things."

"I could say I'd be willing to settle, but if that was the case, we wouldn't still be standing here right now."

She swallowed against a suddenly dry throat. "So we're understood, then," she managed.

He laughed. "Hardly. That's the problem."

"What's not to understand?" she demanded, trying hard to find her righteous anger at his intentional obstinacy. "You want more than I'm willing to give, so it's only fair that we both step back and do our jobs without further entangling ourselves."

"If things were fair," he said, "we wouldn't be attracted to each other in the first place." He crowded her the tiniest bit closer to the back of her seat. "We'd never have gotten entangled to begin with." He shifted a bit more. She didn't stop him. "If things were fair, I'd have turned you in the first time I met you and caught you with that dazzling Columbian diamond."

"A diamond you were also after," she reminded him, though her heart was beating so hard now, she couldn't even hear herself speak.

"The difference is, I was just recovering an item that was stolen from my client and put on the black market." He shifted closer, lowered his head slightly, so she had to tilt her chin to maintain eye contact. "Where did that diamond end up, anyway?"

"Rightful ownership isn't always as clear cut a case as some would like to think," she said, knowing this was already more than she should.

"Meaning what? Finders, keepers?"

"Meaning we both have our own views on what constitutes right and wrong."

That smile flirted around the corners of his mouth again. "Why don't you illuminate me on your personal view."

"You already think you know, so why bother?"

"I don't think I know anything when it comes to you, which brings us all the way back around to my initial proposition."

"I don't recall you propositioning me. Quite the opposite. This time," she added, trying and failing quite magnificently to channel the inner vixen that usually had no problem surfacing around him. Instead she'd come off sounding a bit . . . put out.

"If you're trying to slowly drive me mad, Your Majesty,

you're succeeding quite brilliantly," he told her, allowing a hint of her own accent to color his words as his amused smile once again reached his eyes.

"I'm just trying to get the job done without creating additional obstacles that will only make it more difficult."

His eyes darkened slightly, and his smile hardened. "Interesting choice of words."

She mentally scrambled back over what she'd said, but hardly remembered which words she'd used. He was standing entirely too close, and so she was missing whatever it was he'd picked up on. "Mixing business with pleasure might not be an obstacle for you, but—"

"That's not what I meant. We both know what we're capable of there, and whether we'd prefer it to be more or not."

Now she tensed. What had she let slip?

But rather than illuminate things for her, he merely let his palm slide down her arm until his hand covered hers. He lifted it, turning it palm up, and pressed a kiss into the center of it, never once breaking eye contact as he curled her fingers over the damp spot. "Keep that safe for me, will you?"

With that, he turned around and dug the bag out from under the table. "I'm going to feed the hunger I can. Would you care for anything?"

She stood there, completely bewildered, before thankfully, mercifully, her anger kicked in. He was toying with her, and she most definitely did not appreciate it. "No, thank you. I believe I'll retire and get some rest. Once you've gotten whatever information you can from your partners, I'd appreciate it if you'd use the intercom to buzz me awake. I'll be happy to go over whatever plan you devise." And with that, she turned her back and all but fled to the rear of the plane.

Forty-five minutes later, lying stiffly on her back on a bed that was far bigger and far more comfortable than she'd imagined an airplane bed could be—private jet or no—Felicity realized that she was too pent up to rest. Pent-up anger, pent-up desire, pent-up . . . a lot of things.

She sighed heavily, quite disgusted with her pent-up self, and tucked her arm beneath her head. She was staring at the ceiling, but seeing something else entirely. Someone, actually. Finn Dalton. Of the forever tousled blond hair, blue eyes that should be outlawed for their penetrative abilities alone, and ridiculously sexy grin that never failed to set her pulse to pounding. He wanted her every bit as much as she wanted him, so it made absolutely no sense that he was out there, she was back here, and neither of them was assuaging one bit of the sexual tension and need that had built up to volcanic proportions between them. All because he suddenly wanted more, or the chance at more. And now he was an all-or-nothing guy.

He was the most confounding man she'd ever met.

She curled her fingers reflexively into the palm he'd kissed, then realized what she was doing and instantly straightened her fingers. She didn't want him mooning over her, or doing anything tender and sweet. She most definitely did not want him wanting to get to know her more intimately, at least in any way he hadn't already discovered. Keeping things strictly physical was the only way there could be anything between them. And while she'd tried to push that aside for the good of the job, even she wasn't so foolish as to try to make herself believe she wouldn't be naked and climbing to that always stunning crescendo of pleasure right this very second if that had been his intent.

She shouldn't be disappointed. At least not to the degree she was. She liked her world, enjoyed the thrill her secret life gave her, the balance it provided to the stifling part that was the rest of it. Relentlessly public, relentlessly bound by etiquette and rules and ridiculous protocols, not to mention the endless expectations placed on her by everyone from her board members to every British citizen who read the daily sheets and believed their opinion on how she should conduct her life should weigh heavily on every choice she made. From what she wore, to when and where she ate, to whom she was seen with.

And yet, despite all of that, or perhaps because that was

what she'd been born to bear, she'd always believed, when the time came, it would be that part of her life that would provide her with her future mate and partner. After all, where else would she meet such a match? Or anyone, really, who was willing to take her on, as well as everything else she came saddled with? Of course, when that day came, she'd have given up her other . . . pursuits, in order to devote herself to the relationship and all the new demands it would bring. She was even content with that eventuality. Although, admittedly, she hadn't exactly been scoping out the field, as they say, with any real diligence. Perhaps it was because she truly couldn't envision herself with any of the men who typically crossed her path.

Or . . . perhaps, subconsciously, she hadn't really been all that keen on man-hunting because the man she really wanted, the only one to have ever truly captivated her, and captured her attention, was the one presently sitting a dozen or so yards away in this very plane.

She rolled to her side, restless, far too pent up, and supremely agitated by the whole thing. She definitely didn't need to be thinking this way, certainly not about Finn, and certainly not while there was such an important mission demanding her full attention.

Which left her right back where she started. She needed to find a way to deal with him and succeed in the task at hand without letting either one of them cloud their thinking further by reactivating their dormant physical relationship. Tell that to the pulsing, demanding ache that wouldn't subside no matter how tightly she pressed her thighs together. Perhaps Finn was right, and they should just—no. No, she told herself firmly. Don't even go there. He'd already made it clear he was going to want more. Far, far more than she could give.

Shockingly, she felt a sudden burn behind her eyes and squeezed them immediately, tightly shut to ward off any ridiculous tears that might think to form there. What a hopeless case she was! Finn was out of reach. Completely. Felicity could in no way allow herself to think their lives could entwine, other than like this. And this wasn't enough. Finn was right about that. In fact, this, what little she'd had of it, of him, was already too much. It was true. If he couldn't be everything, then he had to be nothing.

She rolled to her back and stared once again at the ceiling, dry eyed, jaw set, fingers digging into the bedspread, knowing what she had to do. It was the only thing she could do. To save herself, save them both. To regain their focus on what was really at stake here. And that was to get as much information as she could from him while they were in the air, and then, at the first possible chance that presented itself after landing, take off on her own. It was where she should have remained all along.

And let the better man, or woman, win.

Just then the intercom buzzer went off, making her jump. But she quickly gathered herself, stood, and smoothed her skirt. A quick look in the mirror confirmed what she already knew. Eyes steely, chin set, resolve firmly in place. It was time to put that resolve into action.

Only, as she slid open the accordion-fold door and stepped into the hallway, she came flush up against Finn, who had just stepped out of the attending conference area and was lifting his hand to rap on the frame next to her door. Instead, his knuckles brushed against her hair, a touch she moved instinctively, naturally, into, before she could marshal any rational, cognizant thought. The instant she did, a mere split second later, she tried to correct the motion, but it was already too late. He was smoothing a strand of her hair back in place, and his face was far too close to hers as he leaned in. In violation of her personal space, he unrepentantly took one step farther as he drew the ends of her hair across her bottom lip, only to drop the soft curl and replace it with his fingertips.

"Sleep well?" he asked, his tone amused and dry, as it often was, yet completely at odds with the intensity of his gaze.

"I—no." She should step back. Or at the very least bat his hand away, make it clear she wasn't to be toyed with. Only her body wouldn't respond to any command she gave it. It was too damn busy responding to Finn. But she still had a voice in this. "Finn, I can't—"

"Won't," he corrected quietly.

"Can't," she averred. "Nothing can come of this. And you're right in that if what little there has been isn't enough, for either of us, then it's not fair to continue. So, no, I really can't."

"Why are you so certain there isn't anything else there? You're not even going to give yourself a chance to find out?"

She shook her head. Big mistake, in that it caused his fingertips to brush along her cheek. It made her want to bury her face in that wide, warm palm of his, rub against it like a kitten seeking warmth. She wanted to grab the front of his shirt, drag him back to the bed behind her, and indulge in every animal craving he'd ever inspired within her, knowing he'd fulfill each and every one.

"Our lives are so very different," she said, her voice not much more than a hushed whisper. She lifted her gaze to his, hoping he saw the sincerity in her plea—and it was just that, a plea, because if he pushed, she wasn't sure she could resist. "Our paths cross in a place that exists only outside those normal boundaries. You can straddle those boundaries because your regular life and this are one in the same. Mine aren't. And I can't."

"So, that makes me what? Your dirty little secret?"

"Finn—"

"No, the dirty little secret isn't me. It's this." He gestured to their general surroundings. "This alter ego life you lead. You're right. What I do—all of what I do—and who I am aren't mutually exclusive. I know you think we're worlds apart outside of this moment, this place, this mission. I don't happen to have such a narrow view. Of either of us. As far as I see it, what prevents us from exploring the possibility that there might be something more here than an exceedingly intense physical connection isn't your life in London and mine in Virginia. We're both fortunate enough to be in a situation where overcoming geographical boundaries isn't that big of an obstacle, should we want to. What's preventing you from pursuing this is being unable to bring any part of this world into your regular world."

"It's a valid concern," she said, which was nothing but the truth, no matter that he didn't understand the real reasons why.

He leaned in closer. "I know, but if I were going to turn you in, or do anything to threaten your existence in this little alternate life you've created for yourself, I already would have. And I sure as hell wouldn't be standing here asking you to consider developing any kind of relationship with me. Don't you get that?"

She felt a fine trembling begin in her fingers and start to spread. He wasn't going to give up. Not easily. Not unless she gave him no other choice. "Even if I trusted that this wasn't some kind of ploy—"

"I'm not lying to you. My words and actions have always matched."

"In the few short times we've been together, yes, they have. But you've also pursued your own interests in each matter, as have I. Which isn't surprising, nor would I have expected anything less. But I'm not foolish enough to believe—I can't allow myself to believe—that whatever interest you've developed for me would eclipse getting the job done, especially if both were to come to a crucial point at the same moment in time." Despite the tremors rippling through her, she held his gaze. "Can you honestly tell me otherwise?"

"There's another solution to that dilemma."

"That's not an answer."

"It's not meant to be."

"So, what you're saying is, I must give up this 'little alternate life,' as you call it, if I want to be with you, or even explore the possibility that there might be something more worthwhile between us."

He shuffled closer, trapping her between the door frame and

his body. "If it's thrills you're seeking, perhaps we can find another avenue that will satisfy those cravings."

Her body responded instantly to his suggestion, which wasn't surprising since she knew damn well he could deliver on it. Without question. Quite thoroughly. And repeatedly. She could only imagine just how inventive he could be, given the challenge.

It was a struggle to find some sense of balance. He was far too close, and every facet of her equilibrium was threatened, physically, emotionally, intellectually.

"I wish it were that simple," she said, as sincere in that moment as she'd ever been.

"I don't understand why it isn't."

It was there, right on the tip of her tongue, the truth. And the desire to tell him, to reveal that truth, was so strong it actually made her insides cramp. She knew he couldn't possibly guess what was really going on, and that in an odd sort of way, she should be flattered that he was actually going against principle in his pursuit of her—not that he'd be willing to accept her apparent flouting of the law in any actual relationship, but he hadn't dismissed her out of hand simply because he thought she was engaging in activities he could never morally sanction.

But there was still the thread of disappointment that he hadn't yet conceived that there could be another explanation for her actions. That it had to be greed, or thrill seeking, or even something as simple as boredom that drove her to do what he thought she was doing. Hell, to some men, being an international jewel thief might even seem sexy and exciting, a real turn-on. But that wasn't the case with Finn. Quite the opposite. He found her appealing despite her apparent avocation, not because of it.

She wanted to grab his shoulders and shake him and make him question her, poke, prod, and dig until he either discovered the truth or pushed her hard enough to reveal it. But it was as if he hadn't even considered such a thing. And, as irrational as it might be, that hurt. It meant he hadn't a clue who she really was. Of course, he'd met her as a jewel thief, and she certainly hadn't given him any indication, given their explicit and extended carnal activities, that she harbored the sort of normal wants and desires most women held out for in a real relationship.

But they were there all the same. And just as he was discovering that he couldn't keep up the pretense that wild flings were satisfying for him, neither could she. She just wished that he sensed that about her without her having to tell him. After all, she'd met him under the same outrageous circumstances, and yet, she already knew him to be decent and honorable.

"What is it you're not telling me, Felicity Jane?" he asked.

Her heart skipped a beat. It was as close to a revelation as he'd had as yet. Her brain scrambled to weigh all the pros and cons; but it was in constant flux with the reactions of her body, and her heart, and it was all such a huge jumble, there was no way she could make a rational judgment. Not with him looking at her like that, and her wanting all sorts of things that were in direct conflict with why she'd been sent here and what she'd promised to get done. But her mind wouldn't stop spinning, teasing her with ridiculous possibilities, ones that should certainly seem outrageous at best, terrifying at worst. And yet she couldn't stop that little voice from whispering, tauntingly, teasingly, that perhaps it was possible she could somehow tell him and they could join forces and he'd be the one man with whom maybe, just maybe, she could have it all—

Then he cupped her cheek and turned her gaze to his when she looked away in a vain effort to regroup. "Do you need help?" he asked, never more sincere, real concern outlined in every inch of his handsome face. "Have you gotten into something you can't easily extricate yourself from?"

This time her heart didn't skip; it stopped altogether, then thundered on with such ferocity she felt it might explode from the sudden intensity of it. Not to mention the anger that accompanied it. He not only hadn't expanded his thinking about the motivations behind her actions, but he was worried that in all her lawlessness, she'd gone and gotten herself into a spot of trouble. My, my, what an opinion he held of her.

"No," she said flatly, and pointedly extricated herself from the tight space he'd cornered her into. "I'm more than capable of taking care of myself, but thank you ever so kindly for your concerns. I think we've deliberated this point to its only conclusion." She was all crisp business and haughty demeanor now. It helped hide the hurt and disappointment that shouldn't be the crushing blow they were. "I'd appreciate it if we could sit and discuss our strategy upon landing. I'd like to hear what you and your partners have come up with, and see if I have any alternate suggestions I'd like to make."

She didn't wait for him, but moved back into the main cabin with a deliberate calm that cost her more than he would ever realize.

Whatever happened over the next few hours, she'd already resolved one thing: as soon as she was able, she was going back to working solo. It was pure fantasy to have believed, even for that one shining split second, that there was ever going to be another way.

Chapter 9

Finn stood in the now empty passageway, wondering what in the hell had just happened. One second her barriers had fallen, revealing something quite surprisingly vulnerable beneath that confident surface. The next moment, not only were the barriers wholly back in place, but they'd been reinforced with a fair amount of anger. Only he had no idea what he'd said to provoke it.

He knew she had a lot of pride in her abilities, well earned, but he hadn't thought she'd bristle quite so ardently at the mere suggestion that perhaps she'd gotten in over her head and might need a helping hand. If anything, he'd have thought she'd have laughed at the offer.

He played back over the moment just before that, when he'd asked her what she wasn't telling him. He might not understand the rest, but he needed no additional clarification for that particular moment. There had been something quite . . . naked in the expression that had crossed her face. He had absolutely no doubt he'd hit on something there. The question was, what was it? Clearly, the very mention that whatever it was might have put her in jeopardy had pushed her in the entirely opposite direction. Which he didn't understand.

What he did know was that there was more going on here for her than an adrenaline-punching jewel heist. This alternate life, or maybe just this adventure, mattered to her somehow. The image of her face, her eyes, the way her lips had instinctively parted when he'd asked her what she'd left unsaid, played through his mind again. And again. There had been both fear and yearning in her eyes. Whatever it was, for a second there, or two, she'd wanted to tell him.

Then he'd offered to help her with whatever it was, and wham, bam, the conversation—and any sway he'd gained with her—was over. *Fini*. Done.

He stared out into the main cabin, watched as she seated herself quite stiffly—regally, really—in one of the central chairs, her back to him. As concerned and confused as he was, he found himself smiling. So she was pissed at him. Royally. It wasn't necessarily a bad thing, in that it was also telling. Because that kind of anger could be fueled only by one thing: passion. If he didn't matter, he wouldn't rate that kind of response.

All he had to do now was figure out the source.

And hold fast to the knowledge that while she was busy saying no and constructing walls, in that moment when she'd looked into his eyes, there had been confusion and longing plainly there for him to see. And that said otherwise. There was something else going on here, whether or not she could tell him, whether or not she'd even admitted it to herself. He just had to figure out what it was.

He walked over to the table and seated himself, deciding as he did to proceed as if it were business only. He'd pressed his case, made his plea. He wasn't giving up, not even close, but she was clearly in retreat and regroup mode. Pushing someone when they're scrambling often worked to break down that resistance, at least enough to get them to the point where they'd ask for help. He knew with someone like Felicity, it would only make her rebuild those defenses twice as fast, and twice as sturdy. Now was the time to back off and do a little regrouping of his own.

He pulled a sealed roll of English biscuits from the bag on the chair next to him and a bottle of water. "It's not much, but it might be a good idea."

Her eyes widened, and she looked from the roll of cookies to him. "Where on earth did you find McIvities?"

He slid them over to her, smiling. "I'm magic, remember?" He immediately pulled out his iPhone and tapped on the screen, pulling up the notes he'd taken during his phone conference with Rafe. "I've been in contact with one of my partners, who did a little digging on our art gallery owner."

He was pleased to see her take the water and slide a few cookies from the plastic wrapper, but went on without comment. "I've confirmed that Julia's gallery has been open only two years and is quite successful under any new business standard, but almost ridiculously successful for a young, untried gallery owner."

"Where does her success come from specifically?"

Finn settled back in his seat, only partly relieved to be back on solid footing. The rest of him was still stuck back in that hallway. Wanting things he couldn't have. "Private showings of sponsored artists have provided a good portion of her sales, enough to keep her in the black, even as early as during her first six months in business."

Felicity shrugged. "Lucky maybe. Or really good PR. Do we know anything about that angle?"

Finn tapped on the screen, scrolling down. "No, at least nothing of note popped up on Rafe's first look-see." He glanced up. "And he'd find it if it's there to be found."

"So you've said. Good digger, is he?"

He held her gaze then. "The best." She immediately went back to nibbling the cookie, and he couldn't help but wonder if she was concerned that he might also have asked Rafe to research her. Thing was, he'd been more than tempted. And it was foolish, actually, to have ignored the instinct. He should have put his partners on every possible lead, but instead, he hadn't even mentioned he wasn't working alone. He didn't want anyone or anything intruding on this time, at least until he got a better personal handle on it. Which was true, for the most part. He was also avoiding such information, not really wanting to know whatever Rafe might find out about her. Partly because he wasn't ready to have his fantasy destroyed quite yet, though he suspected that was the only real end he could hope for. And partly because he wanted to at least hear it from her directly.

"Maybe she's just that good at picking talent," Felicity offered, moving them past the moment. "Could she have family connections, perhaps? Important friends helping the new business along as a favor to the family?"

"No family connections that we've found. No family at all, for that matter. She has degrees in both business management and art history. For all we know, opening her own gallery has been a longtime goal."

"Plausible. So what explains her success? Are the artists who show in her gallery the type that would show in a new, small place? Or is she somehow getting name recognizable talent?"

"That's more Rafe's arena than mine. I don't know that much about art, much less the West Coast artist community, but from the printed reviews he dug up, it doesn't seem that any of the critics are raising eyebrows in that direction. She had a few successful shows with relative unknowns, which brought more new artists to her door, hoping to be selected for future shows. Several of the artists from her initial shows have gone on to have decent, sustained success. Now she's kind of gotten to be the 'in' place for new talent, and the buyers seem to have her on their list of places to look to be the first to own something by a hot new artist."

"Could be luck, then." Felicity mulled that over as she munched on a chocolate-coated cookie, then sipped her water. Finn was momentarily distracted by her lips, but diverted his attention to his notes as soon as he realized what he was doing. He also kept his gaze away from the damn bag by his

side. He almost wished he hadn't bought . . . the things he'd
bought. It was damn distracting, knowing they were there, un-
likely to be used, all the while watching her mouth do something as innocent as pull on the nozzle of the water bottle.
He'd never wanted so badly to be a water bottle nozzle.

Concentrate.

"Anything suspicious about her liaisons with the local talent? Anything other than strict business partnerships?"

"If you mean are the local artists sleeping with her to get the
coveted space on her gallery walls? Not that we've found so far.
And, just to note, she's as likely to pick female artists as male."

Felicity smiled. "She's in San Francisco. That might not
make a difference."

Finn couldn't help but smile back, but went right back to his
notes when the rest of his body wanted to smile, too. So much
for solid footing. "As for personal relationships, he didn't get
much on that as yet. Apparently she keeps her private life very
private."

"No one hanging on her arm during her showings?"

He shook his head. "She has a reputation for being friendly
and engaging, but strictly business. But if there is a behind-the-
scenes liaison going on, Rafe will find it."

Felicity consulted the slim gold band circling her wrist. Diamonds twinkled from the edge of the watch crystal. Finn
couldn't help but wonder where, exactly, they'd come from.

"We don't have much time for further discovery," she commented.

He glanced at her face, wondering if she was being intentionally provocative. Maybe wishing was more like it. "He'll
beep in if he finds anything."

"Pretty nice bat phone you have. Great signal."

He smiled. "I'm surprised you don't have your own satellite
setup."

She smiled, but only said, "And, in the meantime? Did we
find any previous history between her and Reese? Any kind of
connection?"

"Nothing new." He settled back in his seat. "Do you have any additional insights you'd like to share about the man?"

Her eyes flashed, but she smiled. "Still don't believe me?"

"Oh, I believe you, but you do know him. Certainly better than I do. I didn't know if anything else had come to mind about him that might be of some help."

"No, nothing new. I've told you everything I know about him." She recrossed her legs. "Satisfied?"

"Not for a long time, but I'm trying to be good here."

She did glance at him then, only there was nothing amused to be found in her stare. For some perverse reason, that made him smile anyway. He wondered what she'd say if he told her she was quite adorable when she was annoyed, but figured that would only get him the silent treatment. Or possibly shot. She was a very capable woman, after all.

"We need a plan of attack for when we land," she said archly. "Did you think to ask your cohort to dig up anything pertaining to Reese's possible exploits in California? Any activity out there? Any reason he'd be heading west, instead of east over the ocean and away from your country's rather frightfully decent legal system?"

"He would if it was the only way to hand off the stone with due assurance it would receive proper handling out of the country. If, in fact, it's leaving the country at all." Finn's eyes widened. "That's it."

"What's *it?* You think he's going to try to move it farther personally? As in the Far East? Or north into Canada, then Russia perhaps?"

"I don't know the final destination, but I think I've figured out Julia's role in the transaction."

"Which is?"

"Broker."

"She deals in art. Sculpture, canvas. She brokers showings, not international black market jewelry."

"She's experienced very good success in a short time, which means people with money are in her gallery, buying up art.

Those kinds of people have connections. Perhaps she's providing a whole lot more to her patrons than new art. It would possibly explain the quick success as well."

Felicity seemed to ponder that. "But John is, essentially, the broker. No need for another middle man. Or woman as the case may be."

"Both sides can broker."

"I suppose. But we already know Reese had a deal with Chesnokov. He didn't need Julia for that. So, why was she in New York? Coincidence after all? You don't think she's actively dealing herself, do you? Could she have been after the stone herself?"

"Hard to say, but other than her quick success, nothing suggests it yet. My guess is that she and Reese have possibly jointly brokered other deals in the past. Perhaps when things fell through tonight, he knew she was in town, contacted her. Back-up plan, maybe."

Felicity shook her head. "Possibly, but that still sounds too convenient. I still have to wonder if she wasn't here for the same purpose Reese was."

"Then it stands to reason she'd have her own buyer. Maybe she was tracking Reese, too, knew he lost his buyer, then stepped in and offered some kind of split on the fee if he'd sell the piece to her client."

Felicity's gaze sharpened. "Then that means she might know about us."

Finn shrugged. "Possible, but since we didn't end up with the stone, we're not important to her. She was able to deal directly with Reese, give him a solution to his problem, so they're already on to the next step. I imagine we've been forgotten in the grand scheme of things."

"If Julia is also working this, how is it she's never popped up on the radar?"

It occurred to Finn to wonder then how much research Felicity did when stalking her quarry, and how she went about doing it. He imagined the Foundation had all sorts of resources to check out potential donors as well as recipients. But how did she come to know about the quarry in the first place? She said she'd never bought anything from Reese. That didn't mean she couldn't have used him to find out what was available, then go after it herself. Hence the tea she'd invited him to her hotel room to share. Ostensibly for Foundation business, which she admitted they did share on occasion. Only this time it had backfired on her, and Reese had discovered her ulterior motives. Given the way he'd left her anyway. Finn wondered how much that might have truly compromised her. Now someone else knew about her alter ego, or at least suspected as much. Was that what he suspected she wasn't telling him? Was she afraid that Reese was going to publicly humiliate her? Or worse?

He pushed those thoughts aside. For now. At the moment Reese had more pressing concerns to attend to. And, frankly, Finn thought that a man like Reese would keep his newly acquired information to himself anyway, at least until he could figure out how to use it to his advantage. And given the leverage he now had over her, the possibilities were many.

"Maybe she doesn't typically leave her gallery," he said, in response to Felicity's question. "Maybe she just brokers through other connections, or using couriers like Chesnokov did earlier tonight."

"Any chance she's personally the buyer? Any chance he contacted her to sell her the stone outright?"

"Could be, but why fly her home, then? She was in the city. They'd close the deal; then he'd go his way, she'd go hers."

"Unless there is more to their story."

"Possible. Probable, even, given the champagne and all. But Rafe didn't get anything on her that would suggest she's a private collector, on the record or otherwise. It would make more sense if she's a broker, as that's relatively easy to hide."

"Assuming she does this for a fee, where is the money?"

"Don't know. Maybe she funnels it back into the business. Maybe her showings aren't as successful as they seem and she's rolling the income into the business and stating it as sales as a way to launder it legitimately into her bank accounts."

"So where does the art go if it's not really being sold?"

"She could be destroying it for all we know. Or using it for packing material—" He broke off suddenly and immediately began tapping on his screen.

"What?"

"Well, I was being a smart ass, but it just occurred to me . . . Hold on." He kept tapping for another minute, then finally put the unit down on the table and leaned back in his seat. "Rafe's on it. Hopefully we'll get an answer before we land."

"Care to share your amazing revelation? An answer to what?"

"Whether or not Julia is packing something other than art in the crates she uses to ship things out to clients."

"And if she is?"

"That could be the invaluable service she provides. Not a customer base, though she could be brokering. Ultimately, though, she could just be a mule of another sort."

"Doesn't explain her being in New York."

He shrugged. "We know she's involved with Reese somehow. Maybe she was there in case he needed to move it another way. We don't know when he worked the deal with Chesnokov or when Andreev came into the picture."

"And the shower and champagne?"

"Well, maybe some people really know how to close a business deal." Finn grinned. "In fact, perhaps we should—"

Felicity lifted her hand. "You were doing so well there for a bit, don't spoil it."

Finn reached for the bag next to him and pulled out two half bottles of wine. "I was going to say a toast to our continued sleuthing successes." His grin spread. "Why, what did you have in mind?"

She ignored him, or tried to, by picking up her water bottle and taking another measured sip. "I don't think clouding our heads—and our judgments—with alcohol is a good idea at the moment."

"Afraid you'll take advantage of me?"

"Your wish fulfillment is showing, darling." She took one of the small bottles. "On second thought, perhaps a little libation would be a good thing. Steady the nerves. Do you happen to have a corkscrew in your little bag of tricks? Oh," she said, on a sigh, as she looked more closely at the bottle. "Screw top. How . . . divine."

"Hey, I scored the McIvities, but the supply of wine on such short notice was a bit more limited." He got up and walked over to the small storage and kitchen area in the front of the plane, and came back with two champagne flutes. "Maybe it will taste better in fine crystal."

He could see her fight the smile, but didn't nudge her any further. She poured for them both, then lifted her glass. "To finding Julia and Reese."

"To finding the stone, and the hell with Reese."

She nodded, clinked the edge of her glass against his, then sipped. After a delicate shiver, she sipped again. "This is positively horrid."

"I know," Finn said, downing a gulp. "Fun, huh?"

"I shudder to think what else you scavenged on your little hunt."

He snagged the bag, knowing he was wandering right back into dangerous territory, and not caring as much as he should. They were working together, communicating. Maybe he just needed to trust that tack for a while, and hope for more as they proceeded.

And maybe if she was naked for at least part of that time, it would help her shed the rest of her inhibitions about bringing him in on whatever deal she was really working here.

Of course, he was completely aware how self-serving that newly devised plan would be. And that, as nothing had really changed between them, it made him somewhat hypocritical on his earlier stance . . . but as he watched her throat work, and her slender shoulders shiver as she took another sip, and gave another little shudder, he discovered he wasn't caring much at all any longer about the rest of it.

He wanted Felicity Jane more than he wanted his next breath. He wanted her in more than his bed. He wanted her for longer than the duration of this flight. Or their current caper.

But every journey started with a single step. And he was done denying that the step he was most interested in taking at the moment was toward the big ocean of bed in the rear of the plane.

"Well," he told her, setting his glass down on the table and circling around toward her. "I did have you shuddering in mind when I collected some of it. But in quite a different way." He perched on the edge of the table, his knee grazing hers, gratified when she didn't move it away. "Want me to show you?"

Chapter 10

Felicity stared at Finn over the edge of her glass, pondering whether it was really worth taking another sip of the most awful wine she'd ever had the misfortune to taste. It was a desperate attempt to take the edge off the anxiety growing inside her. Anxiety that had little to do with solving the job at hand, and a lot to do with the fact that despite her little speech earlier, her desire for Finn Dalton hadn't eased one whit.

Sitting across the table from him, watching his quick mind in action, certainly hadn't helped matters either. Wasn't it enough that he had a body that wouldn't quit? He had to have a tantalizing mind as well? She sipped. She shuddered. And her gaze went to the dark blue plastic bag currently clutched in his hands. His long, broad-fingered hands.

She forced herself to look away. "Business," she managed. "We really should stick to—"

He took the glass out of her grasp and set it on the table beside him, then reached for her hands. "The hell with it. Maybe we should stick to what we do best."

It was simple. All she had to do was keep her hands in her lap, or anywhere but on Finn. He wouldn't push her if she didn't want him to. Which was the problem.

She looked up at him. "You said that wasn't enough for you. What's changed?"

"Other than you driving me so crazy I can't think straight?"

"Join the club," she muttered, knowing he heard her when his smile grew.

"I do want more." He wiggled his fingers, urging her to take his hands. "But maybe more talking isn't what's going to do the trick."

She eyed his hands, accepted the shudder of pleasure that rolled down her spine at the image of those strong fingers caressing her flesh, then connected with this gaze once again. "I'm a trick now? A puzzle to be solved? So that is the draw, then? Figure out the mystery of Felicity Jane?"

"I won't deny you intrigue the hell out of me, but my hope is that the more I know, the more I'll want to know. Isn't that how this is supposed to work?"

"I wouldn't know. I don't even know what *this* is."

"And there's no curiosity on your part to find out?"

"We've been through this. Just moments ago, in the hallway."

"Maybe you need options."

What she needed was for him to shut up and drag her into his arms so she wouldn't have to make up her own damn mind about all this. Take the decision out of her hands and drown her in so much sensation and pleasure that she didn't have to think. Not about this.

Of course, for all he was a bad boy personified in some ways, he was also a good guy. Too good to ever do that without her express consent. Which was one of the things that so attracted her to him in the first place. Damn it.

"Options," she repeated.

"At the moment, you have your life all neatly arranged. Your day job," he said, then smiled, "and your extracurricular activities."

She didn't bother to correct him. She couldn't anyway.

"You have no reason to upset the status quo. Why reach for the uncertain?"

"Why, indeed?"

"Because a job, no matter how exhilarating, can't give you

this." He was taking her hands even as she was raising them to his. He lifted her from the chair and pulled her snugly between his thighs in one smooth motion. His hand slid to the back of her neck, and he tilted her head as his mouth descended toward hers.

"What if I don't really want this?" she whispered, just before his mouth took hers. It was a last ditch effort, a plea for him to do what she could not and bring them both back from this brink of insanity. Her heart was beating as fast as hummingbird wings, and her legs had gone all rubbery and weak.

"Don't you?"

She could feel the warmth of his breath, her gaze focused tightly on his lips. She wanted to feel them on her so badly she ached. "I do, but only this."

"It doesn't work that way."

"It did before."

He nudged her chin up, so their gazes met. "It won't now. Not for me. You give what you want, or what you can."

"And you'd be satisfied with that?"

He shook his head, and his lips curved. "No. But I'm willing to take the risk."

"Why?" she asked, never more sincere. Why did this man, who she was certain could grab and hold the attention of most any woman he desired, desire her?

"Because I already know what I plan to give, what I can give."

"Which is?" she asked, her legs trembling now.

"Everything." He pressed his fingers to her nape, urging her lips back up to his. "I hope you're ready for me, Felicity Jane. Because I'm a lot."

Yes, yes you are, she thought distantly, and without much resistance. Because his mouth was finally, blessedly on hers again. And there was nothing tentative about this kiss. But it wasn't a warrior's kiss, bold and aggressive, attempting to conquer through sheer will and force.

No, it was far more insidious than that.

It was confident, certain, and seductive. He didn't just kiss her lips, he feasted on them, and every touch and taste was an invitation for her to do the same. That was something she'd learned about him from the moment they'd first put their hands on each other: he wanted a partner in pleasure, not a passive playmate. She was a strong, confident woman, but in bed, she'd always found herself falling into more traditional patterns. Not because she was shy or uncertain of her abilities, but simply because it had seemed to be what was expected.

Not with Finn. He'd always demanded that she give all of herself, at least physically. She'd learned what it was to be a fully intimate partner with him, and she'd reveled in it. The pleasure it gave her to be with someone who was so responsive to her needs, who pushed her to reach for more, no matter how spent she'd thought herself, but also someone with whom she'd learned the depth of pleasures to be gained from satisfying his needs. She'd felt bold, and innovative, discovering a confidence that being successful in her other endeavors had never given her. She had no idea if Finn knew the myriad gifts he'd given her. Likely he thought she'd always been this . . . conquering vixen in bed. And she'd been privately thrilled to let him think so. It had been quite exhilarating, not to mention liberating.

Now . . . now she wasn't so certain. Now this wasn't simply fun and games. He'd laid down his gauntlet, and it changed completely how this made her feel. How it made her want to react. Her heart squeezed now, engaged despite her wishing it not to be, as he tenderly drew his fingers along the side of her neck, moving his mouth to the delicate line of her jaw, then following the trail of his fingertips.

He'd been gentle with her before, and she'd privately reveled in it, loving how cosseted and adored it had made her feel, but never once allowing herself to believe—or hope—it was anything other than him being a considerate and fully sensual lover.

Now, she had no idea what thoughts were going through his

mind. And so much more of her was at risk of being seduced than her body.

She instinctively eased away from him, pushed at his shoulders. It wasn't a shove, she wasn't strong enough for that, still wanting—craving—what he was giving her, but knowing she hadn't the control needed to protect herself. And she wasn't ready to surrender. Not fully.

He allowed her to shift back, then framed her hips in his wide palms when she stepped back unsteadily. He balanced her, kept his hands there, firmly, but nothing more.

He did balance her, in every way, she thought, struggling for the clarity of mind she so desperately needed right now.

"I—I," she stuttered, then stopped, willing her head to stop spinning, her legs to stop trembling, and her heart to stop pounding. "I still can't." She finally looked at him, and had she found him smiling smugly, secure in the knowledge that he'd proved at least part of his point, it would have made things far easier for her. Instead, his gaze was intense, and as serious as she'd ever seen it.

"I know," he said quietly and, if she wasn't mistaken, with real regret. He slid his hands to her elbows and eased her back, so she could sit down in her chair. "But I'm a patient man," he said, rising, gratifyingly unsteady himself. He touched her hair, then leaned down and kissed her, firmly, deeply, but ending it the moment she began to relax and accept it. "And you're worth the wait."

She swallowed against a suddenly tight throat. "I might never—" she began, needing him to know she was making no promises here. She didn't even know what she wanted.

"I know. It's my risk to take," he told her.

She stared at him, into eyes that held hers so solidly, so certainly. "Why?" she whispered. "Why me?"

His grin was like sunshine peeking out from behind a stormy cloud. His gaze hadn't lessened one whit in intensity, so the gleam from the smile was like a laser beam of light, shining directly, and only, on her. "Why not you? No one has ever captivated me like you have. Two years, and I can't put you out of my mind. We're back here, together once more, and I'm not going to waste my only opportunity to find out what more there might be."

"You think I'm this larger-than-life mystery woman, but I assure you, I'm not so different as all that from other women."

"You're nothing like other women."

With you, she wanted to shout, but didn't. "You'll scrape off the international woman of intrigue, and the woman of means, and discover I'm that girl who likes to dig in her garden and sip tea. I'm hopelessly boring, and there isn't anything memorable—"

In the next instant she was lifted bodily from her seat and pulled fully and tightly into his arms. He spun them both around so he could lower her onto the table. Champagne glasses slid dangerously close to the edge of the table as his body pressed down on top of hers. He pushed her hair from her face and framed her cheeks with his palms. "That's what makes you memorable. You're all of those things. Every complex layer. And I want to peel them all away, while savoring each part, until I get to know every inch of you. Inside and out. Don't you get it? All of you fascinates me. Not what you do, or what you're capable of—though I assure you, you have my full attention there, too. But who you are that allows you to do all of that. To dig in the garden one day and steal a priceless gemstone the next. To be so confident and in control, with what you do, and with me, matching me breath for breath, thrust for thrust when we go at each other, and yet still look at me like you are now, with such vulnerability and trepidation."

"Finn—"

"Call it chemistry, call it whatever you want. But I'm in, Felicity. I'm all in. In a way I've never been in before. If that scares you, fine. It should. It terrifies the hell out of me. So did flying a helicopter solo the first time, but it made the rush that much sweeter. When something intrigues me, fascinates me, I know of only one way to handle it, and that's to immerse myself in it, learn as much as I can about it. I don't ask why, I just go. And do. And enjoy the hell out of every second."

"And when it wears off? When it grows old?"

"Life offers no guarantees. You know that as well as I do. But I wanted to fly. So I do. And it's a never-ending passion for me. I wanted to ride, so I do. I always will. When something fascinates me, grabs me, it's not a matter of getting it out of my system. It's more a matter of integrating it into my life so I can feel that passion every day. About as many times as I'm able to."

She stared up into his eyes, feeling the impact of every word, the absolute truth in them. Marveling at his certainty. Maybe, she realized, she wasn't so different from him after all. She wouldn't be here, on this mission, if she hadn't been willing to tackle something that both intrigued her and scared her. She'd thought working for MI-8 would be the most thrilling and terrifying thing she could ever do.

She'd been so wrong.

Body shaking, lips trembling, she held that passionate gaze, held on to it tightly, and smiled. "Then show me," she said, "show me what it's like to take off and fly into the unknown." She pulled his head down to hers. "Show me what it's like to have all of you."

He took her mouth this time like a man starved. There was nothing tender about it, not that it mattered at this point. She couldn't allow herself to assign motivation or meaning to every little action he took, or reaction he might have. She could only let herself feel . . . whatever he made her feel. Then deal with the fallout afterward.

Even as he pulled back, lifted her off the table, and swept her into his arms, she knew this was as big a mistake as she was likely ever to make. And it no longer mattered. If he was going to be a mistake, best she get on with it and start to deal with the consequences, but telling herself she was strong enough to do anything else was simply putting off the inevitable.

He was nibbling her neck, and she had her fingers in his abundantly thick mane of dark blond hair. "Aren't you forgetting something?" she said, allowing the joy of the moment to push past the fear and anxiety, and holding on to that joy with everything she was worth.

"God, I hope not."

She laughed, feeling suddenly, gloriously free. She was thirty thousand feet in the air, as unfettered and unbound by the world and what awaited her in it as she was ever likely to be. She was in Finn's arms and about to be naked under his equally glorious body. Honestly, what more could a woman want? And in that moment, she didn't want for anything.

She didn't dare.

"The bag of goodies, darling," she reminded him.

"Oh," he said, his voice already huskier, his body already harder, "right." He spun around, held her close with one arm, and scooped up the bag with the other. "If we're lucky, we might even get to the contents before landing."

"We've at least another three hours or so."

He wiggled his eyebrows and nipped at the side of her neck. "I know."

She laughed, even as she shivered in anticipation of what was to come. Namely, her. Several times, if past history was to be repeated. She used her foot to nudge the accordion-fold doors open so he could swing her into the bedroom and onto the bed, wondering why in the hell she'd let herself get so caught up in his emotional whirlpool. They could have been doing this, having each other, all along.

She started to unbutton her dress, but he pushed her hands away. "I'm going to undress you."

"Okay."

But rather than starting with the buttons, he nudged her back onto the bed and motioned for her to scoot back, so she was stretched fully on the mattress. She arched a questioning brow, to which he merely said, "Humor me."

He'd been the perfect playmate in the past, aggressive when

warranted, and gentle when necessary. She trusted him. Here, anyway. Here is where she knew him best, after all.

But there was something else in his eyes now, something beyond the teasing, playful bad boy she'd previously known. Something far more . . . evolved. *No*, her little voice said. *No analyzing, remember?*

She still didn't believe there could be more to this than . . . this, no matter how optimistic Finn was. After all, that was his nature. There was no obstacle he couldn't supersede, no outcome he couldn't impact in his favor, either with money, skill, or sheer force of will. Or a cunning combination of all three. She was more a pragmatist, a realist, who understood the odds weren't always in her favor, no matter how much power she wielded. But if this was the only way they could each discover what needed discovering, then she was all in, too. At least that far.

She let her heels slip to the floor and scooted back.

He leaned over her, then covered her wrists with his hands before pushing them up along the bedspread, until they were over her head.

"There had best not be any cuffs in that bag," she warned, though teasingly. For some reason the idea of him restraining her held entirely different overtones—all erotic—than it had earlier when it simply meant failure of a mission.

"No cuffs," he murmured, his mouth next to her ear, then drew his hands down her arms, making her skin tingle at the warm contact.

She had to work to keep still and not arch into his hands as he drew them along her sides. He didn't cup her breasts. His knuckles barely brushed the swell as his hands continued to move down to frame her waist. Her nipples tightened almost painfully as the expected contact didn't come. The lack of direct stimulation was almost more erotic than if he'd teased and tweaked them.

He massaged his thumbs into the muscles of her stomach, digging his fingers in lightly along her side, before continuing his exploration. Her hips pumped slightly, of their own volition, as he traced his fingers over her pelvic bones. But just as she thought he'd let his thumbs trail down her center, between her legs, he slid his hands to the outside of her thighs and continued to draw his hands lower, until finally, he reached the lengthy hem of her dress.

By now, she was almost frantic for him to directly touch her skin. Any part of her skin. Feeling his hands mold every curve of her body, except those that craved his touch most, was far more stimulating than she'd ever imagined. One thing his slow, methodical journey had done was to dismantle her ability to think about anything other than where he was going to touch her next.

And she was still fully dressed.

It was hard not to be restless, to move her torso, shift her limbs, in an effort to ease the ache that had pervaded her every muscle and pore. The way he'd positioned her hands above her head meant that any move she made felt sinuous, writhing. It made her feel wanton, sexy, voluptuous even, though she was most definitely not.

He teased his fingertips along the edge of her hem, so she could occasionally feel his hands brush against the bare skin of her legs. Thank God she'd chosen to skip putting on stockings. It was almost unbearable just having this much of a barrier between his touch and her bare skin.

As he continued toying with her dress, it took an increasing amount of restraint not to either rip the dress off herself or beg him to do it for her. She fought a smile, wondering if that was his goal. It wouldn't surprise her. Her eyes drifted shut. It was much easier to analyze and think about his motives when it was just about sex. Especially when she knew he had taken very good care of her needs in the past, so there was little doubt of a repeat performance, no matter what route he took.

Her smile didn't fully materialize, however, as without warning, her thoughts veered dangerously toward the area she desperately wanted to avoid. Wondering about things like what he'd be like as a lover over an extended period of time. And she didn't mean a long weekend. Would he remain a considerate, seemingly inexhaustible partner, or would passion ebb, along with his interest in her? More disconcerting was why it mattered?

It mattered, she realized, because if she allowed this to progress the way he wanted it to, lowering barriers, letting him get close, risking . . . things that weren't really in her power to risk, only to have him bounce off in some other direction the moment he grew bored, it would devastate her.

And she knew that, because he was already starting to matter to her.

"Felicity," he said, his voice smooth and soft, like a warming sip of cognac.

"Mmm," she replied, realizing he'd stopped toying with the hem of her dress.

"Don't think," he said. "Just feel."

"I was," she said, being honest. He was the one who wanted more, not her. She just wanted . . . this. For as long as she could get it. And, at the moment, he was willing to let her. "Am," she corrected herself, then tilted her head back, pressing her eyes more tightly shut. She'd waited two years; she wasn't going to screw this up. "Just . . . don't stop."

He responded by slipping free the button closest to the hem of her dress. The garment buttoned—and unbuttoned—all the way up the front. She wasn't sure she'd survive it.

"No slip," he mentioned as he slid another button free.

"The dress . . . it's lined," she managed, a little short of breath just feeling the brush of his fingertips nearing the sensitive skin along the inside of her knees.

"Lucky me."

Oh, she was pretty sure the lucky one at the moment was her, but she didn't give voice to the thought. Besides, he'd already seen her in the lingerie she was wearing, with no dress. She'd felt the full weight of his body on top of her while wearing nothing more than the silk bra and panties she currently had on. Which did nothing to explain how incredibly erotic this slow striptease was.

He continued unbuttoning her dress, carefully parting it as he went, but also careful not to do more than casually brush his fingers against her skin. She felt the cooler air of the cabin brush her skin as he bared it, which did little to soothe the heat that was pervading every inch of her body. When he got to the button ever so helpfully positioned at the top of her thighs, he paused. She wanted to squirm, or scream, already dying for him to do far, far more than lightly brush any part of her with any part of him.

She curled her fingers into her palm, resisting the urge to reach down and push his hand where it would do a fair amount of good right at the moment.

She felt his warm breath blow softly against the tender skin of her inner thighs. Then he slipped open that button—*that* button—brushing against her just enough to make her entire body twitch and a soft gasp escape her lips. He parted her dress, then dropped the softest of kisses to the inside of either thigh, before shifting up and moving on, opening another button, followed by a kiss below her navel, then another, and another, until she thought she'd surely lose her mind.

"Finn," she choked out, not certain if she could stand him opening the front of her dress and not touching her nipples, either. She needed something, anything, to ease the ache that was almost physical pain by now.

"Mmm," was his only response as he did, indeed, unbutton the last few buttons between her breasts, then draw the material slowly across the front of her silk bra, so gently abrading the tight tips of her nipples, sending little shockwaves of pleasure through her. She moaned now, and didn't care what he made of it. She dug her nails into her palms, determined not to sink her fingers into his hair and drag his mouth back to her nipples. Even through the silk, the sensations of his lips tugging on them would be exquisite.

Maybe she'd been right, and his goal was to make her lose

control, lose whatever inhibitions she might have left with him, to demand that he give her what she wanted, so he, in return, could make demands of his own. Only she had no idea what those demands might entail now that he'd made his intentions clear, and she was in no position, or state of mind, to risk finding out.

So she squirmed, and she twitched . . . and waited breathlessly to see what he'd do next.

Chapter 11

She was lovelier than he'd remembered, which was incredible considering he'd been fairly certain he'd romanticized and immortalized every moment they'd shared in the hundreds of dreams and waking fantasies he'd had since last being with her.

The contrast of the midnight blue silk made her skin appear almost translucent, and he wanted to lick every creamy, smooth inch of it. She smelled like a combination of the lavender scent she wore . . . and the musky scent that was simply hers. Her soft moans, and the gasps every time he so much as breathed, told him she was in as heightened a state of awareness as he was. Which was exactly what he wanted.

He wanted her to respond to him at the most basic level; then, from there, he could take her to places accessible only to those who felt more than physical pleasure. She'd come to understand what he knew was there, because she would no longer be able to deny it. He'd imagined it wild and tender, carnal and sweet. A rollercoaster of sensation, emotion, and primal responses, where barriers of any kind could no longer exist. And when he had her there, in that moment, as defenseless as he was, he'd ask her again. Push her again.

But she wasn't letting go. She was clinging, desperately if the fists above her head were any indication, to the patterns they'd established in the past. Wild and carnal they'd been, yes. Primal as well. But with no foundation to build on, except seeking even greater pleasure. Which they had, to sublime, almost ridiculous levels. That, in and of itself, should have told her something.

It had him.

This was likely not the time, or the place, to mount such a delicate and critical mission. He wouldn't get another chance to get it right. But sometimes a person had to take the only moment available and find a way to make it work. They'd be on the ground all too soon, and the job would take center stage again. And they didn't have a really good history of sticking by each other when things got down to the wire, with the spoils going only to one victor. In fact, they had zero history of that.

What he wanted her to see was that there were treasures far greater than priceless gemstones. And that sharing victories made them doubly sweet.

He leaned down and gently bit the tip of her chin, thrust upward as it was, while she arched against the need for his touch. She moaned, and her legs moved restlessly against his, while he fought an equally challenging battle against going ahead with this and risking losing it all.

"Felicity—" he began, only to be surprised when she lowered her chin and claimed his mouth. He hadn't been expecting an offensive maneuver, and it caught him off guard just long enough for her to make serious inroads into destroying whatever common sense and rational thought he might still have. And he wasn't too certain he'd ever had any of that around her. After all, he was campaigning for the affections and possible commitment of a woman he knew to be a thief.

A damned good one, too, he thought as she gently bit into his bottom lip, making him groan, then stretch his body along hers, bracing her wrists to the bed with his hands as he plunged his tongue into her mouth and gave in to his raging need to consume her.

She met his thrust with a sinuous kiss of her own, taunting

and teasing him with her tongue, becoming the wanton, confident vixen he'd seduced in Bogota and bedded in Prague. Gone was the uncertain Felicity, her vulnerability vanished and almost hard to believe existed.

She slid her ankles along the backs of his calves, urging him to snug his bulging erection tightly between her thighs. She gasped at the direct contact, the increased pressure, and he silently swore, wishing he'd removed his clothes before he'd started unbuttoning hers.

He slid his hands down her arms and wove his fingers into her soft, fine curls, holding her where he wanted, so he could taste those lips, plunder that mouth, fully and completely. She responded in kind, sinking her slender fingers into his hair, lightly raking his scalp with her nails, making him shudder in pleasure as she drew them down to his neck and urged his tongue more deeply into her mouth.

He grunted with the need to free himself, constrained as he was now to the point of serious discomfort, but unwilling to leave her long enough to take care of it. Instead, he dragged his mouth from hers, biting her chin, harder this time, then sliding his fingers between her lips to continue that wet invasion, his cock jerking as she immediately continued sucking on his fingers while he slid down to take a silk-covered nipple into his mouth.

She moaned and arched into him, sucking his fingers deeper into her mouth. He flipped open the front clasp of the bra, needing to taste her like a man starved for food. Sweet, so damn sweet. He pushed both silky cups aside, rolling one nipple between his fingers while teasing the other with his tongue. She groaned and moved against him, her hips pressing up, pushing at him, demanding he push back.

This, they knew how to do, this almost mindless need to mate, to join, to give and take pleasure. This they could give themselves over to completely. Actually, it was as if they almost didn't have a choice in the matter. She pushed at him, and he moved downward, trailing his tongue along the delicate line of her abdomen as he slid his wet fingers out of her mouth and used them to continue teasing her nipples. He dipped his tongue into her navel, then along the lacy edge of her panty line. He could already breathe in the sweet scent of her and knew she'd be wet and wanting when he finally worked his way there.

He slid his hands along her waist, lifting her hips so he could press his mouth against the damp silk covering her. She sucked in her breath on a little gasp, then moved beneath him. He knew just how wet she would be, just what it would feel like to sink into her, to feel her take him all the way in, holding him so tightly, so perfectly. He thought he might burst behind the zipper of his pants, but he wasn't about to leave her now. He knew that if he pleasured her this way, brought her screaming right to the edge, then pushed her over, let her tumble, fall, regroup, then pushed her over again, even when she thought she couldn't, when he climbed up over her body and thrust himself into her, she'd keep coming, and the way her body would grip and convulse around him in an almost constant roll of aftershocks would jerk him so hard and fast over the edge he'd see stars.

Mindless. Primal. Basic. Essential. That was what this was.

And yet he wanted so much more.

And he planned to push and push plenty hard. But right now, the only thing he was going to push hard was his tongue. Right into the wet, hot center of her.

He slid his hands down, taking her panties with him, all the way down and off, trailing his tongue along the inside of her thigh, the back of her knee, the sensitive spot below her ankle. He yanked off his shirt and, finally, blessedly freed himself of his pants, while nipping the side of her toe, biting her arch, making her squeal and laugh. Then he teased his way back up the inside of her other leg, making her gasp and moan. She was twisting now, writhing as he drew closer, and closer still, panting, knowing what was coming. He wondered if it made it twice as good for her, already knowing how fantastic, how deeply, insanely pleasurable it was going to be. It did for him.

And it was the knowing, the wanting, that made it possible for him to take his time, when all he wanted was to climb over her and slide back into the one place he'd wanted to be since the moment he'd left her two years ago.

If this was the only way to get to her, to get to any part of her, then he was going to get to all of it that he could. And that meant taking his sweet time. Knowing the reward that awaited them both made that an easy decision to make. He pressed the throbbing length of his erection into the bedspread, accepting what little friction he could get there as a means to assuage the ache, at least a little. Then he focused his attention on her, and only her.

He nudged her legs a bit farther apart, then dropped the softest of kisses along the inside of each thigh, so close, but not brushing against where she wanted him most. He felt her fingers twine into his hair, playing with it, toying with the ends, sending little skitters of pleasure through him, but not directing him or pushing him, trusting that he'd take care of her. He pressed a kiss against her soft curls, then slowly, gently drew the tip of his tongue downward. Her hands dropped away, clutching instead at the bedspread on either side of her body as he continued to play, teasing her with his tongue until she was twisting beneath him, then finally sliding one finger inside of her as he suckled and toyed some more. He pushed her to the edge with long, slippery strokes, both with his finger and his tongue, until she finally couldn't hold back any longer and went shuddering and moaning over the edge.

He had to press his hips firmly into the mattress to keep his twitching cock still, gritting his teeth as he slid his thumb over her and kept her vibrating, fighting against the need to climb up and take her now, while she was still quaking. Instead, he started all over again, kissing softly, teasing gently, even more so now as she was twitchy and pulsing. She didn't push him away, but steeled herself against his touch, so ultrasensitive now that the slightest brush of any part of him against her was almost too much. But he took his time, and she slowly relaxed and began to climb again. When he slid his finger inside her this time, he had to swallow a groan of need, so badly did he want to be there right now. He thrust gently into her, pushing up just enough to hit that other spot inside her, so sensitive, all the while kissing, teasing, tasting, until she cried out as her hips jerked almost violently off the bed. He stayed with her until she was just past the peak, then finally, almost shakily, climbed over her and pulled her calves around his waist, lifting her hips completely off the bed, then thrusting into her so hard it drove them both half a foot up the mattress.

She cried out, and he grunted as she took him, held him, moved beneath him, matching him stroke for stroke as she continued to pulsate and shudder around him. He had no recourse, no way to stop the climax rushing to overtake him, and didn't even try. She sank her nails into his back, her heels digging into his lower back as he came with a long, jerking groan. It was as if he couldn't get deep enough, couldn't pour enough of himself into her. It was beyond seeking physical pleasure and well into some sort of primal mating ritual. Earthy, essential, basic. With her.

He idly thought about the bag. He'd actually thought to buy condoms. Just in case. In Bogota, they'd taken care to protect each other, as they had in Prague. At first anyway. But their joinings had been so fierce and so frequent, they'd eventually found any barrier between them to be too much. They'd shared so little of themselves except the physical, but they'd talked then, and he'd learned that she was protected, and healthy, as was he, so they'd decided to trust each other enough to continue without any barrier between them. As he lay almost trembling on top of her now, so thoroughly spent he couldn't imagine lifting much more than his head at the moment, he could only hope nothing had changed in the past two years, or that she'd have warned him otherwise.

He shifted off of her, rolling to his side and pulling her with him. Cuddling wasn't something they'd done much of—any of, really. They'd usually just lain there gasping. Then one of them would get up to use the bathroom, and things would usually commence again in the shower, and on it went until they collapsed and slept. There had been laughter among the gasps and moans, and they'd been by turns playful and forceful, animal and reverent, but at the core of it was pleasure seeking. And only that.

This time it was different. For him, anyway.

She shifted a bit, and he thought she was pulling away, but realized she was simply shrugging out of her open bra and dress. Still, once she was done, she didn't seem to have a really clear idea of how to move into his arms.

So he rolled to his back and tugged her to his side, pulling her arm across his chest, nudging her leg over his. She tentatively laid her head on his shoulder, which made him laugh. So confident a lover, and yet so unsure of herself as a partner in other ways. She propped her chin on his chest and looked at him. "What's funny?" she asked, only partly able to hide her dismay.

He smoothed the damp tendrils of hair from her temple, then traced his fingers over her cheekbones and along the side of her chin, ending by drawing his fingertip across her bottom lip, pressing slightly in the center. "Not funny, endearing. There's a difference."

She nipped at his fingertip. "Endearing, am I?"

She started to pull away, but he held her tightly against him. "Immensely."

She didn't struggle, but didn't relax entirely against him, either. It was as if she was prepared to spring into action, if necessary, at any moment. So, she was already back at work, or at least part of her was. He supposed he shouldn't let it bother him, as it was a bit selfish of him to expect her to give all of herself instantly, but it did, a little bit, anyway. He was on a mission, as well, but at that very moment, there was nothing either of them could do, and it was the last thing on his mind.

He supposed she might be thinking of him as part of her mission, which bothered him even more. He didn't think she had that in her. As femme fatale as she was in bed with him, and as confident as she was in handling herself in pretty much any situation—dinner with Reese came to mind—it wasn't such a stretch to think she could.

But he'd seen glimpses of the other part of her. The part that had a hard time simply laying her head down on her lover's shoulder. An accomplished seductress wouldn't have blinked at that sort of intimacy, knowing it for what it was, using it to get closer at a time when her partner would be his most vulnerable.

Perhaps she was worried he was trying to do the same. That this whole thing had been a ruse on his part.

Instinctively reacting to that notion, he lifted his head and tugged hers closer, so he could kiss her. And not for a reassuring peck on the lips. He kissed her once, gently, but firmly, then again, more slowly, softly, until she finally unbent enough to relax against him slightly. "I know you have no reason to trust me," he murmured against the side of her cheek, keeping her nestled closely, "but my intentions are sincere in this. I'm not playing you. I couldn't."

She shifted, so that their noses bumped, before pulling back just enough to look at him, but not enough, he noticed, so that she wasn't still tucked under the crook of his arm, leg casually hooked over his. "Isn't that precisely what someone trying to play me would say?"

There was amusement in her tone, and in her eyes, but along with that humor was trepidation, whether she thought he could see it or not.

"You could have a point." He rolled to his side, tipping her to her back, but keeping their legs entwined as he propped his head on his hand. "So, how do I prove to you that I mean what I say?"

"You don't," she said. "I simply have to decide to trust you, or not. Then, time, I suppose, would tell, which is a commodity we don't really have."

"Felicity—"

She pressed a finger across his lips. "I do believe you mean what you say. It's just . . . the rest of the situation we find ourselves in isn't exactly conducive to trust or foundation building." She pressed her finger harder against his lips when he tried to interrupt. "Allow me to have my say." He smiled against her finger, then pulled the tip between his teeth for a gentle nip. She slipped her finger free, but was smiling even as she admonished him. "Play fair."

"I always do. But that doesn't mean I won't press my advantage when and where I can. I go after what I want, Felicity Jane." He brushed a thumb over her cheek, pushed at the hair on her forehead.

Her eyes darkened, and he noted the light quiver of her chin as she took a steadying breath. "As do I," she said, somewhat shakily. "What bothers me is how your sense of fair play is going to work once we're in San Francisco, when what we both want is a certain priceless gemstone. What do you do when presented with one want versus another?"

He rolled to his back and pulled her on top of him, making her squeal in surprise. He laughed, and kissed her soundly, then rolled her to her back and kissed her again. She was pushing at his shoulders, but she was laughing. And she was kissing him back. "Off me, beast," she said, still laughing as he finally pulled away from her. "I call not fair using distraction techniques to avoid answering difficult questions."

"You're right. All I can do is ask you to trust me. And to think, perhaps, a bit more broadly where solutions to problems are concerned."

"We're hardly going to cut the gemstone in half."

"Hardly," he said, in a good imitation of her accent.

She swatted at him, but he was happy to see that humor was still the basis of her actions. Not that she wasn't still wary, but she was relaxed, playful, and willing to tackle the subject rather than simply pass judgment.

"Come here," he said, pulling her back into his arms.

"You think I'll give it to you, don't you?" she asked, allowing him to tuck her under his arm again. He noted she settled far more naturally against him, her head resting easily on his shoulder this time. He wondered if she even realized it.

"I think no such thing. But I do think there is a possibility for an outcome to this that would satisfy us both."

"You do, do you?"

He tipped up her chin and kissed her, gently but firmly, all playfulness gone. "Yes," he said, lifting his head and looking into her eyes. "I do."

"And what, pray tell, is your grand scheme?"

He started to tell her, when the plane hit an air pocket and quite suddenly dropped and jerked hard to the side. They clutched at each other and did their best not to roll to the floor. Before they could do much more than regroup and resettle, they hit another pocket, then another.

"Well," Finn said, holding her tightly against him and trying to brace them both in the center of the bed, "this could have been really interesting if it had come about twenty minutes earlier."

"Indeed," she said, then clung to him again when the plane shook once more.

Captain Steve's voice came over the intercom next to the door. "I suppose it goes without saying that we've run into a bit of turbulence. Might be a good idea to strap yourselves back into your seats. I'll give you an all clear as soon as I can get us out of this. Shouldn't be longer than fifteen, twenty minutes."

Finn looked at Felicity, then scanned the small bedroom to where their clothes were scattered literally everywhere. "I'm not sure which is more dangerous, staying here and holding on for dear life, or trying to get dressed so we can go out to our seats in the main cabin."

The plane dipped again, and her nails dug into his arms. "You have a point."

He pinned her to the bed, grinning. "Well, I could, if we had a little bit more time."

"Very amusing," she said, but didn't push him off of her. Probably because the weight of him would keep her in place. "What do we do?"

"We could wrap ourselves in the sheets, toga style."

"I'm not going toga style in front of Captain Steve, regardless that I'm quite certain he didn't think we were back here playing gin rummy. I don't care which team he plays for."

"Okay, okay. Follow me," he said as another idea formed. He slid from the bed to the floor, then shifted around so his back was to the wall by the door and braced his feet against the bolted frame of the bed. He reached out his hand to her. "Come on."

She was lying flat on her stomach, clutching at the bedspread. "I'm afraid my legs won't reach from there to—"

He wiggled his fingers. "Grab a hold."

She did, just as the plane rocked again, sending her off the bed and sprawled across his lap with a bit more force than he'd expected.

"Sorry," she said as he grunted on impact.

"Don't," he said as she tried to scramble off of him. "Come here. Turn around."

"Finn, this is hardly the time for some kinky new position—"

"I know, but keep it in mind, will you?" He gripped her hips and turned her so she straddled his lap, facing away from him. "I'll hold you, and you lean over and drag our clothes over here. I'll brace you while you dress. I can stay braced between the wall and the frame of the bed."

"What about you?"

He grinned. "I'll be okay. Just—" He groaned a little as she leaned forward to reach for her dress and bra, which had the unfortunate—at least at the moment—result of pressing her backside snugly against his belly, and the rest of her . . . He tried not to think about it, or he'd never get his pants on again. "Grab it," he managed, sighing in relief when she snagged her dress. The bra remained out of reach.

"This will do for now," she assured him. "But how do I get from here to the main cabin? Crawl?"

The plane jerked and dipped again, making him clutch her tightly against his chest. "You know," he whispered in her ear, "if there was even a little predictability to this, it could be fun."

She snorted at that, but didn't refute it, then dragged her dress on and began buttoning it as fast as she could, before the plane took yet another short drop. But she also wiggled her hips a little on purpose as she slid it down over her body, and he heard the little laugh when he bucked instinctively against her.

"You just wait," he warned her. "Keep playing."

"And you'll what?" she tossed back over her shoulder.

The plane rocked. He held her against his chest and cupped her breasts with his palms, through her dress. "I'll think of something, I'm sure."

She gasped, and swayed just a little, and he wished like hell Steve would call the all clear. They didn't have much time, and he knew he still needed to check in to see what Rafe might have dug up, as well as form a more specific plan for after they landed. He wondered what would have happened if he'd been able to keep Felicity here longer, if they could just fly in circles, where there was no chance of her leaving in the middle of the night, where she'd have to confront what was developing between them. And though it had been explosive sex, just as it had been before, there were nuances now, complexities, things that hadn't colored their time together in the past. And he was quite certain he wasn't the only one who felt that way.

"Okay, let me go, so you can get your pants."

He didn't want to let her go. He wanted—

"I think we're through the worst of it, folks," came Steve's cheerful voice through the intercom. "Sorry for the inconvenience. Might still be a good idea to strap in, though. With the new flight plan, we should be in San Francisco in approximately one hour, possibly a few minutes less. I'll keep you informed."

You do that, Finn thought, irrationally disgruntled by the news. For the first time, the job held little appeal.

Felicity slid from his lap and quickly gathered the rest of her belongings, tossing his clothes to him as she got to them.

"Thanks," he said, which made her smile. "What's amusing?"

"You sound like you've lost your favorite toy." She tossed his shoe to him. "And if you follow that with a crack that involves me in any way, I'll take even greater care with where I aim this other shoe." She smiled as she wiggled it next to her head.

Why can't it be like this? he wanted to know. With them laughing together, playing together, and then working together?

He pulled on his clothes as he watched Felicity make an effort to smooth and tame her now wildly tangled hair. Why couldn't she see that it could, indeed, work between them? At least worthy of a try, anyway. Wouldn't she favor using her well-honed skills for the good of others? He was well aware she performed altruistically through her foundation, and that working with him legitimately wouldn't garner the thrills she got from operating on the other side of the law, or right on the fringe of it, at the very least. But many, if not most, of his missions required a great amount of skill, and cunning, to devise just the right plot to win the day. He did a bit of edge walking himself. He and his partners very specifically took on the types of situations that would otherwise be considered hopeless. Righting wrongs, skating along on the finer points of the law, along with exploiting a few loopholes, in order to see that the good guys won.

If he presented it to her in just the right way, maybe she'd see that there was fun and excitement to be found in his pursuits. She just couldn't keep the spoils afterward. Surely, with her wealth, that wasn't the point anyway.

He watched as she carefully, and seemingly effortlessly,

transformed herself back into the proper British lady who spent her days writing checks to charities and her nights at this soiree or that ball. He knew otherwise. He knew what she was like beneath all that. Earthy and vulnerable. Cunning, with a need for excitement. And he didn't want to rid her of that, as her complexity was a large part of what attracted him to her.

All he had to do was figure out how to combine the best of both . . . and then convince her to share it all with him.

Chapter 12

Felicity buckled her seat belt and prepared herself for landing. If only she could as easily prepare herself for what was going to happen after that. Her head told her to make a clean break of it as soon as possible and go back to working as she always did: solo. Her heart wasn't as clear on the matter.

She tried telling herself that what happened back in the bedroom wasn't anything that hadn't happened between them before. It had been every bit as explosive as it had always been, he'd pushed her to places no one else did, but, at the end of it, nothing had changed.

So what if he'd made an effort to be emotionally intimate after their physical urges were sated. He wanted what he wanted. And, yes, it had been somewhat surprising how easy he'd made it to slip into the role of lover and friend, not just sex partner. But just because she had let her guard down a little, enjoyed herself some, didn't mean she had to change her course of action. Nor should she.

She looked out the window and tried to ignore the sounds of Finn clicking himself into his seat. Images of his body, how he'd looked, felt, tasted, laughed, smiled, kissed . . . were still too potent, too close. She needed to clear her head and erase those images. For now anyway. She knew she'd trot them out later and examine them more fully. Dream about them, most likely, if the past was anything to go by. Repeatedly.

He'd sat where he had before, on the opposite side of the plane, for which she was grateful. She needed a chance to regroup. Still, she couldn't help but wonder at the tactic, telling herself it was that and not disappointment that had her analyzing the decision. He said he wanted more from her and had made no effort to hide his determination to succeed in his quest to win her over. He had to know he'd gotten her to lower her defenses, especially afterward, before the turbulence had hit them. So why allow her the chance to rebuild those defenses now? Especially when they were so close to landing. From a strategy standpoint, it made no sense.

No matter what his agenda was, whether it was truly to woo her rather than merely seduce her, or whether there really was some elaborate plan in place to keep her close as a means to secure his success in the mission, allowing her any time to build and execute her own strategy wasn't going to help his cause.

And Finn was no dummy when it came to mounting a good offense. Which could only make her wonder what he was up to with all this space he was suddenly giving her. Damn the man for not being more predictable, anyway.

She glanced over to find him tapping on the screen of his satellite unit.

"Any new information?" she asked, wanting to sound like the professional she was, and not the daft girl who was trying too hard at pretending she wasn't interested in the cute boy.

"Not as much as I'd like." He glanced over at her and immediately smiled. "So serious."

"We have serious work to do," she replied, determined to keep her game face in place if it killed her. It was her only hope at the moment, especially considering she was currently imagining him naked, while also trying to ignore the renewed ache growing inside her as her thoughts strayed to the bedroom in the back of the plane. And that plastic shopping bag of goodies that he'd left behind. Damn the man for that, too. And the flight for not being a wee bit longer. And less turbulent. On several levels. It was rare she got to have fun. She needed more fun. Finn was fun. A shame she couldn't have more of that part of him without risking the rest.

She swallowed a sigh and crossed her legs. "So, what have we learned?"

Finn held her gaze for a moment too long, a moment that told her he was probably reading every last thought in her mind. At least he had the grace not to look overly amused. "We can't seem to find any evidence of a past liaison of any kind between Julia and Reese, business or pleasure."

"Maybe they're both just adept at maintaining their privacy. I doubt they just hooked up and he offered to give her a ride home in his plane."

"Me, either. I'm just saying that if they've done business before, personal or professional, there's no record of it and no one is talking about it."

"Do we know more about her business practices? Was your partner able to line up any of her trips or shipments to clients with known black market trade activity?"

Finn frowned then, as if something had just occurred to him, but when he went on, she had a feeling that it wasn't about whatever revelation had just taken place. "She does travel, but it's on gallery business, as far as her documented activities. Not much information on how she spends her personal time."

In opulent hotel bathrooms sipping very expensive champagne, Felicity thought, and not entirely kindly, though she certainly had no platform from which to pass judgment. "And her trips don't sync with other activities in the same location? What about shipping schedules?"

"Not directly, no. But if she's playing middle man, there might not be such a direct correlation. And not enough time yet to line up shipping manifests with known black market activities."

"Do you still think that's the link?"

Finn lifted his shoulder. "It makes the most sense. It doesn't explain how she happened to be in New York right when Reese needed her, but it might explain what services she could provide."

"Getting the sapphire out of the country in one of her art shipments, so it can be safely delivered to whomever John is selling it to, you mean?"

"It plays."

"But there's still that initial coincidence." Felicity took a moment to analyze the situation. "And I'll bite that maybe it's just that. Or maybe they have a personal relationship they've managed to keep hush hush and set it up to meet there if their paths were otherwise crossing."

"It makes just as much sense as any other explanation."

She looked over at him. His clothes were rumpled, his hair a bit of a tousled mess, and he had a hint of beard stubble lightly shadowing his jaw now. She'd seen him in a tux, she knew how well he cleaned up, but this was the real Finn. So different from her, so different from the men she knew and socialized with. Ironic, given his silver spoon background. "So . . . beyond that, where do we begin? Do we look at her clients for potential buyers? Do we look at her shipping schedule? Do we try and track Reese's actions?"

"Well, we could try and track down Reese himself, but I'm doubting he's keeping any kind of public profile at this point. Besides, I had Rafe dig more on him, and, as it happens, he doesn't appear to spend any time in San Francisco, so no known favorite restaurants or hotels."

"Odd for a man having a liaison with a woman who lives there."

"Unless the reason there are no favorite hotels popping up is because he has private digs."

"Meaning Julia's."

"Yes. And we could dig there, too, see if anyone has seen him there, but that will take time we don't have. It's best if we just assume there is a partnership both professional and personal, and focus on the stone."

"First up?"

"Target the whereabouts of her best clients, see who is in town, who might be up for a late night or early morning meeting. In case it's just a direct sale and we're making it too complicated."

"And second?"

"Shipping. Find out where she ships from, watch the area for activity in case she is going to package the gem and conceal it with artwork."

"So . . . it might not be a bad idea to divide and conquer." She watched him carefully for his reaction.

He looked at her, expressionless. "And?"

"You track clients and any potential meeting sites. I'll watch the shipping dock."

He didn't respond right away, but went back to tapping on his iPhone when it beeped. "It's not a bad plan," he said at length, still keeping his gaze averted.

"But?"

He glanced up, his expression still unreadable. She wouldn't have thought him capable of such a good poker face. "But nothing. We still have a short time to gather information before landing. If nothing else comes in to steer us in a more concrete direction, then we'll follow your plan."

She stared at him, until he finally said, "What?"

"You're okay with us splitting up?"

"I don't see where we have a choice. It would be foolish not to tackle as many avenues as we can. Time is critical."

"And if one of us tracks the stone down?"

Finn smiled then, and she was gratified to see that the smile reached his eyes. "I would hope whichever one of us that is would contact the other, and we'd figure out together how best to retrieve it."

And then what? she wanted to ask, but knew better. "What if waiting means losing the opportunity?"

"Then do what has to be done."

She leaned back and folded her arms. "You don't seem too

concerned that I'm going to take off with the stone if I get it first."

Captain Steve interrupted, announcing that landing was imminent.

Finn shifted back in his seat, but she stayed turned toward him, until finally he looked back at her. "I guess I'm not."

"You guess? Why would you think that? We've both certainly proven what we're capable of when we want something the other one also wants."

"I know. But it's different this time."

"How?" She lifted a hand to stall his response. "I mean, I know you think we should embark on a personal relationship, but, clearly, if I run off with our quarry, I would assume your personal interest in me would wane somewhat."

"Last time you took off, I let you."

She bristled at that, but didn't engage him in that battle. "Meaning?"

"Meaning I didn't follow." He shifted so he faced forward as the plane's thrusters kicked in, making conversation difficult over the rushing roar of sound.

"It wouldn't have done any good," she said, shouting to be heard over the engines, not sure why she was bothering with the argument. He was going to do whatever he thought he should do, no matter what she said, but it irked her that he thought that by not chasing her in Bogota, he'd let her win the prize.

"Maybe not where those diamonds were concerned," he said, looking back over at her. "But it might have kept me from spending the past three-plus years wondering about you."

She'd already opened her mouth to respond, all geared to argue her point, when what he said sank in. "But you take your work very seriously," she said, frowning. "You left me in Prague."

"Yes, I do. And yes, I did. What does that have to do with me pursuing you now?"

"You'd have me believe that you'd put your personal needs before your professional ones?"

"I would, depending on the situation. Family, friends always come first with me."

"I don't mean in choosing career over family or friends, or taking on a certain job if you had other things that were pressing for your attention. I mean, if you were currently on a job, and there was a personal conflict of interest, you'd do what you wanted for yourself, even if it meant failing your client."

"Why do you think I'd have to make that choice?"

She shifted to look more fully at him, grabbing the arms of her chair as the plane touched down on the runway and gave them a good bounce. "If you had the choice of getting your hands on that sapphire, or keeping track of me, pursuing me, you know you'd take the stone."

· Finn just grinned. "I'm thinking if I play this right, I could get both."

Felicity remembered then, right before the turbulence hit, he'd been about to tell her his grand plan for making them both satisfied with one stone between them. She couldn't see how that could be, and she should be turned off by his confidence in the matter, but there was something so charming about that smile, that twinkle in his eye . . . Damn the man anyway. "Did it occur to you that I might be a bit put out if you take what I feel is rightfully mine? I didn't come all the way over here to go home empty-handed."

Finn's grin grew even wider, if that was possible. "Oh, I don't intend for you to be empty-handed at all."

Her frustration seemed to only fuel his amusement. "Fine, if you're not going to take this seriously, I certainly don't see why I should even bother discussing it with you. All I'll say is this: don't be too sure of yourself. You say you want it all. Well, best keep in mind that what I want is to go home with what I came here for. Despite your claims to the contrary, I'm quite certain, barring there being two priceless Byzantine sapphires up for grabs, that it's not possible for us both to have what we want here. Even if my personal desires were in line with yours, which is ground I believe we've also previously covered."

The plane rolled to a stop, then slowly taxied around to its gate. Finn waited until it came to a full stop, then unbuckled his seat belt, stood, and stretched. He stepped over and offered Felicity his hand. She looked at it dubiously, and then even more warily up at him.

"I don't bite," he assured her. "Much. And then only by request. In fact, I thought you rather liked it when I nibbled—"

"Oh, for heaven's sake." She swatted his hand away and got up without his assistance, stepping around him with the intention of quickly using the lavatory before debarking. She had no idea what the rest of the night and early morning hours would entail, so best to hedge her bets where she could.

He didn't look remotely abashed at her rebuke, far from it, in fact. It didn't help much that his general geniality was making her feel crabby and unreasonable. When, in reality, she was generally far more like him, grabbing for the joy in life and doing her best to let the rest roll off.

She just couldn't see there being a future in grabbing for him.

Which meant it was time to let him roll off.

She was just stepping into the bathroom when he moved up behind her. "Can I ask you one thing?"

She stilled, feeling him so close, knowing it would likely be the last time she was in his personal space like this, unable to keep her thoughts from revisiting his little comment on the nibbling . . . which she had, in fact, enjoyed a great deal. Letting him go meant there would be no more of that. Ever. She tried not to feel so disappointed about that, to put it in proper perspective, which was that she was fortunate to have experienced any of it at all. But it proved to be beyond her compartmentalizing capabilities. She'd get past it in time. She had before. Kind of.

"Ask," she directed him, reaching for what he termed her "royal" tone.

He took her elbow and turned her to face him, so she was wedged just inside the tiny doorway, and he filled the entire hallway. She purposely didn't look past him, to the rumpled bed she knew lay just beyond.

"You said you felt the sapphire was rightfully yours. Once before, you characterized this mission as a job. Care to illuminate?"

She'd been expecting another personal volley, so it took her a moment to respond. "I didn't mean anything by it," she said, one of the first untruths she'd ever spoken to him. But she had no choice. She hadn't realized her slip, either of them, and silently cursed herself for making such a potentially costly one around a man as tuned in as Finn. "We both want the piece."

"Yes, but I want it because I think it rightfully belongs to my client. Do you know anything about him, by the way? Or why I'm here trying to get it back for him?"

She knew there were others who felt they had a claim to the piece, but didn't know anything specifically about which of them Finn might be working for. This particular stone had been the subject of a family quarrel dating back several centuries. It was also the centerpiece of evidence in a case MI-8 was building against one of their own, who had used his insider information on the extended family issues to push the stone back onto the open market where he could personally profit from its subsequent sale. Without it, they had no case.

She supposed she should have asked Finn sooner about his side, his client, if for no other reason than additional intelligence on the mission. But she hadn't. She'd been so busy thinking about everything from her viewpoint, from the mission to Finn's declaration of wanting to see if they could develop something personally, that she hadn't really given much consideration to his standing in all this. Or his client's. Which spoke volumes to her about how ready she was—or wasn't—for any kind of relationship with anyone.

"Why do you think I want it?" she countered. It was that one thing, she realized, his refusal to believe there could be a moral reason for her actions, that primarily stood in the way of her even entertaining his proposition. Not that she could fathom breaking the silence she'd been sworn by MI-8 to keep. But it still personally rankled. *Maybe he just needs to know you better,* her little voice added. But her immediate next thought was, *For a man who has professed wanting more from me, there should at the very least be a foundation of respect.* A man like him didn't tolerate liars, cheats, thieves. In fact, he'd dedicated his life to righting the injustices caused by just such a group of people.

So, how could he truly want her if he thought her morally corrupt?

"I don't know why you want it," he said truthfully. "Making a case for absolute honesty here, I would have said, coming into this particular mission, that your interest hasn't really been owning or possessing, even briefly, something priceless. My guess is what I said before, and which you deftly avoided commenting on."

"Which is?"

"That it's the thrill of the hunt, the satisfaction of victory, beating the odds, not getting caught, more than ownership of the quarry itself."

Though it certainly wasn't the motivating factor in why she was doing what she was doing, it would be a lie to say that the element of thrill wasn't at least part of it. Her real life, while very rewarding given the philanthropic nature of the trust she oversaw, was busy, tedious, and filled with never-ending lists of meetings, committees, fund-raisers, charity events, and so forth. Getting to play Jane Bond, even on the minor level she was able to, was thrilling, certainly. Nothing in her real life would ever give her the kind of adrenaline rush she got from casing a place out, staking her mark, making her move . . . and coming back with the spoils, and a mission won.

Doing that made her feel as though she was directly, and very personally, contributing to the betterment of others. It was strictly her contribution, not a check drawn off of family accounts full of money obtained decades and, in some cases, centuries ago by her ancestors. It was only the fluke of being born into the Trent family that gave her even that much power.

This, however, was all her. With rare exceptions, her name got her nowhere in this job and was, more often than not, a detriment to getting things done the way she would have otherwise liked. The accoutrements of wealth came in handy for jetting about the globe, that was true, but in lieu of a salary, she billed MI-8 for her expenses, so even there, the Trent money didn't play a real role.

"Awfully quiet. Have I hit on the truth?" he asked.

She responded with a question of her own. "Are you saying that the adrenaline rush of putting yourself out there, at times in quite the sticky spot, isn't part of what you love about what you do?"

"It plays a part on some cases," he conceded easily, "but it's not the sole motivation. Or even the primary one."

"And yet," she said, easing back into the small bathroom, "you can't seem to fathom that the same could be said about me." She slid the door shut between them and was relieved when he didn't block her. "Now, if you'll excuse me, I'd prefer a bit of privacy."

Chapter 13

Finn wanted—well, he didn't know what he wanted, but he damn well wasn't going to stand there and let her drop that kind of comment with no follow-up. But just then his satellite unit beeped twice, informing him he had urgent incoming data waiting to be retrieved.

Rafe's latest report, no doubt. He slid the unit from his pocket, but was still staring at the closed door between him and Felicity, his mind refusing to budge from her parting shot.

She hadn't denied his summation of her motives, which rang like an endorsement in his mind. What other motivation could she have? Was she playing some sort of modern day Robin Hood? Stealing from the rich to give to the poor? He understood the premise, given that was largely what he and his partners did every day, well, sans the stealing part. As in this particular case, he was merely returning an item obtained illegally in the first place to its original owner. His methods might not be entirely orthodox, but they stayed on the right side of the law. At least as he interpreted them, anyway.

In Felicity's case, she already gave away tens of thousands to the less fortunate every day in her role as administrator of the Trent Foundation. What real motivation would there be in risking life and limb, even for the rush, to steal priceless antiquities, gems, and who the hell knew what else, only to give them away again? Did she fence them and make some anonymous gift of the proceeds? If so, why refer to it as a job?

He swore under his breath when his unit continued to beep insistently. There was no time for this kind of analysis now; they both had a job to do. Which brought him full circle to her earlier question, which was what he would do when faced with choosing to trust her over the job at hand. He knew how he planned to handle the eventuality of them retrieving the stone. He just hoped that if she got to it first, she gave him a chance to at least put his idea on the table.

He stared at the closed door, then abruptly turned and stalked back into the main cabin. Captain Steve stepped in from the control booth at the same time. "You're free to debark," he said. "Sorry for the turbulence earlier."

Finn was still so distracted by . . . well, everything, he didn't really look to see if Steve seemed to be aware of exactly what they'd been up to when the turbulence hit, merely saying, "No problem. I really appreciate you getting us out here. We . . . have a few things to wrap up, but we'll be out of here shortly. Don't wait for us if you need to get inside and see to other details."

"You need a return trip anytime soon? I'll likely be in town for at least the next twenty-four hours, maybe longer."

"I don't know yet, but I'll give you a call if and when I do, and if that works out, great. But don't wait for us."

Steve merely tipped his fingers to the brim of his hat, then grabbed his black leather satchel and climbed out through the open hatch door, disappearing down the metal stairs.

Finn slid the stylus free and tapped on the tiny screen, humming impatiently as Rafe's file downloaded and opened. He quickly skimmed the details, zeroing in on the list of names his partner had come up with as the prime clients who would be probable buyers. It wasn't quite as long a list as he'd feared, and the list grew shorter still when distance was factored in. Reese might have dismissed the two of them as a threat once he made his deal with Julia, but Finn and Felicity Jane weren't the only ones who'd initially gone after the stone. A man with Reese's experience and business savvy wouldn't rest until he'd moved the stone safely out of his possession. To that end, if Reese was selling to one of Julia's clients, Finn doubted he would waste time setting up a courier for one of Julia's out-of-towners. Not if he could find an in-town buyer first. So Finn would focus on them.

Felicity would take the mule angle and work the shipping docks that Julia used, which Rafe had also listed in this most recent transmission. They weren't as close to her gallery as he'd have liked, which was where he'd likely be hovering about, but there was no certainty they'd use the gallery as an exchange point anyway, if the sapphire was staying local.

Felicity came out of the rest room, looking remarkably crisp and fresh for a woman who'd just spent five hours on a plane, in a dress that had spent at least part of that time crushed beneath the weight of both of their bodies.

"You look amazing," he said, quite sincerely, which seemed to take her aback. That made him smile as he looked back down at the info still scrolling onto his screen, suddenly feeling a bit steadier. "I have the list of potential buyers," he continued. "Not as many as I'd thought, but enough to make it tricky on where to start."

"You've got addresses, contact info?" She didn't seem to know what to do with herself, and he looked up in time to catch her starting to fuss with her skirt, then her hair, only to check both motions.

He looked back down so she wouldn't see his smile grow. Good to know she wasn't so steady either. There was hope yet. "Some, not all."

"Set up a radius with the gallery as the central point and work your way out from there. As good a plan as any. Or focus on any one area that has the most clients per square whatever. You want to follow my plan on the rest? Did we get the shipping dock information?"

He looked up then and held her gaze very directly. At least

she'd said "we." "I haven't changed my mind on that. Would you rather handle the clients and I'll take the dock? That might be more your strength than mine. And if things get sticky on the docks, that might be more my area."

She held his gaze in return, and they wasted another few seconds playing visual chicken, but neither backed down. Also good to know, he thought. They were both a bit shaky about their personal situation, but rock steady when it came to the job at hand.

"Actually, I do think that's a better plan." She looked at him a bit longer, and he wondered if she was thinking he'd gotten some kind of intel from Rafe that pointed to the mule angle being more likely. But she didn't press, and he respected that for now, she seemed to be trusting him.

"Good. Then that's how we'll handle it. We'll use the drive in to coordinate the list and make a plan from there."

"We'll need two cars. With drivers."

"Why drivers? Won't that complicate things?"

She smiled lightly. "Okay then, I'll need a driver. It will give me more latitude in dealing with Julia's client base."

"Walk the walk, and all that."

"Precisely."

"Fine, we can hire two cars here, then have one follow us to whatever point we pick. We'll split up from there." It was on the tip of his tongue to ask her to elaborate on what she'd meant before she'd ducked into the bathroom. Despite all the planning and apparent teamwork here, he was well aware this could also be his last real chance to ask her anything.

"Are we done here?" she asked, ending the moment of opportunity.

He pocketed his satellite unit. "Here, yes," he said pointedly. He wasn't giving up just yet, and he wanted her to know that. "Give me a moment." He ducked into the lavatory and took a few minutes to clean himself up, nodding at her as he stepped back out and motioned toward the open hatch. "Ladies first."

"Aren't you forgetting something?"

He patted his pockets, but didn't feel anything missing.

She motioned to the bag, sitting on the chair next to the table.

He lifted his eyebrows, but she cut him off just as the grin started to spread across his face.

"I was only asking because they are your purchases."

"How . . . thoughtful of you." He stepped over and fingered the bag, taking a peek inside, then looking at her. "I suppose I should hold on to them. Be prepared, and all that."

She snorted, delicately, but it was a snort. "Like you were ever a Boy Scout."

"Actually, I was." He swung the bag over his shoulder and moved in behind her, herding her toward the door. He leaned in close to her ear. "Wanna see my service badges?"

She tried to huff, but it came out as more of a laugh. "Honestly," she muttered as she ducked and stepped out of the plane and onto the metal steps.

He followed her, using her descent in heels as an excuse to touch her elbow in a steadying gesture. Given she could likely tap-dance across a tight rope in those things, it was completely unnecessary, pathetic, even, but he took solace in the fact that she didn't brush him off.

There was a town car idling less than twenty feet away across the tarmac.

Felicity looked back over her shoulder at him. "Yours? Your partner thinking ahead perhaps?"

Finn frowned. "I didn't see that in his notes, but maybe I missed it. I was more interested in names and locations."

They both frowned and looked at the car. A driver stood stoically beside the passenger door.

"How does he see wearing those sunglasses?" Felicity whispered. "It's the middle of the night."

He paused them both halfway down the stairs. "Something's not right," Finn murmured.

"I was just thinking the same thing."

"Back in the plane?" he asked, too casually.

"The captain is gone."

"I can fly the damn plane."

"Aren't there flight plans that have to be filed and fueling to be done, not to mention hijacking a plane with your country's current security—"

"I don't have to take off, I just want to play chicken with a bigger vehicle than they have."

"Ah." She glanced at him. "Then plane it is."

But just as they turned, the rear door of the limo opened. Finn immediately pulled Felicity behind him. "Get up the stairs as soon as it's clear."

"Finn, I can—"

"No need to go running off." The deep voice with the recognizable British accent floated easily across the short expanse of tarmac.

Finn kept Felicity behind him, but that didn't stop her from peeking over his shoulder. "John?"

Reese climbed out of the limo. His hands were empty, but that didn't mean he wasn't armed. What in the hell was he doing here? Felicity tried to slip free and at least move next to Finn, if not in front of him. Finn kept her pinned right where she was.

"No need to be a Neanderthal," she muttered.

"I thought you liked it when I went all hunter-gatherer," he murmured back. Then he looked to Reese, a partial smile on his face. "Thanks for the offer of a lift, but we have our own ride."

"It won't be necessary to track me any longer."

Finn laughed. "Track you? Oh, we just flew out so I could take Felicity for some seafood. Can you believe she's never been to Fisherman's Wharf?" Finn kept the casual smile on his face despite the disappointment. Not that he necessarily believed Reese. They couldn't have gotten here that much sooner. If the deal was, in fact, done, they must have made arrangements during the flight out to make the exchange right here at the airport. If he was telling the truth. But why the visit? Reese didn't strike him as a man who needed to prove anything, much less the type to gloat.

Reese merely stared at him, and he heard Felicity sigh. No one wanted to have fun anymore.

"I appreciate the heads up," Finn went on. "I'd loan you the plane, but I understand you have one of your own."

"You didn't go and trade away my bauble, did you, darling?" Felicity cooed from behind him.

Finn wasn't much on the cooing. To Reese, anyway. In fact, he pretty much hated it. "Congratulations, by the way. I'm sure the commission was sweet. So, local or international sale?"

"I don't know." Reese was looking at Felicity. "I'm afraid I didn't take quite the care with your 'little bauble' as I should have."

"What?" Finn demanded. Then he smiled. So that was why Reese was here. Clearly, things had changed. But why come to them?

He put his hand on Felicity's arm when she went to step past him. Until he had a better handle on what was going on, they were staying right where they stood.

"That's not like you, John," Felicity admonished, though Finn could hear the thread of tension in her tone. "What happened?"

Reese moved to one side and motioned to the open door. "I thought perhaps we could discuss the matter on the way into the city, and see what might be done about it."

Finn just smiled. "You'll forgive me if I don't jump at the offer."

Felicity patted the hand covering her elbow. "Now, now, darling, perhaps we shouldn't be too hasty in turning down Mr. Reese's willingness to team up."

He glanced at her. "Because we're doing so well with the partnership we already have."

"I know of its most recent whereabouts," Reese reminded him.

"So, what happened?" Finn asked. "Was Ms. Julia Forsythe more interested in stealing your rock than getting them o—"

"Finn," Felicity admonished, squeezing his hand, though he swore he heard the amusement in her tone as well. "Why enlist our help?" she asked Reese, quite logically. "If you're the one with the trail, why not track it yourself?"

"My business expertise lies in the area of setting up the perfect deal between seller and buyer. I'm not in the habit of having to track down errant merchandise."

"But . . . you believe we'd be happy to do that for you," Finn intoned. "For what, a handsome finder's fee? Perhaps you're not aware, but money isn't a huge motivator where Ms. Trent and I are concerned." He glanced at her, then back at Reese. "We'd rather hold on to priceless treasures ourselves. We're funny like that. So are our clients."

He felt Felicity glance at him at his use of "our." Yes, it was a bluff. It could pan out later. Or not. At the very least, it would bring on an interesting conversation with Felicity later. And he wasn't done having those with her yet.

"You can keep the stone," Reese said, quite seriously.

Both Finn and Felicity looked to Reese, then at each other. "I beg your pardon?" Finn asked, looking back at Reese. "Ours to keep. Just like that?"

Felicity took only a second longer to regroup. Then she clasped her hands around Finn's bicep and tugged a little, a big smile on her face. "Why, that's lovely news, darling!" She looked at Finn. "He said we could keep it." She looked back to Reese, the smile still on her face, but harder now. "Why ever should we believe that?"

Reese didn't find her nearly as amusing as Finn did. "Hard as this may be to understand, I'm not so much interested, at this point, in recovering the stone, or my percentage. I do quite well. One botched transaction won't send me to the poorhouse."

"But your reputation—"

"Can take it. This is more . . ."

"Personal?" Finn queried. His smile grew. "Ah, now I understand. You don't want the stone; you just don't want Ms. Forsythe to have it."

Reese didn't even pause. "Or profit from it."

Finn glanced at Felicity. "Seems we're taking on more clients. We should consider hanging a shingle. Dalton & Trent, Professional Treasure Trackers."

"I'm sure your other partners would be thrilled," she said. "Although, shouldn't it be Trent & Dalton? Ladies first, brains over brawn?" She turned back to Reese, not giving Finn a chance to reply. "How do we know you're not sending us on a wild goose chase to throw us off the real track?"

"You don't," he said simply. "Although, generally, when I make a deal, and the deal is done, I move on. What my competitors do about it isn't any of my concern. My role is over."

Finn considered that, and knew the truth of it. That was his immediate thought when Reese stopped by to see them in the first place. It wasn't his style. "Seems to me a man with your resources would prefer to take on his personal issues personally."

Even with the distance between them, Finn could see Reese's jaw tighten. "I've been associated with this artifact quite enough. I trust that you'll take care of it. What you do with it once you obtain it is of no concern to me."

"And Ms. Forsythe?" Felicity asked. "What of her? Any special directives there? Messages you'd care to deliver?"

Reese held their gazes for a few long seconds, then said, "Retrieve the stone. That will be message enough."

"And what proof would you require for the deal to be considered done?" This was from Finn. He wasn't exactly entertaining the idea of really taking this on, but the more he knew about where Reese's head was in this whole mess, the better for them. He hoped Felicity was of the same mind and wasn't really considering teaming up with him.

"We'll worry about that when you have it."

"And what is the deal, exactly?"

"I give you my leads, you get the prize."

"What would keep us from working with Julia ourselves?"

Reese's smile was anything but sweet. "She's already stolen from me. I'm not thinking it would be real smart to team up with her. But, by all means, go for it if you think that's your best shot. It's not like I've got anything to lose. But you certainly do." He motioned to the open back door once again. "Time is of the essence. Shall we discuss the rest during our ride into the city?"

Finn didn't want to cut Reese loose—yet—but he wasn't too keen on giving the man that much control of the situation, either. He still wasn't sure he was buying Reese's story. But he couldn't come up with an alternate one that would make any more sense. In the end, Felicity solved the problem by ducking past him.

"Come, darling," she said to him as she glanced back over her shoulder. "Like the man said, time is wasting."

Finn didn't move right away, so she paused. "Would you like me to go with John and see what we can find while you pursue our earlier plans? We can drop you at the rental agency, then meet up later once things are more sorted out."

Reese merely smiled.

And Finn swore under his breath, not at all liking where his brain was going with this. Had Felicity somehow contacted Reese? Was this whole Julia thing a red herring to divert his attention from the two Brits teaming up and putting one over on him? It seemed rather an elaborate scheme, when all she had to do was take off the moment his back was turned and meet up with Reese. But this way, they kept him close and his activities monitored . . . He stared at Felicity's retreating back and wished like hell he didn't have any doubts about her. He wouldn't have thought it of her, but he still hadn't reconciled her alternate life with the woman he thought she was. Of course, as heavily influenced as he was by a fog of pheromones and an almost constant state of arousal, who the hell knew what he was willing himself to believe?

At the moment, the only way to find out was to join her and

Reese in the car. He followed her onto the tarmac, palming her lower back as he steered her toward the car. "I should have given this case to Mac," he muttered.

Felicity laughed as she ducked down and climbed into the car. "And miss out on all this fun?"

"Is that what this is?" He climbed into the car beside her, purposely leaving Reese to take the seat opposite them. "I was having a hard time telling." He'd briefly toyed with the idea of letting them sit next to each other so he could keep an observant eye on both at the same time, but in the end, his inner Neanderthal won out.

"Funny," Felicity said, leaning her shoulder against his. "I could have sworn you were having a very good time when I did that little—"

Finn gently squeezed her knee, a bit surprised she'd given that tidbit to Reese, wondering what her angle was. Certain she had one. He chuckled. "Now, darling, let's not talk of such things here and now. He's just been dumped, after all." He smiled at Reese, who, he discovered, was staring out the window, apparently oblivious to the two of them.

If Finn didn't know better, he'd have guessed that their surprise client wasn't merely pissed off at being swindled. He was hurt. Along the lines of being devastated, actually. Or heartbroken. Or both.

It took a bit to really wrap his mind around that possibility. Sure, they'd thought Reese and Julia had a thing going, but— and maybe it was the whole international man of mystery thing—Finn didn't really see Reese as the sort to fall head over heels for anything that wasn't at least a few centuries old. And worth millions.

He glanced at Felicity, who was studying Reese as well. He subtly nudged her knee with his own. She gave the briefest of nods, without looking at him. So, she'd figured it out, too.

"So why don't you fill us in on the chain of events leading up to the sapphire leaving your possession," Felicity said, all business now, though she left her hand on Finn's knee.

He liked it there. For once, it wasn't wreaking havoc with his body. But it was doing a little number on his heart. It felt . . . steadying. Maybe it was for her, too.

"That won't be necessary," he said, looking to his hands, glancing at them. One brief notice of Felicity's hand on Finn's knee had his gaze drifting back out the window.

Finn actually felt bad about the "dumped" remark now. But, who would have guessed the real truth of it?

"I know where you need to look, or who to start with anyway."

"Julia," Finn said evenly, without inflection of any kind.

Reese gave a curt nod, but said nothing.

"So . . . was there a business deal between you?" At Reese's glare, he clarified. "I need to know the technicalities, not to mention the legalities, of what I'm walking into."

"Business deals. Personal relationships. They get messy," Felicity interjected. She glanced at Finn, then smiled quite charmingly. "I know a little something about that."

Reese didn't respond to that. Instead, he looked to them again, holding their gazes squarely this time. "I chose the two of you because you have the most to gain, and want it the most. Plus, against a team, Julia is less likely to . . . be persuasive."

"John—" Felicity began, only to have him cut her off.

"Trust me, Ms. Trent."

She held his gaze a moment longer, then nodded.

"About the business deal," Finn prodded.

"It seems you know something of her," Reese replied. "Tell me what you know, or think you know."

They didn't have anything on Julia that would be damning to their chances if he was, in fact, playing them in some way. Nothing he didn't already know, anyway. Finn started. "We know she runs a very successful gallery in the city, quite successful given her young age and relatively recent entry into the art world. We couldn't find anything linking her to you."

"I assume you searched my hotel room." He didn't make it a question.

"Yes," Finn responded. "There were lipstick prints on the champagne glass."

Reese fell silent for a moment; his expression remained unreadable.

"Business partners first?" Felicity gently queried. "Or did that element come into play later?"

Reese looked to her. "Not that it matters here, but I would have to say they rather went hand in hand. As it were."

"Then this wasn't the first business arrangement you've made," Finn reiterated. "How long have you worked together?"

He didn't answer immediately, and Finn thought he'd push that off again. So he was a little surprised when Reese said, "For the past year." He straightened in his seat, seemingly pulling on his mantle of control before their very eyes. "But I don't really see what that has to do with anything. We made a deal. She broke it and used the information we'd shared in setting up the deal for her own personal gain. She stole from me. And I want the item retrieved. Then it's yours. It's as simple as that."

It was anything but simple. Finn felt the slightest pressure of Felicity's knee against his and pressed back.

It occurred to him that he and Felicity had balanced each other well in this situation. He approached Reese from the professional angle, and she had smoothly gone with the more personal route. They hadn't planned anything, couldn't have, so had just naturally fallen into the most productive approach. Hang a shingle, indeed.

"Do you think she expects you to come after the stone?"

"Or her?" Felicity added. She didn't clarify whether she meant with the intent to get her back . . . or get back at her.

Reese looked to Finn, then Felicity. "I clearly have no idea what she's thinking in regards to me, but I do know she won't be expecting you."

Felicity started to ask something else, but Finn covered her hand, still on his knee, and squeezed lightly. It was just as well that Reese was done talking about the personal side of his liaison with Julia. The last thing he needed was for Felicity to sit there and hear all the reasons why their international, wheeling-dealing relationship hadn't panned out. To be honest, given his earlier suspicions of there being a possible partnership between them, he didn't need to hear it either.

Although, at least those questions had been put to rest. If they were playing him, then Reese deserved an Academy Award. For that matter, so did Felicity.

"Where do we start?" Finn asked.

"It would help if you'd explain the deal itself," Felicity added, on the business angle now, too. "What her role is. Was."

"I had a backup, to Chesnokov. But I'd missed the window, which meant it was up to me to get it shipped."

"Julia regularly ships art overseas," Finn supplied.

"I see you made that connection."

"It was one of the probables we'd intended to pursue."

"Can I ask how she gets the pieces out undetected? Aren't there pretty stringent guidelines these days?"

"To a degree. But the pieces moved aren't hidden, if that's what you're referring to. They're legitimately moved."

Finn leaned back. "Really."

Reese pinned him with an equally steady gaze. "Really. I know about the rumors, but I work within the bounds of the law. Sometimes just within the bounds. And I can't help it if sometimes those bounds are a bit gray. I work with what I'm given." Now he leaned back. "But then, that's something you're familiar with, aren't you, Mr. Dalton?"

So, he'd done some checking, too. Finn wondered when he'd had time. On the flight, most likely, just as he had.

Reese's claim of legitimacy was possible, if not probable, given all he'd been reputedly connected with. The legitimate trading and selling of artifacts, vintage pieces, heirlooms, antiquities, and the like was a multibillion-dollar industry that functioned on a global scale at a blistering pace made even more frenetic with the advent of advanced communication technology. It was also a business riddled with loopholes and gray areas that allowed a great deal of latitude in operation as well as the interpretation of various laws and boundaries. All of which Finn was intimately aware of—Reese had that much right. He had walked those boundaries and stretched those interpretations for the sake of his clients on numerous occasions.

"How are the items legitimately shipped? You claim them as art?"

Reese turned to Felicity with cool regard. "I would think you'd have figured that one out by now, Ms. Trent. Seeing as you are far more . . . clever than even I'd assumed."

So, Finn thought, he really hadn't known about Felicity's sideline before this little adventure.

"John—" she began, but he waved her silent.

"I don't ask questions that don't concern me. And what you do in your spare time doesn't concern me. Beyond the next twenty-four hours anyway."

Felicity wisely didn't push further. But they all knew where they stood, which was, individually, on shaky, yet ultimately solid ground.

"The pieces become part of the art," Reese said at length. "They're incorporated."

"Then later . . . unincorporated?" Finn asked.

Reese nodded. "And I'm not sharing for the greater good, but so you know to be on the lookout for something much bigger than a simple necklace."

"What is it being shipped with?"

"My guess is, at this very moment, it's being welded to an iron and plaster sculpture of a somewhat largely proportioned satyr. Only the top half isn't exactly . . . traditional."

"Clearly not if the sapphire won't look somewhat amiss."

"It won't," he said, but didn't elaborate.

Finn didn't press. How many sapphire-wearing satyrs could there be floating around the city, after all?

"Do you know where the work is being done?"

"Several possibilities."

"And the shipping docks. We have several locations. Is there one in particular she typically uses?"

"I don't know. I don't generally have anything to do with that segment of the process. Once it leaves my hands—"

"Your role is over," Finn repeated. "Understood."

The intercom buzzed from the driver. "We've arrived, Mr. Reese."

Reese looked outside, as if just remembering they'd been in a moving car and were not still sitting on the tarmac.

"This isn't the gallery," Felicity commented, peering through the tinted glass.

"Or a loading dock," Finn added.

They were in a warehouse district. It had rained recently. The empty parking lots were dimly lit, with most of the lighted poles not functioning at all, but just well enough to show the pavement was still wet and the blacktop was covered in numerous puddles. A light fog hung in the air, misting the most heavily just beneath the lights.

Reese pressed a button to his right. "Kill the lights."

"Kill. Not a word I'm particularly fond of," Finn said dryly. "Especially in settings such as this."

"Why are we here?" Felicity asked. "Is this where you think the sapphire is being added to the sculpture?"

"These are my warehouses," Reese said.

Finn's eyes widened briefly, and he glanced around through the rear window. "All of them?"

"The ones circling us, yes. I maintain depots in several regional areas on both coasts. This happens to be one of them."

"Makes storage easier, I suppose. How close are we to the shipping docks?"

"A couple of miles."

"Why not take us there?"

"I prefer a bit more privacy."

Felicity was still staring out the window. "Do you really move such a high volume that you require this much space?"

For the first time since climbing into the car, Reese smiled slightly. "I personally handle only a small percentage of my actual trade business."

"Determined by?"

"My choice. Certain clients will deal only with me. And certain transactions are more appealing to me than others."

Finn had a pretty good idea which ones those were. "And Julia? Does she have access to your warehouse locations? Does she share storage?"

Reese sighed. "She's aware of them, but she has her own setup." He didn't go into any further detail.

Felicity glanced outside. "Looks pretty deserted. You're not thinking she'd use your space."

"I wouldn't think. But it's clear I don't know what she's thinking."

She looked back at Reese. "Are you dropping us off, then? We will need transportation."

"I've arranged that. And yes, we will part ways here."

Finn didn't like the sound of that, either.

"Why do you think she will stick to the same plan?" Felicity asked. "Wouldn't she switch things up to keep you from tracking her down?"

Reese looked out the window. "As I said, I honestly don't know what she's thinking."

"What I think is that privacy or not, we don't need to be sitting here like the big elephant in the room," Finn said. "Unless you think maybe she'd use one of your warehouses instead of her own, believing you'd never think to check here."

Reese turned a look on Finn that actually made him shift back slightly. "I might not have been aware of what she was capable of, or understood the lengths she'd be willing to go to, but I assure you, Mr. Dalton, neither is she aware of mine."

Another town car pulled into the lot and rolled into a spot a few feet away.

"How will we get in touch with you," Felicity asked, "when this is done?"

"I'll be in touch." He reached inside his jacket, and Finn tensed, but Reese came out with a business card. "Her business card. The additional addresses of interest are on the back."

Finn took the card and gave it a cursory glance. He'd do more with the information once they were alone and away from Reese. He was going to comment that Reese didn't have their contact information either, but at the moment, his radar was pinging all over the place. He just wanted to get out of the damn car.

The driver opened Finn's door. Finn looked at Reese, who was still staring out his window, his thoughts seemingly a thousand miles away, but said nothing before climbing out. He reached his hand in for Felicity, who slid most of the way out, then looked back at Reese.

"I'm sorry," she said.

Finn couldn't see Reese, but he heard him say, "Take care of this, Ms. Trent, and I'll owe you a favor. Feel free to collect at any time."

"We're all just doing our job," she said quietly, so quietly it barely reached his ears. "I just want to continue to do mine."

Finn ducked down then, in time to see Reese look at her and say, "I'm not in the habit of burning bridges." He looked away again. "Some are simply burned for me."

Felicity squeezed Finn's hand and looked up at him, concern and determination etched on her face. "Let's go."

Chapter 14

Felicity made herself comfortable in the back of the other town car, smoothing her skirt more out of habit than because she cared, at this point, about her appearance. She waited until Finn had settled across from her and the driver had closed the door before she spoke.

"I think we should check her studio out first, before the shipping docks. It would take some time to convert that satyr."

"I think we should follow Reese. This whole thing isn't feeling right to me."

Felicity looked at him. "In what way? Certainly he's being honest about Julia betraying him. You can't fake that kind of pain."

Now it was Finn's turn to look more closely at her. "He seemed more pissed than upset."

"Then you weren't watching closely enough."

"What do you know about the pain of betrayal?"

"If you're asking me if I'm personally identifying with what he's going through, then the answer is no. But, in my work with the Foundation, I've dealt with a lot of people going through a lot of misery. Pain being a fairly universal element of their misfortune, despite there being an assortment of sources. I'd think, given your vocation, both current and former, you'd be similarly aware." She looked at him more closely, then huffed a little. "You did notice, didn't you? You're probing. Me. And we don't have time for that right now."

"You're a tough woman to get to know. I won't apologize for probing."

"We both saw the look on John's face, the stunned tone of his voice. He was thoroughly gobsmacked. So what is it you don't think he's being truthful about?"

"I didn't say he wasn't being truthful. I said this wasn't adding up. A man like Reese—I don't care what his background or usual role is in these kinds of things—isn't a guy who sits around and lets other people fight his battles. If he's been betrayed, by anyone, but most especially by someone he was emotionally vulnerable to, he strikes me as a man who would take it upon himself to seek justice, revenge, vengeance, whatever he felt was necessary. In whatever manner he needed to."

"He is."

"He's farming it out. Doesn't sound like him."

"You don't know that."

"You do. Can you honestly say he strikes you as the kind of man to let other people do his dirty work?"

"This is hardly dirty, it's merely—"

"You know what I mean."

She sighed. She did know. And she happened to agree; she just didn't want to share her viewpoint with him. Felicity was still undecided on just how she planned to see this particular mission through, so the less shared between them, especially as it concerned a potential adversary, the better.

She just wished she felt more at ease with that plan.

"Maybe it's because of the personal nature of the betrayal that he's not willing to get directly involved," she said. "But if you want to follow John, his car is leaving now."

Finn looked out the window, then at their driver, then at Felicity, then back out of the window, and swore.

"What?"

"We're in Reese's car." He nodded to the screen. "Using Reese's driver. Not a good situation."

"It's not so risky as all that." She tapped the button on the intercom to the front of the car and rattled off the address John had given them of Julia's personal studio location. "As swiftly as you can manage," she added, her accent crisp and formal, before looking back at Finn. "Do you think he's somehow monitoring our actions via his driver?"

"I wouldn't be at all surprised. You don't actually think he's flying back out tonight, do you? He might not be willing to involve himself directly, but I'd bet money he'll stay somewhere within reach until his problem is resolved to his satisfaction."

"I have no idea what he's planning to do. As long as he stays out of our way, I don't know that I care. I just want to track Julia down and get our stone."

Finn smiled.

"What?" she asked, nonplussed.

"*Our* stone. I love it when you get all sentimental."

She rolled her eyes, but had to fight the smile that wanted to form. He was the most contrary man. He was so focused on business, sorting things through with such a keen mind, that it became difficult for her to not want to confide in him, strategize with him, and yet, at the same time, he remained constantly and consistently emotionally connected. To her. Quite contrary. Worse, he made her feel contrary as well.

She watched John's car leave the lot going the opposite direction, toward uptown, then lost sight of him all together as they turned a corner and headed farther into the warehouse district. While she wasn't as unconcerned about John as she'd portrayed herself to be, she felt certain her plan of action was the best. But she couldn't quite squelch the small pang of doubt that maybe Finn was right and Reese was the one they should be following, though that might be tough to do in matching black town cars.

"You're worried, too," Finn said.

She looked over to find him watching her and once again realized how unused she was to being so closely observed.

"It's okay, you know," he added, quite sincerely and without a hint of patronization, "you don't have to pretend otherwise. You'd be foolish not to be, and you're anything but foolish."

Oh, you have no idea, she thought. Because she was actually contemplating sticking with Finn after all, at least until they recovered the sapphire, then pleading her case to him—whatever that might be, she hadn't exactly come up with her defense as yet—hoping to play on his fair and honorable nature. If she could find out a little bit about his client and discredit any of his reasoning for the stone belonging in the hands of his client versus her government, more the better.

Which was all very strategic and smart. And not remotely the reason she really wanted to stay with him.

Foolish, indeed.

She refocused her thoughts on business. "What if he still has it?"

"What?"

"I just . . . I was listening to you, you know, and I just thought, following your line of concern, what if John still has the stone?"

"He wouldn't be talking to us. He'd be making a deal. Hell, he'd be trying to sell it to us if he thought he could. It's not like we both don't come with built-in funding."

"If we'd wanted to buy the stone, we'd have been dealing with him from the beginning. He knows we wouldn't play that way. This isn't about bartering, but rightful ownership."

"Exactly. So, if he has the stone, why is he wasting our time in any way, shape, or form if we're not his targeted buyers?"

"To distract and steer us down the wrong path while he sets up his deal? We didn't land too long after he did. Perhaps his deal with Julia didn't pan out and he needed to buy some time to set up another one and didn't want us on his heels. He could be putting us on Julia's track, knowing she's out of the game and it's a dead end lead. Or, for all we know, she's in on the plot and will intentionally lead us on a merry chase."

Finn thought about that for a second. "Possible, I suppose." He glanced from the window directly at her. "But, if that's the case, then what about all that pain he's supposedly in?"

She didn't flinch under his steady regard. "I still maintain something happened with Julia, but . . ." She stopped talking and mentally went back over their conversation with John. He wasn't the most demonstrative man she'd ever come across, but she couldn't shake that look on his face as he'd talked about her. She shook her head. "No. He doesn't have it. She does."

Finn folded his arms.

"I mean it. I was going your way, looking at the possible scenarios, but I know what I saw on his face. She betrayed him. In more ways than one."

"My original point still stands. Why use us? We both know he knows where she is. Or can certainly figure it out a lot better than we can."

"I don't think he's used to being in the position he's in at the moment. I think he's hurt. I think he's angry. Really angry. Maybe in ways he's not used to feeling, much less coping with." She held Finn's gaze, certain now, as she spoke the words, that she'd hit on the truth of it. "I don't think he trusts himself at the moment."

"Trusts himself how? What is he afraid he'd do? Hurt her?"

"I don't think he trusts himself to be around her in any capacity." She looked out the window then, knowing it was a cowardly move, but suddenly unable to hold Finn's gaze any longer. "And no, I don't think hurting her is what he'd be afraid of doing. It would be more the risk of further hurting himself."

From the corner of her eye, she saw Finn open his mouth to speak, but then he stopped and settled back in his seat. And said nothing.

How she wished this wasn't so complicated.

Even more, she wished she knew what he was thinking right that very second.

"Okay. So, we let Reese go," Finn said at length. "Focus on Julia. I don't know what impression she thinks she's left behind in taking the stone for her own purposes, but unless she somehow thinks she'd have Reese's blessing in this, I don't think she'd use her usual facilities. Or his. She has to know he's quite capable of tracking her down."

"I agree, but I'm not sure where else to start. Her business addresses are all we have from John. And we haven't got much more ourselves. You have the list of her best clients. Do you think we should go that route directly? If she's going to dump it, and does it locally, she won't need her shipping facilities or to disguise it on the satyr."

"Reese seemed to think she was going to follow through on their plan with the satyr, which means her target isn't a local client." He turned over the business card. "There isn't anything else here to go on."

"Then let's check the private studio off the list, then scope out the docks while your partner digs up a list of possible other connections she has in the area where she could do the same kind of work. Maybe one of her featured artists' studios. Specifically, the one who created the satyr."

"Makes sense. But first we should—" Finn broke off as the limo slowly bumped over the uneven entrance to the industrial park where Julia's other studio was situated. The car slowed to a stop in the middle of the road leading in. "Well. That doesn't look good," Finn said, staring out the window.

Felicity didn't have to ask him what he was talking about. Even in the middle of the night, she could see the huge plumes of black smoke billowing from somewhere deeper inside the park. "I guess it would be too much to ask for that to be just a coincidence and it's someone else's building going up in flames."

"I'm thinking yes on that."

"Do we go back there? Verify it's her warehouse?"

"No." This time Finn leaned forward and pressed the intercom button. "Nearest car rental agency, please."

"But—"

"But, nothing. I want out of Reese's leased town car, if you don't mind. Given what we know, the list of who would want Julia's building burned down is a very short one."

"If the driver is staying connected to John, then what makes you think he'll just drop us off anywhere we—"

"Why don't we find out." Finn cut off any further response by rapping on the tinted screen between them and the driver, then punched the intercom button. "Change of plans, you can just pull over here."

The driver immediately pulled over.

"Well, that answers one question." He opened the door. "Come on."

"What? What are we doing?"

"You made another good point. Why give Reese any indication of what we're doing, or where we're going?"

"You've already made it known you're renting a car."

"The minute I ditch the limo, he's going to assume that much. He doesn't need to know where we're getting it from, too."

"Well, I'm fairly certain it will be quite the walk if we hoof it from here."

Finn smiled. "Oh, ye of little faith." He slid out, then reached his hand in for her. Once she was safely next to him, he waved the driver on.

The limo pulled quietly away from the curb a moment later.

Felicity hadn't really believed that it wouldn't, but she did sigh a little in relief, nonetheless. "I think you're being overly cautious, which could slow us down."

Finn already had his iPhone in his hand, tapping away at the tiny keyboard. "Someone is torching warehouses. I'll take overly cautious, thanks." He stopped tapping and looked at her. "Rafe is sending us a car."

"It's three in the morning."

"Six A.M. at home. Not that it would matter."

"A taxi service could get us to the closest rental place faster."

"I think, given what's going on a few hundred yards from here, that it's better if we leave as little a paper trail as possible."

She didn't argue. He had a good point. He usually did. She'd like to believe she'd be thinking more clearly if he wasn't around, but the fact was, they did make a good team. They both had sharp minds and strong instincts, but they followed up on them in different ways. He made her think differently, which wasn't such a bad thing. "What do you propose we do while we wait?"

He grinned.

Okay, he also made her think about that. A lot. Which should bother her more than it did. Visions of their plane ride swam through her mind, so she swatted his arm in defense. Of all of it. "Insufferable."

"I didn't say a word."

"You didn't have to." She started walking in the direction of the industrial park. And the fire.

"Now, Jane, honey," he sang out from behind her, "don't go off in a huff."

"Don't honey me. Or Jane me, for that matter," she said. "And I'm not in a huff. I simply think we should use this time wisely."

"And that means go rubbernecking at the scene of the crime? I hate to tell you this, Red, but you stand out. And if you open your mouth, you're downright unforgettable."

She turned and batted her lashes at him. "Why, thank you, kind sir." She faced front and continued walking. All the better to hide her smile. *Unforgettable, hmm?* "I have no intention of letting anyone see me, much less hear me. Given my success rate in my field, I'd think you'd give me at least that much credit."

He easily caught up to her and walked along beside her, his long legs more than matching her marching stride. "Field. Job. You really see your recreational pursuits as an occupation, don't you?"

She really just had to stop talking to him all together. In fact, she was already realizing just how bad an idea her new plan was going to be. If she'd been thinking with her head instead of with every other part of her body, she'd have found some way to get out of his range for a few moments, pull out her own little personal digital assistant, and get her own damn car.

She'd purposely kept her little unit hidden as Finn was far too clever for his own good, and the last thing she needed was for him to get his hands on that little gold mine of information. To anyone else who happened across it, it would appear quite generic. The main screen would lead to nothing but personal numbers of friends and business associates, with a Foundation business e-mail and file folders all tidily lined up.

Only Finn would know to dig deeper. Not only that, but he would know how. Or find someone who did. Likely one of his own partners. She doubted it would take him any time at all to unlock the information and private files she'd encoded on her little unit. Which was why it was staying right where it was, secreted away in an invisible lined pocket of her skirt. It was a miracle he hadn't found it on the plane. Even worse, she hadn't even thought about it at the time, only later, when she'd been crawling around on the floor, half naked.

She'd thought about raising a signal from the plane after they landed, but couldn't be certain he wasn't standing outside the bathroom door the entire time. The only contact she'd been able to make since meeting up with him was a brief message about her new destination when he'd gone off to get his little bag of goodies.

She tried very hard not to think about that damn bag. Which, she belatedly realized, he was still carrying. She was tempted to snatch it from his hands and throw it into the nearest refuse bin. The plane ride had been fun, but fun time was over. Forever.

"That was a particularly plaintive sigh."

She didn't look at him, just kept walking. "If it was plaintive, it's because you can be quite wearisome."

Finn chuckled.

"And I have no idea what you could possibly find amusing about the situation we're presently in, but—"

In the next instant, she found herself spun directly into his arms and being very soundly kissed. By the time she got her senses back, he was already lifting his head.

"What on earth did you do that for?" she demanded, not sounding remotely as put out as she should be.

"Did I ever tell you that you drive me crazy when you get all haughty on me?"

She pushed at him, but his arms didn't budge. "Don't patronize me, it doesn't reflect well."

"I wasn't patronizing you. I was kissing you. And you were kissing me back, if you hadn't noticed."

"Reflex action. You caught me off guard."

He tugged her closer when she wriggled against him. "Felicity."

She purposely didn't look at him. She didn't know what her eyes would give away at that moment, but she didn't dare risk it.

"Felicity," he repeated, quietly, but also quite seriously. There was nothing remotely patronizing or even overly patient in his tone.

She stopped struggling and took a small, steadying breath, then faced him. "What?"

He grinned then. "Reflex action?"

She wanted to smack him. She also wanted to laugh. "You're mad, you know that? And not in a good way." Her lips threatened to curve when his grin didn't abate. She should be quite tiffed at him for toying with her, and yet she couldn't seem to find much mad to grab hold of. Probably because his teasing was always playful, never demeaning. And because he meant it. Every delightful, mischievous moment of it. "Most of the time, anyway," she finished, then punched at his shoulders when his rich laughter made her snicker. "Oh, you are so incorrigible. I don't know why I put up with it."

He finally released her, then hauled her right back in and kissed her again, only this time he lingered before lifting his head. And damn if she didn't let him. She might have even sighed a bit, swayed a bit, as his lips left hers. "Maybe that's why you're so reflexively hooked on me. If I was anything less, you'd dismiss me out of hand."

"I'm dismissing you, anyway."

His grin simply grew. "Okay. In the meantime, can I check your reflexes again?"

"You don't take me seriously at all, do you?"

"Oh, I take you very seriously. I also take you playfully, demandingly, patiently, and decidedly willingly. In fact, I take all of you. All that you'll give me, anyway." Then he did the damndest thing. He kissed her nose. The very tip of it. And then the middle of her forehead. Then the highest curve of her cheek. And then the spot just below her ear. It was completely disarming. He nipped the tip of her chin, then dropped the softest, sweetest, most thorough kiss on her lips she'd ever experienced. She was literally reeling when he finally lifted his head.

The only saving grace at all was that he looked a tad disoriented himself.

"What you do to me, Felicity Jane," he said, his voice a bit more gruff now. "What you do."

She couldn't have formed words even if she'd tried.

"Let's go check out this fire," he said, "from an anonymous viewpoint." Then he took her hand and set off across the lot, toward the buildings a row behind the burning one.

And, still reeling, she let him.

Chapter 15

Her hand felt all too right tucked into his. So Finn focused on the flames ahead and not the ones licking at his heart.

"Won't we be just as obvious ducking down a row of darkened warehouses? And what about the car Rafe is sending?"

"Weren't you the one who thought we should look into this?"

"Yes, but—"

"The car will wait for us."

"If even one official comes in or out of here and sees a town car idling at the curb . . ."

He squeezed her hand and pulled her a little closer so they bumped hips. "Give me and my guys a little more credit than that," he said, parroting her earlier words, but with a hint of a smile. He was a little surprised she hadn't pulled her hand away. He was sure it was only a matter of time. So he held on while he could.

"Point made," she said wryly. "My thinking was to get close enough to overhear what the firemen are saying, but it would depend on the size of the crowd."

"Not sure there's going to be much of one out here, other than the crews working the fire and maybe some media."

"And maybe Julia," Felicity said. "It's her building, after all. Maybe they called her."

"Or maybe she was already here."

He felt her shudder slightly. "I hope—you don't think she was in there, do you? I mean, the stone isn't worth killing for." She looked at Finn. "Your guy . . . he wouldn't—"

"My guy, meaning my partners? Or meaning my client?"

"Client," she said, as if she couldn't believe he'd even question that.

He held her hand a bit more tightly. "No, he wouldn't. His is a convoluted story, but it checks out. He has documentation no one else would be privy to. The sapphire is definitely rightfully his. Not so much the setting it's currently in, that's not the original. But the stone itself, yes."

"Okay," she said easily. "Anyone else we could think of?"

"You mean besides Reese?"

"He wouldn't."

"No, I don't think so, either," he agreed. "Not in this case anyway."

"Finn."

"Anyone is capable of anything, given the right motivation, but hurt or not in this situation, I don't see him reacting to that degree. He might be ruthless, but I think that's just business. And murdering people is bad for business."

She didn't respond, but she didn't pull her hand away either.

"So the fire serves what purpose, then? Killing Julia would be counterproductive to anyone who wants the stone."

"Maybe the intent isn't to kill, but intimidate."

"And risk her or the sapphire in the process?"

Finn shrugged. "Maybe they knew she wasn't on premises. Or maybe it's someone who was tracking her and Reese together and doesn't know she's not working with Reese any longer. They might have sent a warning that no longer mattered, as she's no longer planning on coming out here anyway. If the local agencies haven't gotten a hold of her, she might not even know."

"All possible, even probable," Felicity said. "So, if it's not John, then who set the blaze? Not her client, I wouldn't think."

"Do you think Reese knew there was another player on the

field and didn't tell us? Never mind, don't answer that. Of course it's a possibility."

"Maybe it's his back-up client," Felicity mused. "If they'd made a deal and she double-crossed him, that would force Reese to renege on that deal. Maybe someone isn't all that happy about losing out on the opportunity and decided on a little payback."

"Seems like if there was a chance of the buyer being that upset, Reese would have gone after the stone himself to honor the deal. Which makes me think they didn't have the back-up plan entirely set up yet."

"So, following that line, and the fact that John assumes she's going ahead with altering the satyr as planned, then she's setting it up anyway, just on her own. Which puts us back to square one, with no one else on the playing field with a grudge to bear. Except John. And, I agree with you, hurt or not, I don't see him doing something like this. I doubt he'd send us out after her, knowing what we'd stumble across."

"Then we're back to intimidation," Finn said. "If the back-up knows he's dealing only with Julia now, maybe he's angling for a better deal."

"Because she's a woman and whoever it is would conclude she doesn't know what she's doing?"

Finn smiled. "I'd never say that."

"You didn't have to. And . . . point taken. Given the way men think, it is possible." She huffed a little, mostly for show.

"We are an incorrigible lot," Finn replied.

"Your accent is atrocious."

Finn just kept smiling. "This is nice."

"The bickering, you mean?"

He tugged her closer, then lifted her hand and kissed the back of it. "The partnering."

She didn't say anything, but she didn't exactly move out of his personal space. He considered that a step forward.

They slowed as they reached the scene of the fire. The crews had cordoned or taped off the surrounding area, and other than crossing the line, which would be quite conspicuous, there was no way to get close without going around the front of the buildings where everyone was assembled. There was still a fire going, but from what little he could see, and gauging on the level of activity, it was mostly out.

"Looks like it was mostly contained in the center of this row."

Finn started edging them toward the front of the building, keeping them in the shadows of the warehouse that ran perpendicular to the area where the fire was. They passed a sign posted on a grassy median at the entrance to that section of warehouses. Finn got closer so they could read it.

Felicity pointed. "Julia's number, right there."

They both turned and looked down the long row. It didn't take a lot of calculating to deduce which one was on fire.

"I don't think we're going to be able to get much closer without standing out," Finn said. "There isn't a lot going on other than the firefighters. No media trucks."

"I guess it's only a big deal to us."

"And Julia."

"And whoever set the fire." She looked to Finn. "Should we try and contact John?"

Finn shook his head. "We do this our way. I appreciate the lead, but we're not doing this for him."

"Agreed. But perhaps his reaction would be telling."

Finn thought about that for a moment, then shook his head. "I say we play this our way and keep this to ourselves. Without a face-to-face, it would be next to impossible to gauge if he's hiding anything, and I don't want to inadvertently give anything away if he is, in fact, involved in this somehow. If he wants to follow up on his own, he's more than capable of it."

She didn't argue that. "So, what next, then?"

"We go find our car, and I'll put Rafe on seeing what report he can get on this fire. See if arson is suspected or confirmed."

"And that no one died."

"No medical personnel here, other than the fire trucks, and the EMT they bring with them. We didn't hear any sirens earlier. More importantly, no coroner's van, either."

"An ambulance could already have taken off before we got here."

"Rafe'll find out one way or the other, but I'm betting if there was a fatality here, or even serious injury, some news outlet would be on the scene."

"True." She skipped a little to keep up with him as he increased his pace. "So, we're off to where now?"

"We're off to find out if the rest of Rome is burning."

"Shipping docks or gallery first?"

He paused for a second and pulled out his iPhone. "You know, to save time, Rafe could probably find out . . ." He trailed off and tapped in a message to Rafe to find out if there were any emergency calls to Julia's other addresses. "I'm having him check her home address as well."

"We're going to check on her clients, then? See if we can figure out who the buyer is?"

"It's the only thing we have to go on at the moment, until we hear something back from Rafe on the fire, and whatever else he can dig up."

They reached the entrance to the industrial park, and Finn tugged her hand and kept going across the street, into another industrial park. Behind the first row of warehouses there was a row of dumpsters. Idling quietly behind them was their town car.

Once settled inside, Felicity said, "Who is on the list?"

Finn punched the file up, skimmed it again . . . then held it out for Felicity to take. She lifted a brow in surprise, but he continued holding the unit out to her until she took it. If he was going to talk the talk about her trusting him and letting guards down, then he had to walk the walk himself.

"Any of those names ring a bell or mean anything to you?"

Felicity was quiet as she carefully reviewed the list. "Nothing that stands out to me." She looked up. "They're sorted by proximity and the amount of business they've conducted. Which takes precedence?"

"Considering the scene we just left, I'm giving edge to proximity. Everyone on that list has the funds to make the purchase."

"Maybe we should cross reference and go to the one who hits first on both lists?"

Finn nodded. Just then his unit beeped. "Incoming file, should be from Rafe."

She immediately went to hand it back to him, but he just said, "Click on the icon next to the message."

She held his gaze for an extra beat, then did as he said. Her eyes widened a bit as she read.

"And?"

She glanced at him, then patted the seat next to her and went back to reading. "It'll be faster if we both go over it together."

Finn slid over to the opposite seat, thinking a lot of things went better when they did them together. She leaned into him and held the unit between them.

"It was Julia's warehouse. Says here that early reports suspect arson. Too early to know anything else like why or how. They're checking her insurance to see what she might have to gain from it burning down."

"No other reported guesses on who else might have had an axe to grind," Finn said as he continued to read.

"But take a look at this," she said, and tapped the screen. "There was a break-in at the shipping dock location. Nothing reported stolen or damaged. Just a routine check after an alarm going off. But when you add in the fire . . ."

"Which they'll put together shortly, which means we have to find her before they do."

"No statement by her or anything mentioning her name in the official reports so far. And nothing going on at the gallery or her home address," Felicity noted. She looked up at Finn.

"How does your guy get all this information? I mean, the fire isn't even out yet."

"I'm fairly convinced Rafe could hack into NASA and chat with the astronauts if he were so inclined."

"Do you have a bit of a boundary issue with him, then?"

"No. He keeps it legal. He's just . . . creative."

"I see."

Finn wished he saw. *She* was asking about boundary issues? "What is it like?" he blurted out.

She shifted to look at him directly. "What is what like?"

"Working alone. I mean, Mac, Rafe, and I go our separate ways with cases far more often than we work together on one, but we give each other input all the time, utilize each other's strengths, maximize skill sets. I don't know what I'd do without them, but I'd certainly be less productive and a lot less successful. I'd be far more limited in the types of challenges I could take on."

"I imagine so," she said, a bit warily. "And yet you were . . . operating solo in these kinds of endeavors before you set up shop with them. Bogota and Prague both were before then."

"I know. That's what drove me to create Trinity. I was in the midst of dismantling my father's estate, on extended leave from the district attorney's office, when I heard about the situation with Angelo and his wife's family's ancestral jewelry."

"Bogota."

"Yes. I thought I could help. I tried regular channels, but even with my background both legally and personally, I couldn't get anything set in motion."

"So you took matters into your own hands. Literally."

"I did," he said, but he was thinking, *I took you into my own hands, then, too.* "And nothing was the same after that."

"But you didn't get the diamonds back."

"Exactly."

Her expression shuttered a bit, but he pressed on.

"I knew, even then, that I could have helped. I just needed broader resources. I wasn't as prepared as I should have been." *Though nothing could have prepared me for you.*

"What about Prague? You succeeded there, working solo."

"I had already started networking on cases with Mac and Rafe by then, but strictly friend-helping-friend. Mac had already left the NYPD and was working private security for a very high tech firm. He's very . . . technologically and mechanically inclined, but he wasn't really happy with how he was applying those skills. Neither was Rafe. So, we got to talking, and that led to us teaming up, and Trinity was born."

"You obviously enjoy what you do, sounds like all three of you have found a calling." She smiled. "I think that's great."

Finn kept his gaze on her, and when she looked back to the PDA, he pushed. "What about you? What got you into doing . . . what you do? When you go . . . hunting, do you have anyone you can go to for help?"

There was a momentary flicker in her expression at his description of her activities, but he couldn't decipher what it meant. Her expression was unreadable now, her gaze steady, but definitely wary.

"I rely on my own wits," she responded.

"How do you decide which artifact to go after? What's your source?"

Her expression shuttered completely then, which only made him want to press harder.

"We're wasting valuable time," she said.

"Felicity—"

"Finn," she parroted back. "We need to focus on finding Miss Forsythe before the local agencies, or, worse, before the arsonist and/or burglar finds her first."

Finn held her gaze another long moment. "I'm not going to stop pushing. You know that."

Her shoulders drooped ever so slightly. And he thought he heard the softest of sighs. "I know."

He pressed a finger under her chin and turned her face gently to his. He smiled, but he knew his gaze was serious. "You've said it yourself. I'm incorrigible. Why don't you just tell me? If you're worried you'd be dragging me into something, I'd say I'm already dragged. I can take care of me." He drew his fingertips up to her cheekbone, then tucked a loose curl behind her ear. "And if you need help taking care of you, I can do that, too." He cupped her cheek, lowered his mouth to hers. "But I can't do anything unless you let me in." He brushed a soft kiss across her lips. "Let me in, Felicity."

She sighed into him, accepted his kiss, then returned an impossibly sweet one of her own. His heart dipped, then squeezed tightly.

"You're further in than you know," she said, briefly cupping his face with her hand. "As in as I can let you." She stroked her thumb over his cheekbone and looked into his eyes. "All I can do is ask that you trust me to know what I'm doing. And trust your own instincts. They're not letting you down, Finn." And then she dropped her hand and ducked her head, removing herself from his touch, if not his personal space. "Now, please, we need to figure out her trail before something else happens."

Finn stared at her bent head for a long, silent moment. She didn't give much, but she asked for even less. So when she did, he listened. She'd asked for his trust. Or, more to the point, his faith.

Now he had even more questions. And fewer answers. It was driving him insane. She was driving him insane.

"Why couldn't I do something easy?" he muttered. "Like falling for a mob heiress."

She reflexively glanced up at him, then immediately looked back at the PDA screen. Given that he knew she had no mob connections, he could only assume it had been the other part. The part about falling.

"I know that unnerves you, but it's there anyway. You'll have to find a way to deal with it, Felicity Jane," he said, wanting to shake her. Wanting to take her. Wanting . . . everything. "You're going to have to find a way to deal with me."

"I'm working on it."

Chapter 16

"I don't know about this," Felicity said as their town car eased down a winding street lined with high stone walls and gated entrances. It was past dawn now, and the sun was rising toward the tops of the trees, burning off the fog that had cast everything beyond the curbs in a gray shroud of mist.

"What's not to know? This has to be it. Besides, none of the other clients panned out. Julia's nowhere to be found. This is the last solid lead we have. Hell, it's the only real lead we've had from the beginning. I just wish Rafe had found it sooner."

"The Russian was never a client of Julia's, so it wouldn't have come up. I'm more surprised he found it at all."

"I know, but we've wasted so much time. I never even thought to check that connection." Finn sipped his coffee and forced another bite of their makeshift breakfast. "This is the driest damn bagel I've ever tasted." He pushed the bag toward Felicity. "Have one, anyway. You need to eat something."

She would have argued, except he was right. She was jittery from lack of sleep, too much stress, and having little to nothing in her stomach. He'd insisted they stop at a small coffee shop, where he'd surprised her by coming out with coffee for him and their driver, but hot tea for her. She nibbled at a sesame seed bagel. "You're right. These are awful."

"I would have had them toast a few, but then I got that

damn message from Rafe. We need to get to Chesnokov's place before he goes anywhere this morning."

Felicity shook her head. "I still can't believe he has an address here in the States."

"Not just in the States, but right here in San Francisco. Too big a coincidence for me."

She nodded. "I wonder why he used a Russian mule and set up the meet in New York?" The fact that Finn had been certain from the start that something was off with John's offer was starting to look quite probable. She should have listened to him.

"Who the hell knows? He uses Andreev often enough that we connected the two when we knew he was handling the transfer. Maybe, in this kind of deal, Chesnokov would only use someone that he trusted."

Felicity dumped the bagel back in the bag, suddenly not hungry. "A deal that failed because of my interference. You'll have to pardon my lack of optimism that chatting him up is going to go well for us."

"I'm not planning on chatting him up. I'm planning on following him."

"If he used an agent before, what makes you think he wouldn't again?"

"Because, if we're right and he was Reese's target out here, then this is Chesnokov's second shot at it," Finn said. "He won't take chances."

"And now Julia has gone solo with the stone. Given that Andreev bailed out when he saw we knew about the deal, why do you think Chesnokov would deal with Julia, when he was supposed to deal with Reese?"

"I guess it all depends on how badly he wants the stone. But he's the only one out here with a direct connection that we know about, so I say we go for it."

"Do you think she'll follow through with a deal with the Russian if he was Reese's target, rather than get a new one of her own? Or maybe she had someone lined up all along."

"Considering we've been through the list of clients she might have gone to and come up empty-handed, I'd say she's planning on going directly to Chesnokov. But who knows? If it's someone else, then we're screwed unless we get another lead."

"Wouldn't she be afraid of Reese coming after her if she tries to communicate with Chesnokov?"

"You could argue either side. That, if this was Reese's plan, she wouldn't go to Chesnokov because he'd know right where to ambush her. Or that she would, assuming Reese would never think she'd be so bold and would dismiss Chesnokov as her buyer. Or you could argue that Reese had a different plan entirely, and Julia went solo to sell to Chesnokov herself."

"Meaning that Reese doesn't know the Russian is here, but Julia does? How? He wasn't on her client list, so—"

"Maybe he used an agent to purchase art from her. Hard to say how she might know about him, but I do think it's safe to assume she knew he was Reese's buyer in New York and she knows the deal went south. Maybe she lured Reese out here on the pretext of selling it to one of her clients, knowing as soon as she got the stone out here, she could hijack it and sell it to the Russian herself."

"Why not propose that deal to John?"

"Greed? Could be many reasons."

Felicity pondered his train of thought. "Well, it would explain why we can't find any evidence of the satyr, the sapphire, or her shipping anything out, or even any activity from her gallery in that direction at all the past forty-eight hours. If she knows her buyer is here, then it's all quite convenient."

Finn nodded along with her reasoning. "The more I think about it, the more I wonder if Reese didn't have another buyer in mind. After all, he was sure she was shipping it, hence the need for the satyr. If he had any idea about a plan with Chesnokov as buyer, he'd know they'd be making the deal direct. No shipping or satyr required."

"True, although given the initial meet was set in New York

with a Russian agent, maybe Chesnokov wanted it off American soil, so they had to agree to ship it out of here for him." She shook her head. "Too many possibilities, not enough information."

"All of which revolve around Chesnokov. I think he's still our best bet."

"I wish we could talk to John, see what he'd make of this connection, get more information on what his initial plan was."

"Until we know more about what's going on, I don't think that's a wise idea."

"I suppose you're right, but he's the one with the answers right now."

"I don't trust him. And I don't trust him bringing us into this the way he did. If nothing pops with Chesnokov, then we'll consider going that route. Last resort."

She nodded, reluctantly agreeing. "The greed angle, that I'm just not sure about. Without knowing her, or having more information on them as a couple, it's hard to say, but given how blindsided John was, I don't know why she would double-cross him so suddenly and badly. How much could she stand to make on this one transaction, versus a lifetime of future work with him? She had a decent working relationship with Reese and, from what it looks like, a serious personal relationship—"

"One that Rafe couldn't find a single trace of," Finn pointed out. "So clearly they kept their liaison very private. It's also possible that she did propose it and Reese turned the idea down. There was a reason, after all, that the meet was in New York and not here. Maybe he knew the Russian wouldn't go for it."

Felicity went with the idea. "So, you're saying she was frustrated by that and decided to strike out on her own?"

"Yes. It's even possible that she took the stone with plans to sell it direct to Chesnokov as a way to prove herself to Reese. Maybe she wasn't betraying him at all. In her mind, anyway."

Felicity frowned. "She had to know he wouldn't take well to finding her and the stone gone with no word as to what she'd planned."

Finn looked at Felicity. "Maybe she wanted him to trust her."

She held his gaze for a long moment. Too long. Then finally looked away as she sipped her tea and wished she could untie the knot in her stomach. "So, we follow him . . . then what? If it is Chesnokov, how do we know the deal hasn't already happened while we were chasing after Julia's wealthiest client base?"

"From what we dug up on Chesnokov, the one thing that came through consistently was that he's known for his exceedingly high standards when it comes to taste, refinement, and style. I doubt, despite his desire for the sapphire, that he's the sort who'd agree to some clandestine, middle of the night rendezvous. He would consider that gauche. If Julia contacted him, I'm thinking he'd push for an early morning meeting, probably over breakfast. Far more civilized, and it would keep Julia dangling a bit while he checked out her story."

"She's got the stone, so she has the leverage."

"She has Reese potentially on her tail as well, though, so she needs to make a clean sale to someone who won't be bullied by him or anyone else, if Reese figured out who she sold it to and decided to make things difficult."

Felicity tried to keep her optimism afloat, but battle fatigue was starting to set in. She tore off a chunk of bagel. "I just wish we'd been able to track down Julia. Any trace of her."

"Certainly would have made things easier, yes. But she's either smarter than we credited her for, for a novice, or—"

"Or she's using Reese's connection to Chesnokov to make the sale." She chewed, swallowed, and thought. "You're right, it does make the most sense."

Finn polished off his bagel, but paused before taking a sip of his coffee.

"What?" Felicity asked, noting the sudden unfocused expression. She was learning him, bit by bit, and she'd already come to know that expression meant he'd just made a mental connection of fact to fact, or had some other revelation.

Finn's gaze focused outward as he turned to look at her. "There is a third possibility why we can't find any trace of her. One we really haven't discussed."

Felicity didn't have to work too hard, given the somber tone, to make the mental leap with him. "I know things don't look so good here, but let's not assume the worst just yet."

"Not assuming, but at least acknowledging."

She took another bite and nodded as she swallowed. "If something untoward has happened to our Ms. Forsythe, then we're all screwed, so to speak. So we might as well think positively until we're given good reason not to any longer."

"Agreed, but we need to think that possibility through, if for no other reason than to come up with a list of who, so we'd know what track to jump on."

"If someone got to her already, I doubt we'll ever get our hands on that sapphire. Not this go-around anyway."

Finn grinned. "Spoilsport."

She wrinkled her nose at him. "Realist. It's taken over four decades for this stone to surface. I imagine it will be easily that long, if not longer, before it shows its lovely facets again. Likely not in our lifetime, anyway. Or your client's."

"Which is why we're sitting at the corner of Chesnokov's street and hoping we're wrong about Julia's potential fate. But, playing devil's advocate here, if someone got to her, it's a pretty short list on who. The same list we came up with for the warehouse fire and shipping dock break-in."

"You could add the Russian now."

"True. So that makes two people."

Felicity's eyes widened as another thought came to her. "You know, that list could get expanded by two more names. Ours."

"We've got an alibi."

"Right. The same one who would put our names on the list in the first place. John Reese."

"I meant his driver." He lifted a hand. "I know who pays his salary, but if push came to under oath, it might be a different story. And it's not like we're not capable of making it worth his while."

"Bribe him, you mean?"

Finn grinned again. "There goes that tone of yours again. Maybe we should have skipped breakfast and—"

"Focus."

"I am focused." He kept his gaze on hers, totally unrepentant.

She just sighed. Mostly self-directed, because, truth to tell, her thoughts had gone in much the same direction. But he didn't have to know that.

"And we wouldn't be bribing the guy to lie. We'd be encouraging him to tell the truth."

"Still, it's not something I'd want to bank my freedom on."

"Which brings us back to Chesnokov."

She tapped her chin and gave voice to her other fear. One she hated to even admit she was thinking, but Finn made too much sense where this entire scheme was concerned. "What if this whole thing is a setup by John to target us?"

"Meaning?"

"Meaning if he set the fire and did something nefarious to Julia, then we'd be set up as being the ones that went after her. Complete with showing up at the scene of both crimes, albeit after the fact, but don't they say that the perps usually like to show up at the scene and bask in the glory of their dirty deeds?"

"You read too many crime novels in your garden," Finn said, grinning, but he didn't sound truly cavalier about her supposition.

"What if I'm right?" she asked quietly.

"Then nothing we do now is going to change anything."

"We could go after John."

"If he is capable of what you're suggesting, then it's not our job to go after him. We have to go after the sapphire."

"If he is capable of what I'm suggesting, then he has the sapphire."

Finn lowered his coffee cup to his knee and gave her a steady look. "If you were working this alone, what would your next step be?"

Startled by the question, she took a moment to answer. "Knowing what we know? About Julia's place burning and Chesnokov being in town?" She paused, then sighed. "I don't know. I'd probably be sitting right where we are. Albeit perhaps a bit more inconspicuously."

Just then not one, or even two, but three town cars eased down the road from opposite directions. Finn chuckled. "Oh, I think we blend right in to this particular community."

Her lips quirked. "You might have a point." Her gaze sharpened as the gates at the end of the street ahead of them slowly swung open. "Action time."

Finn glanced at his watch. "Pretty early for a breakfast meeting. It's not even eight." He pressed the intercom switch. "Follow whatever comes out of the drive, end of street, on the left. A discreet distance, please." He clicked off, then fidgeted a bit in his seat, looking out the side window, watching, waiting.

"It's making you crazy, isn't it?"

"What is?" he asked, never taking his eyes off the gleaming Rolls Royce Silver Cloud that slowly rolled through the gates, then mercifully turned away from them and off down the street.

A second or two later, their town car eased through the intersection and quietly rolled down the same street, about two blocks behind the Rolls.

"Not being in control," she said.

"Who said I feel out of control?" He spared her a quick glance and a fast smile. "I can play well with others."

"I wasn't referring to our partnership. You want to be the one driving the car."

"Actually, I was thinking my helicopter would have come in damn handy. We should have rented one of those instead."

"And so inconspicuous, too."

"But think about how much time we'd have saved all night and morning long, checking on Julia's client list."

"The firefighters at the warehouse might have paid us a bit more attention, however."

All of a sudden Finn rapped on the security glass between them and the driver. "Left! Not straig—shit. He missed the damn turn!"

The speaker crackled. "There's a shortcut, sir. A block ahead, that cuts over. The Rolls is on a one-way. We'll come in a bit closer this way. Once we get uptown, we'll have to stay tight if we don't want to get left at the lights."

It was a good move. In case the Rolls had noticed them following, turning off would throw that. They could reenter the scene from a new angle, and hope Chesnokov would think it was a different car. "Stay with that plan," he said, then clicked off.

"Your partner seems to have chosen well with the driver."

"Yeah, well, Rafe has possibly accused me of having control issues as well."

"Ah," Felicity said, her lips curving as she looked out the window to track their progress herself. "How surprising." With her back to the driver, she was having to crane her neck to see what was in front of them. Then Finn took her elbow and tugged her toward him.

"Sit over here. Better view. And you also won't be blocking mine."

"Such a gentleman," she said dryly, then made a little squealing sound when he tugged her into his lap instead of the seat next to him.

His arms snaked around her waist to keep her on his lap.

"Now we both have the same view." He kissed the side of her neck. "Just being a gentleman and all."

She started to smack at his hands, but then his lips trailed around to the sensitive skin at her nape, which had her catching her breath, and maybe pressing her hips down just a little as she wiggled back against him.

"You know," Finn murmured just beneath her ear, "we could say the hell with Reese, Chesnokov, and the damn sapphire, and book ourselves into the Four Seasons for a few days." He nipped at her earlobe. "Weeks." He tightened his arms around her waist and snuggled her more tightly against the growing bulge in his trousers. "Maybe a month would do it. Maybe."

"Maybe," she repeated a bit breathlessly as his palms flattened on her stomach and started to slide upward. She was trying like hell to keep her gaze focused, if somewhat unsteadily, on the Silver Cloud, now three cars ahead of them. But Finn wasn't making it easy.

Nor was she scrambling to get off his lap.

He cupped her breasts, gently catching her nipples between his fingers as he squeezed. A moan slipped out as she arched into his hands, and any thought of the Rolls Royce and her all important mission dimmed substantially.

"Finn—"

"Shh, the driver's on it."

No, she thought, *Finn's on it*. And she wanted more of him on her. He nibbled at her nape, making her shudder, then slid one hand down between her legs, undoing a button or two to allow him to slide his fingers along the inside of her thigh.

"We—should—"

"Do more of this," Finn murmured roughly. "Come for me, Felicity." He stroked the silk panel between her legs as he continued to toy with her nipples and nibble her neck. She was going to stop him and focus on the job, really she was. But she was tired, and hungry, and needy as all hell, and this felt way too damn good to stop. So she let her eyes drift shut, let the sensations take over, let Finn take over, and promised herself that she'd regain control the moment it was over. Promised herself that she'd come to terms with Finn and his effect on her.

Just as soon as he made her climax. Again.

She was still shuddering, still jerking against his hand and the oh-so-clever fingers he'd slid inside her, when he was already slipping them out and shifting her around so she faced him, taking her mouth with his, even as he slid his hand between them to unbuckle and unzip. "Let me in," he breathed against her lips.

And she could have told herself that it was only fair to let him have his, since he'd so thoroughly seen to hers, but the raw truth of it was she was craving the feel of him, filling her up, as she'd never craved anything before. She would have pushed his hands away and torn at his pants herself if she'd thought it would get him inside her any faster.

She was hiking up her skirt and he was tugging at his pants, and they'd barely freed what had to be bared when he was jerking her down on top of him. She pushed down as hard as she could, grinding on him, glorying in the long groan of satisfaction she wrenched from him as she clenched her still twitching muscles tightly around him and rode him until every last spark of need was sated to its fullest extent.

His hands were on her hips, his mouth on hers, his tongue deep inside, just as he was, thrusting, just as he was, and she took both as fast and deep as she could. She felt him gather beneath her as his own climax built. She bit his bottom lip, making him growl and buck higher, which made her cry out as he reached a place even deeper inside her. She tightened her fingers in his thick hair and held on as his fingers sank into the soft flesh of her bum, likely marking her there as he tugged her harder, faster, against his now bucking hips.

He reached some spot that sent sparks shooting all over again, and she arched back, trying to keep him right there, on that spot. And her arching took him over the edge, groaning,

growling, as he pistoned inside her while coming in a shuddering fury.

She clung to him when it was over, and he clung just as
tightly to her, clutching her to him, even as she struggled to
stay upright in his lap, her fingers still in his hair, her face
buried in the crook of his neck.

Their breaths came in heavy pants, and she slowly became
aware that she was damp and sweaty. The air inside the limo
had grown humid with their body heat, the windows fogged
beyond visibility.

She half expected a chuckle from Finn, something to put the
ferocity of what they'd just done in some kind of proper perspective. It was always like this. So, it shouldn't have been
shocking or felt like anything other than what it was. If anything, she should be bashing herself for letting him sidetrack
her to such a wanton degree when they were right in the midst
of tracking down their quarry. Of course, the danger and sus-
pense certainly heightened their sensations, so there was that
element, as well, feeding into all this.

None of which explained the burning sensation that gathered behind her tightly squeezed eyelids. Nor her reluctance to
let him go, to look him in the eye and once again force herself
to put this—whatever the bloody hell it was with him—back
into some kind of contained, heart-proof box.

But he wasn't laughing. He was still holding on to her, his
face buried in her hair, as if he wasn't ready to let go, either.
He's still recovering, that's all.

Not that it mattered.

She willed herself to move, to gather herself, put her head
back in the appropriate place—on the job and not leaning on
his shoulder. But at the first hint of movement on her part, his
arm tightened around her, his fingertips dug more deeply into
her hair. So she did what felt natural and right. She pressed her
lips against the damp, heated skin of his neck, the kiss far
sweeter and gentler than she typically shared with him. And
when she felt him kiss her hair, she kissed him again, drawing

her mouth closer to the hard edge of his jaw, before nuzzling against his cheek, until he turned his face and met her lips with his own.

They kissed, softly, silently, reverently. Every moment of which quenched her thirst for him in a way that the most fierce, rocking orgasms could never hope to match.

"The Rolls is entering the parking garage for a Talbot, James & Warrick. Follow?"

Felicity had startled at the sound of the driver's voice coming through the speaker next to her head.

"Yes," Finn said, his voice raspy and sounding gruff. "Thank you."

She did move then, but he captured her face between his palms before she could slide completely off his lap. His expression was as serious as she'd ever seen it, his gaze locked on to hers so intently it was as physical a connection as the kisses they'd just shared. There was a stunned silence between them, the power and essence of which she saw reflected in his gaze as well.

It was both a relief, to know she wasn't alone in reeling from the magnitude of what she'd felt had happened just now, even if she couldn't define it, and a threat to what little sense of self she still maintained. She had no idea what would happen now, what meaning he might draw from this, or what actions it might motivate him to take. The breadth and depth of which both alarmed and thrilled her.

He said nothing, just held her gaze for the longest moment. Then he took her hand and pulled it up to his mouth. He nipped each fingertip, then kissed them each, too, all the while holding her gaze. Then he closed his eyes and kissed the center of her palm before curling her fingers—still damp from his mouth—over it.

He wrapped his hand around hers as he looked up into her eyes, his own an almost impossible cerulean blue now through the thick fringe of his dark blond lashes. "I trust you. I trust us. That's a promise. Don't lose it. Keep it safe."

She was torn by the almost overwhelming instinct she felt to pull his hand up and give him the same gift, demand the same vow, startled by how strong the urge was to bind herself to him in such a significant way. Ultimately . . . she couldn't. There was so much between them, but even more still left unsaid. And if she couldn't tell him the rest, then she had no business making promises. Of any kind.

And yet she curled her fingers tightly into her palm, knowing he felt her do it. It was as much of a vow as she could make. That she did, indeed, want what he wanted. She just had no idea how to go about getting it.

Not without putting at risk the trust that had already been bestowed on her, and the vows she'd made to others first.

Chapter 17

"**P**ull over to the side and watch where the Rolls parks, or if they do a dropoff," Finn instructed the driver, then released the intercom button so they could both quickly put themselves back together. He watched the Silver Cloud pull over in the drop-off zone by the bank of elevators, then tapped on his PDA, doing a quick search for Talbot, James & Warrick. His eyes widened when their home page popped up. "Well. That's . . . interesting," he said, skimming the home page of their Web site, trying to absorb this latest curveball.

"Interesting, how?" Felicity asked, frowning as she tidied up her hair a bit. At a glance it was hard to believe she was in the second day of wearing the same clothes, with little time for personal maintenance. A closer inspection would reveal the crumpled fabric in the skirt of her dress and the tiny lines of fatigue feathering the corners of her eyes and tugging at the corners of her mouth. All he could see was how well kissed her lips looked and the rosy glow flushing her cheeks.

He returned to the screen before he gave in to the urge to pull her back across the space between them and demand the driver take them to the nearest hotel. First for a long, hot shower, followed by as many courses of room service as they could stuff themselves with . . . and then whatever extended period of time it would take for him to convince her to open up the rest of the way and tell him whatever it was she was still hiding from him.

"Looks like Talbot, James & Warrick is a private company that specializes in, well . . . matchmaking. For lack of a better word."

Felicity had been peering out the window, looking in the direction of the Rolls Royce, too, but jerked her gaze to Finn's. "They what?" She looked back to the gleaming silver car, and they both watched as an older gentleman, bald head, somewhat portly in stature and stooped in posture, was helped out of the backseat by his driver. "Chesnokov," she murmured. "But . . . what is he doing at a matchmaking service?" She looked to Finn. "And what, exactly, do you mean by 'matchmaking'? As in, 'hired help' kind of matchmaking?"

"No," Finn said, scrolling down through the information on his screen. "It's not a call service. I meant exactly what I said."

"And they operate out of this entire building? From the name, they sounded more like an investment firm or something."

"Appears to be a pretty upscale operation, so I imagine that is exactly the tone they wish to set. They operate internationally. Their specialty looks to be arranging matches between U.S. citizens—mostly men, from what I gather, based on the focus of the pictures on the home page—"

"And foreign women," Felicity finished, sounding slightly disgusted.

Finn flashed a smile. "Says the foreigner here."

She glanced at him. "It's not that, it's just . . . I mean, it goes on in Britain as well, but it all seems so rather . . . overly specific, don't you think?"

"As long as both sides are consenting, and it's legal, I guess it doesn't really matter what I think."

"Oh, I'm sure it's lovely for those who get what they want, but . . ." She rubbed her arms. "There just seems to be something rather . . . off-putting about specifically looking for some-

one who is of a culture other than your own as your main criteria for selection, rather than simply finding a mate who fits you,
regardless. And the idea that that single criteria is so important
to enough men to warrant an entire industry devoted to it just
seems . . . depressing somehow." She looked back out the window. "Rather like adopting a spouse for the sake of having one,
rather than finding your true love."

"To each his own, I suppose." Finn watched her watching
Chesnokov and thought about what she'd said. *Finding your
true love.* "But, speaking for myself, I couldn't imagine settling
for anything less."

She glanced at him and got caught up in his gaze for a moment, as they often did, before quickly shifting her gaze back
to the window. He smiled and reluctantly returned his attention to the window as well. He wanted to retrieve the sapphire
because it was the right thing to do for his client, but mostly he
just wanted this damn case over so he could get on with convincing Felicity that there was more to life than running a
Foundation and occasionally stealing priceless antiquities.
Namely, him. Of course, once the case was over, so might his
chance be to see her, much less speak to her, ever again.

That was what was depressing.

They watched as Chesnokov moved slowly toward the elevator, relying heavily on his cane.

"So, do you think Chesnokov is a client? Or—" Felicity
looked to Finn. "Tell me, do they work with a large percentage
of Russian imports? Maybe he's helping them 'procure' their
matches."

"There seems to be a focus on Asian and Far Eastern cul-
tures, but Europe and Russia are featured, too. Without some
digging, I can't say about a possible business connection here,
personal or professional. What I can say is that this feels like a
dead end. Whatever his involvement is with Talbot and crew, I
don't see this having anything to do with the sapphire."

Felicity sighed. "Me, either. If he just made that deal, or was
planning to do so today, I don't see how a visit here connects

to that in any way." She slumped lightly back in her seat and folded her arms across her stomach. "So . . . now what? Should we stay here until he leaves, continue to follow him, see if we can connect him to Julia or the stone?"

"I'm not giving up on him entirely. He's still our best bet at the moment. But I think we could use a brief time-out here." He pressed the intercom button. "We're going to grab a cab, but I'd like you to sit here and wait for that same gentleman to leave. When he does, contact me, and follow him. We'll meet up at his next stop. I'll make sure you're compensated for your trouble."

"Not a problem, sir. Your partner, Mr. Santiago, made me aware I might need to be . . . flexible when he hired me."

"Excellent." Finn rattled off his cell phone number, then popped open the door to the town car and slid out. He reached in for Felicity. "We can grab a cab out front. Find a nice hotel. Recharge a little."

She lifted one eyebrow, but said nothing as she took his hand, making Finn smile.

"Not that kind of recharge. It might take me a while to . . . recharge enough for that."

The corner of her mouth curved. "I've never noticed a particular problem with that before."

It's never been . . . whatever this is now, either, he wanted to say. But when she looked down and smoothed at the folds of her skirt, as if suddenly thinking about that as well, he opted to leave it alone.

"A hot shower, a hot meal—"

"Yes," she said instantly, her green eyes sparking to life.

"Done." He took her hand, and they ducked out of the parking garage and went around to the front of the building, grabbing the next cab making a dropoff. "This will give me a chance to check in with Rafe directly, and from there, we'll figure out what our next move will be. He should have something more on the police and fire marshal reports from the fire, as well. We can do some further checking on the Talbot thing, too, just for information's sake. I'm not holding out much hope on that angle, but you never know what may pop up." He got them both settled in the backseat. "The nearest hotel please," he instructed the driver. "Nice hotel," he amended.

The driver smiled as he glanced back at them. "How many stars?"

"As many as you can manage in as short a drive possible."

He nodded and pulled into traffic.

"I think we might want to go back by the gallery now that it's almost time for normal business hours to begin," Felicity said. "What time does it open today?"

"Eleven." He looked at his watch. "That gives us a few hours. Depending on what happens with Chesnokov's next move, maybe we can swing by the shipping docks first."

"Okay." Her shoulders were a little curved, arms folded once again, her gaze directed out the window. "We're not going to find Julia in either of those places," she said, sounding more dispirited than he could ever recall her sounding.

He knew it was probably fatigue talking, but it still made him wish he had a better handle on the situation, and better options available. He did not want to track down Reese. "We'll talk to whoever is there, get a feel for what's going on, maybe find out when she last made contact, see if there's anything that sounds like it's not business as usual. We can check the shipping locations to see if there's been any activity at the docks since the police were there for the alarm."

Felicity nodded.

"You don't seem overly optimistic."

She lifted her gaze to his. "I know you're against this, but I can't help but think going directly to John might save us a lot of time. He's the one in the middle of this. I'd think he would be our best bet right now for getting some answers. At least about whether or not Chesnokov was his intended buyer out here."

"Except we can't trust anything he says. We have no idea what his involvement in this really is, or if his story about Julia is even true. We talk to him and it's just an opportunity for him to give us more useless information. Or worse, misdirect us."

"We can ask him if he's heard from her, or knows anything new about the moves she's making. We might be able to glean something from how he responds."

"Last time we thought he was in a lot of pain and telling us the truth. Now, we're not so sure. I don't think seeing him face-to-face will give us a distinct advantage, but his knowing we're grasping at straws certainly will give him one."

Felicity sighed. "If he's telling the truth and she does have it, and the deal hasn't already happened, she's definitely going to hand off or ship out today. She can't risk having it on her any longer than that. Even a novice would know that much. Too many people know of its whereabouts, and that it's still potentially available."

Finn drummed the stylus against his thigh. "The more I think about it, something still isn't adding up with Chesnokov for me, either."

"I agree. Maybe Julia hasn't connected with him yet and his stop at Talbot's this morning was just something already on his schedule, and completely unrelated."

"Maybe. That's why the driver is staying on him. I'm still trying to connect bringing Andreev in from Russia to carry the stone when Chesnokov's already here."

"That's not all that unusual. Andreev could have been taking it back to Chesnokov's home in St. Petersburg. Chesnokov being here in the States, with the sapphire a continent away, would provide him with a decent cover if things went wrong with the deal, or if Andreev was caught trying to transport a gemstone of questionable provenance out of the country. Then that deal never even got off the ground, so Reese, now with Julia in tow, brings the stone directly to him, hoping he'll go for it."

"And yet, I'm still not satisfied." Finn stared up at the buildings they were passing, playing back over the fact that Chesnokov was visiting a matchmaking company. "Is there any other reason he might have been meeting with the Talbot group that could be connected to the sapphire? Maybe we're not thinking far enough outside the lines. I mean, it's not even eight o'clock in the morning. Pretty early for a matchmaking strategy session. And why would someone of Chesnokov's stature be using such a service anyway?"

"Maybe the connection is professional, not personal. As I said before, maybe he's helping them procure women from his side of the pond."

"But what would that have to do with the sapphire?"

"I haven't any idea. It might be unrelated."

"On the surface, it certainly would appear to be. But that doesn't feel right, either." He swore under his breath. "Nothing about any of this does."

"So . . . do you want to go back? Stick close to him?"

"No, I'm going to put Rafe or Mac on it, see if they can make any kind of connection. With those two digging and Rafe's guy following Chesnokov, we can get back to tracking Julia."

"And John?"

"No, I told you—"

She lifted her hand to stall his rebuttal. "I don't mean to contact him; I meant to track him down. Find out where he is and what he's doing. Maybe that will be our path to finding Julia."

Finn fell silent as he thought that over. "Not a bad idea. But we're short a little help on that, and I can't get either of my partners out here fast enough to—"

Looking a bit hurt, Felicity said, "What am I? Chopped liver?"

Finn had already gotten so used to working with her, he'd forgotten their original plan to split up, divide and conquer. "Right," he said, "I'm sorry. I just—" He smiled. "I'm kind of getting used to bouncing things off of you, working with you. I wasn't thinking, but I didn't mean to insinuate . . . anything, really."

She smiled briefly and made a point of curling her fingers into her palm and squeezing them tightly. "Good."

Trust. He'd meant what he said, but she was clearly calling him on it. "We'll get a hold of Rafe and Mac, then figure out our battle plan from there," he said, and meant it. He just didn't know quite what that plan was going to be yet. The idea of them splitting up didn't sit well with him, but not so much because of the trust issue, but for more personal reasons. He had this gut feeling that if he let her out of his sight, he'd never see her again. And trust had nothing to do with it. Things were happening here, things they didn't understand, including burning buildings and a missing gallery owner. Until he had a better handle on who the players were and what the stakes were, he didn't really want to let Felicity out of his sight.

The cab eased into a circular drive in front of a regal-looking old hotel. It stopped at the curb, and several bellmen immediately moved in their direction.

He smiled at Felicity as his door was opened. He could see the fatigue etched on her face quite clearly now, and knew he didn't look much better. "But first, hot shower, hot food."

"No," Felicity corrected him as she took the bellman's hand and slid her legs out of the car. "First, we go shopping."

Finn paused, but Felicity was already out of the car, a renewed spring in her step as she explained there was no luggage, but that she would be remedying that shortly.

He caught up to her and put his hand on her lower back as the bellman held the lobby door for them. "We don't have time to—"

Felicity smiled up at him, tired, but a bit of a gleam in her eyes now. "Oh, darling, it won't take any time at all." She patted his cheek. "Trust me."

"It's not that, it's just—"

"You get us a room and go up and shower. I'll be up shortly."

"But—"

She shooed him off and ducked into the first boutique off the grand lobby.

He was all set to go in after her, or hover outside, just to keep an eye on her, but realized that trust was about more than believing she wouldn't dupe him. It was also trusting her to take care of herself. She wasn't exactly fragile or helpless. Which was a great part of why he was so drawn to her. But it didn't make him feel any less conflicted. He wasn't used to feeling so proprietary or worrying so much about anyone.

On the other hand, while Felicity might be touched to know he was concerned, he doubted she'd be all that thrilled to know he didn't have enough faith in her to take care of herself. He did. But just because she'd clearly done a good job taking care of herself up to this point didn't mean bad things couldn't happen. They could happen to anyone. He swore under his breath. Partnerships could be tricky at times, he knew that from working with Rafe and Mac, discovering their boundaries and limits, as well as developing trust and faith. But with Felicity there was the added emotional element, which was as huge as it was confusing. It was the part that wasn't rational or reasonable, more like a primal directive to protect and defend. He snorted at himself. Neanderthal.

He stared after her as she disappeared among the racks of clothing, thinking about that, which led him to also think about what would likely happen if they both went up to their hotel room at the same time. And finally, resigned, he sighed and turned toward the registration desk. "Yeah, I'll just go up alone."

Thirty minutes later he stepped out of the hottest shower he'd taken in a long time, happy to be clean, but not feeling as rejuvenated as he'd hoped. He knew that part of that was the latent anxiety he'd tried to ignore, quite unsuccessfully, waiting for Felicity to show up. She hadn't come into the bathroom, but maybe she'd been respecting his privacy. Or maybe she'd known, as he did, what would happen if she did. More distraction they didn't need right now. And he was already feeling far more distracted having been through the emotional rollercoaster of the past half hour than he'd like to be. Falling in love was a bitch.

Then he stepped into the master suite and found Felicity stretched out on the bed, fast asleep. And thought it was also one of the best feelings in the whole world. The relief was far greater than it probably should have been, but he was human. She'd come back. And she was okay. In some ways, on some levels, that was all that mattered to him right now.

His body, however, was even happier, if its reaction to seeing her all flushed and relaxed was any indication. In fact, it felt quite rejuvenated. Perhaps a cold shower would have done him more good.

He hated to wake her, but he was pretty sure she'd rather use what little time they had freshening up rather than sleeping. At least he assumed she would. Again, he was struck by how little he really knew her. And by how badly he wanted to correct that. It would take a lifetime to know everything about her, and he just happened to have one handy and available.

He rubbed the towel over his hair, dreading putting back on the same clothes, but paying far more attention to her sleeping form than to the pile of rumpled clothes he'd left thrown across one of the bedroom chairs. It wasn't until he almost tripped over them as he rounded the foot of the bed that he realized she'd left an entire row of shopping bags on the floor there. Between checking in and getting to their room, he couldn't have been in the shower for more than twenty minutes.

He glanced up at Felicity and smiled. Benefactor to the poor, acquaintance of the Queen. Jewel thief and champion shopper. He glanced back down at the bags. Hopefully she'd paid for everything in there.

"So pensive," she said, her voice all soft and drowsy with sleep.

He glanced up at her in time to watch her stretch. Parts of his anatomy stretched right along with her. His emotions were far too turbulent to deal with that temptation at the moment, so he turned and sat on the bed and started poking through the bags. "I was just thinking that if shopping was an Olympic sport, you should really be scouted for the team."

"It's not all for me. I figured you wouldn't mind a change of clothes yourself."

He glanced over his shoulder.

"Why do you look so surprised?" She pushed up on her elbows. "Don't I strike you as the sort who'd do a chap a favor?"

Her cheeks were a little rosy with sleep, her hair softly tangled around her face, her eyes a bit unfocused. And all he could think was that she struck him as the sort that called to him, quite strongly, to say the hell with clothes altogether and climb up the bed, right into her waiting arms, and into her warm and willing body.

"Thank you," he said. "I didn't mean to look ungrateful. I just—how did you even manage it? You don't know my size or—"

The most provocative smile curved her lips, sorely testing his willpower. "I knew enough to assume I was close. We can always call down and have a different size sent up."

Oh, he was just the right size, that he knew. He looked back at the bags and quietly cleared his throat. *Head in the game, Dalton.* Time was ticking again.

He picked through the first bag, but it was full of soft fabrics and things lined with lace. Yeah, that stuff he didn't need to be fondling right now. In the third bag over, he found boxers and socks, both perfectly suitable and sized properly. A glance in the last bag revealed two white T-shirts. He chanced looking at her again. She'd sat up now, her legs off the side of the bed. "So, boxers, socks, and a clean T-shirt. Good start, but

I was thinking maybe something a bit more . . . professional might be optimal for today's adventures." He was teasing, but realized she didn't know him that well, either, and added, "Of course, if that's all they had, that's fine, I can recycle the rest—"

She laughed. "Don't get pouty. Pants and shirts are hanging in the closet."

He tried not to look overly relieved. "Thank you. I'll be happy to reimburse—"

"Don't be silly. We're partners. You got me McIvities and tea. We're even."

"I hardly think—"

"Good. I like you better that way."

"Very cute." But he grinned as he stood and turned to find her standing now as well. A sea of bed between them. *Danger, danger*, his inner voice warned. Like he needed a warning.

"Yes," she said with a smile, "you are that." She scooped up two bags and skirted by him on her way to the shower.

It took almost superhuman control not to reach out and snag her and her bags full of lacy things and toss them all on the bed. Instead, he grabbed a pair of what turned out to be silk boxers out of the bag.

"You'll love the feel of them against your skin," she told him.

To which his body responded with a resounding hurrah. In an effort to keep from taking her up against the nearest wall, he made a show of modeling them in front of the towel he'd wrapped around his hips. "Well, if you're the brains of this outfit, I guess one of us has to bring the pretty."

She shook her head, and simultaneously they both said, "Incorrigible."

If she only knew just how much restraint he was showing right now.

She was still laughing as she closed the bathroom door between them.

He looked back down at the silky black boxers, then tossed them back in the bag, opting for cotton instead. The last thing he needed was something slinky and slippery sliding all over him the rest of the day. He heard the shower go on and tried to block the mental images that accompanied the sound. "Right." Disgusted with his inability to get his head back on straight— and leave the other one out of it—he tugged on socks and T-shirt in record time, then checked out the closet to see what she'd picked out for him. It was a necessity, a favor. And yet looking at the fine linen shirts and selection of freshly creased and pressed trousers felt stupidly personal. Intimate even. "You are so gone," he muttered.

He finished dressing, raked fingers through his drying hair and rubbed a hand across his chin, silently thanking whoever had decided to include a disposable razor in with the standard room amenities. He tossed his old clothes into one of the empty bags, then after another lingering look at the bathroom door, stalked out into the main room of the suite and punched the button on his iPhone that went directly to Trinity. He didn't care who answered; he just needed a distraction from the sound of that damn shower. And the woman presently enjoying it.

"About time," Mac said.

"Hello, to you, too."

"Sapphire all safe and sound yet?"

"You're a funny, funny man."

"So I've been told. What can we do for you?"

"Rafe get anything more on Chesnokov or Julia? Or the fire and break-in?"

"He's still running through stuff."

"Well, tell him to add this interesting little tidbit to his list. Have him check out Talbot, James & Warrick and see what connection he can come up with between them and the Russian."

"Sounds like a stuffy legal firm, but given your tone, I'm guessing not."

"Hardly. Trust me when I say it will brighten your day immensely."

"Usually that's reserved for sex, so—" He broke off, then

chuckled. "I don't even think I want to know how that connects. Besides, isn't Chesnokov like ninety or something?"

"Eighty-two."

"Exactly. So what gives? This a private medical group that's going to get his mojo back?"

Finn tried not to shudder. "It's early here, you know. I could have gone all day without thinking about Chesnokov's mojo."

"Hey, you brought it up."

"Well, I don't think 'up' is the operative word in this case. At least I'd like to think there was some other reason he was there at seven-thirty this morning."

"Something that a nice sapphire would be connected to?"

"I don't see how, but yes. If you or Rafe can make that connection, Santa will be very kind to you this year."

"I don't believe in Santa. But I do believe in Christmas bonuses. And a whole week in some unnamed spot alone with Kate would be a very nice thing to find under the tree."

"You do that voodoo you do so well, and it's done."

"Okay, now you're starting to scare me."

Finn chuckled now. "Fair's fair. Let me know the instant you have something. We're going to check out the gallery just as soon as—"

"We?"

Shit. He'd been trying so hard to distract himself from the temptation in the other room, he'd distracted himself right past remembering that Mac and Rafe had no idea he wasn't handling this case alone any longer. Or ever, really.

Thinking quickly, he said, "Rafe got me a driver, and let me tell you, kickin' A with this guy, so keep his name handy. Anyway, like I said—"

"You're so full of shit I can smell it from here. Who is she?"

Finn was silent for a tellingly long moment. "The driver really does kick ass."

"Great. Rafe will be thrilled. But it's the piece of ass I want to know about. Spill."

Again, he paused, not ready to talk about any of this. Mac

and Rafe were the two people closest to him, knew him the best. Well enough to see through anything he said. And he wasn't ready for their all-too-keen insights right yet. "It's not like that," was all he said, knowing his tone brooked no argument. Also knowing it was a tone he'd never once used with either of his partners.

Mac wasn't remotely offended. In fact, when he got done laughing, Finn thought it was just as well he was three thousand miles away. "So, it's like that," he said, still chuckling. "Hallelujah and welcome to the club, my friend."

"It's not like anything." *Anything I've ever known, anyway.*

"Right. You forget, you're preaching to the choir here, friend. And boy will Rafe be relieved."

"Why is that? If anything, he's the one who'd understand that not everyone's head is turned by—" Then he paused as Mac remained silent. "Don't tell me."

"You'll meet her when you get back. It's like the greatest thing ever." He chuckled again. "You just wait and see. Come in, by the way, the water's fine."

"I'm not interested in the water right now," he said, though that was a bald-faced lie and Mac well knew it. Not to mention it was killing him not to ask more questions about what the hell was going on with Rafe. He hadn't even been gone that long. "What I'm interested in is finding some kind of crack in this case that we can break open to—"

"There you go with that 'we' again. So she's not just along for the ride—speaking metaphorically, of course—she's actually engaged in the mission. Interesting."

Finn wisely remained silent. Better to let Mac have his fun than inadvertently give him so much as a speck of information to grab hold of. Mac liked to play the laid-back kidder of the group, but his mind was as ridiculously agile as his hands. The most evolved technology, along with mechanical objects of all sizes and complexity, bowed before his overly indulgent, God-given talents.

Not that Finn didn't want them to know about Felicity

Jane. At some point, they would. Just not yet. Not now. If he told Mac anything, they'd do a complete check on her. And when—not if—he found out the rest of Felicity's story, it was going to be from Felicity herself. Not from one of Rafe's well-documented reports.

"Get back with me when you know something. And wipe that damn smug-ass grin off your face."

"Will do. And you must be joking." Then he clicked off.

"Good thing I love you guys like brothers," he muttered, then slid the stylus out and started doing his own digging.

Chapter 18

Felicity rinsed the shampoo from her hair and told herself she had absolutely nothing to feel guilty about. Finn trusted her, which was great. She trusted him, too. But she still had a job to do, and contacting her superiors to give them an update and ask a few questions was hardly a breach of that trust.

She knew he still had questions about her—in his position, he'd be a fool not to—but the fact that he'd given her any latitude with that impromptu shopping trip had been gratifying, to say the least. He'd wanted to balk, and that had given her a momentary pang, but despite whatever misgivings he was still harboring, he'd stood by his promise and let her go.

What was bothering her even more was the fact that while she'd used her time away from him to transmit a request for further information on Chesnokov, Julia, Talbot & Company, as well as John Reese, she hadn't taken the opportunity to inform them she was working with someone. Much less who that someone was.

She could tell herself all kinds of things about why she'd made that decision, and most of them would even be true. But she was having a very hard time ignoring the most important reason she hadn't mentioned her new partner, which was the fear that her immediate controller would issue a direct order to leave him and continue working solo. She'd never ignored or gone against a direct order. She didn't want to find out whether that fact would have changed.

She also could have used the time to not only notify them about Finn, but attempt to convince them that he should be taken into her confidence. She had rejected that plan as well. Her superiors knew she and Finn had crossed paths before. Although they weren't privy to the more intimate details— any of them—they did know that he'd made completing her mission a challenge once, and a failure the second time. She doubted that even if she'd had an extended period of time to communicate with them, she could have accomplished any amount of real convincing, much less during the few scant minutes she had while throwing clothes on the counter of the hotel boutique.

She finished rinsing off and stepped out of the shower, only to be assaulted by the heady fragrance of freshly prepared food. Even the smell of coffee had her stomach grumbling. She shoved aside her concerns about her superiors and Finn and quickly dressed. She ran a fast comb through her curls, squeezed out the extra water, then shook them as loose as possible. She still looked like a drowned poodle, but it would have to do. She did a quick check of her PDA, but nothing had been transmitted during the short time she was in the shower. She wasted a moment wondering what she'd do if her controller did send along useful information. How would she tell Finn without him wondering how she'd come upon such information?

Deciding she'd cross that bridge when and if she came to it, she stepped out of the bathroom to find the bedroom empty, but she could hear Finn talking in the main room of the suite. She wasn't sure which was more enticing, the sound of his deep voice, murmuring something to someone in the other room, or the intoxicating scent of the food, but fortunately she didn't have to choose and followed both.

There was a room service table set up in the middle of the room. Finn was standing over by the large picture window, talking on his cell phone. From the sounds of it, he was talking to one of his partners. She moved over to the table, confident he'd share any pertinent information with her when he'd concluded his call. She felt another little stab of guilt, knowing she couldn't be a hundred percent certain she'd do the same, but quashed it as she sat and spread a linen napkin across her lap.

"Go ahead and start," Finn mouthed, motioning with his hand for her to eat.

Any other time, she'd have done the polite thing and waited, but just the smell of the bacon alone had her stomach growling so loudly, she selected a piece and crunched it merely to silence the unseemly noise. Finn ended his call and joined her a few moments later.

"News?" she asked, putting the bacon down as her stomach tightened a bit. Her own PDA hadn't vibrated in the pocket inside the short-waisted jacket she'd donned, which only meant she just felt partially guilty asking him to share all.

"The fire was arson. No leads on that, or the break-in, as it doesn't appear they've been able to locate the owner, either."

Felicity let her hands drop to her lap. "Oh, my."

Finn poured more coffee and nudged the teapot and sugar closer to her. "I know. No leads there, but I do think going to the gallery is imperative at this point, gauge how her employees are behaving, and what, if anything, they say when we ask about the owner."

"And the shipping docks?"

"They stay on the list, too."

"No word from the driver on Chesnokov?"

Finn shook his head. "I checked in with him before calling Rafe. No sign of him yet."

Felicity looked at her watch. "It's been a little over an hour since he went in. Maybe we should go in, or one of us anyway.

Pretend we're a client, see if we can figure out where in the building Chesnokov is. At the very least we might find out what his connection is, if he's not in the clientele area."

"If the gallery and docks reveal nothing, and he hasn't budged, then we can give that a shot. He doesn't know either of us directly." Finn paused with a piece of toast halfway to his mouth. "Does he?"

Thankfully, she didn't have to make a decision on this one. "No, I've never met the man. Although, I can't guarantee he isn't aware of me. From my research, I know he spends a fair amount of time in the U.K., and, as you know, I tend to pop up in the papers there from time to time."

"Then I'll go in if it comes to that. No point risking things unnecessarily." He crunched his toast and helped himself to some eggs, so she did the same and bided her time, willing her phone to vibrate with information they could use . . . and praying it didn't, forcing her to go along with Finn's intel and saving her from making a choice.

They continued in silence for several surprisingly comfortable minutes. Comfortable enough that she actually ate a decent amount and drank some very lovely tea. But as she was dabbing her mouth with her linen, Finn said, "If I end up going after Chesnokov, I know you'll want to go after Reese. I also know you're going to call me on the trust thing, but I'm telling you, I don't want you to go off alone after him. And trust has nothing to do with it."

"Meaning you don't think I can handle him? I realize our last one-on-one didn't end well for me, but I'd like to think I'm a fast learner."

"I know better than anyone that you can handle yourself. It's just . . . I don't want anything happening to you."

The way he'd said it, the look on his face, made her heart squeeze. She tried to ignore that and focus on business, even though she knew that wasn't at all what he meant. "But you just said you knew I could take care—"

"I didn't say it was logical, or even rational. It's . . . Neanderthal." He smiled. "And, trust me, it's not something I'm entirely comfortable with, either."

"Then don't," she said, even as her insides were melting a little. No one had ever cared enough to be that concerned about her, not like that. "Worry about Julia. Worry about the sapphire."

"I do. I am." He reached across the small table and covered her hand with his. "But that doesn't stop me from not wanting you put in situations that we don't fully understand."

"We don't," she repeated. "You're right. So why am I any safer with you than without you?"

He lifted his hand away from hers.

"I didn't mean it like that," she said. "I'm aware you can handle things, and handle me as well."

"I know what you meant." He leaned back in his seat, his gaze on his plate, but she doubted he was seeing anything on it. "And you're right." He lifted his gaze to hers. "I can't guarantee anything, your safety included. I just feel that if we stick together, we have a better chance of dealing with whatever is going to come our way." His smile returned, but there was something tender, almost vulnerable in it. "We make a good team, Felicity Jane. I like us together. On and off the playing field."

She couldn't manage to look away, couldn't seem to find whatever it was she had left that would keep her head strictly on business. "I think we do, too," she said, relieved to be honest with him. "But I don't think we're going to resolve this particular situation staying joined at the hip." That mischievous glint surfaced in his eyes, and she couldn't help but smile. "Or wherever we're joined."

He tossed his linen napkin on the table and finished off his coffee. "So, docks, then gallery." He stood and reached his hand out to her. "Then we'll figure out what's next from there."

She put her hand in his and wished things weren't as complicated as they were. Because, he was right, if the gallery and docks revealed nothing, and no other leads came in, then he would go after Chesnokov.

And, like it or not, she would go after John Reese.

As it turned out, neither scenario went into play as planned. They were halfway to the docks when the driver buzzed in to Finn . . . and not thirty seconds later, she felt her own phone vibrate in her pocket.

Finn listened to what the driver had to say, then said, "Follow him. We're not that far away; we'll cross paths at some point. Keep me informed on the direction he's heading."

"He's not heading home, I take it?" Felicity asked as he hung up.

Finn shook his head. "He's actually heading in the same general direction we are." He instructed their cabbie on what direction to go, then turned back to her. "We'll meet up with the driver, and I'll follow Chesnokov. You head to the gallery in the cab. I'll either come and get you there, or we'll make other arrangements."

"What about the docks?" She stopped him before he could answer. "If you tell me it's too dangerous there for a woman, I'm—"

"I didn't say that."

She folded her arms. "Didn't have to. So, let me tell you that—"

"Let's get through with the gallery and see what Chesnokov is up to before we plan further." He looked out the window when the cabbie swung a left and started heading out toward the warehouses lining the docks along the harbor. He swore under his breath.

"What?" she asked.

"I just realized, how are we going to keep contact? You could use the gallery phone to contact me when you're done, but I really would rather you—"

Felicity's stomach cramped in a knot at the potential implications of what she was about to do, but she spoke before she could change her mind. "I have a phone."

Finn's eyes widened.

Felicity shrugged, and tried to play it off as if it were nothing out of the ordinary, which, normally, it wouldn't be. If anything about this whole escapade could be considered normal. Which it most decidedly could not. "You never asked. And I haven't needed to use it since we teamed up."

Finn held her gaze a beat longer, so she casually pulled it out of her jacket pocket. "I've had it on me the whole time. I'm not exactly hiding anything here." Which wasn't entirely the truth, but not exactly a lie, either. She held it out to him, praying he didn't notice the fine trembling of her fingers.

"Okay," he said a moment later. "Good."

He didn't take it from her, and she tried not to breathe an obvious sigh of relief. If he'd even glanced at the screen, he'd have seen there was a message waiting to be read. "Good."

He turned his PDA on. "Number?"

She rattled hers off and took his as well. "There," she said, and pocketed the phone again as nonchalantly as she could manage. "Now, if we're heading toward the docks, then maybe we should just wait and see where Chesnokov is heading before splitting up. We can just follow the town car in the cab."

Finn smiled then. "See? Teamwork. Good idea."

Felicity smiled, and it was sincere, but it didn't lessen her anxiety one whit. She needed to read that message and couldn't until she was alone. She should have angled for them to separate as soon as possible, but her gut told her that any answers they were going to find weren't going to be at the gallery. Better for her, regardless of whatever intel was on her phone, to stick with the higher percentage plan for as long as she possibly could.

The fact that that plan kept her with Finn was secondary. *Right.* Fortunately she was saved from having to think about that any longer when Finn's phone buzzed again.

"It's Sean." At her confused look, he added, "The limo driver." Finn put it on speaker-phone. "What have you got? Where are you now?"

"He's on Graves. Warehouse district, off Advent. I'm one block west. Not enough traffic here to shadow him. One block closer to the bay and I'm going to lose him. He's got to be going to one of the warehouses back here. I can give you a grid, narrow it down."

"He still in the Rolls?"

"Yes."

"We'll find him."

Finn listened while Sean rattled off the intersecting streets surrounding the area that Chesnokov was in. Then he signed off and tapped rapidly on his screen.

"Is this close to Julia's shipping location?"

"That's what I'm trying to figure out." He tapped a few more times, then urged the information to pop up faster. "Satellite phones are great, but they aren't always the fastest with linkups."

Felicity scooted closer and looked over his shoulder. He smelled like fresh soap and shampoo. She tried not to let that distract her, but it was every bit as tantalizing as breakfast had been. She'd been starved for that. She shouldn't be starved for Finn. She'd just had him. But tell that to her body, which was reacting as though he hadn't touched her in a week.

The map popped up on the screen just as she was leaning in a bit more closely, saving her from behaving any more unprofessionally than she already had.

"Same general area, but not the same place," Finn said. "A few miles off, actually." He tapped the screen. "Julia's place is here."

"The two places don't even connect. He'd have to come back out to the main street to cut over to that industrial park."

"Maybe she's using a different location. It's too much that he's near any shipping docks on the day the sapphire shows up in San Francisco." He leaned over. "Your hair smells really good."

She smiled at him, but internally rolled eyes at herself. He made it seem so effortless, which made her feel as if she was making it way more complicated than it had to be. Except if she went around saying everything she felt about him when she felt it, then he'd know that she—She pulled herself up short there. He'd know that she *what?*

"So does yours," she blurted out, then laughed.

He smiled, looking a little surprised at her outburst. "Thank you."

When her laughter didn't subside right away, he laughed, too. "What's funny about our hair smelling good?"

She waved her hand, knowing it was partly fatigue making her giddy, but also realizing that that same fatigue was causing her to lower her defenses. And, now lowered, she sensed that the harder she tried to tuck her feelings for Finn in one neat little box, so she could concentrate on her work, the more impossible the task became. Because there was no compartmentalizing her feelings for Finn. The only difference between the two of them was that he was the one being honest with himself. And her.

That sobered her up. "Nothing. It was charming and sweet. You're charming and sweet. It's just me. I'm being ridiculous." *What's ridiculous is you staring a perfectly good man in the face—maybe the best man you'll ever know—and not acknowledging what is really happening here.*

"I've lost him," came Sean's voice over the speaker-phone, jerking their attention back to the matter at hand.

"Where?" Finn demanded.

"Last spotted turning into the Bayside Industrial Park." He rattled off the address.

"We can be there in five minutes. Stay close, but out of sight."

"I'll . . . do my best. Standard form of transportation around here is front-end loaders and paneled trucks. I stick out a little."

"So does a Silver Cloud, I'm guessing. Just do your best. I'll let you know what's up next." He clicked off, then gave the cabbie directions.

"This isn't such a great part of town," the cab driver said. "I can drop you, but I'm not waiting."

Finn and Felicity exchanged glances. Then Finn said, "I'll double your rate. We won't be long. Ten minutes, tops."

Felicity hoped he was right about that. But then, she doubted Chesnokov would want to hang around the area for very long, either.

The driver looked at them in his rearview mirror, clearly still skeptical despite the increased fee. "Half up front. After ten minutes, I leave."

"Deal," Finn said.

She leaned closer to Finn. "We have the other car, do we need to keep him here?"

"Until we find out what's what, I say we keep all our options open. Worst case is it takes longer and he splits and we go find Sean."

She nodded, then looked out the window when the cab slowed down as they entered the warehouse district. "How do you want to approach this?"

"Pull over here," Finn said.

By her estimation, they were still a good half mile or more away.

It was close to midday, and there was a fair amount of activity in and around a few of the warehouses. Some of the sections were abandoned and had become quite derelict, but there were a few in operation, with trucks going in and out. Still, it wasn't exactly a tourist spot, and they were in the only cab she'd seen since they'd left midtown. Once the cab pulled to the side of the narrow road, Felicity put her hand on the door.

Finn put his hand on her arm. "I don't think it's such a good idea for you to go along."

"I thought we went through this."

"That was before I knew that Chesnokov was going to visit boarded-up dockside warehouses." He ran his gaze over her. "You stand out just a bit, you know. It's attention we can't afford to draw."

"And you look so like a dockworker."

"I could be an investor, owner, city official. I've been there, done that, in worse locations than this."

"I can hold my own, just the same."

"Not this time." He pulled cash out of his wallet and peeled off a few twenties, which he handed to the cabbie. "Ten minutes." He looked at Felicity. "If I'm not back by then, find Sean and wait there for me."

"Finn, let me—"

"If the situation were reversed, what would your professional assessment be?"

She scowled. "Not fair."

"I know, but such is life." He leaned in and kissed her hard. "Keep your phone handy," he said, breathing a bit less steadily when he lifted his head. "I'll stay in contact. If you don't hear back from me, don't come in after me, go find Reese. Make him talk."

"Finn." But there was nothing else to say. The trust and faith he was putting in her, leaving her here, complete with driver at the ready—a driver not on his company's payroll—was enormous. And she knew, despite his smile, that it wasn't lightly placed. That kiss he'd just planted on her had said as much. He turned to go, and she abruptly pulled him back and kissed him, quickly, but intently.

"And that was for?"

She stared at him, knowing this was her personal moment of reckoning. Nothing in life was guaranteed. Not her safety. And not his. "Just . . . don't let anything happen to you."

His response was an immediate broad grin. "Of course I won't. We've only just started."

He slid out of the car, and she scooted over after him. "Finn."
He turned.

"We are a team," she said, realizing, fully, that it was true.
In every sense. She just had to figure out how to make it all
work. And, in that moment, she determined that whatever it
took, she would find a way.

His smile stayed, but concern clouded his eyes as he said,
"The best."

She squeezed her hand into a fist so he could see. And the
grin reappeared, the concern gone. Then he was loping across
the street and cutting through a scrawny hedgerow before
ducking behind the nearest row of warehouses and finally,
completely out of her line of sight.

She waited a few moments longer before sliding her phone
out to check the incoming message. Whatever the intel was, she
was going to find a way to incorporate it into what they were
doing together. She would simply have to find a way to make
her superiors understand why she was bringing him into her
confidence. The one way she knew how was for them to get
the sapphire back together, irrefutable evidence that her faith
had been well placed.

Then she'd do whatever she had to, to broker a deal between Finn and her government. They could use the stone as
evidence in their case . . . after which, if his documentation
was what he claimed it was—and she couldn't imagine he'd be
risking himself like this if it wasn't—the stone would go to
Finn's client as rightful owner.

She smiled then, feeling calm for the first time since Finn
had walked into her hotel room. This was the right thing to
do. She kept her fingers curled into her palm, so certain of her
decision it should have surprised her, but instead made her feel
as though she'd simply been blind to it for too long. She'd
never been a partner to anyone before, in any real sense. With
Finn, she wanted that partnership, in every sense. And that
was going to start right now.

She punched in the code that unscrambled the text of the message.

Then her mouth dropped open on a soft gasp. And her stomach knotted right back up again as she read the words on the screen.

Find John Reese. Bring him Home. Mission completed.

Chapter 19

Finn caught sight of the Silver Cloud two buildings over and immediately stopped and ducked back around the corner of the building he'd been skirting. He transmitted the exact location of the warehouse to Felicity and Sean, then crept closer while trying to determine exactly how to handle this.

First, he wanted to see what kind of business Chesnokov was visiting, banking that this was some kind of back-up facility of Julia's. Probably owned by a friend or contact, as it hadn't shown up at all in any of their background searches on her. And if Reese knew anything about it, he certainly hadn't shared. In this case, given the situation, it made more sense for Julia to be going off trail with the location than sticking with anything that Reese had been privy to.

And it was that point exactly that had his hopes rising that maybe they'd finally managed to track down both target and seller. What exactly he was going to do with them now that he'd possibly found them was another story entirely.

There were no windows on the backsides of the buildings, allowing him the freedom to move across the open area between one and the next without worrying about being seen. At this end of the lot, all the buildings were either boarded over or vandalized. His guess was this place was far more active at night, with the main business being drug dealing. And he doubted anyone was exactly paying rent on the space to conduct said business. At this end of the row, there was no real activity of any kind. Except for the beat-up white pickup truck and Silver Cloud parked in front of the building he was presently behind, the immediate area was deserted. *Wonderful.*

He stayed in the shadows and slowly scanned the edges of the target building and those around for any mounted detection cameras. Not that the area seemed to warrant any high-scale security, but someone was conducting some kind of real business out of this building, and so it was hard to say what measures they'd felt compelled to take. Especially given the location.

Seeing nothing obvious, he quickly crossed the last section of open ground and flattened himself against the building Chesnokov was currently visiting. Coming in the way he had, there was no way to check for any group signage like there had been at the warehouse development last night. And the only way to see any sign posted on the front of the building was to put himself in plain sight. And he wasn't prepared to do that quite yet. Brick and cinder block buildings also didn't lend themselves well to voices carrying, and metal roofing didn't play well for alternate forms of silent entry. He crept closer along the side of the building, then crouched and tried to eyeball the parking lot without being seen.

Luck was on his side. An external, block cement staircase leading up to an elevated front door gave him enough extra cover to duck around front and, by risking a quick pop-up, check out the sign above the bay door. *Nelson Studios.* Great. He crouched back down and quickly tapped the name into his PDA, but nothing popped up on the Web for it. He transmitted the info to Rafe, but didn't hold out much hope on getting anything back in time to help with his decision on how to go about entering the structure. If he had any clue what kind of business it was, he could play a role accordingly. Going in blind, with there likely being, at best, a handful of people inside, wasn't wise.

He thought again about his intel on the Russian. This was

not exactly a classy meeting place. Which meant either Chesnokov was desperate enough to agree to any meeting place. Or he'd had no choice.

Finn leaned back against the building and let his mind play out the possible scenarios. The stone was rare, and Chesnokov had certainly desired it, but he didn't see the man being that desperate to own what was, for him, simply another piece in the vast collection of antiquities he'd already amassed. Especially given the unusual circumstances surrounding the continued availability of this one. Which left coercion. But what in the world could coerce a man of Chesnokov's stature and wealth to agree to deal on a level that must certainly feel beneath him? Blackmail? But, in what way? Why would someone be forcing him to buy the stone? It made no sense. Finding another buyer couldn't be that difficult.

And yet, Chesnokov was definitely here, on the wrong side of the tracks, doing business of some sort.

"Finn."

Finn's hand went to his heart as he swiveled his head to see Felicity poking her head around the corner. "What in the hell are you doing here? I thought we agreed—"

"You agreed," she said, keeping her voice to a whisper. "I—"

Just then the front door opened right above where Finn was crouched. They both froze. Then he jerked his head, motioning her to duck back around the wall as he shrank into a corner of the staircase and building as best he could.

There was a sudden, angry burst of Russian as the door banged against the staircase railing. First by a deep, raspy voice, probably Chesnokov, followed by a decidedly feminine, much younger sounding woman. Finn knew a little of the language, but wasn't nearly conversant enough to follow their rapid-fire exchange. The girl came down the stairs first, but all Finn could see were mile-high black spike heels and black-seamed stockings on very long, slender legs. Next came the thump and slow progress of Chesnokov with his cane, though it didn't slow his shouting.

Then a third voice joined the first two. "Mr. Chesnokov, I understand you aren't happy with Natalia's decision, but you can hardly just—"

The old man turned rather quickly for someone of his advanced age and girth and, using the railing for support, jabbed his cane in the direction of the man's voice. "You have no idea what I can do," he said in heavily accented English. He turned toward the girl. "I did not spend a lifetime building my empire to have my one and only great-granddaughter shame the family name by making such an outrageous alliance. I will not stand for it." He motioned now toward the girl. "Get in the car. We will discuss what will be done about this—this travesty of a union once we've departed this ... place."

Finn was surprised he hadn't spit in disgust after that last point, and found himself trying not to smile.

"She is my *wife*," the man shouted, coming down the stairs after them. Finn got a brief glimpse of a young man with shaggy brown hair, wearing jeans and a plaid shirt, with what looked like several cameras slung around his neck. "I chose her over hundreds of other women. She agreed to marry me. I didn't force her to do anything. You can't—"

Chesnokov turned, his voice deadly cold now. "That is where you are wrong again. I can. And I will. It is enough you had to use some kind of service to find yourself a partner. Then you fill her head with ideas of becoming an international model. A *model*, Natalia?" He all but hissed the word, as if he'd found her in a brothel, hoping to be a hooker. "You allow him to photograph you like this? It is beneath you, as is this place, this—this *studio*."

The girl spoke again in Russian, but the pleading tone in her voice said it all.

"I will not discuss this further," he said, then began moving toward the Rolls again. "Get in the car. And, for God's sake, cover yourself."

There was another angry string of Russian from Natalia.

"You can't interfere like this," the man tried once again. "We are consenting adults. You can't stop us from—"

"She is not an adult of any kind. She is not even of legal age. For that alone, I can have you imprisoned." Chesnokov paused to let that sink in. "Do you care to continue this conversation?"

Finn couldn't see the other man, but the silence that ensued said enough.

"Natalia?" the younger man said at length, his voice shaky and broken.

In response, Natalia burst into tears. There was a soft moan from the man above; then he swore loudly and stomped back up the stairs and into the building, the door slamming shut behind him.

A few moments later, Finn heard the door to the Rolls shut. He experienced a moment of panic that his position would be revealed as they left the parking lot, but the driver swung them around the opposite direction. He doubted Chesnokov was looking back, but on the off chance Natalia glanced back for one last possible glimpse of her supposed true love, he remained crammed as far back in the corner as he could.

Once they'd left the parking lot, and he was as reasonably certain as he could be that the other guy wasn't going to come storming out, he quickly hustled around the corner of the building, only to find a silently laughing Felicity leaning against the cinder block, arms folded, waiting for him. "Well," she said, "I suppose that answers the question of why he was at Talbot & James at the crack of dawn this morning. That poor man is fortunate Grandpapa wasn't carrying a weapon."

"I think Chesnokov being Chesnokov is weapon enough."

Felicity fell into step beside him as they quickly made their way back toward where the cab was parked.

"You look awfully chipper for a woman who just lost her last solid lead," he said. "What possessed you to come after me anyway?"

"We didn't lose our last lead," she said.

He paused, and turned to her. "What do you mean?"

"I mean, I know where to look next. Or at least, who to look for. That's what I came to tell you."

"I know I told you if this didn't pan out that we'd hunt down Reese, but—"

"I found out Chesnokov wasn't our link. So I thought I'd better come get you out of here before you inadvertently did anything to put yourself in a difficult situation."

Finn held her gaze. "What are you telling me? How did you know about Chesnokov?"

There was a flicker of hesitation on her part; then she took a breath and said, "I received some intel of my own. I know John Reese is the man we need to find."

Finn took a moment to process what she was telling him. Both spoken and unspoken. "I'm guessing you don't mean that Rafe contacted Sean, and he told you—"

She shook her head. "No. My own intel." She paused, then said, "From my people."

"You have people."

She nodded, but held his gaze. "I have people."

"People you've had all along."

She nodded.

He shoved his hands in his pockets. "And you're telling me now, because . . . ?"

"Because I want us to go find the sapphire. Together."

A part of him was deeply relieved to know his instincts had been right all along. At least, he assumed her "people" were part of a legitimate setup. And yet, another part of him still felt a bit betrayed that she'd held back when he hadn't. Which made no sense, since he'd known all along she was hiding something, and it certainly hadn't slowed him down any.

"And before?" he asked.

"Before, I wanted us to find the sapphire. I just had no idea what we'd do with it when we did find it."

"But now you do."

She smiled, though it was a bit shaky. "I do."

Just then the white pickup truck came roaring out to the entrance of the parking lot, squealing wheels as it took a hard turn onto the street where they stood. Finn slipped his hands out of his pocket and took her elbow, pulling her toward him and away from the curb as the truck roared past. "No need to follow him, I'm assuming."

"I feel sorry for him," Felicity said. "He really seemed upset."

"I thought you said men like him depressed you."

She looked at him and shrugged. "The idea of it is depressing. He really seemed like he cared."

The truck rounded another corner and sped off. Finn looked back at Felicity. "So," he said. "Are you going to tell me? About you?"

"I've wanted to all along. I—I didn't have clearance for that kind of thing. It's never—been an issue before."

"And you do now? Have clearance, I mean?"

Her eyes twinkled, and that smile of hers, the one that got him every time, surfaced. "Not exactly. But I will. I hope."

"Felicity, if you can't—"

"What I can't do is wait any longer. I could have just told you I got the information on my own, made something up. But you've trusted me when you had no reason to. You've shared everything with me, made me a full partner in this, despite not knowing what we'd do with the sapphire when we got it back. You believed in me. And, all along, I believed in you, trusted you. I just—I didn't know if I could risk it. I would have if it was just me, but it's not just me I'm making decisions for."

And it hit Finn then, how truly cavalier he'd been in his own client's best interests. It was one thing to trust his gut instincts when he was the only one risking anything, but this time, he'd been risking someone's entire heritage. He ducked his chin, then looked at her. "You've actually handled this better than I have."

"What do you mean?" She looked worried.

He took her hand, and they crossed the street. "Let's talk

when we get back to the limo." He looked at her and tried to smile. "We do still have a limo?"

"Yes, but no cab. He wasn't interested in waiting around if I left, so I had Sean come around. He's right over there." She pointed, and Finn could just make out the front end of the limo in the rear parking lot across the street.

Still holding hands, they hurried across the street, and Sean pulled around to pick them up.

"Where to?" he asked.

Finn looked to Felicity, who turned to Sean. "Back to our hotel."

Sean just smiled patiently.

"Oh," she said, "that's right, you don't know where that is."

Finn gave him the name, but Sean waved a hand before he could give the address. "I know it," he said.

They both slid into the backseat and were on their way moments later.

Felicity didn't even bother with smoothing her skirt or her hair. She shifted to the edge of her seat, leaning toward him, her focus exclusively on him. "I'm sorry."

"I'm not sure you have anything to be sorry about," he said, and realized it was true. "You were already involved in this for your own reasons when I came along. You had no real reason to change that just because I decided we should be partners and wanted . . ." He trailed off, feeling like the idiot he'd apparently been. Not that his feelings were anything less than authentic. Now, or then. But he'd been wrong to force his viewpoint, his feelings, his need for more, on her. Especially in the middle of what, apparently, was every bit as much a job for her as it was for him. "I'm the one who owes you an apology."

"Finn—"

He lifted a hand. "Don't tell me anything that will breach trust with your—whoever it is. Not that I can't be trusted. You were right about that much. I would never do anything to intentionally thwart—"

"I know that," she broke in. "That's why I want to tell you. Should have told you."

He sighed, torn, because she was offering him everything he wanted. Or at least the first important step toward it. But, to do so, she had to violate other trusts, other agreements, and that wasn't fair. To them, or to her. "Just tell me what I need to know that will get us to the sapphire. I don't need to know the rest."

She stared at him, disbelief clear on her face. "You've wanted my trust, pushed me to open up, and now that I am—"

"I realize it was wrong to do that to you. It's not my business to know. When—" She started to speak, but he talked over her. "When it's all said and done, and you've cleared it on your end, then yes. I'll want to hear everything. If you still want to tell me."

"What does that mean?" she asked warily.

"It means, we need to find this sapphire and figure out how that will solve both of our problems. Then we'll work on sorting the rest out."

She stared at him for the longest moment, then rolled her eyes and flopped back in her seat and folded her arms across her chest. Only Felicity could make such a move look elegant and graceful. If he hadn't been so distracted by this latest turn of events, he'd have smiled.

"You're being incorrigible again," she said, "but in a way I find immensely unattractive."

"I'd like to think I'm recovering the integrity I should have had with you all along."

"You thought I was a jewel thief," she all but shouted. "With very good reason, I might add. Why on earth would you have thought you'd needed to have any integrity around me? I couldn't fathom why you'd trust me as far as you could throw me. I'd certainly given you absolutely no reason to, despite your being very open and up front with me." She eyed him, quite put out. "Why did you? Trust me, I mean. You're not a foolish man given to foolish behavior. What did you know?"

"Not nearly enough to jeopardize what I did."

Her face fell then, and he immediately reached across the space between them and took her hands in his. "I didn't mean that as a reflection on you. Only on me. I won't say I don't know what got into me, I do. You got into me. You did from that first night we met at the museum gala. But I shouldn't have let that cloud my better judgment. Not because I was wrong about you. But because I put someone else's future at risk."

"You are being so perverse. I thought you'd be happy that I was bringing you in."

"I am," he vowed. "But, right now, I can't let you knowingly risk what I foolishly risked. Even though we know we can trust each other, we have to handle this as professionals first. That's why we're here in the first place, and what the people who sent us here expect of us. Do you understand?"

"I do." She slid her hands free. "I just don't think you realize what you're asking."

"Meaning?"

"I work solo. My superiors expect me to use whatever resources I need to in order to complete the job, but bringing someone else in, sharing my intel in any fashion, that crosses the line."

"So, what are you saying?"

"I'm saying that if you truly want to put job before us, with all our professional integrity intact, then this is where we part ways. I go after the sapphire with my own resources, and you continue on with yours. Let the better professional win."

The car had pulled into the hotel's driveway, and Felicity popped open her door and exited before Finn could reply. He was out his door a second later. "Wait," he called out, but she was already stalking through the entrance to the lobby. "Sean, grab something to eat, but I'd like you to stay on call."

"I'm here as long as you need me."

Finn rounded the front of the car, and two bellmen looked as though they might want to interfere on her behalf, but Finn skirted them both and caught up to her by the elevator. "Now, wait a minute, will you?"

The doors slid open, and she stepped coolly inside, folding her arms and looking straight ahead.

"Felicity, I think this is taking things to the extreme, don't you?"

The doors slid open on their floor, and she exited smoothly and swiftly, marching down the hallway to their door, not waiting for him before going inside. He had to catch the door from closing in his face.

"We've worked together up to this point, why—"

She rounded on him. "Why? Because you have some misguided notion that working together has somehow weakened our integrity in getting the job done. Did we handle everything perfectly? No. But then, no job goes perfectly, does it? You say you want to do what is right for our clients first. I think we were on our way to doing that, and, if you recall, I said I had a plan to make it work for us both, in the end. But no. Only now you say you want us to still be a team. Well, my apologies if I don't understand. We're either a team all the way, or we work solo. I don't see how you can have one, but not the other." She got right up in his face. "You want to work with me? You want to be part of my personal life? Then you get all of me, all the time. All or nothing, Finn. I know it took me a while to see what I was risking losing. And it wasn't the sapphire. So, I'm all in. What about you?"

Finn just stood there, absorbing the fiery volcano that was Felicity Jane Trent in full tilt, explosive action. It was something to witness. "Are you armed?"

His question caught her off guard if the sudden confused look on her face was any indication. "When necessary."

"Now?"

She frowned. "No, not now. Why?"

"Because I don't want to get shot when I tell you that you're really amazing all the time, but when you get angry, really angry, you put the royal in royally pissed in a way that is absolutely breathtaking."

Her eyes narrowed. "There are other ways to maim a man, you know."

But, angry as she was, she was still fighting a smile, which probably only served to piss her off more. It would have if it were him. She'd just laid her heart bare before him, and he'd teased her in response. But it was a lot to absorb, she was a lot to absorb, and so he'd taken a sidestep to give himself a moment to truly take in what she was offering. Because it was everything he wanted . . . and he wanted a lot. He took a cautious step closer. "I'm glad you're on my side."

"Says who?"

"But mostly," he said quietly, reaching out to brush a finger along her cheek. "Mostly, I'm glad you care enough to get that angry at me."

"You idiot, of course I care! I—"

The rest of whatever she was going to say was cut off when he tugged her into his arms and kissed her silent. He was gratified that it took less than a second for her to respond and kiss him back. It took both of them a while longer still to come up for air. "I'm not sure," he said, panting a little, "but given our track record, makeup sex might be lethal."

"We're not making up," she murmured against his lips. "I'm still royally pissed." But she wove her fingers into his hair and tilted his head so she could gain greater access to his mouth.

He held her tightly and let her have her way with him. He had halfway decided to scoop her up and head to the bedroom, when she broke the kiss and pulled back. Not from his arms, but enough to look at him. "You make me insanely crazy, you realize that. It's all your fault I'm a screaming shrew."

"Join the club."

She grew serious. "What are we doing, Finn?"

"We're doing what comes next. Whatever that is. Nothing else has gone along any kind of normal path, and I'm certain whatever happens next won't either. Maybe we should just adopt a wait-and-see attitude and roll with it."

"Roll with it, hm?"

"Roll with it. I do know what I'd like for us to be doing."

Rather than roll her eyes, she actually tugged his hips closer and said, "Me, too. It beats the bloody hell out of figuring out how to work with each other."

"I think we work together just like we do everything else together. Passionately, fully, and quite amazingly well. I don't want to lose you as a partner, in any sense, I just—" He broke off, and took a moment, pushing the wild, windblown curls from her face and tucking them behind her ear. "I want to do what's right for my client. I want to do what's right for you. I don't usually put what I want ahead of what others need. And when I realized I'd done just that, I—maybe I went a bit overboard in the opposite direction, but I don't want to work solo. Not this time. Not any time I don't have to."

"So, you're happy then. That I confided in you? Because, with all that back in the car, I wasn't sure."

He spun her around and backed her up against the door, making her squeal in surprise. "I'm ecstatic about that. It's everything I want. You're everything I want. And I want everything with you, from you."

"Well, then?"

"We have other obligations. And I don't want you putting something else at risk, or someone else, because I'm pressing you to—"

She laid a finger across his lips. "I can handle my job, thanks." Her smile was a bit saucy. "You, I'm not so sure about. But I'm willing to try."

He nipped the ends of her fingers. "I just don't want to put you in a tough spot. We can resolve this case. And I'll still be there to deal with when it's done. That's all I was trying to say.

I wanted to go back to putting the job we came to do first, as it should be, then us. But I didn't mean we had to go back to working alone." He smiled, and kissed her fingertips. "In fact, I think we work better as a team. Which, if you think about it, is an advantage to the people we work for."

"That was exactly the argument I intended to make."

He pulled her closer and tilted her face up to his. "So, are we all done fighting now?"

"If I say yes, is makeup sex out of the question?"

He smiled. "Well, given your intel, how critical is it that we leave the room in the next, oh, fifteen or twenty minutes?"

"Actually," she said, weaving her fingers through his hair and pulling his head down even closer. "We have to wait for another report to come in, so we might actually have a few hours."

"Hours," he said, savoring the very idea.

"I know. Being professionals first and all, whatever will we do with all that down time?"

He pulled her legs up around his hips and walked them both into the bedroom. "Strategize." He dropped her onto the bed, and she pulled him down with her.

"Well, you are a master . . . strategist." She tucked her feet around his ankles and wriggled beneath him.

"I love it when you call me master."

Her eyes widened at that, but she was laughing as she used their locked ankles as leverage to roll him to his back. "Honestly," she said, pushing their joined hands up over his head, bringing her face close to his in the process.

"Incorrigible," he said. "I know."

"We'll see who's the inveterate one . . ." She grinned quite wickedly and nipped his bottom lip. "And who's calling who master."

He rolled her to her back, pinning her tightly to the bed, hands joined, pressed next to her head. "I have no problem letting you boss me around. Especially here." He leaned down and took her bottom lip into his mouth and suckled it. "But I rather thought you liked it when I got a little . . . What would you call it? Neanderthal?"

He pushed his hips into hers and dipped his tongue into her mouth, once, then again, then finally took her in a kiss so deep, and so intense, they were both moaning a little bit when he finally lifted his head.

"Yeah, about that," she said, a little short of breath. "Don't stop."

He grinned, and said, "Yes, master," and gave her exactly what they both wanted.

Chapter 20

Felicity clutched at the hand rail in the shower as Finn soaped her breasts. She'd given up questioning why it was like this with them. Insatiable didn't begin to cover it. They'd finally crawled from bed twenty minutes ago, after playing "master strategist" for a good hour and a half. They were supposed to be showering off and cleaning up in anticipation of her report coming through any minute now . . . but, at the moment, he was pushing her right up to the edge. Again.

"I thought it was . . . your turn," she gasped, her thighs quivering as he slid his hands down her torso and over her hips, while sliding himself down between her legs.

"Lost track," he said, then took the showerhead from her and rinsed off the suds as he let the warm water pulse directly over her still pulsating, sensitive parts.

She started to slide down the wall, but he replaced the gentle spray of the water with the even gentler touch of his tongue, and she immediately peaked. She clutched at his head, trying to keep her balance as the waves rolled through her again. "Illegal. Must be," she gasped, clutching at his shoulders, shaking and shuddering, as he kissed her thighs before finally standing and gathering her into his arms.

"I don't think there's a climax police," he said, chuckling. He sat down on the built-in corner seat and pulled her into his lap.

Heart still pounding, she tucked her head on his shoulder and blew out a long, shaky breath. "Thank goodness for that." She smiled against his warm, slippery skin. "I'd be taken into custody for sure."

Finn tipped her chin up and kissed her. But this time it wasn't meant to incite. Instead, it was slow, tender, the kind of kiss that made her want to curl up with him and fall asleep in his arms.

She wondered if they'd ever get that chance, but forcibly pushed that thought away. There was so much to do, so much yet to sort out, before the reality of what they wanted could even be discussed. So she'd decided to enjoy the moment rather than waste a single one worrying about future moments.

She was just about to suggest a short, restorative nap, when her phone buzzed from its spot by the sink. "I told you we should have left it by the bed," she groused, but she was already climbing off of him and reaching to turn the showerheads off. "I know, I know," she went on, before he could remind her. "We're professionals. Job first."

Finn wrapped a towel around her from behind and pulled her back against him, nipping the side of her neck. "I'm pretty sure what we were just doing had nothing to do with the job."

"True, but—" The phone buzzed again. "Oh, sod it."

Finn laughed at her less than ladylike epithet, so she whipped a towel at him, which he neatly caught, then pulled her against him again.

"I'm sensing a pattern of behavior here," she said, pushing him away, when what she really wanted was exactly the opposite.

"And this is a problem, because . . . ?"

"Not a problem. I'm a creature of habit, after all."

He snaked her towel off and snapped it at her. "I pretty much like all the habits of yours I've discovered so far." He tucked his towel around his hips and pulled a fresh one off the rack and stepped up behind her to gently rub her hair.

"Stick around, I'm sure there are a few that will drive you mad."

He pushed her head to one side and dropped a warm, damp kiss on her neck. "Deal."

Her phone went off a third time, and she snatched it up.

Finn put his hand on her wrist before she could flip it open. "Promise me you'll handle this in whatever way works best for you. We'll get the sapphire, one way or the other, so if me being on a need-to-know basis is what makes life easier for you in the long haul, then . . ." He raised an eyebrow until she nodded her understanding. "Good. I need to check in with Rafe anyway. So, I'll give you your privacy."

He went to step out of the room, but she halted him this time. "Do your partners know? About me, I mean?"

"Not yet, no."

She wasn't sure why it mattered, or why she'd even asked. But now that she had, she realized she wasn't the only one who had things to sort through with coworkers or superiors. "Was it because you thought I—were you embarrassed to tell them?"

"No. It's because you and I had more to talk about first. And they didn't 'need to know' until that happened."

She thought about that, and nodded. "Okay."

"Okay," he said, then smiled and closed the door between them.

She appreciated that he was always direct with her, and vowed to be the same with him. It was new, being responsible to someone like that, but she wanted the same from him and found it wasn't so hard to do when the rewards were so great. He was doing everything he could to make this easier on her, like the space he was giving her, and that it mattered to him that things went well for her professionally beyond just recovering the stone. She wanted to do the same for him, with his partners, but wasn't sure where to even begin.

She picked up her phone and flipped it open. For the first time, she wasn't as anxious to dive headlong into whatever they threw her way next. She looked toward the closed door between her and Finn and realized it was because she finally had something more exciting to dive headlong into.

Smiling, she looked back at the screen and punched in the descramble code. Her smile faded as she read the very sparse report. She'd responded to their last message with a number of what she considered to be pertinent questions. Namely, when they said it was time to bring John *Home*—meaning MI-8 headquarters in London—she could only take that to mean that it wasn't just her home base, but possibly his. Only she couldn't see how that could be. Because that would mean they'd put two agents on the same mission without telling them, and for what purpose? And what was John's mission? He'd tried to sell the stone to Andreev, while she was supposed to bring it back with her.

And had they answered her vital questions? No. All she'd gotten was a list of places where it was anticipated he might show up. She'd asked them about Julia, if they had any intel on her, or hell, if she was working with them, too. She'd gotten no response back on that. Sometimes the "need-to-know" predicate was frustrating as all hell.

But there was nothing she could do for that now. Asking again wouldn't net her any additional info. And given what she had to tell them about Finn at some point, annoying them now would not be a grand scheme.

She looked over the list. The next time there appeared to be a possible rendezvous point was over dinner this evening. It was almost impossible to believe that it was just twenty-four hours ago that she and Finn had crashed John's dinner with Andreev. That felt almost a lifetime ago now. And given the lifetime she was now contemplating, perhaps, in some ways, it had been.

She pulled a comb through her hair and brushed her teeth, but gave up on the rest. Instead, she put on one of the hotel robes and headed back into their bedroom to find Finn. How odd it was, really, already so used to having him around, that she missed him when they were apart, even for a short time. She wanted to discuss the latest information with him, bounce ideas off of him, and, yes, just be in his personal space for as long as she could manage. She'd berate herself for being so silly and foolish, except she felt pretty damn good at the moment. So she went with that, and, smiling, went to find him.

But the bedroom was empty, so she walked into the main room. Also empty. She experienced a moment of panic, before reminding herself that Finn was hardly the love-'em-and-leave-'em sort, much less the kind of man who'd play her into submission, then take off on his own after their quarry. He might have been willing to do that before—they both would have— when they'd been professional adversaries, but no way would he do that to her now. She knew that, didn't doubt that. Which left her to sort out where he would have gone without telling her.

She looked around for a note of some kind, even went back into the bedroom to look there. No note or message. But his towel was on the back of the bedroom chair, and a quick look inside the closet showed he'd dressed in fresh clothes. She went to the hallway door and looked out, thinking maybe he went for ice, or to get something off the maid's cart, but no sign of him there, either. And when she walked back into the main room, the ice bucket was where he'd left it after filling it earlier. So, if he hadn't left on his own . . .

Her heart picked up its pace again, but for entirely different reasons, when the sound of a sliding door behind her made her jump and spin around, wishing she'd dressed first so she could better handle the intruder.

Finn stopped just inside the balcony door and smiled at her assumed karate pose. "You're probably a black belt, but, I must say, you look a lot cuter in the white terry cloth one, Grasshopper."

She all but slumped to the floor in relief. "Where the hell

were you? I mean, never mind, I didn't know there was a balcony, but for the love of all that is holy, next time—"

He grabbed the loose ends of her robe and tugged her to him. "Miss me?"

"Worse." She smacked his chest with her open palm. "I was worried. Don't do that to me."

"You didn't think I'd taken off on you?"

"No. I knew you wouldn't. Which left you leaving under duress."

He covered her hand with his own, trapping it there. "Don't take this the wrong way," he said, turning her hand over and pulling it to his mouth.

"If you say one word about my being cute or royal—"

"Actually," he said, dropping the sweetest of kisses into the center of her palm—he was really disarming when he did that—"I was going to say that while I don't ever want to worry you, because I'm learning I don't like it a whole lot either, it's kind of nice knowing you would."

She opened her mouth, all prepared to argue, then closed it again as his words sank in. "Oh. Well." She curled her fingers into her freshly kissed palm and slipped it into her robe pocket. "I do. Worry. And, you're right, it's not a lot of fun."

He used the tail of her terry cloth belt to swat her across the butt. "But we have plenty of that, so it sort of balances out." Then he slowly reeled her back to him. "And, to be honest, like it or not, I'm okay with having someone out there who worries about me. Puts things in a whole new perspective."

"Yes," she agreed. "Yes, it does."

"So, what's our next move?"

"Dinner, with John."

He raised an eyebrow, but only said, "Same move, new coast."

"Apparently."

"When?" he asked.

And, once again, she was struck with gratitude for how he

was handling this. He didn't argue or ask a million questions
she couldn't respond to; he just nodded and went from there.
Perversely, it made her want to share everything with him all
the more. He had a cool-headed way of sorting things out and
coming up with viewpoints and possibilities she didn't always
see or think about. She was still very confused about John's
role in all this and would feel a hell of a lot better if she had a
better handle on it before she went barging in again. Too many
things weren't adding up, and most of them had to do with her
direct chain of command.

"Felicity?"

She jerked her gaze to his and realized he was still waiting
on an answer. She was waiting on a ton of them. "Six, but we
need to get there first."

"Why is that?"

"I'm not exactly certain what's going on. I'll feel better if I
see him come in, gauge his demeanor. See if he's with someone,
before he sees us." Another thought occurred to her, making
her pause.

"What?"

She looked at him, worried all over again. "It occurs to me
that I shouldn't take for granted that I'll be the one breaking
news of our liaison to my superiors."

He started to ask, but then paused as the light of understanding dawned. "You mean Reese would inform them?"

"He knows I'm not merely Felicity Jane Trent, Foundation
director and the Trent ancestral heiress. He knows. Other than
you, he's the only one who has ever put those two things together."

"But how would he tell your superiors, unless—" Now he
broke off. "Sorry, I'm venturing into territory—"

"Bollocks to that," she said abruptly. "I need help." She
looked at him. "I need your help. Right now, you're the only
one I know I can trust. Things aren't adding up. Important
things. And it seems foolish for me to try and figure them out

myself, when I have another clever mind sitting right next to me." She held his gaze. "I think the bigger risk now is that I make the wrong move because I didn't use my resources wisely. And, if my chain of command doesn't like it, then they can find themselves another thrill-seeking, philanthropic heiress to do their dirty work."

"I know I should be arguing, given our recently struck agreement, but you're making very good sense." He grinned. "Besides which, it's killing me, you know."

She smiled then, despite the nerves currently twisting her insides into knots. "Is it now? Well then, there should be some way we both benefit from that."

"The goal is to get the sapphire back. And not put you at risk. Beyond that, I'm game for what you think will work best. You know more about the playing field at the moment than I do."

"I'm afraid I'm already at risk. In fact, I'm not at all certain I'm not being intentionally used as a pawn. And while I understand that that is generally my role on this particular chess board, I can't say in this instance I like it overly much. Especially when I fear our Mr. Reese is something of a rook. Appearing to move to the side, when, in fact, he's still making forward progress."

"Where does that leave you?"

"Somewhat out in the cold, I believe."

Finn took her hand and walked over to the settee, where they both sat and turned to face each other, knee to knee. "Okay. So tell me what you need to, so that I can help figure this out. I can put Rafe on it, Mac, too, if you'd like. They are family to me, and you can trust them the same as me. I won't have to tell them anything that jeopardizes you. They don't even know who you are. Just what to dig for, where to go, or who to look at."

"I'd like to say no, and not drag anyone else into what might potentially be a . . . difficult situation. You, included."

"I'm not going anywhere." He smiled. "And difficult situations are what we excel in."

"Which is exactly why I'm going to do the wisest thing and pool resources. I don't know what the fallout will be, but it's a risk I'd take regardless of our personal situation. You do believe that."

"I don't think I've ever seen you so spooked. So yes, I do believe you."

"Okay, then." She took his hands in hers. The steadying strength she found there made it easier to do what she'd never done before. "I work for M—"

"I'm still okay with need-to—"

She held his gaze intently. "This is my decision. What *I* think is best. And what I think is best is that you know. If it turns out I'm wrong, then I take the consequences. It's not your choice to make."

He nodded, and she squeezed his hands.

"Are you sure, though, that you're willing to be privy to what I'm about to tell you? I know you want to help, but I honestly have no idea what I've gotten myself involved in here. It could be that my making this decision will put you at risk in some way I can't foresee, and—"

"Felicity."

Her lips quirked. "You're quite patient with me, aren't you?"

Finn barked a laugh at that. "I'm certainly glad you see it that way. I feel like I've pushed you about as hard as a person can, and rushed you the whole way."

"So," she said, quite serious now. "You're certain? And you might be speaking for your friends as well, so—"

"I'm certain. They'd respond the same in this kind of situation. Have, actually. And I'd do the same for them."

"Okay." She took another steadying breath, and this time he squeezed her hands. She looked into his eyes and found exactly what she needed there. And then, it was suddenly quite easy. "I work for a division of our country's national security department known as MI-8."

Finn grinned. "So, you are Jane Bond."

She knocked his knees with their joined hands. "Very amusing."

"Quite, and I rather like it. Go on."

"Your accent is truly atrocious, you know." He nodded, and she fought a smile. "This is quite serious business."

"I know. But it's our business, and, as such, considering our past exploits together, not so shocking as all that. Would you rather I gasp and splutter?"

"*Our* business?" she asked. "You don't mean to say that you also work for your government, do you?"

"No. I've already done my time with them. My partners and I operate entirely privately, getting things done that our system, wonderful though it is, sometimes can't. But you know the history of that. How did you get started? Did they recruit you?"

"In a manner of speaking, yes," she said. "I was at a royal function in Copenhagen, doing Foundation work, and a man pulled me aside and asked if I'd be willing to help him out in the name of the Queen and national security."

Finn grinned. "And you believed him?"

"I certainly believed the ID. And the gun he was carrying was quite persuasive as well." She took some pleasure in the way his face blanched a little at that. "You know, you're right. It's not fun, but it's quite nice knowing that someone cares enough to worry."

"Is lethal force often required in the types of jobs you do for them?"

"Rare to never. I'm employed more for my . . . diplomatic skills."

"So, you helped, and I'm guessing someone was impressed and asked if you'd be willing to continue on a more routine basis?"

"I was invited to help them from time to time first, and then, yes, we made it a more formal agreement."

"How often—" He stopped, lifted his hand. "Never mind."

"Not, too," she answered anyway. "In fact, it's been very occasional of late."

"How do you square your time spent helping your country with your other duties?"

"I manage. It's not so frequent that anyone gets suspicious when I take a little trip. They usually think I'm shopping, or vetting potential future Foundation beneficiaries. It's really not as hard as all that. Outside of Britain, I'm not well known, except in certain circles. But I do have contacts, and experience that allows me to move pretty freely in those circles."

"What's different this time? Have you ever been this confused by your directives?"

"I haven't always understood why I was being asked to accomplish certain goals, and, seeing as I was never asked to do anything I had a personal or moral issue with, I don't know that I cared, as long as it helped them get the job done. As you said, the thrill of it can be quite intoxicating, and a bit addictive. Which, given how staid and proper my regular life is, has been quite something for me. But it's also been a personal thing with me, something I can do that has nothing to do with commitments that were preordained by a fluke of birth."

Finn smiled. "I understand that better than you could possibly know."

"I'd like to hear more about that, you know. Fair being fair and all."

"I promise to bore you with my family history at great length if you really want to know, but right now, you need to tell me what's gone wrong with this mission."

"I'll hold you to that, don't think I won't. But yes, things are getting rather critical, it seems, and I can't figure out what's really going on here."

"Your job was to get the sapphire, bring it back, right?"

"Correct."

"And now you think Reese works for them, too. Except he was trying to sell the piece to Chesnokov's agent."

"Right. Here's the rest. The reason they want the sapphire is because they believe one of their own agents—" She stopped, her mouth dropping open. "Oh, my Lord. It's John! John is the one they suspect of treason."

'Treason?" Finn said, looking truly shocked. "How does a sapphire necklace, even one as old as this, have anything to do with jeopardizing your country's security?"

"I don't know. In fact, it's amazing to me that I know anything beyond just retrieving the piece. But I got information from a different handler this time, and he told me that it was a matter of utmost security, that they're trying to nail down evidence against one of their own, for using secure information for personal gain. Apparently the sapphire plays a dual role, in that it would be evidence against the agent, as well as whatever it is that makes it a matter of national concern in the first place."

Finn was silent for a moment. "So, Reese selling the stone would play along with that supposition, that he's an agent, and that he's on the take. I just can't figure out what the stone would have to do with national security. Why would your country have been researching it, or tracking it, in the first place?"

"I don't know. I know prior to going on the market, it was owned by a Greek man—"

"Capellas," Finn supplied. "Alexander Capellas."

"He's not your client, is he?" Felicity asked.

"No. No, my client is a second generation American, Theodore Roussos. The stone rightfully belongs to his family and can be traced back to the Ottoman occupation. He's the final descendant. It's been the center of a feud between his family and the Capellas that dates back well over a century and was, at one point, used to destroy Theo's family's honor and, because of that, their financial security."

"So, he wants it back to sell it to pay off family debt?"

Finn shook his head. "No, he just wants to clear his family's name. He plans to donate it to the Met. Where it will be on display forever, secure, and proving the provenance was his line, not the Capellas."

"Sounds like it had quite the tempestuous history."

"It did. Still does, apparently. If it's okay with you, I'll put Rafe on looking at a connection between Capellas and your government, see what we can make pop."

"I don't know that it's important at this point. He doesn't have it any longer."

"But your country wants it back. If they can claim treason for stealing it, then we should know exactly what it is we're dealing with. And it matters to my client, as well. He's been fighting Capellas in court most of his adult life, trying to get the stone back. I don't think he'd have much luck against your entire government if they think it's a matter of national security."

"How did your client know the stone was surfacing on the market?"

"He's known all along who had it, but, as an American citizen, his success in pressing Capellas, who is a Greek citizen, to prove provenance has been limited. Capellas sent notice recently, in response to another attempt by Theo to bring him to court, that he was no longer in possession of the piece."

"Did Theo offer to buy it?"

"He's in no position to do that financially. And, for him, it's about honor. He shouldn't have to buy what is rightfully his. It's as much about restoring the family name as anything, and, even if he could, simply buying it back wouldn't do that."

"If the piece is at the center of a centuries long family feud, then what would provoke Capellas to get rid of it? Sounds like he was doing everything he could to hang on to it."

"That's the part we don't know. When he got the notice, Theo was shocked. Capellas would give him no further information, other than that he'd sold it to a middleman who was going to sell it on the open market."

"And that's when you came into play."

"Well, the stone is rightfully, legally, his. Whatever leverage he had, though, was against the Capellas. Trying to go after the new owner would likely get him nowhere, and that was only if he knew who the owner was. It's an ancient artifact, and as such, priceless. Whoever could afford to buy it would likely be in a good position to protect it, financially and in every other way." He paused. "Of course, your government could bring more pressure to bear, so that's a possible avenue, if we knew why they wanted it. But I would imagine the new buyer would be made aware of this, and it will disappear from sight. Who knows when or if it will ever surface again. As it is, Theo's legal bills are already staggering from the protracted battles he's waged thus far."

"So, I take it you were the wiser investment."

"We don't charge people for what we do."

"Right. Your own Foundation, of sorts."

"Yes, but privately controlled. We choose who we want to help. We're not a charity. It's more about—"

"Righting wrongs that would otherwise go unfixed. I remember. Lucky he found you."

"His lawyer found me. I . . . still keep in touch with some of my former colleagues and adversaries."

"Ah. They contact you with their lost causes."

"Sometimes. So, what else do you know about it? Anything?"

"Well, now I know that—or strongly suspect—John is the agent they're after. It makes sense. And I spoiled his plan to sell it, initially anyway, but also managed to tip him off to the fact that I'm more than I appear to be."

"Do you think he knows you work for the same agency?"

"I have no idea. I certainly had no idea he might work for MI-8. He might think just as you did, that I'm in it for personal gain."

"What if the agent sold it to Reese? Or is just using him as middleman?"

"Could be," she said, "but it makes sense that he might be working with them. It would explain why he's ended up in situations where he's walking a fine line with the blackmarket trade, and how he knows about so many items newly on the market. I'm not understanding why he'd want to pull a double cross, though. Especially if the item is critical to some other case."

"Maybe he doesn't agree with whatever it is they're trying to do with it, so he's getting rid of it so it can't be used."

"Possible." Felicity shrugged. "I honestly have no idea. I just think that if it was still just about the sapphire, they'd keep me focused on that. But they said to 'bring him Home.' Capital H. That means home base. No one goes there who isn't already cleared to go there. So, I can only assume that was their way of letting me know that he's one of us."

"Wait a minute. Does that mean that Reese, himself, is now the proof? The evidence?"

"I don't get your meaning."

"I mean that you're assuming, since they want him back, he still has the sapphire, correct? And bringing him back with it will prove what needs proving."

"I—yes. I guess. Why, what do you think?"

"I think maybe they have some kind of documentation proving he tried to sell it, or that he has already sold it, and that's all they needed. You're just bringing him back to answer to the charges."

Felicity sat back and let that possibility play out. "Maybe, but then they lose the sapphire, and whatever that jeopardizes is jeopardized. Unless they know, somehow, that it's already sold and out of their hands and reach." She sat up. "That could be the Russian connection. If Chesnokov did end up with it, then maybe it's out of their reach. And now they want Reese back to work on him about the details, maybe try and get it back. Or at least prosecute him."

"Possible, even probable." Finn sat forward. "There is one other thing."

Felicity looked at him.

"Was it a regular part of your job to bring, let's say, undesirables, back to the homeland?"

"No, never. Why?"

"How do your superiors assume you're going to persuade Reese to come back with you?"

"I don't know. I hadn't made the full connection until just now, but I'm not certain they realize that he knows I'm not the same Felicity Jane Trent the rest of the world knows. Maybe they think he'll be unsuspecting until we return home. They know we've done Foundation business in the past and that we are acquaintances."

"You're sure they mean to bring him to MI-8 and not just home to the UK? Because, strolling into headquarters would certainly tip him off."

Felicity smiled a little at that. "Maybe they clued me in, so I'd understand why I was bringing him back, for my own safety."

"No other information?"

She shook her head. "I responded to that message with questions about the sapphire, about Julia, about Chesnokov, Andreev—"

"Me?"

"No," she said. "I had no reason to put you on their radar."

Finn nodded. "What did you get back?"

"Frustratingly little. They sent a list of possible locations for an interception with John."

"Nothing on Julia? On anything else?"

"No. Which, I suppose isn't surprising. But, again, they aren't privy to all that has transpired, either."

"Maybe you should tell them."

She looked at him as if he were daft.

"No, I'm serious. Tell them that your cover is blown, at least in part, with Reese, and, given that, how do they want you to proceed? What are they going to do if you admit a failure, or partial failure, of mission?"

"I don't know. Not that I haven't been unsuccessful in the past—you know that—but I've never given myself away. Perhaps they'd terminate their need for me, assuming I'm too big a risk."

"Is that why you haven't told them?"

"I didn't know there was something to tell until the transmission this morning. Yes, I would have debriefed them in regards to John Reese once the mission was over and completed. I wasn't honestly worried about that. But that was before I knew John, himself, was central to the case, and a possible agent, as well. I was more worried about telling them about my partnership with you." She rubbed her arms. "And add to all that the fact that John came and found us here, and asked us to track the stone. Why? He didn't want it back, but didn't want Julia to have it."

"Or, maybe, it was Julia's buyer he didn't want to have it."

"But if I had it, and Reese is who I think he is, it would have damned him for me to take it back."

"Which is why I still think it's possible he doesn't know who you work for, any more than you did with him. Maybe, in contrast to Julia, you seemed safe. Or a nonthreat, at least."

Felicity sighed. "I don't know what to think."

"Well, it would seem that finding Reese tops the To Do list. Even if we don't choose to make direct contact until we have a better idea about what's going on, locating him and watching his actions would be a good place to start."

She leaned closer, resting her hands on his knees. He immediately covered them with his hands, and she took strength in that, no longer even trying to pretend she didn't want or need it. "What about the sapphire? What if he doesn't have it? If he's my target now, then maybe it's best I track him, and you go after the stone."

"It could still be one and the same. I don't have any other

leads. Chesnokov didn't pan out, there is still no sign of Julia, and given this latest information, we don't know who might have the sapphire."

"Maybe that's still your best bet. To work that angle and track her down while I track Reese." When he hesitated, she said, "Job first, remember? You still owe Theo his family name back. You can't give up. We don't know for sure it's out of reach."

"How were you going to square that, anyway? If we both found the sapphire?"

"My hope was, with your client's documentation, that we could strike a deal whereby my country kept the stone as evidence in whatever case they were building, until it was no longer needed, then agreed to turn it over to your client. It might be a long while before he got it back, but he'd be guaranteed its safe return."

Finn thought about it, then nodded. "Sound plan."

"Only now, as you say, maybe they just want John. Which has the benefit of leaving the sapphire free and clear for you."

"If I can find it."

"I'm sorry," she said. "I didn't mean to stall your search. If I'd had any thought that the transmission meant anything other than Reese had the sapphire, I'd have told you straightaway. You've already wasted enough time with me. Maybe you should see if Rafe or Mac has found anything promising. At the very least, we—or you—should track down Julia Forsythe."

"She might provide you with some necessary information as well," Finn said. "It would be interesting to know what she knows about John Reese. Maybe her taking off didn't have anything to do with the stone. Maybe she found out something about him that sent her running."

"Like he's a double agent for the British government." Felicity chewed on her bottom lip. "That would do it for most women."

"We still don't know that he doesn't have it. Maybe they do intend for you to bring back both." Just then Finn's phone buzzed. He clicked on the screen, and a second later a broad grin crossed his face. "Well, it's about time."

"For?"

"For our lucky break."

"I thought we had that with the Chesnokov info."

"Except it didn't pan out. I think this one will deliver." He turned the screen around so she could read the message.

She gasped. "Your lovely partners have tracked down Julia."

"Seems they have." He chuckled as he read the rest of the note. "Yeah, amazing detective work on their part. They called the gallery after it opened, and she answered the phone."

Felicity gaped. "She's at the gallery? Where the hell has she been all night, then?"

Finn shrugged. "Don't know. She wasn't home, or at her shipping dock, and we know she wasn't at the fire. The reports Rafe had this morning said no contact had been made, so she wasn't answering her cell."

"Kind of odd, but maybe not. Maybe we worried for no reason."

"Or maybe Reese is full of shit and Julia was never in it at all."

"Guess we should ring her up and ask a few questions ourselves."

She glanced up at him when he didn't respond right away. "That's a rather devilish look you're sporting. What plot are you hatching now?"

"Well, I was just thinking that if Reese was put out by our appearance at his dinner meeting with Andreev in New York, imagine how he'll feel if we show up tonight, with a special guest in tow."

"You don't mean . . ."

"Oh, yes, I do mean. What say we get dressed and go round

up one Miss Julia Forsythe on our way to dinner? We can catch up on the ride over."

"But how will we get her to agree to such a thing?"

"Oh, I'm sure we'll think of something." He tugged her close and gave her a resounding kiss. "That's what great partners do."

Chapter 21

Finn stood, and pulled Felicity to her feet as she stifled a big yawn. "We've got a few hours; why don't we get a little rest before we head out."

She eyed him warily.

"I do mean rest. We're running on fumes at this point, and I'd like us to be a little fresher before we tackle this evening's events."

"What about Julia?"

"I'll put Sean on her location. If she leaves, he'll let us know."

Felicity looked as if she was going to argue, but her rebuttal was cut off by another yawn. She smiled around it. "I guess you win."

He made a quick call to Sean, then tugged her gently to his side and put his arm around her shoulder as they walked back into the bedroom. "Sleeping together. I don't think we've ever actually done that."

She laughed. "Do you hog the covers?"

"I have no idea. But if you stay close enough to me, it won't matter."

"Good plan," she said, and reached up to kiss him.

He marveled at how easy and natural it was between them, when, just as recently as on the plane ride out, she'd been awkward and unsure. It was probably, he realized now, because of the position he'd unwittingly put her in, rather than because she didn't know how to relax with him.

"Rest time, no working," she said.

"What?"

"Your mind drifts and you get that unfocused look on your face. It means you're working."

They quickly undressed and slid beneath the covers. He immediately pulled her to his side, and she moved willingly into his arms. "Actually, I was thinking about you," he said.

"Oh?" she murmured, yawning again as she snuggled more closely and pulled the covers up higher.

"I was thinking about this," he said, liking how her head felt tucked in the crook of his arm, and the weight of her leg draped across his.

"This?" she said, already drifting.

He scooted down and wrapped her more fully in his arms, his eyes drifting shut as he buried his nose in her sweet-smelling hair. "Mm hmm. This."

The next thing he knew the alarm was rudely going off, and three hours had gone by in a blink. He reached over and smacked the alarm off. It took Felicity a bit longer to rouse herself. So he used the time to watch her, and think about the dramatic turn his life had taken since he'd left Virginia a few weeks ago to start tracking the stone. If he was honest, the dramatic turn had really happened several years ago in Bogota. It had just taken them this long to finally do something about it.

"Caffeine," she grumbled, her face still plastered against his chest.

"Hmm," he said, grinning, "not a morning person."

"And you're insufferably chipper," she retorted, finally lifting her head. "And it better not be morning."

Finn pushed the mass of curls off her face, then leaned down to kiss the tip of her nose. "Tea?"

"Get me some espresso, and I'm yours."

"Had I only known it was so simple."

She smiled, still drowsy, with a crease mark on her face and a flushed pink in her cheeks. "Oh, you've spoiled me with the rest, so don't think you're getting away from that."

"I wouldn't dream of it."

He started to roll her to her back, but she anticipated the move and slithered off the bed before he could catch her.

"We need to be perky and on our game," she said, standing there, looking anything but. "That takes me some time to achieve."

"So I gather."

She grabbed a pillow and tossed it at him, then retreated into the bathroom.

He caught it against his chest and hugged it. "Nice bum you have there, Ms. Trent," he called after her.

She grumbled something in return. Then he heard the shower come on. He thought about joining her. His body was well past that idea given its ready state, but there was, unfortunately, a job to be done first.

"I swear, Theo, this better all work out." He swung his legs over the bed and reached for the hotel phone. "Although I suppose I should thank you." If he hadn't gone to New York after the stone . . . He glanced at the bathroom door and smiled. "Yeah, I definitely owe you."

Forty-five minutes later they grabbed a cab in front of the hotel.

"Julia's still at the gallery?" Felicity asked as she slid across the backseat.

"I know, hard to believe."

"Either she's incredibly confident, or she doesn't really have anything to hide."

"According to Sean the police and fire marshal have been by, along with someone else driving a county car."

"Sounds like standard follow-up to the fire. And they didn't take her with them, so perhaps she's not a suspect."

"Maybe. We'll be able to tell more once we see her. I hope."

"We're meeting Sean there, then?" She smiled. "Didn't anyone think it odd that a limo complete with driver has been hanging 'round all day?"

Finn shrugged. "I don't think Rafe hired just anyone. I'm pretty sure Sean's done some, shall we say, *offensive* driving before."

"I was wondering about that."

"Yeah. I've been wondering if he's interested in moving to the East Coast. We could use someone like him."

Felicity nodded, but Finn noted she glanced away then, shifting her gaze out the window as they pulled into the steady stream of traffic heading downtown.

"You okay?" he asked after a few more moments had passed. "I know you're worried about getting Reese to agree to—"

"No," she said, glancing back at him, a more tentative smile playing around her mouth. "It's not that."

"What, then? You don't think I should hire Sean full time?"

The smile spread at that, which he'd intended. Whatever it was that had caused her withdrawn reaction, he doubted it had anything to do with their young driver.

"No," she said. "I mean, yes. I mean, do whatever you like with Sean. I think he's great. If you don't employ him, I might."

"And?" Finn prodded.

"And, you mentioning him moving east made me think." She took another pause, but Finn had already made the mental leap as well, and didn't push her to continue. His heart was suddenly rising into his throat, making conversation a bit difficult.

She looked at him fully then. "If we're to . . . proceed, you and I, once this is over, what would you want? I mean, have you thought about that at all?"

"Not really," he admitted. "There hasn't been much time for that." He smiled then. "I was too busy trying to get you to even contemplate the idea, to allow myself to stretch the fantasy out much beyond that."

"Fantasy," she repeated. "Of course, then you thought I

dabbled on the wrong side of the law for kicks, so perhaps it was wise to hedge your bets on any future happening between us."

"Clearly it didn't slow me down any, but I will admit it was the one part I couldn't make jibe with the rest of you."

"It never occurred to you that I might be working in some way?"

"You danced all around it, and gave enough clues, but no, never once did I fathom you were really a secret—"

She covered his mouth and jerked a nod toward the cabbie.

"Right," he said. "Sorry. I thought maybe you'd gotten in over your head in something that walked the line and had maybe stepped over. That's why I offered to help."

"But you weren't certain of that. You honestly thought I was just in it for the sheer thrill."

He tipped his head. "I didn't know. Not for sure."

"And yet—"

"Yeah," he said. "And yet. My instincts are rarely wrong about a person. I just told myself to be patient until I had all the facts, and then I could decide. Other parts were already well on their way to making up their minds, however, and—"

"I'm well aware of what parts those would be," she said dryly.

He took her hand and placed it on his chest. "Those weren't the parts I was referring to," he said quite seriously.

Her eyes raised to his, then widened as she looked from her hand, her palm spread over his heart, back up to his face. "Oh."

"Oh," he repeated.

"Well."

He grinned. "Well, indeed."

She smiled then, too, while still looking a bit stunned. "Your accent really does need a bit of work."

"Perhaps when we're in London, you can help me with a bit of private tutoring."

"When we're in London?"

"I thought maybe you'd want company escorting Reese back." He lifted a hand. "Not that I don't think you're perfectly capable. But I was also thinking that if it's okay with you, I'd like to be present to mount my own defense when you tell your chain of command about us."

She just sat there and stared at him, as if unable to grasp everything he was saying.

"You don't have to decide now, just—"

"We're here," the cabbie loudly interrupted. "Forsythe Gallery."

Felicity darted a look at the cabbie, then back to Finn. She looked . . . poleaxed, for lack of a better word.

"So, maybe some things I did think about," he said, by way of explanation. "We'll talk later."

"Yeah," she said, the word coming out a little choked. "Later."

Finn's smile faded. "Don't backpedal on me. I know I move in leaps, and you—"

"No," she said quickly, having to clear her throat. "Leaping's not all bad. I just . . . I'll catch up. You . . . caught me off guard. No one has ever—"

"You all gonna pay me or what?" the cabbie said. "Time is money, you know."

"We know," Finn said, then paid the man and opened his door. He slid out and then reached in for Felicity's hand, helping her out after him. "Maybe no one has ever," he said to her after the cab had pulled away and he'd stepped into her personal space. "But I do. And I can't imagine ever stopping. I'm . . . incorrigible that way." He slid his hand under the hair on her neck and tipped her mouth up to his. "As long as that's okay with you . . ."

"It is," she said softly, then lifted up on her toes to close the gap, kissing him first.

Because that's what great partners do, he thought. And returned her kiss.

There was a quiet clearing of a throat just behind them, and

Finn turned to find Sean standing about five feet away, hat in his hands. "Sorry to interrupt, sir, but I thought you'd want to know. Ms. Forsythe is leaving." He turned and pointed to a dark-haired young woman standing in the open doorway to the gallery, having a conversation with someone still inside. She was wearing large, dark sunglasses, brown slacks, and matching fitted jacket, with a long, brightly colored silk scarf around her neck.

"She knows how to dress," Felicity murmured. "Vera's Lavender label, and Hermes. The bag and briefcase are both Coach, if I'm not mistaken."

"I'll trust you on that," Finn said. "Thank you, Sean."

The driver nodded, then stepped back over to the limo, several yards away.

"Show time," Felicity said, then took a deep breath and started off down the stone walkway leading to the front stairs.

"Wait," Finn said, lifting a hand, but she was already beyond his reach. "We should discuss—what are you—"

But Felicity was already skipping up the steps, arms outstretched. "Why, Julia, darling!"

Finn just smiled at Sean, who nodded and lifted a brawny shoulder in return, as if to say, "What are you gonna do?" Finn turned back to Felicity and decided what he was going to do was follow her lead.

Julia had been speaking to a slender man in a very nicely tailored suit, standing just inside the door. She turned in obvious surprise at the sound of Felicity's voice. Finn was several steps behind her, but didn't interfere.

Felicity kept on going up the stairs and straight into Julia's personal space, air-kissing both cheeks, then leaning back to take her in, as if thrilled to see her. "Finally, we meet!" she said, all sparkling eyes and cheery smiles. "And who might this be?"

"Francois Benetton," the young man said, his accent quite heavily French. He was smiling uncertainly, clearly unsure how he should behave around the sudden intruder, but he swiftly took in Finn, and the limo at the curb, and erred on the side of caution. "I'm the manager here at Forsythe Gallery." He extended his hand, and when Felicity went to take it, he took hers instead and kissed the back of it.

Felicity gave a delighted laugh and even managed a blush. "Quite the charmer," she said in an aside to Julia.

At Julia's frown, she quickly went on. "Oh, my, you don't know who I am. It's Felicity Jane, darling. Trent. From the Trent Foundation." She glanced back at Francois. "We've been setting up a Foundation grant to help Julia with some of the underprivileged artists in the area." She turned back to Julia. "Perhaps you didn't get my message, about arriving today? Anyway," she went on, as Julia watched her in stunned silence, so overwhelmed by The Felicity Show that she hadn't even glanced past her to Finn, much less the limo waiting at the curb behind him. "We're all set for dinner, and I've brought my own ride, as you can see."

She waved at Sean, who gave a little wave back. Then she appeared to remember that Finn was right behind her. "Oh, silly me, jet lag." She pulled Finn up a step. "This is Finn Dalton; he'll be handling all the legal details." She leaned in closer to Julia and whispered. "Former district attorney, but honestly, he's so lovely, who cares about his credentials, right?" She laughed gaily and put her hand on Julia's arm, then glanced briefly again between her and Francois. "Are you all set to go? I don't want to intrude on gallery business." She turned her attention back to Julia, sincere concern etched on her face now. "I heard about the fire. Dreadful business, that." She glanced between them again. "You've probably been tied up all day with the officials."

Julia had frozen at the mention of the fire, and Francois was frowning now, too.

Felicity took advantage of the moment and began to steer Julia toward the steps. "Well, you'll enjoy a nice dinner all the more, then. But we really must go." She glanced back at Francois. "Sorry to dash off, darling. I'll be sure to get the entire tour later on. It was a pleasure meeting you. I've heard such wonderful things."

Francois was still frowning, but smiled briefly at the compliment.

She turned her attention back to Julia. "We've a bit of a dash to make. Our reservations were hard won, despite my best wheedling, and I'm afraid if we're late they'll give our table away."

Julia started to say something, but Felicity slipped her arm through hers and steered her down the stairs. "I understand The Loft is the best place in town."

Finn was still facing them, and he didn't miss the sudden pause in Julia's motion, or the way she almost tripped down the next step.

Finn moved forward and took Julia's arm. "Watch your step there." He smiled at her. "Everything okay? You do like The Loft, right? Felicity mentioned it was one of your favorites."

He was close enough now to see her eyes through the dark sunglasses. She wasn't at all happy with what was going on, that much was clear, but with her manager standing in the doorway, and her unexpected guests knowing a hell of lot more about her than she did about them, she let them shuffle her along.

Finn gave a brief wave to a nonplussed Francois, who waved back more automatically than anything.

Sean opened the door with a flourish and nodded at Julia as she approached. "Evening, ma'am."

Julia just stared at him. Then Felicity slid in, and Finn gently pushed down Julia's shoulders, more or less putting her into the car behind Felicity without appearing to manhandle her. "Mind your head," he said. Then he climbed in behind them and nodded at Sean, who closed the door.

The instant it clicked, Julia exploded. "What in the bloody hell is going on? Who are the two of you, and what in God's name do you think you're doing?"

Felicity and Finn's mouths both dropped open in shock. "You're English," Felicity said, unnecessarily, but echoing Finn's thoughts exactly.

Julia just gaped at them, then lunged for the door.

"Don't be hasty," Finn said, regrouping quickly and blocking her exit with a well-placed arm.

"You can't keep me against my will. And if you think I'm going to quietly accompany you anywhere, much less out to dinner—"

"We just want to ask you a few questions," Felicity said quietly. "About the sapphire. And John Reese."

Julia had been all set to argue, but that caught her up short. She sat perfectly still and looked between the two of them, clearly uncertain on how best to proceed. "Who are you?"

"We know you flew out here with John, from New York City. We know which hotel you were in there, even which room."

Her defiant pose lasted another moment; then her shoulders dipped slightly as she leaned back in her seat. "How?" she asked, her tone still defensive, even if her posture said otherwise.

"We're not the police, or from any American law enforcement agency," Felicity assured her.

"Meaning you are associated with a different one?" She glanced between them. "You seemed rather surprised I was English."

"How do you know John?" Felicity countered.

"Old friends."

"And occasional business partners, as well?"

"Legitimately. Is there a problem with that?"

"What happened with the sapphire?" Finn asked.

She looked at him. "John sent you, didn't he?" Then she looked back at Felicity, her eyebrows lifting. "You're the ones who spooked the deal in New York, aren't you?"

"Did you sell it?" Finn persisted.

"How about you answer a question for every one I answer?"

Finn had thought they'd be dealing with a novice, and that perhaps, their joint appearance would be enough to fluster her into telling them whatever they wanted to know. The woman sitting across from him was no novice. He really needed to confer with Felicity, but unfortunately, there was no way to make that happen. "What was the plan in coming out here?" he asked, wanting to ask her about Chesnokov directly, but not wanting to give away everything they knew. "Who was the new buyer?"

"Has it already changed hands?" Felicity asked. "Or did the fire last night slow that down?"

She studied them both, but didn't answer.

Finn noted that she didn't accuse them of setting the fire, which meant it either hadn't occurred to her yet, or she already knew who was responsible.

They pulled up to the restaurant entrance.

"I'm not going in there," Julia stated. "I don't think you want a scene, and I can promise you a big one."

Finn's attention strayed beyond Julia, through the rear window. "Well, as it happens, that won't be necessary." He waited a beat, then lowered his window. "Reese."

Julia startled, as did Felicity, both of them swiveling and jerking their gazes toward the side window. Finn glanced at his watch and noted that Reese had arrived ahead of his scheduled dinner reservation. Which meant he could have simply arrived early . . . or he could have been watching the gallery himself and followed them here.

"Care for a ride?" Finn asked. Then he lowered the window farther, allowing Reese to see who was in the car with them.

Reese stilled for a split second, then stared into the car. Finn wasn't certain, but if looks could be lethal, there was a good chance Ms. Forsythe would no longer be with them.

"Don't allow him in here," Julia hissed. "You don't know

what you're doing. I'll talk, but tell your driver to pull away. Now!"

But it was too late. Finn had no idea what the full ramifications were going to be, having them all in such a confined space. But he did know that one way or the other, they weren't exiting the limo until he had a hell of a lot more information than he did right now.

"Hello, Julia," Reese said, quite coolly, as he opened the door. "Miss Trent."

Finn slid over to make room, which left the men facing the women.

Julia tried to get out again, but this time it was Reese who blocked her way. "It's time, don't you think?"

Now it was her turn to stare daggers at him. "Time for what, exactly? Time to be falsely accused of betraying my own country? I hardly think it will ever be time for that, thank you very much." She sat heavily back in her seat and folded her arms, looking quite defiant.

Finn and Felicity shared a look, which told Finn she was thinking exactly what he was thinking. Julia was MI-8's target, not Reese. But then, why had they directed her to bring Reese home? Or *Home*, as the case may be? Unless they were all spies.

And since Felicity had unknowingly linked Reese to Julia in her requests for information, they'd decided to pull Reese in to get him to turn on Julia. It still didn't explain the whereabouts of the sapphire, or why, specifically, they'd wanted it in the first place.

Finn smiled, and scanned the lot of them, focusing especially on Julia and Reese, then made a gut decision and went with it. "So, everyone here who doesn't work for MI-8 raise your hand." He raised his, and was met with a steely gaze, a shaded one, and Felicity, who simply looked at him as though he'd lost his mind. "I just thought we might as well get past all the posturing and prancing." He lowered his hand. "The way I see it, we four are the only ones who control what happens next, to whom, and where. So, I suggest we all put everything we have on the table and see what's what. That is, unless, one of us is guilty of treason, and then, well, I'm afraid it's bad news for you. Three against one, your odds of not paying the piper aren't looking too great." He leaned back and parroted Julia and Reese by folding his arms. "In which case, you might as well fess up anyway. So . . . who wants to go first?"

Chapter 22

Felicity stared at Finn as if she'd never seen him before. And maybe she hadn't. Not clearly anyway. She couldn't believe he'd just taken the information she'd held so dear, that she'd shared with him in absolute secrecy, and outed her right in front of the very people who were suspected of betraying their own country. *Her* country. She wanted to demand what in bloody hell he'd been thinking, but just then, he winked at her. As if to say, "Trust me, go along with it."

Well, it was one thing to expect him to go along with her little charade in front of the gallery, but he'd just exposed her and jeopardized not only her future with MI-8, but possibly her future drawing breath. Treason wasn't exactly a mild offense.

She glanced quickly to John and Julia, to see if they'd picked up on Finn's signal, but they were still both quite wrapped up in glaring at each other.

She could only hope he had some grand scheme in mind that would make all this okay in the end. But, for the life of her, she couldn't imagine what that could possibly be.

"No one? Okay, then I'll go first." Finn pressed the intercom button. "A nice sightseeing tour, if you don't mind." The limo pulled smoothly away from the front of the restaurant and back into the flow of traffic. Finn settled back and propped an ankle on the opposite knee. "So, the way I see it, there is a marionette operator pulling strings, maybe multiple operators, and you guys are the puppets."

Reese shifted in his seat to stare at Finn, but his expression was unreadable now. There was no doubt, however, that he was paying attention. As, Felicity noted with a quick glance, was Julia. Felicity turned her attention back to Finn as well. What had he figured out that she hadn't?

"Given the fact that you each have relatively high profile, alternate careers, I'm guessing you're all part-time puppets, brought on stage when you have something of specific value to offer." He looked at her and smiled a genuine smile. "Felicity was fortunate enough to be born a Trent, which gives her entrée into a realm of society barred to most people. Then there is her Foundation work, which opens doors on every level, on every continent. She moves comfortably through these worlds with grace and elegance, and no one would ever suspect that in addition to dedicating her life to helping those less fortunate, she also moonlights on occasion, lending a hand to her government on some rather . . . delicate missions."

He shifted his gaze to Julia, and his smile shifted a bit as well. More bemused now. "There is Julia Forsythe, with a largely untraceable and perhaps questionable past, who popped up out of nowhere on the San Francisco art scene several short years ago, and now runs a ridiculously successful gallery, featuring previously unheard-of artists who are immediately sought after, once their art hangs on her walls. Her clients cover a broad spectrum, but have wealth as their common denominator.

"They, themselves, also have a broad range of connections, which are assumed to broaden Julia's contact base as well. She also ships her art to destinations worldwide, and, it is that ability, along with her important contacts, that makes her a valuable asset to her government, as she has been known to incorporate certain items that need to be moved internationally, without raising any eyebrows, into artwork being ostensibly shipped overseas to new owners, thereby becoming a legitimate and quite legal mule service, of sorts. It is presumed that her government returns the favor by providing her with this apparently new life in the States, complete with, and, I'm just guessing here, name and background. And livelihood. Win-win for everyone, there.

"Which brings us to John Reese, a well-established global entrepreneur in the import-export business, which gives him access to, well, just about everything and everyone. Quite handy having a fellow like that on your team, I must say." He smiled at the three of them. "Have I missed anything? Good." He uncrossed his legs and leaned forward. "So, on to the rest of it. Felicity typically works solo, but has, to my great good fortune, agreed to team up with me, a guy who does privately pretty much what she does governmentally. Which gives me and my team access to things you don't have, and a far greater latitude, as we only follow orders from ourselves, and there is no need-to-know crap."

He looked between Julia and Reese. "From what I understand, you two also work together from time to time, both personally and professionally."

Neither Julia nor John confirmed his comment, nor did they deny it. They simply continued to stare at Finn, but they also remained silent and interested in what he had to say.

So, Felicity admitted, was she. She still didn't know where he was going with this, but the potential damage done to her had been done. There was really nothing more he could give them on her, so she might as well see where this would lead.

"However," Finn went on, "though Felicity and I managed to find a way to make our unusual partnership work, the two of you apparently had a falling out. And then Felicity here was instructed to bring one of you home."

Both Reese and Julia looked at Felicity. Okay, so she'd been wrong. There had been more information he could reveal. She glared at him, making it perfectly clear what her feelings were on the matter, but decided there was no point in making a scene. Just yet, anyway.

"In the middle of all of this are two things," Finn went on. "One, supposedly someone hasn't been playing fair and has been using secure information for personal gain. Two, there is the sapphire. Which, for me, is merely an answer to a client's prayer of restoring his family's good name, but for your government is apparently a matter of national security; otherwise one of you stealing it and selling it wouldn't be grounds for treason."

Felicity eyed both John and Julia for reactions, but both were completely stone-faced.

"What I can't help but wonder is, why your chain of command needed three agents on one mission. Each with a different personal task assigned to them, none of whom apparently knew about the tasks assigned to the others, or even that the others worked for their same employer." He looked at Julia and Reese. "I'm assuming you two were both working, correct?"

John merely held his gaze, but Julia, glaring at John, jerked a nod with her chin, arms folded even more tightly.

"Ah," Finn said. "Now we get somewhere." He looked to John. "Did you know you were both working for the same team? I'm assuming you knew of the other's affiliation prior to this. It would explain why there is little to no public record of your personal relationship."

Julia's gaze darted from John to both Felicity and Finn. As if she was suddenly concerned that their personal relationship was going to be put under the microscope. Interesting, Felicity thought. Why would she still care, given that she'd taken off? And gauging from John's steely-eyed stare, it would appear that this was strictly professional for him, but she'd seen him in the wee hours this morning, clearly hurting over her betrayal. No, this was personal for him, too.

"But did you know you were both assigned to the same task this time?"

"No," Julia blurted. "No. *We* didn't know. Only John knew."

"You're wrong about that," he said quietly, suddenly not looking quite so steely or inscrutable. "I didn't know."

Felicity's mouth dropped open, and she immediately looked at Finn, who shot her a smile. She wanted to ask him how he'd suspected, but knew that would have to wait for later. Her irritation with him, however, and her feelings of being hurt and betrayed diminished a great deal. It had been a huge risk, but, then again, at this point, it was likely to all come out anyway.

"Then why did I get intel telling me that you'd gone renegade?" Julia blurted. "They led me to believe you were using me to cover your tracks."

"And you believed that?"

"Of course not!"

Everyone fell silent, but no one looked more stunned than John. "Then why did you leave?" he asked. "Why did you take the stone? To give it to them as proof?" His eyes widened. "You didn't give it to them, did you?"

"No," she said. "And I took it because I thought if I got rid of it, then they'd have nothing to pin on you. I was protecting you."

"But—I was protecting you."

She frowned. "What do you mean?"

"When you took off with the stone, I thought maybe—"

"*You* thought *I* was the one?"

"I never would have. But you took off. With the stone. Without a word."

"Because if I'd let you know, you'd have information they could get out of you. If you had no idea—"

"Then they couldn't pin any of it on you," Felicity said, her tone hushed. "But why would they ask me to bring you back if they suspected Julia?"

"Because you asked for information on both of them, providing them with a link and an insider source. Maybe they just wanted John so he could roll over on Julia," Finn said.

"I swear, I only took it to protect John. I've never—would never—do anything to bite the hand that feeds me. I have a life because of them. They rescued me from—they made a life possible. I'd do anything to repay that."

"Even give up your life?"

She looked at Finn. "What do you mean?"

"The fire."

"I wasn't there, I was—"

"But, if you hadn't taken the stone, you would have been there," John said. "We both would have been there."

She leaned back then, folding her arms now, but more because she looked shaken than because she was angry. "I don't understand. Any of this."

"So, if none of you is on the take, then that means you're being framed by the person who is. And the only one with that kind of power would be in the chain of command," Finn said calmly.

"The puppet master," Felicity said. "But which one? And why?"

"Clearly they know something is up and are on the hunt. Maybe he's trying to cover his ass by targeting one of you. Then things started to go south—largely, I suppose, because of my unexpected entry into this little scenario—and he had to scramble."

"So I was directed to sell it to Chesnokov's agent as a way of damning me. Except it was a direct order."

"Your word against his. And maybe it served a dual role of framing you for the sale and getting the stone where he needed it to go, keeping your government from using it," Finn said. "I just wish I knew why in the hell they wanted the damn thing. Do any of you have any idea?"

"No," John said. "I did tell them about the situation in New York." He looked to Felicity. "I had no idea you worked for them. I was afraid you'd been conned. Honestly, I had no idea what to make of you. You totally took me by surprise when I found you snooping." He glanced to Finn. "I'm sorry about the manner in which you found her, but I had to make it look as if it were a matter between lovers. Had I left her tied to a chair or something, fully clothed, it would have been far easier to convince hotel staff that she'd been a victim of some other sort, and I couldn't chance that."

"I understood," Felicity said, speaking for Finn. "So, you're telling MI-8 about me and Finn, and I'm asking them about the two of you . . . and we've all gone racing to the West Coast, the entire case now clearly spinning out of control—"

"Our puppet master panics, maybe?" Finn said. "And decides, perhaps, to cut his losses and pin the thing on John or Julia. Posthumously, if necessary."

"Or maybe us," Felicity said. "Either way, he's clear."

"Only Julia takes off with the stone, John drags us back into things, and—"

"Nothing is going according to anyone's plan or back-up plan."

"So, I get word to bring you in," she said, looking at John. "I assume—when the fire failed, and with Julia on the run with the stone—as a last ditch effort to nail you with it, somehow, using me as a witness."

"I wasn't on the run," Julia said. "I checked into a hotel so I could have some time and space to sort things out."

"Did you contact your handler?" Felicity asked.

"No. I made no contact with anyone. Nothing was making sense to me. I was debating contacting Chesnokov and just getting the damn thing out of the country, but the fire spooked the hell out of me. I didn't know what was going on." She looked to John. "Or who, at that point, was doing things. To me. To us. I was just really confused. But I was going to stay clear of you until I figured it out."

"To keep me from being connected," he said.

She nodded. "I had the stone, so—"

"Had?" Finn asked. They all looked at Julia. "Where is it?"

"Hotel safe. By this morning, I had decided to go to work as usual, deal with the officials, maintain as normal a front as possible, and try and figure out what to do next. I had no further intel, and I wasn't sure if I wanted to contact them with the information that I had taken the stone, as I was directly in violation of orders and . . . nothing seemed right. My instincts were all over the map."

"Then we showed up," Finn said. "And here we are."

Everyone looked at each other, but no one said anything.

"So," Felicity said at length. "I say we put our heads together and figure out who is really behind this. Then we figure out how to nail him."

John looked at her, then at Julia for an extended moment, in which she held his gaze quite intently as well. "I'm in." He turned to Finn. "I owe you."

"How do we figure out who is behind this?" Felicity asked.

"I say the first thing we need to do is figure out why your country wanted this artifact in the first place and why it has anything to do with national security. If we know that, figuring out who else might have wanted it, for any reason, might be more easily pinned down."

"Except we don't know who we can trust," Felicity said.

"I do," Finn said, and pulled out his PDA.

Chapter 23

Finn landed the helicopter gently on the pad at Dalton Downs. It was good to be home. It wasn't the way he'd have planned things when bringing Felicity here for the first time, but there wasn't much he could do about that. Mac was waiting a few yards away and ducked to come closer as the blades slowed overhead. Rafe was coming up the path.

Mac grinned as the door opened and first Felicity, then Reese, then Julia debarked. "It's the British Invasion, all over again. Welcome."

Felicity smiled. She extended her hand. "You must be Donovan MacLeod."

He took her hand. "Mac, please. A pleasure to meet you, Miss Trent." He shot a look at Finn, who was coming around the front of the bird. "In fact, you have no idea."

She took his teasing in stride and smiled more broadly. "Thank you. And it's Felicity." She stepped back. "This is John Reese and Julia Forsythe."

Mac shook hands with both of them, then stepped over to Finn. "Finn and Felicity, John and Julia. Cute."

"Ha ha," he said, then shook his best friend's hand and accepted a quick hug and clap on the back. "It's good to be back."

"It's good to get you back."

Rafe arrived, and introductions were made again. He gave Finn's shoulder a squeeze. "Good to have you back, man."

"Same. So," Finn said, "no smartass commentary from you?"

Rafe's gaze flickered down to the paddocks, where Kate's ranch manager, Elena, was putting one of their horses through its paces. He glanced back at Finn, his smile warmer and more relaxed than Finn could ever remember seeing it. "Uh, no. I believe in karma. I'll just welcome you home." He glanced at Felicity Jane. "And hope you're half as content as I am."

He was clearly sincere and sounded so . . . yes, content was the right word, that Finn didn't know what to say to that. It was a lot to process. "I take it I'm not the only one whose life got a bit . . . interesting over the past few weeks."

"Interesting is one way to put it."

"More later?"

"We can swap stories, but for now, I've got things set up to run those tests you asked for. Did . . . everything make it okay?"

"Yep." He stepped back over to the helicopter and pulled a leather satchel out of a small storage net. "Right here."

"Good." Rafe stepped back. "Shall we, then?"

"Always working, that guy," Mac said. "I had dinner set up for about an hour from now. And we prepared rooms for everyone. I know it's been a marathon of flights from California to New York to here, so if you'd rather—"

"We'd like to get started with the testing," Reese said. "If that's all right with you," he added, including Finn in the request.

"It's going to take some time to run everything—" Mac began.

Julia stepped forward then. "It's not that we question you or your facility; we couldn't be more grateful. It's simply, after all we've been through, we'd be able to relax and enjoy your hospitality far more if we could observe things getting under way."

Mac looked to Finn, who nodded, then turned back to the group and spread his arm wide, gesturing to the stone path that led down to the main house. "Absolutely. Please, right this way."

They all walked up to the house, with Finn and Felicity letting Reese and Julia take the lead, allowing Mac to play tour guide. Rafe hung back with the two of them. Finn noted that Reese had his hand on Julia's lower back. After their initial discussion in the limo, once they'd decided to team up, he didn't think Reese had allowed more than a few feet to separate him and Julia since. Finn smiled, and put his hand on Felicity's lower back as they walked down the path toward the house. For once, he understood exactly how Reese was feeling.

"It's lovely, this place," Felicity said, looking fresh despite the fact that they'd spent most of the past few days flying or driving. "The rolling fields remind me a bit of home, as do the horses. But your mountains are a different backdrop. Quite beautiful, really."

"Thank you," Finn said, wondering, for the first time, what her home was like. He knew the Trent ancestral holdings were outside London.

"You grew up here?" she asked.

"No, I grew up in boarding schools and summer camps. This was my father's home." He looked down at the house he'd hated coming back to as a child. "But it's my home now." And, thinking about the people he'd brought together here, he realized how true that sentiment really was.

"And you love it here now; I can hear it in your voice."

"Finn has worked hard to create a family here," Rafe said. "We all feel strongly about this place. It's become a foundation to build on, for all of us." He looked to Finn. "More so now, than ever."

Finn thought about Mac, who'd brought Kate home a year before, and now Rafe, who, from what little he had been able to get from him, had Elena, who was also here permanently now. He glanced to Felicity and wondered what she was thinking. They hadn't talked about their future. There was too much to be done first, before any decisions about that could even be discussed. But it didn't mean he hadn't thought about it.

He slid his hand into hers. "Yes," he said. "I do love it here." *But I'm falling in love with you, too*, he thought silently, wishing the rest would fade away so he could have some time alone with Felicity. But now was not the time for that conversation. He tried to take heart in the fact that she was here and the conversation would happen at some point. That was all he could hope for, and, for now, it would be enough.

"Flight down from the city go okay?" Rafe asked.

"Fine. But I'll be happy to stay in one spot for more than twenty-four hours for a change."

They'd left San Francisco last night, as soon as they could arrange a private flight out. Finn had spoken to Rafe before leaving to get him going on the research. Then they'd spent the flight back catching up on some much-needed sleep. Or trying to. The flight down from New York in the helicopter really hadn't been conducive to much discussion either, so there was still a lot of brainstorming to be done on what the connection was between Britain and a Byzantine-era sapphire necklace. It had been Mac's idea to check the stone and setting, to see if they could find anything on it, or any inconsistencies with it, that would explain its value to British intelligence.

"Anything else pop up?" Finn asked.

Rafe shook his head. "Alexander Capellas runs a restaurant. The same one his grandmother ran, and her mother before that. The necklace came to him through his father's side of the family. His father stepped out of the picture when he was a child, but the extended family stuck around, and, as the last son, he inherited it along with other possessions from his grandfather."

"No clue why he suddenly parted with it? His family has hung on to that thing for over a hundred and fifty years. Any financial worries with the restaurant? Relatives ill and needing medical care? Gambling debts?"

Rafe shook his head. "Nothing. He's comfortable, but he doesn't live the high life by any standard, and there is nothing to indicate he suddenly wanted to change those circumstances. He's known as a hard worker, loyal, honorable."

Finn nodded. "He's as stubborn and as strong on protecting his family name as Theo is about restoring his. That's why I can't figure out what could possibly make him change that, after decades of legal battles that had to hurt him financially as much as it hurt Theo."

"Maybe my government convinced him," Felicity said.

This had come up on the plane ride, with no good rationale coming out of it. "It makes sense, but with what?"

"Blackmail?"

"He lives in a small Greek village and runs a family restaurant—"

"The one thing he is the most stubborn about is his family," Rafe said. "If your people had something on a member of his family, and threatened to take it public, even if just in his immediate village—"

Finn nodded. "That could do it. He'd hate it, but it might be enough. It would have been for Theo, I think, if it were damning enough and there was no other alternative, or the pressure was just more than he could surmount. And, as you said, his resources were very limited."

"I'll do some more digging, look at that angle. I started digging back on his father, but so far, I can't track the guy at all. It's like he—"

"Disappeared?" Felicity and Finn said at the same time. "Sort of like they made Julia disappear from her former life," Finn finished.

Rafe's expression changed. "Except, as far as I can tell, his father's life until that point was pretty routine. Yes, his wife died giving birth to Alexander, but from what I've dug up, his family was quite close and they all dealt with the blow. I don't know that his answer would have been to also abandon his family. He seemed to be cut from the same cloth as the rest of them in terms of loyalty."

Finn thought about that, then had another idea. "What if he was convinced to leave, or go down a different path, for the same reason his son was convinced to give up the necklace."

"To protect the family name?"

"In their culture, and his was especially Old World, it could follow." He looked at Rafe. "Maybe we need to dig more on the father, but also start tracking back. Theo has the provenance on the necklace up to the point where it left his family's hands in the early eighteen hundreds. So it would have to be something that happened with it after that."

"With it, or to it," Felicity said.

Both men looked at her. "What do you mean?"

"Well, you've talked about testing the stone, and the setting, the necklace, to verify it is in fact an artifact and not some kind of duplicate, or something that would be out of the ordinary. I'm thinking that if the necklace proves authentic, it doesn't rule out foul play in the same vein."

"I'm not following," Rafe said.

"I think I am." Finn paused on the path and turned to Felicity. "You mean you think something is hidden in or on the necklace."

"Something like that."

Rafe said, "But microtechnology didn't begin until—"

"It doesn't have to be a micro dot or chip," she said. "It could be something encrypted, scrolled into the metal, or—"

"Or designed right into the jewelry. I know something about that."

They turned to find Julia and Reese behind them.

"You think it's not the necklace itself, but information being passed along with it?"

"What else about a gemstone and some jewelry could jeopardize security, or, by passing it along to someone, be seen as a betrayal of one's country?" Reese countered.

"We've been discussing it, too," Julia said, "and I think you've hit on something." She looked to Rafe and Mac. "Do you have equipment that could scan for technology?" She glanced at Felicity. "We also can't rule out that Alexander's father worked for his government, in the same capacity we do for ours. Microtechnology did exist in his day." She looked back at the men. "I can go over it and look for inconsistencies in the metal work. If you have a really good magnifier, we can examine it for possible micromessaging."

"You mean engraved right into the setting? Or, the stone?" Felicity looked properly horrified at the thought. "That piece is over a thousand years old. Would they really desecrate it like that?"

"If it's even the original setting. No one knows. It's been in Capellas' family for over a century."

"I didn't have it authenticated," Reese said. "I did verify it was in the case, and I had the provenance paperwork direct from Capellas as well."

"So, you got it straight from Capellas?" Rafe asked. "Or did someone else play mule getting it out of Greece?"

"No, I was sent down there to get it. I got it out—"

"Did it go to headquarters before coming to the States?" Felicity asked.

He shook his head. "No. Direct to New York for the meeting with Chesnokov's agent."

"And you knew he'd be using a courier," Rafe stated.

"Yes. I knew to expect Andreev. Chesnokov uses him frequently. There was nothing out of the ordinary there."

"He didn't demand any kind of proof it was authentic?"

Reese turned to Mac. "I have an impeccable reputation. He relied on that."

Unfazed by Reese's cool response, Mac pressed. "You weren't concerned that you might jeopardize that impeccable reputation by not personally guaranteeing its authenticity?"

"There was no time for that. And no, I was following orders as I always did. I trusted they would not set me up." He looked to Julia. "A misplaced trust, it would seem. For both of us." He looked back to Finn and Mac. "But, at that time, I had no reason to believe it wouldn't be in their best interests as well to maintain my integrity. I worked with them often enough, it was to their advantage as well."

Mac nodded, as did Rafe, satisfied.

Now it was Finn's turn. He looked to Julia. "I know you have a background of some kind in art, but this is jewelry, and—"

"My background is actually in ancient studies and archaeology." She smiled. "With a second master's in art history."

Even Reese looked surprised by that little tidbit. "New revelations," was all he said, though.

Julia flushed a little. "You never asked," she told him.

"You're so young to be so accomplished," Felicity said, then quickly added, "I didn't mean to presume anything, but you've done a lot, especially considering a past that you've alluded wasn't perhaps a good one."

She looked to the rest of the group, somewhat warily, then said, "My past was unique, and definitely threatening, but not in the manner you would ever assume. I was considered something of a prodigy as a child. I tend to pick things up rather quickly. Some people tried to use that skill for gains that weren't exactly legal."

Finn had a feeling "some people" might have been her own family. "I'm sorry," he said.

"It's in the past now," she answered with a shrug, clearly ending that conversation. "So, I can help you with authenticating it, at least to some degree, and looking for signs of alteration. I did have a brief look at it while it was in my possession, but I had no tools to use, and I couldn't bring it in to work. Anything I had that would have helped me with that went up in the fire at my other studio."

"Another reason, perhaps, for the fire," Finn noted.

"I say we get inside and start things up," Mac said. "Then, dinner."

"Always food with this guy," Finn said, smiling and try-

ing to ease the tension and strain. At least they were all getting along with one another, and the source was situational
and not temperament oriented. Still, it was exhausting. And,
admittedly quite selfishly, he was getting impatient to be
done with this, so he could focus his energies where his attentions were most interested at the moment: on Felicity
Jane.

But first things first.

After dinner and another brainstorming session that didn't
net any new possibilities, but did give them a chance to get to
know one another a little better, they all headed over to where
the Trinity offices were housed, and the temporary lab that
Rafe and Mac had cobbled together during the latter part of
Finn's expedition.

"Nothing else coming in?" Finn asked Felicity as they followed Rafe and Mac down the hall. During dinner MI-8 had
attempted to make contact with all three of their errant agents
on their individual PDA's.

No one had responded to the transmissions.

"Nothing new," she said.

There had been some debate on whether they should even
decode and read the messages, on the off chance there was any
way, given they were MI-8 issued units, they could be tracked.
They'd moved back to the East Coast leaving little to no trail
behind them, and they wanted to keep it that way for as long
as it took to get a break in the case.

She glanced up at him. "I'm still not sure about leaving the
messages unscrambled."

"I think I might be able to help with that," Mac said, looking back at her. "I need to do a bit more tweaking to the pro-
gramming, but we might be able to load them directly into our
system, then put the code in to unscramble, so there can be no
direct connection of any kind. I should have it functioning by
morning."

They all nodded, then paused as Rafe stopped in front of a set of double doors.

"It's pretty basic, haven't had time to do more than move stuff from other places all into one room, but it will make this a lot simpler if we can consolidate." He opened the doors, and even Finn was impressed. "Nice."

Felicity walked in, her mouth open in a silent "O." Julia and Reese were a bit more reserved in reaction, but Finn thought they looked suitably impressed as well.

"You have the case?" Rafe asked. "I thought we'd start over here with a simple magnification." He turned to Finn. "Close the door, will you? This is the only room with no windows, so we control the lighting. I also redirected the air, and we have our own system, which should keep the stone and setting as protected as possible while they are exposed."

Mac turned to Finn with a "Look, Pa!" smile on his face. Finn nodded and gave him the thumbs-up. His family never let him down, but that didn't mean they didn't surprise him from time to time.

"Julia?" Rafe said, all business.

She brought the case over, and everyone crowded around. They'd decided to wait until they got it back to Virginia safely before opening the case again. She pushed it over to Reese, who dialed in the combination on the lock and opened the outer, airtight case that held the actual jewel case.

"This case is actually only a few centuries old," he said, leaving the jewel case in the specially designed airtight casing. "The original has long since rotted away. This one is holding up okay." Rafe handed him a pair of protective gloves, to keep any oil from his skin from getting onto the case or the necklace. A moment later, everyone was staring at one of the largest sapphires Finn had ever seen.

"The engraving and setting is typical of the time, and the workmanship is outstanding," Julia said. "The stone isn't cut nearly to today's standards, but—"

"It's stunning," Felicity said.

"On sheer size alone, it's impressive," Finn agreed.

"Let's move it over here, to this table," Rafe said. They kept the old case sitting in the airtight case, with the necklace still resting on the crushed satin backing. "For now, we'll leave it sit, as is. See what we can see."

Everyone pulled stools and chairs over and clustered in front of a flat screen that Mac had mounted on the wall. "Julia, tell me if you want to see anything in more detail," Rafe said, maneuvering the overhead scope. Mac seated himself at a computer keyboard and loaded a digital pointer and grid onto the flat screen.

They spent the next four hours straight going over every last-minute detail of both setting and stone. Julia was responsible for moving and turning the piece, but despite the broad-ranging capability of the equipment they had, nothing untoward came up.

"I can scan it for any technological elements," Mac said, "but I wouldn't hold out too much hope."

"Should we look at the case?" Reese suggested. "It's been around long enough that several Capellas generations have had contact with it."

"Not a bad idea," Finn said. "I wish there was a way to lift fingerprints without causing any potential damage to the surface. Who knows what we might find?"

Rafe smiled. "I can help you with that." He went over and got a kit. "I had this sent out for a case I was on last year, never had a chance to use it."

Another three hours elapsed as prints were excruciatingly carefully lifted and the case was examined as thoroughly as they dared. "I don't have X-ray capability, but that might be an option. As would dating it, but that takes time and materials I don't have."

"But could get?"

"I'm not sure we're going to be given the luxury of an extended time to figure this out," Reese said. He lifted a hand to stall Finn's rebuttal. "I realize the care we took to cover our tracks here, including blocking any signal that might be transmitting from our cell units, while still receiving incoming transmissions. You've been more than generous," he said to Finn. "But I've worked with my agency long enough to know that they are very good at tracking something—or someone—down, when they want to. And they have three someones in this case. We won't have long. Mark my words. We need a break, and we need it soon."

Yet, by three in the morning, they were forced to call a halt when nothing had come up on the fingerprint search, and, without more delicate technology, they couldn't continue without potentially harming the artifact.

"We're still digging on the Capellas," Rafe said. "Maybe something will pop up there by morning."

"You mean later in the morning," Mac said on a yawn. "I'm heading down to the cabin. I'll be back in a few hours." He looked to Finn. "I'd like to bring Kate."

"I'm not sure it's a good idea to involve any more people than we have, just because it makes us more vulnerable—"

"Being here makes them all vulnerable. She'd like to be here, and I think maybe a fresh brain—a very sharp one, by the way—and a fresh pair of eyes might do us good."

Finn nodded in agreement.

Rafe stood. "I'll introduce you all to Elena another time, but I'll be back up here in a few minutes."

"You've been running nonstop since we left San Francisco," Finn said. "If you want some down time—"

"I want to figure this out," he said, then looked from him to Felicity, and back. "You'd be doing the same for me."

"I wish I'd been here to do so. And you're right. See you in a few."

Finn showed Reese and Julia to their suite and explained how to operate the security system that was independently wired for their set of rooms, as well as the one that ran the entire house.

"Very . . . layered," Julia said, quite approving of the intricate system.

"We've had occasion to house clients that require certain levels of safety," Finn responded. "I'm just glad we had this handy. Sleep well."

He backed out of the room, then turned to a yawning Felicity. "Just one day," he said.

"One day what?" she responded.

"One normal, not sleep-deprived day. That's what I want with you."

She smiled sleepily.

"Of course," he said, pulling her into his arms. "I'll want a bunch more of them, probably all in a row, so perhaps we really need to get rid of some of our guests first."

She nodded, then leaned her head against his shoulder as he put his arm around hers and steered her down the hall. "This isn't my usual set of rooms, and I'd really rather have you over there, but it's on the other side of the house, and I think it's best to keep us all in the same general vicinity."

"Given the level of threat they've used already with the fire, I think that's a good idea."

"Rafe has external security on. And we have good perimeter security around the entire farm, very recently updated from what I understand. But it never hurts to keep alert."

She yawned again, then laughed at herself as he steered her through another set of double doors into a sitting room and, after setting their personal alarm, right through that room into a nicely appointed—he knew some would say rather grandiose—bedroom. "I'm not so sure alert is something I could aspire to at the moment. Or I'm certain I'd be making some kind of comment about this room." She sank onto the edge of the bed and dropped straight onto her back and stared up at the fresco ceilings, each ornate section painted with a mural of angels. "Looks like something my family might have dreamed up. I wouldn't have ascribed it to you, however."

"I've renovated all the areas we use. Haven't made it to this wing yet. This was my father's idea of good taste."

"Glad to know it's not yours. A bit . . . opulent."

"Yes, it's the Donald Trump school of decorating. The more gilt the better."

She laughed at that and started fumbling with the buttons on her dress, still lying flat on her back.

Finn loomed over her, planting his hands on either side of her. "Scoot back," he urged.

"I'd love to, but I don't think I'm able." She raised her arms to him. "I don't think I'm capable of anything at the moment. I don't think I've ever been so bone weary."

"So, shower in the morning?"

"Mmm hmm," she said, yawning again.

Finn slipped off her shoes, then brushed her hands away and finished unbuttoning and unzipping and untucking.

"I feel like a sleepy child," she said.

"Trust me, you don't look anything like one. And it's a testament to how tired I am that I can't do anything about it, either."

He quickly undressed and turned down the bed, then scooped her up and tucked her in, climbing in on the other side of her. She was rolling toward him and curling into him before he could even reach for her. "It's not my bed," he murmured, pressing his lips to her hair. "Which is where I want you. But it's—"

"Shh," she said. "You're home, and that's all that matters."

And then she slept.

And Finn didn't. He lay awake, contemplating what she'd just said. And where home was going to be if he wanted her to remain in it.

He was finally drifting off when the bedside phone buzzed.

Felicity roused first and rolled over to check it out before he could lean past her. "I think I'm still asleep," she said, looking back at him over her shoulder. "Or does this say the pool house is calling?"

"Rafe," Finn said, levering up and across her to get it.

"He lives in the pool house?" she said, but he was already pushing the intercom button.

"What's up?"

"I am," Rafe said. "And now you are. Get Reese and Julia. I figured it out."

Chapter 24

It was a very bleary-eyed group that reassembled in the makeshift lab. Mac entered with a young, pretty blonde who Felicity immediately assumed was Kate. He confirmed that by introducing her to the rest of them. "She can't stand being left out of the fun," he explained.

"My white knight," she said, smiling and leaning against him as he tucked her under his arm. She looked at the group. "Thank you for allowing me in. If there is any way I can contribute, I will."

Felicity knew she ran a school on Dalton Downs property that helped children with severe disabilities increase their aptitude to communicate, among other things, by working with horses. She understood from Finn that they had all known each other as children and that Mac had recently reentered Kate's world when her life had been threatened. He was such a direct man, with great charisma, so it was interesting seeing how Kate softened his edges a bit. His teasing was clearly part of their natural banter and, Felicity was certain, under normal circumstances, was easily returned. "It's a pleasure," she told Kate. "I'm glad you could join us. Julia and I were feeling a bit outnumbered."

Kate shook her hand. "From what I hear, the two of you can more than hold your own. I mean that in a good way," she added quickly. "I look forward to getting to know both of you better."

Rafe entered, finally, with a dark-haired woman stepping in just behind him. "Hi," she said. "I'm Elena and don't blame this on Rafe." She bussed his cheek, then stepped past him and extended her hand to Felicity. "Not how I wanted to make first introductions, but I hate being left out of the fun."

Everyone smiled or chuckled, and she looked around and said, "What?"

"I'll explain later," Kate said.

Elena looked more shyly at Finn. "I don't know what Rafe has told you, but—"

Finn stepped forward and hugged her. "He's happier than I've ever seen him," he said quietly. "Thank you."

Elena flushed and stepped back, then seemed to notice everyone was still staring and said, "Well, now that we've evened up the teams, we'll get out of your way." She and Kate moved over beside Felicity and Finn, and Rafe motioned them over to the case, which they'd closed up again when they'd ceased their examinations earlier.

"It occurred to me that we'd checked out every micrometer of this thing, and the case it came in, but we neglected the rest."

"The rest of what?" Finn asked.

"This." He put on the table the portfolio that had traveled with the artifact.

"The documentation of the stone's provenance. But it's not that old. What does that have to do—"

"Old enough," Julia said. "So, that's where he hid it."

Felicity was already nodding.

"What British Intelligence was looking for is embedded in the documentation," Rafe said. "It hit me that we never even looked at it, so I came back and took a page out to my office to run some checks before I got everybody up." He glanced at Elena, and Felicity noted the immediate warmth that entered his gaze. "Well, the rest of everybody."

She smiled back at him, clearly not remotely upset to be part of his world, even if it meant getting up before dawn. More than likely, seeing as she ran the stables, she was used to it anyway.

Felicity struggled not to look at Finn, to see if he was noticing, wondering if the two of them had the same obvious connection that the other pairs in the room shared. She knew they did, but . . . She shut that path down. She was tired and being foolish when she needed to be anything but. She didn't know where things would lead, or how they'd sort through them, but first they had to resolve this case. And resolve it in a way that put her, John, and Julia in the clear.

Rafe slid one of the sheets out and put it on a mat in the center table, then nodded to Mac, who turned out the lights.

A moment later he switched on a light wand that bathed the room in an eerie blue glow. Felicity wasn't the only one who audibly sucked in her breath when he waved the wand directly over the page. A series of letters and symbols popped up, all of it illegible to Felicity. But not to Julia.

"An old Greek code," she murmured. "Are you sure this was his grandfather's and not his father's?"

"The stone was last passed down by Alexander's grandfather, directly to his grandson. But that doesn't mean that Alexander's father didn't have access to it while he was still at home. I haven't been able to decode more than the top corner and a few words in the first two lines, but the dateline says London, and it was written in the late seventies."

"Isn't that right around the time that Alexander's father vanished?" Mac asked.

"Exactly when," Rafe said.

Julia leaned farther over the page. "This is a message detailing . . ." She trailed off, but kept reading.

"What is it?" John asked quietly, when she lifted a hand to cover her mouth.

"It's a list," she said, awed, and from the sounds of it, not in a good way. "Complete with details. Explicit details." She looked up. "Of certain illegal activities some of our agents were involved in. Very . . . illegal. Trading in contraband, stealing priceless antiquities . . . even murder." She became silent as she kept reading.

Felicity stepped up, but there was no hope she could make sense of anything on the page. "Does he name them?"

Julia nodded. "You'll recognize one of them." She looked to John, then back to Felicity. "Thomas Wharton."

Felicity's mouth dropped open. "As in, Director Wharton?"

"Who is that?" Finn asked. "Someone in your chain of command, I assume."

John nodded, his expression tight. "Right at the very top of it. He runs the entire MI-8 Division. But he started out like the rest of us."

"How was Capellas' father privy to this?"

Julia was still reading. "He was an agent, for his own country, but he worked in tandem with some of our guys and apparently got caught up in their black market schemes by accident, not realizing the tasks were unauthorized. When he figured it out, he wanted out. He left this detailed list while at home, but they'd threatened his family. So he took off. At the end of this . . ." She kept reading, then motioned to Rafe to put the next sheet down. "He says he was concerned for his own life, but couldn't bear to think of anything happening to his beloved son, after just losing his wife."

Finn and Felicity naturally gravitated toward each other, and she slipped her arm around his waist, even as he was tugging her close with his arm around her shoulder. A quick glance up showed her that the other couples in the room had instinctively done much the same. *So,* she thought, *we are a bonded pair, just like them.* The confirmation gave her more comfort than it probably should have, but which she took, and refused to think beyond.

"So . . . what do we do now?" she asked.

Kate stepped forward. "I—my mother had a fairly wide

range of contacts, garnered over the years, through several husbands." Her smile was deprecating, but direct nonetheless. "She did unto herself for most of her life, and rarely unto others, unless it was poorly, but perhaps this will make up for that a bit." She looked at Mac, then at the rest of them. "My brother still maintains contact with most of those people. I don't know if they'll talk to me, but I happen to know that a few of the men are currently fairly highly placed in the State Department. Hopefully they will remember me more fondly than my mother, but if I bring this to their attention, maybe they can use their leverage to—"

"Not to cast aspersions on your government," Julia interrupted, "but how do we know we could trust these relative strangers with information so delicate that our lives could be at stake if it fell into the wrong hands? They already are at stake. What's here is very serious. So much so that I'm not surprised Director Wharton thought he might have to commit murder to cover it up. Which he's already tried once. And, according to these documents, it's a solution he's used before, long ago."

"I agree," Kate said. "What I was going to suggest was that maybe we could get them to see if they can find out what happened to Alexander's father." She looked at Felicity and Finn. "Maybe he's still alive."

"I seriously doubt if he's been successfully hiding all these years, he'd be willing to come forward now," Finn said.

"What I don't understand is," Mac said, "if he was so worried about his family, why leave the incriminating evidence with them?"

"No one knew he'd even made the list," Julia said.

"Someone had to suspect, or they wouldn't have started looking for the stone."

Finn shook his head. "I think I know what might have triggered it." He looked up. "Me."

Felicity's eyes widened. "How?"

"When I took on the case, I made contacts of my own, trying to get Theo more highly placed help to assist in his legal battle."

"But how would MI-8 know any of that?"

Finn shrugged. "It's a pretty small world. And who knows who else is on that list that might care if it sees the light of day? Alexander's father worked for the Greek government. Maybe this list has agents from a number of other allied countries, ours included. It's possible they did know about it, or suspected its existence."

"But as long as it stayed buried in a tiny Greek village, who cared, right?" Elena said.

"Until Theo wanted his stone back," Mac finished.

"And, suddenly, someone had to make sure that didn't happen," Felicity murmured.

"So," Julia went on, "they pressure Alexander, probably threaten his family—"

"Again," Finn put in. "But why have Reese sell it to the Russian? Why not just destroy the document?"

"Maybe they didn't know how he secreted it, just that he did. Maybe they couldn't risk actually destroying the artifact without someone knowing, or questioning its destruction. If it goes to Chesnokov, who is notorious for hoarding his little collection, it stays buried."

"Or . . . Chesnokov was on the list, too," John said. "He's in the right age range. A bit on the upper end, but . . ."

"So, maybe he set the fire," Felicity said.

"Possible."

She leaned more heavily into Finn's strength and warmth. "Then who knows how high this reaches? And how far reaching it goes?" She looked to John and Julia. "What do we do with it?"

"We decode all of it," Rafe said decisively. "Or Julia does. We have to know who we're dealing with. We'll go through the names, do research, find out who's who."

"Then we go public," Finn said abruptly.

Everyone turned to him.

"You're smiling. Why are you smiling?" Mac asked warily. "He gets crazy ideas when he smiles like that."

"We make the smallness of the modern day world and the new age of technology work for us." He hugged Felicity closer. "We do what any self-respecting spy coming in from the cold does. We hold a press conference."

Chapter 25

"Are you sure this is a good idea?"

Finn stood to the side of the helipad and watched the skies for the incoming chopper. He glanced down at Felicity. "No, but it's the best one we had. And it's kind of too late now. Besides, it will be up to them how they handle it. They deserve the chance to find out."

She nodded, and tightened her arm around his waist. "I just hope they remain open-minded about everything."

"Me, too. The fact that they all agreed to come here seems to be a good start."

They both looked back down the hill, over to the house and beyond, at the sea of media trucks and news vans crowding the road into the farm, the yard, and every other available space they could inhabit.

"I'm surprised they're not in the trees," he muttered, but was happy to see them as it meant his idea held merit. Everyone wanted to hear the news when the news was dirty laundry.

"I can't believe we put this together so quickly."

It had been only seventy-two hours since Rafe had started to put the pieces together. But time was critical. The messages had stopped coming in to the agents' cell phones over thirty hours ago. Which meant they'd given up the diplomatic route. And who the hell knew what other means they might be willing to try. He didn't doubt they'd put together Finn's little press conference with their supposedly undercover case. Officials from his own government hadn't shown up, making any kind of noise about protecting national security, so he took that as a good sign.

Not that he'd asked anyone's permission in the first place.

As it turned out, the list Julia ended up with had included more than one highly placed official, both in and out of the spotlight. They'd thought about alerting the various government bodies affected by the coming fallout so they could be prepared, but none of them was willing to risk just what their version of "preparing" might entail. They had no way of knowing how complete a list Alexander's father had compiled, and who else might come out of the woodwork if word got out privately, before it got out ever-so-publicly.

The sound of helicopter blades drew his attention back to the skies. Once it had touched down, Finn and Felicity ducked and moved closer. A familiar-looking young man got out of the pilot's seat and sketched a quick salute to Finn.

"Thanks for helping us out, Sean."

"Glad to be on board," he responded, then opened the other door to allow his passengers out.

An older Greek man and an even older Greek woman debarked. The woman looked quite pale and uneasy. She made the sign of the cross on her chest, then turned to face Felicity and Finn.

"Greetings, Mrs. Capellas," Finn said, taking her hand, then shaking Alexander's. "Thank you for coming all this way."

"You are putting my family back together," he said in very broken English. "For this, I would travel to the moon and back."

"Sean, can you take them down to the house? Mac is there."

He nodded, and the trio made slow progress toward the house.

"I hope the translator has gotten here," Finn said. "I want them to feel as comfortable as possible, which is close to impossible in this circus. She's never even been out of her country before; this has to be bewildering to her."

"She's stronger than she looks," Felicity said, watching them leave. "It was her decision to accompany her grandson here. She'll be okay."

Finn nodded, then looked back to the sky. "Come on, come on. One more to go."

"When is Theo getting here?"

"He said he'd call from the airport. He wanted to drive in. I offered to send Sean, but—"

"How is it our limo driver knows how to fly helicopters, anyway?" Felicity asked, clearly bemused.

"Apparently he has all kinds of . . . specialized skills."

"It was great of him to come out here."

"I knew I could trust him."

"He's agreed to stay on?"

Finn pulled her into his arms and kissed her on the forehead. "Yes. You can't have him." He kissed the tip of her nose, then tipped up her chin. "Well, you can share. But there are conditions . . ."

"Conditions, hmm," she said, pretending to mull that over.

They'd had precious few moments of complete privacy, and Finn was wondering if they ever would, or if they were simply doomed to live forever in the center of chaos.

The sound of another helicopter had them moving over to the second pad. "God, I hope I'm doing the right thing."

Felicity hugged him. "They need to have the chance. You're right. What they do with it is up to them."

The larger helicopter landed, and out of it stepped the Greek ambassador to the United States, the U.S. ambassadors to both Greece and the U.K. . . . and a very tired, very nervous looking Dmitri Capellas. Alexander's father.

Introductions were made, and Finn did his best to reassure the older man that he would be safe.

"So many cameras," he said, and visibly shuddered. "I do not like spotlight."

"Don't worry about that. The cameras are for us. Would you like to see your son? And your mother?"

His face brightened, and he looked terrified all at the same time. Tears made his eyes glassy. "They know?"

Finn nodded. "They're at the house. They just arrived."

"My sainted mother . . ." Dmitri crossed himself, and Finn wondered if he knew just how like his mother's that mannerism was. "She flew in that?" He nodded to the smaller helicopter.

Finn smiled. "She's a pretty amazing woman, your mother. She's held your family together."

Felicity stepped forward and put her hand on Dmitri's arm. "You'll be proud of them. They are proud of you."

A single tear tracked down his heavily wrinkled cheek. It wasn't so much age, as stress and extended exposure to the sun, that had weathered him so badly. They'd found him on a small island in the Caribbean, working on a banana plantation. Finn hoped that his next plane ride would be taking him back home to Greece.

"Come," Finn said, "let's go inside. If you need some time—"

"No," Dmitri said quite adamantly. "I am nervous, yes, but there has been enough time. Too much time." He shook his head and walked with his ambassador down the path. "Too much time," he repeated.

Finn welcomed the other ambassadors and thanked them for coming. "I'm not sure we'll need you to say anything on camera, but your presence will go a long way."

"You're stepping up to the plate and doing what's right and to hell with the rest," the U.S. ambassador for Greece said gruffly. "We need more patriots willing to do that. I'm happy to be here."

Felicity stepped up and spoke with the U.S. ambassador to the U.K., whom she knew personally from her work with the Foundation. Then, with Finn, they led the small contingent to the house. "What do you think is going to happen with the necklace and stone once this is over?" she whispered under her breath. "Theo still wants it, and Alexander wouldn't talk about it."

"I don't know," Finn said. "I'm hoping that the magnitude of what is about to happen here today puts their families' ancient histories into some kind of perspective and they come to an equitable solution."

"Theo has the family Bible, and all the proof about how the Capellas ended up with the Roussos' family heirloom. So the Capellas can see it firsthand."

"He does. We'll have to play it by ear on when or if we're going to pull that out."

"But—"

They reached the house just then, and Rafe met them at the side door. He merely lifted a questioning eyebrow and glanced at the group behind Finn.

Finn lifted a shoulder as if to say, "Who knows."

"We're all set to go live at five o'clock. Did I mention how much I hate the circus?"

"You did. Several times," Finn said dryly. More seriously, he added, "Elena, is she okay? I know this is a little close to home with what she went through—"

"She's fine. More than fine. Is there anything else you need?"

"Just baby-sit the ambassadors—"

"I'll stay, too," Felicity said. "A familiar accent won't hurt. Besides, they don't know how to act around me now that the word has spread about my clandestine activities. I can use that to my advantage."

Finn smiled. "Oh, I'm sure you can. Then I'll leave you to it." He turned to Dmitri. "Are you ready?"

He nodded decisively.

"Okay, then. Come with me."

Felicity leaned up to give Finn a quick, reassuring kiss on the cheek, and she patted Dmitri on the shoulder, then turned a most charming smile toward the ambassadors. "Gentlemen, if you'll follow me, we have drinks and a light lunch waiting for you."

Rafe leaned close to Finn as he passed. "I don't know how you managed it, but don't screw that up. She's the only woman I've met who can not only keep up with you, but probably surpass you." He grinned. "I'm kind of liking that."

"Careful, funny man."

Rafe kept smiling, quite unrepentantly. "I'm bulletproof these days."

Finn laughed. "Yeah, smug bastard."

"Don't worry. You two will figure it out," he said, then followed Felicity into the small salon they'd set up away from the madness.

He hadn't spoken to Rafe or Mac about his worries regarding his future with Felicity, but it didn't surprise him that they'd picked up on it. He smiled, and gestured for Dmitri to follow him. And prayed Rafe was right.

Two minutes later he encountered Sean outside the door to one of the other quiet rooms they'd set up. "Mac just got word that Theo changed his mind. He's getting a bit spooked now that it's almost time. So I'm going to get him. That okay?"

"More than okay." He clapped Sean on the shoulder. "Thanks."

Sean smiled and nodded at Dmitri, then excused himself.

Finn looked down at the shorter man, who was clearly bracing himself for what lay on the other side of the door.

"They both love you. And you love them," Finn told him. "You can't go wrong with that foundation."

He jerked his gaze up to Finn's, then nodded, rubbing his palms on his pants. Finn opened the door, and Dmitri walked in.

There were several other people in the room. Kate and someone Finn took to be the translator he'd hired to help them understand what everyone else was saying, particularly during the press conference. But from the almost instantaneous sobbing and hugging going on in the center of the room, he didn't think it was going to be immediately necessary.

Alexander looked over at him, then back at his father, tears streaming down his face. "Thank you," he mouthed.

Finn nodded, and thought Theo probably didn't have much to worry about. Alexander had gotten his family back. Finn didn't think it would take much work to persuade him to give Theo back his.

Mac stuck his head in the door just then. "One hour to showtime."

"We'll be set. Where are Julia and Reese?"

"Next door. The area around the tent we pitched to hold the damn thing is mobbed."

"And the A team—"

"Security is in place. Don't worry. I got the best."

"I've got plenty to worry about, but that's not on the list."

Mac smiled, and smacked him on the shoulder. "Don't worry, man. I've seen the way she looks at you. You'll figure it out."

Then he vanished, leaving Finn to wonder if he had a freaking neon sign blinking over his head.

He watched over the Capellas reunion for a few minutes longer, then left Kate to monitor that while he went back down to get Felicity. He wanted to go over things with her, Reese, and Julia one last time before they went in front of the cameras.

There were men and women stationed all up and down every hall, outside every window, every door, on the roof . . . which might have been security overkill, but considering the bombs they were going to drop today, he was happy to have every bit of protection they could get.

Felicity met him at the door to the salon. "It's ridiculous, because it's almost over, but I swear I've never been this nervous in my life."

He rubbed her arms and pulled her out of the open doorway, into a guest bathroom across the hall. A security agent was already silently moving into place in front of it, even as he closed the door between them. Finn blocked Felicity from turning on the light, pulling her instead into his arms and kissing her more passionately than either of them had had the energy or privacy to do since they'd left San Francisco what felt like eons ago.

They were both a bit breathless when he finally lifted his head, but he was already crowding her back against the sink, and she was shifting so she could sit on it and pulling him between her legs, without either of them having said a word.

"I miss you," she whispered heatedly. "I know we haven't been apart for more than five minutes in the past three days, but I miss you. Terribly."

"I know, me too."

"We shouldn't be doing this," she said, even as she was unbuttoning his shirt.

"I don't know if I can get through the next twenty minutes without an extended taste of you." He pushed her back so her head rested on the mirror over the sink. "Let me . . ."

"Finn, I want—" Then she stopped talking all together as he pushed up the full skirt of her dress and slid his hands up her thighs.

"We both need," he said, then proceeded to take care of just that, and to hell with the damn security agent. He leaned over and kissed her as his fingers trailed up the inside of her thigh and stroked her through the silk of her panties. Their tongues dueled, while his fingers stroked, and he drove her up to the edge, and beautifully over, still kissing her even as she was shuddering through her climax.

"God, I miss you," he said, pressing his forehead to hers. "I've just barely gotten you into my life, and into my world here, so I don't know how I can feel so—"

"I know," she said, and pressed a kiss to his jaw, then the side of his neck. "I absolutely know."

He lifted his head. "We've had no time, to talk, or . . . anything, but it's not because I don't want—haven't thought—I have, I just—"

She laughed softly then. "Me, too. And we will. After . . ."

She shuddered again, only this time not with pleasure. He gathered her close, and she slid to her feet and folded herself against him. "What if . . . What if it goes horribly wrong?"

"It won't," he said. "It can't. Once we put it out there for the whole world to know, and can back it up with proof, you'll be too public to be a target. And the real targets will be too busy facing down their own interrogations to have any time to do anything else."

"I miss home," she said. "I miss London. But I'm not looking forward to going back." She tucked her head closer as he tightened his hold. "It could take a long time, a lot of questioning, and I don't know what my latitude will be, but—"

Finn tipped her chin and silenced her with a gentle kiss this time. "I do have the luxury of latitude."

"You're still planning on coming back with me?"

"For as long as you'll have me."

"But—what about your work here?"

"We'll work it out. I won't let you go through it alone, Felicity Jane." She started to balk, but he kissed her again. "Let me put it this way, I don't want you to go through it without me. I don't want to sit an ocean away. I want to be with you. As much for myself as to support you."

"Well," she said, the humor he loved so much finally coming back into her voice, "when you put it that way, I'd be a shrew not to allow it."

"Exactly," he said and, for the first time, allowed himself to believe what Mac and Rafe had been telling him all along. Maybe it would work out. Somehow.

"Come on," he said. "Showtime."

Chapter 26

"Vultures," Felicity said as she passed through the great room.

Finn immediately turned off the television, where he'd been watching the incessant coverage of the fallout still falling out even two weeks later. "I don't know how you stand it," he said, never more sincere. "England is beautiful, this place is amazing, but it shouldn't be a prison." And yet it was. Just on the other side of the gated drive was a scene on only a slightly smaller scale than the media chaos at Dalton Downs that had started this whole thing. "I know you explained to me that it was different over here, with you and the press, and . . ."

She crossed the room and sat in his lap without pausing, uncaring that it creased her designer suit or mussed her perfect, lawyer-approved hair. Which was exactly why he would put up with ten times the insanity if that was what it took.

She put her arms around his neck and smiled, wearily, but truly. "Brits adore gossip. We make what you all do to Britney and Paris look like child's play. It will die down eventually, but, as I told you, as a Trent, and a high profile one at that, due to Foundation business, it's always a bit like that, especially when I'm out and about. And now they learn I'm a secret agent? Or was? It's simply too, too delicious, you know. They really can't help themselves."

He framed her face. "You're worth it." He kissed her, then

said, "But maybe we can bring Sean over. No offense to Foster, but we could use a better defensive driver getting around town." Foster was the Trent family driver who Finn was fairly certain had personally been with the family for generations. Four or five, at least.

Felicity smiled at that. "Shh, you'll hurt his feelings."

"We could be sitting in his lap, and I doubt he'd have heard me."

She tried to look scolding, but couldn't quite pull it off. Finn was more distracted by the lines of fatigue etched in her forehead and fanning out from around her eyes. "What more did your lawyer—barrister—have to say?"

"Solicitor," she corrected him. "The barrister is advising the solicitor, but he doesn't—oh, never mind. He's hopeful that we'll have a ruling shortly, but I'll be expected to be available for further questioning, and, eventually, for testimony if necessary. He wasn't sure what kind of travel freedom I'd have, or when I'll have it."

Finn just hugged her. He knew no one was wearier of the whole thing than she was. "No word from or about Julia and Reese?"

"Nothing."

"Are they keeping them apart, still?"

"Last I heard. Which is ridiculous, since they've allowed you to be here with me."

"I'm not a rogue agent like you are, honey," he said, bussing the tip of her nose when she scowled at him. "But I agree, it's not fair for them. I would—well, I don't want to think about what I would or wouldn't do if I was being kept from you until God knew when."

"I'd go mad," she said quietly, then laughed a little at herself. "A far cry from that independent woman I was when I last left here."

"You haven't lost your independence," he said. "You've just gained an advocate, that's all."

The way she looked at him then, as if he was her own personal warrior, made him feel capable of being just that. He would have gladly gone striding from the room to personally slay each and every dragon if he could have. It still struck him every day how deeply he felt about her, how profoundly what she was going through affected him.

And he wouldn't have it any other way.

"What about Rafe and Mac?" she asked. "Things okay on the homefront?"

Homefront. He'd sworn to himself back at Dalton Downs that he'd be here to support her, to defend her, to help her, to do anything she asked of him. But the one thing he'd vowed not to do was pressure her, or even bring up their future beyond the madness they were enduring as everything got sorted out, post-bomb-dropping.

But there were times when it was mighty challenging. It was his nature to see things to their conclusion in the most direct, satisfying, and expeditious manner as possible. Those were the principles he applied to his business life. And he wasn't really equipped with any other way to go about achieving his goals than the ones he used day-to-day.

"What?" she asked, tilting her head to the side. "You have that unfocused look again."

He smiled, and pulled her more tightly against him. "Rafe faxed me some case files to look over." He felt her tense a little.

"That's . . . good."

He laughed. "That was the most unconvincing affirmation ever."

She lifted her head, and though she tried to look amused, he was stunned to see her eyes grow a bit glassy. "I know, that was horribly selfish. I can't expect you to give up your life for me, and you've done that already for far longer than you should have, which also puts an undue burden on your partners, and—"

He cut off her stream of worry in the most effective and pleasurable way he knew how. But gently, this time. She was so strong, and so tireless, in doing what she knew she had to do, but she was also human, and worn out, both emotionally and physically. Which was where the teary eyes came from, he was sure. When he finally broke the kiss, he said, "He faxed me case files to look over so I could give him feedback and opinions on which ones to consider more seriously. Not cases I need to go home to take on personally."

"I'd understand if you had to," she said, but the way she'd relaxed against him when he'd assured he wasn't leaving said otherwise. Not that she wouldn't be understanding, just that she didn't want him to leave.

That made two of them.

"I am sorry, that this makes things harder on you."

"We're fine. That's the luxury of being your own boss and picking your own cases." And then it occurred to him that he didn't need to stop considering cases at all.

She lifted her head and looked at him again.

"You read me too well," he said, but he was really starting to like it. She was very in tune with him, which made him look forward to taking on new work and bouncing ideas off of her like he did with Rafe and Mac.

"The wheels are spinning so fast I'm surprised I don't see smoke," she said.

"I—I just had an idea, that's all."

"About?"

"You. And me. But it can wait. Until after this has settled down and we know what is what."

"You know what would help? Giving me something to think about beyond this madness. It's so all-consuming. I mean, yes, I'm still working on behind-the-scenes Foundation business, but given everything, they are talking about the possibility of hiring someone to run the day-to-day with me remaining a more private advisor."

Finn's eyes widened. "Why? When did that happen?"

"Conference call right before the solicitor's call."

"I know the media glare is crazy right now, but, that's your family's trust; they can hardly—"

"They're right," she said quietly. "And you know what's worse? I think I'm relieved."

"But—"

"I—this isn't the life I chose for myself, Finn. It was chosen for me. And I've done my best by it, but with my current notoriety, I'm more hindrance to the good we do than a help. Yes, it will die down, but that won't be anytime soon, and the Foundation needs to continue to operate if they're going to benefit anybody."

"If people want help, they can bloody well get over it. You were one of the good guys, or haven't they bothered to remember that?"

She bussed his nose. "You're very good for me, you know that?"

"I—I just don't want to see you pushed out. You've lost your future with MI-8, and now this. It's not right that you get left with nothing."

She kissed him and smiled. "Hardly nothing, darling. And the truth is, I think I'll be better served, too. I can still work behind the scenes, and, someday, if it's determined I won't be a gawking, gaping distraction, I'll go back to being the face of the Foundation at certain events. But keeping a low profile and focusing on the work is my best bet." She stopped herself, and looked at him. "But that's not what I need to focus on right now, either. What idea did you have?"

He hadn't even had the chance to think it out, decide how feasible it might be. Or if she'd even be interested. "I was just thinking that if I'm going to be over here for a while, well, there are people in need everywhere."

"You mean . . . take on cases here?"

"Possibly. Maybe your Foundation has people who come for help, but not the kind you can provide. Or I'll put Rafe on it."

"No . . . no, I think I could be some help with that. You wouldn't believe the requests that come in to us. Some are downright heartbreaking, but don't fall under the purview of the kind of help we provide."

Finn grinned. "Well, it's a start." He slid down in the chair a little and tucked her in with him. "You wanna do some behind-the-scenes work for me?"

She wiggled her eyebrows and traced a finger around his neckline. "Is that what we're calling it now?"

Finn barked a laugh. "Actually, I was serious. With the Foundation pushing you into a new role, and your work with MI-8 clearly at an end, I was thinking maybe you could team up with me."

She started to laugh, then stopped. "You're serious, aren't you?"

"Very," he said, the idea rapidly expanding in his mind as he really gave it credence. "We could work here when you want or need to be here, and, if you're willing—" He broke off, realizing he was doing it again.

"Willing to what?" she urged.

"I promised myself I wouldn't push."

She laughed outright.

"I think I was just insulted," he said in a mock wounded voice.

"I should think not," she said, as haughty as she got. "Your drive and determination is one of the main reasons I fell in love with you. If you hadn't pushed, I'd have let myself walk away from the best thing that ever happened to me."

"Wait, back up. What did you just say?"

"That if you hadn't pushed me, I'd have—"

"Before that."

She had to stop and think. Then the most delightful shade of pink stole into her cheeks. "See, and I promised myself I wouldn't say that."

"Why on earth would you promise yourself that?"

"Because these are highly emotional times, and when I said it, I wanted you to know that my judgment wasn't clouded by being bombarded and worn out from all the chaos. I know I cling to you lately, but—"

He framed her face and brought it close. "You're the most nonclingy woman in the world. Physically, we fit, emotionally we fit, but it's because we have our own minds, our own ideas. And I'm glad you told me. Because I love you, too, Felicity Jane Trent."

She broke out, then, in the brightest smile he'd seen from her in, well, maybe ever.

"That felt pretty damn good," he said, maybe a little more surprised than he'd thought he'd be.

"Yeah, it kind of did." She leaned in. "Perhaps we should head up to my suite and, you know, discuss the terms of this declaration."

"There are going to be terms?"

"Oh, yes. Lengthy and quite detailed terms."

"Am I going to like them?"

She wiggled down in his lap. "Oh, I believe you're going to like them a lot."

"You know, don't tell Rafe or Mac, but when it comes to being a fully rounded team player, you really have it all over them."

She laughed. "Ah, now I have leverage."

He stood, and swung her up in his arms, then slid her directly over his shoulder, clamping her legs to his chest. "Good, you'll need it."

He grabbed a canvas tote he'd stashed in a corner back when he'd arrived. He'd felt kind of silly then, but it had been an impulse to bring it along. Now he was glad he had.

"What on earth is that?" she asked, craning her neck around to the side.

He stuck his hand in the bag and pulled out a familiar blue plastic bag.

"Is that the same bag? From our plane ride west?"

"It is." He handed it back to her, then strode from the room and headed to their bedroom.

He heard the plastic rustle; then she giggled. "Good call. I love chocolate sauce, you know. And honey. I didn't know we shared the sweet tooth."

"I'm not so sure it was teeth I was thinking about, so much as tongue."

She wriggled a little, and he picked up the pace.

"But . . . what on earth is the set of children's paint brushes for?"

He grinned. "Arts and crafts."

She laughed. And suddenly, life was pretty damn perfect.

Epilogue

It was just past dawn when they finally arrived back at Dalton Downs. Hard to believe he'd been in England for almost six weeks. But, although there would be continued involvement, possibly years' worth, Felicity no longer had to be available to her governing body on a moment's notice. "Come on," he said, "I want to show you something before everybody gets up and starts the welcome home festivities."

He walked her into the main house, through the central rooms, then down the gallery along the back and through the far back door. He never used this one, despite the fact that it wasn't far from his personal library, where he relaxed in the evening. He'd left specific instructions on what he wanted, and he didn't doubt for a second that his partners hadn't let him down.

She opened the door, and gasped. "Oh." She walked out onto the cobblestone patio he'd requested be laid, complete with the white wrought-iron table and chairs set just to the far side. Across from that was a thickly padded chaise, perfect for reading. Opposite that, he'd strung a wide hammock. And surrounding all of it were richly tilled flower beds, presently empty. She spun around, and into his arms. "My garden."

"Well, it will be. I thought maybe you'd want to grow your own flowers, but we can have them put in if—"

She'd learned the best way to quiet him, too. She kissed him long and passionately, which, considering how they'd spent most of their private flight over, was surprisingly vigorous.

"It's so lovely," she said, her voice choked. "No one has ever done anything like that. It's—" She spun around again, and he wrapped his arms around her waist and pulled her back against him as she took it all in again.

He'd done for others his whole life, and yet he thought that moment might have been one of the most gratifying yet. Sometimes, doing something for the ones who didn't expect it was more satisfying than helping the ones who did. "Everyone needs to know they're loved," he said, pressing his lips to her hair.

She covered his hands with hers and squeezed them. "I don't know what to say."

"Say you'll give up some of that chaise time to lie in the hammock with me. I know that's a bit of a deviation from your place, but—"

"But my place was just for me. This place is for us."

He turned her around then. "I hope you feel that way about all of Dalton Downs."

"You've made this place a home. I know Trent Hall is cold and hollow in comparison—"

"Well, when we're over there, we can work on changing that. If you want."

She threw her arms around him, and he was just spinning her around as people started spilling out of the house, onto the patio.

"Oh, sure, sure, sneak in like thieves in the middle of the night, without a thought to your family," Mac mock scolded.

"Ignore him," Kate said, right behind him.

Rafe and Elena followed, bearing platters of food and tea. "I got a message from John and Julia," he said as he put his platter down on the table. "They're taking a trip to Japan. He has business interests there, and they both said they wanted some time alone."

"I can't say as I blame them," Finn said. "But I'm still disappointed they didn't take us up on the offer to stay here."

"I hope Reese can put work aside at least for a little while," Felicity said.

"Oh, they didn't turn you down," Rafe countered. "They just delayed their acceptance. In fact, he said he wanted to discuss some . . . possibilities with us when they get back."

Felicity and Finn exchanged looks, as did everyone else. "Well, that could be interesting."

Elena poured cups of tea for Kate and Felicity and coffee for the rest of them and passed them around.

Finn lifted his before taking a sip. "We started as a team of three best friends. We've grown and we've grown up." He looked to Felicity, Mac looked to Kate, and Rafe to Elena; then they all looked to each other and raised their cups and mugs. "Rafe and Mac, you saved my life when I was young. I guess we saved each other. And from that bond, Trinity was eventually born. And we became a family in every way that means anything." He shifted his toast toward Kate, then Elena, and finally Felicity. "Now we have the chance to make that family into something meaningful beyond just us. Maybe even outlasting us. Taking what we've learned the hard way, and doing something even better with it."

"Hear, hear," Rafe said, and took a drink.

"Hear, hear," Kate, Mac, and Elena intoned, and followed suit.

"Hear, hear, indeed," Felicity said quietly, from her perch on Finn's lap.

"Home," Finn said, pulling her close. "Finally, we're all truly home."

If you liked this book, you've got to try
WANTON,
the newest from Noelle Mack,
out this month from Brava . . .

London, 1816. The Pack of St. James meets in secret in their elegant lair. An unknown assailant has begun to prey upon the women they love—and a poisoned communication threatens worse things to come. Marko Taruskin begins to investigate and finds the trail leads to a scandalous beauty known as Severin. Well aware of how a clever woman can hide more than she reveals, Marko must employ all of his powers of sensual persuasion . . .

The last chord died away and Marko heard the almost noiseless click of a piano lid closing. The woman who had been playing so beautifully sighed as she put the sheets of music in order before she rose, pushing back the padded bench with a faint scrape. He heard the faint miaou of Severin's cat, following her mistress about the adjoining chamber. Silk skirts rustled over polished floors. Then Severin swept through the double doors that led to her bedroom and stopped, her lips parting with surprise.

"What are you doing here?"

"Waiting for you."

Severin glided past the bed upon which he lay to her mirror-topped dresser. "I do not remember inviting you." She began to take down her hair, looking at his reflection in the silvery glass, her back to him.

"No, you didn't."

"Then how did you get in?"

Marko shrugged. He was quite at his ease stretched out upon her featherbed, luxuriously so, in fact. He rolled to his side, bracing himself with one arm and letting the other rest upon his hip. "Through the front door."

"Hmm. Unusual for you."

"What do you mean?"

Severin gave an unladylike snort. "You're a great one for trellises and balconies. Ever the romantic hero."

Her gleaming hair ripped over her bare shoulders. He longed to bury his face in its fragrant softness, lift it away from her neck, kiss her madly—but he stayed where he was.

"It is raining."

"Oh? I did not notice," Severin said, turning to face him. She put her hands on her hips and looked him over.

Marko could almost feel her gaze. He was nearly as aroused as if she had actually touched him. Since he was fully dressed, from his fitted half-coat to the breeches tucked into his high black boots, the sensation was not entirely comfortable. He drew up one leg and bent his knee to conceal his reaction to her cool study of his body.

"Boots in the bed?" she murmured. "How uncivilized of you."

"I could not very well strip, Severin. You might have screamed."

She permitted herself a small smile. "I don't think so. I've seen you naked before."

He remembered that night with chagrin. "Yes, but—nothing happened."

Her amber eyes glowed with amusement. "You wanted something to happen. But I was not ready."

"Are you ready now?"

The question was bold, but she was bolder.

"Yes," she said. And she came to him . . .

And here's a sneak peek at
Charlotte Mede's sexy historical,
THE MIDNIGHT MAN,
in stores now from Brava . . .

The hand on her wrist was beautiful, large and strong, and male. A sinewed forearm, the shirt cuffs turned back, led to shoulders that blocked her view of the salon. Broad shoulders, but sculpted beneath the fine linen shirt, no cravat, and a waistcoat with the top two buttons undone. A torso she suddenly ached to draw.

She couldn't see his face against the dim light of the chandelier. He was sitting on the chaise, leaning over her, saying something. The deep voice was rough velvet.

"I've seen your work."

She pushed away the haze clouding her thoughts, unable or unwilling to concentrate as a ribbon of fear unfurled deep in her chest. "You have." It was more of a statement than a question. Her artist's eye traced his body, a sculpture that was large-boned, long-limbed, but elegantly made. Like nothing she had ever seen in real life. More like a hallucination or a bronze at the Victoria and Albert Museum.

"It's magnificent."

He was so close that she could detect his scent, the ocean, sun, and something else. Languorousness seeping into her bones, her words were slow to come. "I must have misunderstood." She heard herself laugh, the sound throaty and low. "Most of the critics, not to mention the friends of my late and beloved husband, aren't that generous in their praise."

"You're bitter."

The blue-gray smoke combined in the air between them. "How discerning of you, sir. Whoever you are." The metallic taste in her mouth stung as a flare of panic flickered in her chest.

She tried to sit up and couldn't. Although he wasn't touching her, she instantly felt caged by his body limned in the shadows of the alcove. Closing her eyes, she tried to shut him out, following the shapes and patterns her imagination conjured. A stream distorted by sunlight. A face shattered into geometric planes. A rough-hewn mountain range. She was only vaguely conscious now of the low and constant sounds of strangers humming in the background.

Then the hand skated down her arm and a jolt of awareness pulled her back. And all she could do was focus on his touch, as compelling as the opium in her bloodstream, the calloused fingers moving slowly over the sensitive skin of her wrist before he pressed one finger into her bare palm. A shiver traveled from the top of her spine to the tip of her womb.

She opened her eyes. *What if he is one of them?* The thought crawled out the thick morass that was her reality. She wanted to move, to run, but she couldn't, held down by a force of nature invading her senses. The urge, out of nowhere, was contradictory and overwhelming, to reach up and loop her arms around his neck, then trace the hard muscles and warm skin of this man's body. First to feel and then to draw him.

"What's in that head of yours, Helena? In your mind's eye?" The low gravel voice mesmerized and she'd barely registered that he knew her name. His hard fingers traced a sensual pattern on her palm, the fine veins of her wrist.

From under heavy lids, she strained to discern his features. He was so close she could track the cadence of his breathing, the rise and fall of his chest. "What I see?" Her breath was shallow and the words cost her some effort. "Inspiration? You think this is where it comes from?" She gestured to the small blue pipe with her free hand. "Not from here, not from this."

"Then from where?" The dark voice led her on, as surely as if he'd leaned closer, his lips hot on the curve of her neck. Beneath the heaviness of her limbs, she felt an unfamiliar need, a tightening in her chest that was equal parts desire and dread.

"Most people believe I'm mad." It was more of a whisper than a statement.

"Why?"

She shook her head against the enveloping, smothering cushions. "Because of what I do and how I do it." Explaining anything more would not help, even if she could.

"I saw your entries in the *Salon des Refuses* in Paris." He cupped her cheek, sketching her ear, the slope of her shoulder. Her insides turned liquid and her skin hot.

Desire coursed through her, foreign and frightening, desire for this stranger whose face she couldn't see. His voice and his body, the here and now that could blot out the terror that hovered in the air around her. From far away she watched herself as, with leaden arms, she reached up to pull him down toward her. His muscles were granite beneath her hands.

Her blood rushed and she breathed in his scent. "You're what I need," she murmured. "To escape, just for a little while . . ."

She was on the margins of awareness, her physical senses as keenly attuned as the finest instrument. The heaviness pooling in her abdomen and the swelling of her breasts were exotic terrain, her body suddenly alien to her experience.

She felt the heat of his breath with its tinge of warmed brandy and tobacco. "I can do that for you, Helena. I can do whatever you desire."

There's nothing more irresistible than
EVERLASTING BAD BOYS.
Keep an eye out for this anthology from
Shelly Laurenston, Cynthia Eden, and Noelle Mack,
coming next month from Brava.
Turn the page for a preview of Shelly's story,
"Can't Get Enough."

Ailean didn't know what woke him up first. The two suns shining in his eyes—or the paw repeatedly slapping at his head.

Yawning, he glared at the little monster trying to claw him to death. "Oh, now you're feeling fine, aren't you?"

He yipped in answer and that's when Shalin murmured in her sleep.

That's also when Ailean realized Shalin was asleep on his chest.

Slightly terrified, Ailean desperately tried to remember if they'd done anything the night before. He didn't think so and, when he looked down at her, she still wore the red gown from yesterday, and the fur covering he'd brought with him still lay between them.

He let out a breath, but still didn't know what had come over him. He may not have touched her, but all the things they'd discussed . . .

Ailean never talked about his father with anyone but his brothers, and those two never mentioned the old dragon unless necessary. Ailean definitely never discussed his mother and what happened that awful day. His own kin knew never to mention it. Nearly a century ago, one cousin drunkenly brought it up after a family hunting party and lost both his horns when Ailean snapped them off.

But Ailean had told Shalin pretty much everything. God . . . why?

The puppy yipped again and Shalin's head snapped up from his chest. "Wha—where?"

"You're safe, Shalin," he told her, seeing the confusion and panic on her face. When she looked at him, her panic seemed to pass and she smiled at him with real warmth.

"Good morn, Ailean."

"Good morn to you."

She turned a bit to look at the puppy, but seemed more than comfortable cuddled up on his chest. "And look at you, Lord Terrify Me."

The dog yipped again and Ailean said, "You best let him out, Shalin. Or there'll be more mess to clean up."

"Let him out?"

"Just open the door. He'll find the rest of the dogs."

"All right."

He thought she'd roll away from him, but instead, she moved across him to get to the edge of the bed. Ailean gritted his teeth and willed his body not to react. It had to be one of the hardest things he'd ever done, and he'd gotten in a fight once with a giant octopus.

"Will he come back?"

"I'm sure. He's bonded to you, Shalin." And he knew how the little bastard felt. Ailean knew if he left this moment, he'd probably come back too.

"Come on then, you little terror." Shalin picked the dog up and walked to the door. Ailean heard it open and then Shalin's strangled, "Uh . . ."

"What's wrong?" He rolled to his side, raising himself up on one elbow, and looked toward the door. "Shit," he barely had a chance to mutter before Bideven pushed past Shalin and stalked in, Arranz and the twins right behind him,

"You dirty bastard. Couldn't keep your hands off her, could ya?"

Ailean slid off the bed and stood in front of his kin, the only thing holding up that fur covering his hand.

"I'm not quite sure what it has to do with you, brother."

Bideven moved toward him but Shalin calmly stepped between them. "He never touched me."

Arranz sighed. "Shalin love, could you move? You're in the way of some lovely violence."

Giving no more than an annoyed sniff, she didn't respond to Arranz and instead said again, "He never touched me, Bideven."

"Then why was he here?"

"I needed help with my puppy."

Arranz and the twins started laughing and didn't seem inclined to stop while Bideven's accusing gaze shot daggers at Ailean.

"You bastard!"

Shalin rested her hand against Bideven's chest. "Stop this now."

"Shalin, you're an innocent about this sort of thing—"

Ailean didn't realize he'd snorted out loud until they all looked at him.

He glanced at Shalin and shrugged. "Sorry."

"—and his intent," Bideven finished. "We're just trying to protect you."

Shalin folded her arms over her chest. "Do you think so little of your own brother?"

The confusion on their faces would be something Ailean remembered for ages.

"What?"

"Do you think so little of him? That he'd take advantage of me. Force me,"

"I never said—"

"Is that truly what you expect of your own kin? I thought the Cadwaladr Clan loyal to each other."

"We are."

"I haven't seen it. Not when you barge in here and accuse your own brother of being all manner of lizard."

"I never meant to—"

"Then you should apologize."

Apologize?"

"Yes.

"You can't be—"

Shalin's foot began to tap and Bideven growled. "Fine. I apologize."

Patting his shoulder, Shalin ushered Bideven and the rest out. "Now don't you feel better?"

"Not really," Bideven shot back, but Shalin already closed the door in his face.

Ailean stared at Shalin. "That was . . . *brilliant*!"

Shalin held her finger to her lips while she bent over silently laughing. "He'll hear."

"Good!" Ailean watched her walk across the room. "How did you do that?"

She shrugged before falling back on the bed, her grin wide and happy. "Years of court life, my dear dragon."